An Italian Affair

BESTSELLING AUSTRALIAN AUTHOR
MICHELLE DOUGLAS
& NINA SINGH

MILLS & BOON

AN ITALIAN AFFAIR © 2023 by Harlequin Books S.A.

CINDERELLA'S SECRET FLING
© 2023 by Michelle Douglas
Australian Copyright 2023
New Zealand Copyright 2023

First Published 2023
First Australian Paperback Edition 2023
ISBN 978 1 867 28744 5

TWO WEEKS TO TEMPT THE TYCOON
© 2023 by Nilay Nina Singh
Australian Copyright 2023
New Zealand Copyright 2023

First Published 2023
First Australian Paperback Edition 2023
ISBN 978 1 867 28744 5

Except for use in any review, the reproduction or utilisation of this work in whole or in part in any form by any electronic, mechanical or other means, now known or hereafter invented, including xerography, photocopying and recording, or in any information storage or retrieval system, is forbidden without the permission of the publisher.

This book is sold subject to the condition that it shall not, by way of trade or otherwise, be lent, resold, hired out or otherwise circulated without the prior consent of the publisher in any form of binding or cover other than that in which it is published and without a similar condition including this condition being imposed on the subsequent purchaser.

All rights reserved including the right of reproduction in whole or in part in any form. This edition is published in arrangement with Harlequin Books S.A. Cover art used by arrangement with Harlequin Books S.A. All rights reserved.

This is a work of fiction. Names, characters, places, and incidents are either the product of the author's imagination or are used fictitiously, and any resemblance to actual persons, living or dead, business establishments, events, or locales is entirely coincidental.

Published by
Mills & Boon
An imprint of Harlequin Enterprises (Australia) Pty Limited
(ABN 47 001 180 918), a subsidiary of HarperCollins
Publishers Australia Pty Limited (ABN 36 009 913 517)
Level 19, 201 Elizabeth Street
SYDNEY NSW 2000
AUSTRALIA

MIX
Paper | Supporting responsible forestry
FSC® C001695

® and ™ (apart from those relating to FSC®) are trademarks of Harlequin Enterprises (Australia) Pty Limited or its corporate affiliates. Trademarks indicated with ® are registered in Australia, New Zealand and in other countries. Contact admin_legal@Harlequin.ca for details.

Printed and bound in Australia by McPherson's Printing Group

CONTENTS

CINDERELLA'S SECRET FLING — 5
Michelle Douglas

TWO WEEKS TO TEMPT THE TYCOON — 223
Nina Singh

Cinderella's Secret Fling
Michelle Douglas

Michelle Douglas has been writing for Harlequin since 2007 and believes she has the best job in the world. She lives in a leafy suburb of Newcastle, on Australia's east coast, with her own romantic hero, a house full of dust and books, and an eclectic collection of '60s and '70s vinyl. She loves to hear from readers and can be contacted via her website, michelle-douglas.com.

Books by Michelle Douglas

One Summer in Italy

Unbuttoning the Tuscan Tycoon

Redemption of the Maverick Millionaire
Singapore Fling with the Millionaire
Secret Billionaire on Her Doorstep
Billionaire's Road Trip to Forever
Cinderella and the Brooding Billionaire
Escape with Her Greek Tycoon
Wedding Date in Malaysia
Reclusive Millionaire's Mistletoe Miracle

Visit the Author Profile page
at millsandboon.com.au for more titles.

Dear Reader,

I'm so excited for you to read the second book in my One Summer in Italy duet. In this book, Audrey finds herself living a dream come true in gloriously gorgeous Lake Como.

Who of us hasn't secretly dreamed of being gifted a windfall, of being whisked into a world of wealth and glamour where suddenly anything is possible? Having a chance to wear designer gowns, sip expensive French champagne while living in an eighty-room lakefront mansion. It's what happens to Audrey, though the real prize is the discovery of the family she never knew she had.

The only blemish in this otherwise glorious existence is the forbidding Gabriel Dimarco, the father of her sweet four-year-old niece. Gabriel is disapproving not only of this new world she finds herself in, but of her new family, too. Gabriel has been badly burned by an heiress before and has absolutely no intention of falling for the bewitching Audrey. Forced to spend the summer together, however, they discover hidden depths in each other and in themselves, too.

Cinderella's Secret Fling is a story of hope and forgiveness and new starts, and I hope you love it as much as I do.

Hugs,

Michelle

To Trisha Pender for her enthusiasm, support and a shared love of the romance genre.

Praise for
Michelle Douglas

"Michelle Douglas writes the most beautiful stories, with heroes and heroines who are real and so easy to get to know and love.... This is a moving and wonderful story that left me feeling fabulous.... I do highly recommend this one, Ms. Douglas has never disappointed me with her stories."

—*Goodreads* on *Redemption of the Maverick Millionaire*

PROLOGUE

My darling Audrey,
I know this is going to come as a great shock to you, and I'm hoping you do not blame me too much for not revealing this to you sooner, but I know how much family means to you. And this is not a secret I can take to the grave. The decision for how to proceed is yours, my dearest girl—not mine, not your father's and certainly not your mother's.

My mother? I can almost hear you ask. Yes. She is not who she claimed to be and I have discovered her true identity. I'm sorry to tell you she passed away many years ago, and it was a brief news item reporting her death that prompted my suspicions and subsequent investigations.

Rather than being a poor orphan, as she always claimed, she came from a very old, very powerful and very wealthy Italian family. And apparently, you have an Italian grandmother and a plethora of cousins.

Your aunt Beatrice is now in possession of all the associated documentation, and she has been in con-

tact with your maternal grandmother's lawyers. Your grandmother's name is Marguerite Funaro, and she wishes to meet you. If you wish to meet her, you can now do so. The choice is yours.

Wishing you all joy and every happiness and a life filled with love and family.
Your ever-loving Nonna

AUDREY STARED AT the letter in her hand and then up at her aunt Beatrice. *Aunt* was an honorary title, but Nonna's best friend had always felt like family. For the past month she'd been in Lake Como staying with Aunt Beatrice, and yet all this time she'd had a family she'd never known about?

'This says...'

'Yes.' Beatrice nodded.

'I have...?'

'A family? *Si*, Audrey, it would appear so. Your grandmother wanted me to make contact with them first as she did not want you getting your hopes up if they did not wish to recognise you. On the contrary, though, they very much want to meet you.'

A champagne fizz of excitement bubbled in her chest. And something deeper. Something that made her catch her breath.

If she was being brutally honest—and she was always brutally honest, at least with herself—she'd not fully regained her balance since Johanna had died. Losing a twin... It felt as if she'd lost a part of herself.

She'd been finding her feet again, though, slowly, every step hard-won. Then her father had made the shocking announcement that he was marrying and relocating to America. She hadn't even known he'd been seeing someone!

Then Nonna had died. Her throat thickened. She doubted anything could fill the gap that now yawned through her. It took a superhuman effort to swallow the lump stretching her throat into a painful ache. Her family, never large, had suddenly dwindled to her, her cousin Frankie and her aunt Deidre.

But to now discover her mother's family... *A grandmother and a plethora of cousins.* She'd been searching for something to anchor her, a safe harbour. Could this be it?

'Would you like to meet them?'

It felt as if the sun had come from behind a cloud and bathed her in light. A big extended family? She clasped her hands in her lap. She wanted that more than she'd ever wanted anything. 'Yes, please. How soon can it be arranged?'

CHAPTER ONE

'YOU ARE READY, AUDREY?'

The words sounded more like a command than a question. Audrey glanced at her grandmother and found she couldn't push a single word from a throat that had grown too tight. She'd met Marguerite Funaro a week ago, and Marguerite was as unlike Nonna as it was possible to be.

'Appearances can be deceptive.'

She held that thought close; the voice—Nonna's—made the tight knot in her stomach loosen a fraction. Nonna had taught her the importance of family. Audrey had no intention of forgetting those lessons and abandoning all of Nonna's wisdom now, just because she was nervous and things felt a bit awkward.

Marguerite might not be touchy-feely and demonstrative, but Audrey had felt a bond with the older woman the moment they'd met. Marguerite hadn't felt like a stranger, although the world she inhabited did.

In her letter, Nonna had said Audrey's mother's family was wealthy and powerful. Audrey just hadn't realised how wealthy and powerful. Apparently, the Funaro name was synonymous with all the great aristocratic names of Italy.

She pinched herself. It was hard to believe that *she* was a member of such an old, powerful Italian family. Or that she was now a resident at their impossibly luxurious estate on the shores of Lake Como with its splendid Funaro Villa, extravagant gardens and extraordinary views.

She glanced at her grandmother again and her stomach churned. She didn't want to let Marguerite down. Didn't want to let any of the family down, but what did she know about this world? How would she ever fit in?

Just because Marguerite is regal and proud, it doesn't mean she has no heart or kindness or love.

The thought made her straighten. Marguerite had welcomed her into the Funaro fold without hesitation…and with her own brand of warmth. Lifting her chin, she nodded. 'I'm looking forward to meeting the rest of the family, Grandmother.'

Grandmother was what Marguerite had requested Audrey call her. She had no idea why she wanted her to use the English title rather than the Italian one. Maybe it was so she could tell her apart from the other members of the family.

Because, apparently, there were quite a few of them.

The wriggle of delight was cut short as Marguerite's gaze roved over Audrey's attire. Her lips didn't tighten and her nostrils didn't flare and nothing about her face gave anything away, but Audrey couldn't help but feel she'd been found wanting.

She glanced down at herself. 'Would you like me to change?' Not that she had anything else to change into. Not really. 'I only brought a limited wardrobe with me on this trip.' She only had a limited wardrobe period, but she had no intention of admitting that out loud. 'I've not had a chance to do any real shopping yet and—'

'Audrey!'

She snapped to attention. 'Yes, Grandmother?'

'You are a granddaughter of the Funaro family. You have royal blood flowing in your veins.'

She choked down an entirely inappropriate laugh. Royal blood? *Her?*

'Your attire does not define you.'

Easy to say when you happened to be wearing a delightfully chic Chanel suit in pink-and-white tweed.

'You will walk out there as if you own the room.'

Oh, just like that, huh? Easy-peasy. She had an insane urge to call her cousin Frankie and demand a pep talk.

'You will keep your back straight, your chin high and a pleasant expression on your face.'

She adjusted her stance to meet her grandmother's exacting requirements.

'Ours is a large family and, as with most families, some members get along better than others. You will not allow anyone to ruffle your peace or to allow you to feel inferior.'

Okay, now she really wanted to run back to Aunt Beatrice's and hide under the bed that had been hers for the past few weeks.

'Repeat that, please,' the older woman ordered.

'I won't allow anyone to make me feel inferior,' she obediently repeated. These people were her family; things were bound to be a bit awkward initially. But it wasn't money and position that made a person worthwhile. Just because her dress wasn't the latest fashion, it didn't make her a bad person.

Her heart beat hard. She had family. And she *would* fit in.

It might take some time, but she *would* make them love her. There was strength in family, not to mention security. And a place to belong. Ever since Nonna's death, she'd felt cast adrift. But here was a place where she could find safe harbour and acceptance—where she could love and be loved.

'Remember, you have your grandmother's seal of approval.'

Marguerite might not be all touchy-feely maternal warmth, but her unerring support warmed Audrey from the inside out. 'I'm ready to meet everyone, Grandmother. I'm looking forward to it.'

Once this initial meeting was over, she could work at getting to know everyone on a more leisurely and less formal basis. She imagined lunches, dinners, outings. Hopefully by Christmas it'd feel as if they'd all known each other forever. She crossed her fingers.

'Remember, spine straight, shoulders back...and smile.'

Audrey followed the instructions to the letter, and then waited outside a set of gilded double doors while a butler or footman or...well, a member of staff who wore the most extraordinary uniform, flung the doors open. She half expected him to announce them.

He didn't, of course. This wasn't the set of a historical drama. She wasn't some Jane Austen heroine. This was the real world.

Except Audrey's real world wasn't Lake Como, glittering chandeliers, eighty-room villas and *a new family*.

Marguerite took Audrey's arm, as if for the support— as if she was an old lady who needed to lean on someone. Which was a joke, because *frailty, thy name is woman* wasn't Marguerite. She doubted she'd be able to best the older woman in an arm wrestle.

The thought, though, made her smile.

Then they stepped inside the room and her breath caught. There had to be at least forty people in here. It took all her strength not to clasp her hands beneath her chin and beam at them. How *wonderful*! She'd always wanted to be part of a big, loving family.

Nobody said a word as she and Marguerite split a path through the crowd towards a throne—

Not a throne. A chair. But it was all gold gilt and pink velvet and clearly Marguerite's. The silence raised all the fine hairs on her arms. She concentrated on keeping her spine straight, her chin lifted and her expression pleasant. This odd formality must be the way they did things here in her new world.

Still, she'd never hated her height more. It always made her stand out, gave her nowhere to hide and— Except...she wasn't the only tall person in the room! This stature must be a Funaro trait. Her smile widened. Surely, that meant she was fitting in already.

Marguerite removed her arm from Audrey's and sat. Audrey immediately felt cast adrift.

Don't be a baby.

It'd be easier if she knew what she was supposed to do. Should she sit? Except there was no chair beside her grandmother's.

You're not supposed to sit. You're supposed to mix and mingle and get to know everyone.

Not until she'd been introduced, though, surely? She felt as if she ought to have a sign around her neck saying Exhibit A.

The vision had her lips twitching. Once everyone got to

know her, she wouldn't be such a curiosity. She'd be just another member of the family.

And still, the silence stretched. Though, she couldn't help feeling an awful lot of silent communication was happening among various family members. She hid a wince. Awkward much?

Finally, with an impatient huff, a child broke from the ranks and came hurtling out from behind the crowd to rush up to Audrey, hopping from one foot to the other in front of her. '*Ciao!* Hello!'

The pretty little thing couldn't be older than three or four. Something inside her melted. She hadn't thought, but of course, there'd be children. She knelt down to be eye to eye with her and held out her hand. 'I'm Audrey. And who might you be? A princess, maybe?'

'I'm not a princess. I'm Liliana.' She placed her hand in Audrey's and shook it earnestly. 'And you're my aunty.'

She stared at the little girl and her throat thickened; her eyes burned. She had a niece? She had to swallow before she could trust her voice to work. 'My niece? I have a niece?'

Little Liliana nodded eagerly.

The delight that flooded her couldn't be hidden, contained or otherwise tempered. She clapped her hands, grinning madly. She might've even shimmied. 'That is the best news I've ever heard!'

She had a niece!

Liliana grinned back like she couldn't help it, either.

And then they hugged each other like they meant it.

She had at least one friend here, then. And she had every intention of treasuring her.

* * *

Gabriel took one look at the tableau unfolding before him and wanted to swear long and hard.

One thing the world *didn't* need was another Funaro.

One thing that world *really* didn't need was a Funaro his daughter found irresistible.

Not that he blamed Lili for falling for the statuesque woman who'd folded down to her height with the ease and grace of a ballet dancer. Or who smiled at her as if her very heart's delight had just been handed to her on a diamond-encrusted platinum platter at Lili's announcement.

Even *his* heart had thrilled as he'd watched the scene unfold, and he was a hardened cynic who didn't trust in appearances or believe that anyone in the room had his or Lili's best interests at heart. He watched the stranger rise; watched the way Lili slipped her hand inside her new friend's; noted the way this Audrey's fingers curled around Lili's as if...

He rubbed a hand across his chest.

As if she welcomed that hand. As if she'd keep that little hand safe from all harm. As if...

He swallowed an indigestible lump. It is the way Fina should've held Lili's hand. But even if his wife hadn't died and was still in their midst, that wasn't the kind of woman Fina had been. None of the women in this room were. None of them would hold Lili's hand in that fashion.

He studied the quietly beautiful woman's face with its dark eyes. If one wasn't looking for it, they wouldn't immediately see the beauty there. But he had an artist's eye and recognised it immediately. This wasn't a woman who made the most of her assets by painting her face, by drawing her hair up into a complicated style that took myriad pins and a team of hairdressers to maintain. If her dress and shoes were anything to go by, she wasn't a woman who, before now, had the means to buy designer labels.

Several women in the room exchanged raised eyebrows. As if to say 'Look what the cat has dragged in.'

Mind you, all too soon this Audrey would have access to the funds to rectify every single problem the assorted horde would find with her appearance. And then they'd be jealous of her as she outshone them all.

For a brief moment, at least. Like a star shining its brightest before exploding. Or should that be imploding? Whatever one wanted to call it, it'd be spectacular. And then it'd be spectacularly disastrous.

Marguerite finally made a general introduction to the room at large, saying that she was pleased to welcome her granddaughter Audrey into the family fold. A chair was placed for Audrey beside Marguerite's, and he gave a silent, humourless laugh. Audrey didn't yet understand the honour being done to her with the placement of that chair. But she'd learn. And if she didn't want to be eaten alive by the piranhas in the room, she'd better learn *presto*.

The temperature in the room rose as resentment and *devilry* heated the air. What would most of the people here give to be seated in such close proximity to Marguerite, to have the opportunity to whisper sweet nothings and bitter calumnies in her ear for ten minutes? How many of them would like the opportunity to make a fresh impression on their stately elder?

And because they couldn't, because they'd messed up—in some instances again and again—the feuding family members in the room seemed to momentarily join forces against the newcomer. As if they couldn't wait until she, too, fell from grace.

A bitter sigh welled inside him. He didn't doubt that Audrey would indeed fall from grace. She *was* a Funaro, after all. Falling from grace was what the Funaros did. They knew of no other way of being.

As various family members were called forward to be introduced and pay their respects, he remained in the shadows—where he belonged. He wasn't a member of the family, thank God. He was tolerated as Lili's father, nothing more. Lili might be a Funaro, but she was also a Dimarco. His hands clenched. He would *not* allow her to go the way of her mother. He would *not* allow this family's excesses, their hedonism and extravagances, to destroy his daughter. He would do everything in his power to prevent that from happening.

He kept a close eye on Lili now and it took all his willpower not to call her back to his side. It would bring attention to the both of them, and that was something he'd avoid if he could.

The arrangement—one legally signed off by a team of lawyers—stated that during the summer Lili would spend uninterrupted time with her mother's family. He had no desire to engage in a protracted legal battle with Marguerite if she should happen to take exception to some interference of his, or imagined some slight or infringement to her rights.

Where he could, he'd keep things amicable. To her credit, on this one issue Marguerite had been in surprising agreement. When he'd demanded to be allowed to accompany Lili for her summers at Lake Como, Marguerite had acquiesced. They both knew his being there would keep Lili content and secure. In his turn, he ensured Marguerite could spend time with Lili throughout the rest of the year. They maintained an uneasy peace he would prefer not to shatter.

He glanced again at the newcomer's face and his chest clenched. Her height, the line of her nose and the aristocratic cheekbones pronounced her heritage. He saw Fina there, and her mother, Danae, too.

He would never again fall for a Funaro heiress, never again indulge a fascination for one, or even speak to one longer than necessary. Once had been enough. He would not live that nightmare a second time.

It didn't mean he relished the notion of witnessing another heiress's fall from grace, though. Watching the newcomer succumb to the wealth and sophistication, the petty flatteries and scheming seductions, the endless parties. Breath hissed from his lungs. The drugs.

He loathed the thought of all the potential encased in that elegant frame being brought low; watching as the fire in those eyes dimmed and eventually went out.

'Gabriel!'

His name, an imperial command from the matriarch herself, snapped him back to himself.

'Come! I have a request to make of you.'

He kept his face a study of polite lines. What was the scheming Funaro elder up to now? Whatever it was, he suspected he wouldn't like it.

Lili's wide smile and hopping excitement had him moving towards the trio in the middle of the room, rather than heading for the door like his instincts told him to.

'This is Papa.' Lili leaned against Audrey's legs, smiling up at her with the naive openness and utter assurance of a much-loved four-year-old, clearly believing Audrey adored her every bit as much as Lili did her. It made him want to snatch his daughter up and bolt from the house and lock her in a tower where none of these people could ever hurt her.

'I'm looking forward to meeting your papa,' Audrey said with a wide smile that had a different part of his anatomy jerking to attention. He wrestled with the curse that rose to his lips.

'Good grief, Audrey,' said Marguerite, 'you don't need to stand every time I introduce you to someone new.'

'It only seems polite,' Audrey returned mildly, apparently unfazed by her grandmother's imperial tone.

'Audrey, this is my grandson-in-law. He was married to my granddaughter Serafina.'

'My *mamma*,' Lili whispered. Though four-year-olds apparently couldn't manage a quiet whisper; they only thought they did.

Audrey squeezed Lili's hand. 'And my sister.'

'Half sister,' Marguerite snapped with her customary autocratic tyranny.

Audrey winked at Lili. 'I bet your mamma and I would've been the best of friends.'

A titter went around the room. Quickly quelled by Marguerite's glare. But he silently agreed with everyone else. He doubted Audrey could've made Fina a friend, but he appreciated the kindness to his daughter.

'Gabriel,' he said, extending his hand as Marguerite had failed to mention that key piece of information.

She promptly placed her hand in his and something arced between them. Something that had her eyes widening and him frowning. They reclaimed their hands at exactly the same moment.

'Audrey apparently has some artistic talent,' Marguerite said peremptorily.

Uh-huh. A dabbler. He lowered his gaze to hide the derision in his eyes, the cynical twist of his mouth.

'She's been studying under Madame De Luca for the last month.'

His head shot up, and the way Audrey's lips twitched made him suspect he'd not hidden his shock very well. If she'd been studying under Madame De Luca, though, she must have a degree of talent.

Audrey registered Gabriel's surprise at the fact she'd been studying under someone so well regarded, and it made her smile.

But that didn't stop her hand from continuing to burn at the brief pressure of his, or help ease the constriction in her chest. This odd awareness didn't make sense. Gabriel wasn't classically handsome. He wasn't smooth or clean-cut or smilingly polished like the other men in the room. What he was, though, was thoroughly masculine. Dark haired, olive skinned and sporting several days' growth of beard, he seemed to *bristle*. Something primitive beat beneath the contained demeanour and it thrilled something primitive deep inside her.

She had no idea what that meant—he probably had that effect on every woman he met. Whatever it was, it was far from comfortable. And she had every intention of ignoring it.

She had enough to negotiate this summer. She wasn't adding men and romance to the mix. She wasn't thinking about any of that until she'd worked out her place in the family; had learned to negotiate this new world of hers.

Grey eyes continued to survey her, their colour taking her off guard. They should be dark like his hair. And yet...

Stop it!

'What medium is your speciality?'

The question had her swallowing. 'While Grandmother is correct, and I have been studying under Madame De Luca, it has been as a favour to a mutual friend of ours. Your first impression was the correct one—I am a rank amateur.'

Expressive brows rose as if he'd noted her evasion. It was just...when she told others her artform of choice, they usually laughed. And she didn't want anyone laughing. Not today. There were already enough undercurrents threading through the room that she didn't understand.

'I'd hate for Grandmother's words to mislead you.'

He stared at her for a long moment, flicked a glance at the rest of the room and nodded. She let out a breath, the tension in her shoulders easing. 'Are you an artist, Gabriel?'

Another titter sounded through the room, and she fought back a frown. What had she said now?

The Funaros might not be as warm as she'd hoped, but it was early days. She hitched up her chin. She'd make them love her yet. Resisting the urge to glance to Marguerite for an explanation, she held Gabriel's gaze and awaited his answer.

'I am a sculptor.' He pushed his hands into his trouser pockets. 'I work with recycled materials.'

'Like?'

'Like steel, wood, wire and such.'

Hold on...

Her heart started to thump. 'Do you work on large installations?'

He nodded.

His first name was Gabriel...

She swallowed. 'You wouldn't happen to be Gabriel Dimarco by any chance, would you?'

'*Si*, that is me.'

Her jaw dropped. She couldn't help it.

'Audrey, please,' Marguerite half sighed, half ordered.

'But—' She stared at her grandmother. 'His work is amazing.' She swung back to him. '*Your* work is amazing.'

Her hands fluttered in the air as if searching for all the things she wanted to say; all the things his work made her feel. She could no more control them than she could the sun—or the rest of the room's opinion of her. But the knowledge she was standing in front of such an artist drove all such concerns momentarily from her mind. Gabriel's installations stood in both public spaces and enviable private collections. He could demand whatever price he wanted. He was a *huge* name in the art world.

'I saw your installation titled *Maybe* in Como. It was the most amazing piece. I sat there for an hour watching how it changed as the sun passed overhead.' It sat in a pretty town square, and the sculpture was an Impressionist piece—half human, half butterfly...or, at least, if not a butterfly, something winged. 'It made me feel hopeful but sad. I couldn't work out if the figure wanted to take flight or return to its cocoon.'

Powerful arms folded across an impressive chest. Considering the tools he must use, he'd need every one of those impressive muscles. 'What was your conclusion?'

She pondered the question anew. 'I spent a lot of time trying to work it out.' She'd gone back the next day, earlier in the morning when the sun would hit it at different angles, to see if that would help her solve the conundrum. 'In the end, I decided it depicted the battle between security and adventure, and that the piece was deliberately ambiguous. I don't think the figure knew yet which it was going to choose.'

Grey eyes widened and nostrils flared. 'You—'

He snapped back whatever he'd been about to say with a shake of his head. 'I am glad you enjoyed the piece.'

She wanted to press him for what he'd been going to say, but it wouldn't be polite. And she suspected her grandmother would find it indecorous. Twice already this afternoon Marguerite had heaved a sigh and murmured, 'Dear Lord, Audrey, we're really going to have to take you in hand.'

She had no idea what that meant. She hoped it wasn't as ominous as it sounded. She liked Marguerite, and an additional point in the older woman's favour was the fact she clearly loved her great-granddaughter. She and Lili seemed to have a perfect understanding.

She was far from sure about the rest of the room, however. She'd seen the raised eyebrows, the speaking glances. She suspected she'd been meant to. Why didn't they want to embrace her the way she wanted to embrace them?

Was it about the money?

Surely not. The Funaro family had so much wealth that one more person sharing a portion of it wouldn't make any difference. Not that she wanted a portion of it. She just wanted the family. And she was determined to find a way to bring them around.

'What I would like for you to do, Gabriel,' Marguerite said now, 'is take Audrey's art education in hand. Determine where she's at and what she needs—' that imperious hand waved through the air '—and then use your connections to engage whatever teachers, tutors or experts you deem necessary.'

Audrey blinked. 'Grandmother, that's something you ought to consult with me about first.'

The room froze. Very slowly, Marguerite turned her head

to meet Audrey's gaze, and the expression in her eyes had her gulping. 'It's just...' It took a superhuman effort to not wince, grimace, or backtrack. 'It'll be expensive to hire experts like that, and I've already told you I'm not here for your money. The money might not mean a lot to you, but...' It meant a lot to her and she didn't want anyone here thinking she was only out for what she could get.

Her grandmother gestured for Audrey to bend down. Hiding a wince, she did as she bid and prayed the older woman wasn't going to yell at high volume in her ear.

'Please...'

The word was nothing more than a whisper, but she heard the vulnerability threaded through it and it had tears prickling the backs of her eyes. Straightening, she swallowed and eventually nodded, turning back to Gabriel. 'I would be very grateful for any advice you'd be able to offer. If you have the time.'

When she was sure nobody was looking, she reached down and squeezed her grandmother's hand. 'Thank you.'

'Papa, can Audrey come with us to your studio tomorrow?'

'I think that's a remarkably fine idea, Lili.' A gleam lit Marguerite's eyes. 'Do you have any objections, Gabriel?'

The pulse in his jaw ticked. 'None whatsoever,' he eventually ground out.

Audrey's heart plummeted. Oh, God. He didn't want her invading his studio space. How on earth could she get out of this gracefully and save face for everyone?

'Be ready to leave at nine o'clock.'

'She'll be ready,' Marguerite said.

Before she could think of a way to extricate herself, Gabriel was already striding away. She glanced down at her grandmother, recalled her *please* and swallowed her protests, made herself smile. 'What a treat! Thank you.'

CHAPTER TWO

THE FOLLOWING MORNING Audrey made sure to be sitting on one of the hard-backed chairs in the foyer ten minutes before the assigned time. She had no intention of being late or putting anyone out more than they already had been.

Recalling again the less than thrilled expression on Gabriel's face, she grimaced. She didn't blame him for his lack of enthusiasm. He was an important artist. He was probably working on something amazing. He didn't need the likes of her underfoot.

Biting at a hangnail on her thumb, she made a resolution to do her best to remain in the background and not get in the way.

After pulling the thumb from her mouth, she clasped both hands in her lap. Apparently, Funaros didn't fidget. Apparently, they were always careful to appear composed and at ease, regardless of how they felt inside. The thing was she also happened to be a Martinelli, and they *did* fidget, and they had a habit of wearing their hearts on their sleeves.

She glanced up when the front door swung open to see Lili come skipping through it, her father following close behind. *Not* skipping. She shot to her feet and the little girl threw her arms around Audrey's legs, the little face smiling up at her with big shining eyes. Audrey swept her up in her arms and hugged her back. She had a niece! It made her want to dance.

Before any of them could speak, a door off to the left opened and Marguerite strode out. At seventy-four she was still as erect as she must've been as a much younger woman. Audrey envied her poise. She doubted she'd ever acquire that level of grace and command, no matter how hard she practised.

'Good morning, Audrey and Liliana. Gabriel.'

Clearly, Marguerite wasn't the kind of person to enjoy a morning lie-in.

Audrey set Lili back on her feet. 'Good morning, Grandmother.'

'Marguerite.' Gabriel nodded in the older woman's direction. 'Gently!' he ordered Lili as she raced across to hug her great-grandmother in the same way she had Audrey.

'Leave the child be, Gabriel. I'm not as frail as you and the rest of the family make me out to be.'

Marguerite clearly adored Lili, and while she might try to hide it beneath a crusty exterior, Audrey doubted she was fooling anyone. Least of all, Lili's father. She turned to Gabriel with a grin, expecting him to be amused, too, but he didn't so much as smile. The flat expression in his eyes as he stared back at her had the smile sliding off her lips. Pressing her hands to her waist, she reminded them to neither twist nor fidget.

'Now, Lili, I have a proposition for you. Tomaso informs me it's time to decide which puppy we're to keep from Tippy's litter.'

Lili's eyes grew wide. 'Can we play with them yet?'

'We can.'

The little girl hopped from one foot to the other. 'When?'

'This morning, and as it's the only morning I have free this week, I'm afraid you'll need to decide if you want to accompany your father and Audrey to the studio, or if you'd like to come to the stables and play with the puppies and help me choose which one to keep.'

Lili swung to her father. 'Can I stay with Nonna, Papa? *Please?* I want to play with the puppies.'

His jaw tightened fractionally and Audrey wondered if Marguerite noticed it, too. 'Do you mean to abandon your new friend so quickly, Lili?'

That little face fell and Audrey found herself crouching down in front of her. 'I totally understand, Lili. I mean... puppies, right?'

The little girl's relief was palpable and then her entire face lit up. 'We could *all* stay and play with the puppies!'

'*No.*'

The single word shot from Gabriel's mouth like a bullet and they all jumped.

'I mean,' he moderated his voice, no doubt for his daughter's benefit, 'that I shall be going to the studio today as planned. Audrey will have to make the decision whether to stay and play with the puppies or come to the studio for herself.'

Puppies would win in the ordinary course of events. And the 'No Trespassing' signals radiating from Gabriel in waves would normally seal the deal. But her grandmother drew herself up to her full height and sent her a look that told Audrey in no uncertain terms what was expected of her. Yet, it was that vulnerable *please* from last night that played through her mind.

'I've no desire to change our plans. I'm looking forward to seeing your studio.'

His lips twisted and his jaw clenched as if he was biting back something curt and succinct. His nose didn't exactly curl, but it felt like it did and she could feel herself shrivelling inside.

A Funaro always appears composed.

She planted as pleasant a smile as she could to her face and kept her chin high. She'd get this done—go and tour his studio, have a brief conversation about her artistic endeavours—to please Marguerite. She'd get the names of several suitable teachers whom she could contact, and then she and Gabriel need never have anything to do with each other again.

'Liliana, pop through the kitchen to Maria. I believe she has something special for you.'

With a wave, Lili raced off in the direction of the kitchen.

'A word if you don't mind, Gabriel. We won't be a minute, Audrey.'

Another flaring of those rather savage nostrils had Audrey internally quailing, but when Marguerite turned on her very elegant heel and strode back the way she'd come, he fell into step behind her.

Audrey took a seat and waited. It was no hardship. The villa was utterly extraordinary, and the foyer was all classic white marble with a vaulted ceiling housing a stunning chandelier whose crystals glittered in the light pouring in at the arched windows set high above. And complementing it all was the sweeping curve of a grand staircase.

'I am Cinderella.' She pinched herself. Rather than a fairy godmother, she had a grandmother.

And a niece!

She didn't have long to luxuriate in all the splendour, though. Less than five minutes later Gabriel appeared—turbulent, dark and crackling with barely restrained...um, energy. Without a glance in her direction, he strode out the door.

Was she supposed to follow him? For one brief moment she considered chickening out.

Please.

Marguerite's simple request with its underlying vulnerability pierced through her cowardice. Swearing under her breath, she leapt up and scrambled after him, catching him up before he reached the car.

He didn't utter a word, just slid inside the dark sedan. She moved to the passenger side but when she tried the door handle, it was locked. She had to tap on the window to get him to open it. For one awfully fraught moment she thought he wouldn't; thought he'd drive away and leave her there.

For heaven's sake! There was reasonable annoyance, but then there was also unreasonable rudeness.

He unlocked the door. She slid into her seat, pulled her seatbelt on and folded her hands in her lap.

Don't make waves. Don't rock the boat. Wait until you know how everything here fits together.

It took a superhuman effort, but she bit her tongue and kept her thoughts to herself. She didn't like confrontation. Nobody did, she supposed, but something about this man and his behaviour had her itching to take him to task.

She risked a glance at his profile as he set the car in motion and had to stifle a laugh. Take him to task? He looked like granite—hard and inflexible. She doubted anything she said or did would have the slightest effect on him.

He didn't speak, so she kept her gaze trained directly out to the front.

Comfortable? No. But luckily, the trip took less than ten minutes.

She blinked when he pulled the car to a halt in the carpark of a small marina. If she turned her head, she could see the Funaro Villa back along the lake, its grand arched balconies shining white in the morning sun.

He pushed out of the car so she did, too. Clearing her throat, she prayed her voice would sound normal. 'Where's the studio?'

He pointed at the water, before striding down to the dock towards a speedboat.

Her jaw dropped. An island? His studio was on an island?

And then she couldn't help it; she started to laugh.

'What's so funny?' he said with an irritable twist of his lips, though he did have the civility to help her step into the boat.

Where was she supposed to sit? He didn't give her any hints, so she chose the padded seat beside the driver's seat. It might not be large, but the boat looked built for speed, and this seat had handrails to the front and side for her to hold on to. Did he have any lifejackets?

'Under the seat,' he said, as if reading her mind.

She put it on. To her surprise he put one on, too.

'Can you swim?'

She nodded. 'Can you?'

He nodded back. *That* was the extent of their conversation before he fired up the engine, undid the moorings and turned the boat's nose towards the middle of the lake.

They'd been travelling for five minutes, maybe a bit longer, when he cut the engine and she turned from admiring the view. Lake Como, the lakeside villas dotted here and there, the forests and mountains... Dear God, it was *breathtaking*.

'You didn't tell me why you laughed back there on shore.'

'I didn't,' she agreed, determined to keep a pleasant expression on her face. It would be good practise. If she could maintain her equilibrium around this man, she suspected the rest of mankind would be a walk in the park.

'You do not wish to tell me?'

Be pleasant.

'It's just...the way you people live. It's extraordinary, and so far removed from my usual world it boggles my mind.'

Dark eyebrows rose. '*You* people?'

'The Funaros and—'

'I am *not* a Funaro!'

Wow, okay. 'But you're clearly from the same world and—'

'I did not grow up with the kind of wealth and privilege that the members of the Funaro family were fortunate enough to enjoy.' Stern lips became positively grim. 'I am not of the same social standing or—'

He broke off, breathing hard. She'd clearly struck a nerve.

Keep your equilibrium, Cinders.

'Well, let's stick to the facts, then,' she said *pleasantly*. She held up one finger. 'You're ridiculously successful and wealthy.' She held up another. 'You have an art studio on an island in the middle of Lake Como.' She held up a third finger. 'And you're famous. This is not the usual state of affairs for the majority of people.'

Hooded eyes surveyed her for a moment. 'The studio is not on an island. It's simply located farther around the lake.'

'Oh, well, then that makes everything *ordinary*, then.'

Her eyeroll and the loud breath that shot from her lungs ruined the pleasant thing she'd had going. She comforted herself with the thought that she was a work in progress and that the poise would come with time.

'Signor Dimarco—'

'Gabriel!' he growled, a scowl darkening his face.

In that moment she decided pleasantness was highly overrated. With a superhuman effort, she didn't growl back. She folded her hands in her lap and met his gaze. 'Do you have friends?'

He blinked as if the question was the last thing he'd expected. 'Of course, I do. I have many in Milan where I live. Not so many here around Lake Como, that is true. Why?'

'Are they nice, good, decent people?'

Grey eyes narrowed. 'I think so. Why?'

'It's just that I'm interested in how you manage to keep them if this is the way you treat people.'

His hands clenched so hard he started to shake. Reaching down, she trailed her finger through the water. 'At least the water temperature is pleasant.'

'For what?'

'For if you really do plan to throw me overboard.'

The thunderous expression that raced across his face had her eyes widening, and no amount of coaching herself to remain composed could prevent it. But a moment later she was released from the fierce glare when he ran a hand over his face.

With a soft curse he eventually met her gaze once more, his expression milder. Or at least what she suspected he hoped would appear milder. It was debatable if *mild* was something this man could achieve. 'This is something you fear from me?'

Not really, but... 'I don't know you. I've been thrust upon you in a way that you obviously resent, and yet for some reason you didn't refuse when Marguerite made her request yesterday. You don't want me here. You've made that very clear. You've barely been civil. One could even say you've been actively rude.'

He blinked. 'I—'

'I'm sorry I couldn't find an excuse to get out of the studio visit in a way that would've seemed polite to my grandmother. But you have my assurance that I will do my best to stay out of your way when we reach your studio, and to take up as little of your time as possible.'

Grey eyes throbbed into hers.

She swallowed when he didn't say anything. 'And then, when we return to the villa, we need barely see each other again.'

'That will be impossible.'

She stared down at her hands and huffed out a laugh. 'Oh, I'm sure you'll find a way.'

'Lili.' He said his daughter's name as if it explained all. 'Unless I'm very much mistaken, you are as taken with my daughter as she is with you.'

Damn.

'She will wish to spend time with you.'

She wanted to spend time with Lili, too. She studied his face, blew out a breath. 'And you don't allow your daughter to spend time with people you don't know.'

'I do not,' he agreed.

She couldn't blame him for that.

'I owe you an apology, Audrey. I did not mean to take my bad temper out on you. You are right. I have treated you abominably and I humbly ask your forgiveness.'

It was her turn to blink. She, um…wow, okay. 'Consider it forgotten,' she mumbled.

They stared at each other. She couldn't read the expression in his eyes at all. 'What does your grandmother have on you?' he finally asked.

She wasn't sure she'd heard him correctly. 'I beg your pardon?'

'Why do you feel compelled to do Marguerite's bidding? What does she blackmail you with?'

'She's not blackmailing me!'

She leaned towards him, but it brought her in too close. His scent hit her and it was like a shock of cold water to her senses. She shot back, her heart pounding.

Stop being ridiculous.

And yet a strange new energy filled her, and it took all her strength to not lean forward and breathe him in a second time. Something about him invigorated her like a cold alpine breeze and sea spray, but it carried the heat of chilli peppers. That heat stole into her veins now.

She did what she could to shake the sensation off. 'Marguerite has unreservedly welcomed me into her family and her home. She's been kind and generous and everything that is benevolent. In asking you to assist me with my art, she's hoping to provide me with something that will make me happy. It would be ungrateful, not to mention ungracious, for me to refuse her that.'

He remained unmoved.

She started to lean towards him again, but caught herself in time. 'We're family, Gabriel. Family should pull together and look after one another. I know it's only early days, but that's what I would like to work towards with Marguerite.'

It's what she'd like to work towards with all of the family.

'Then you are a fool.'

She turned and stared at the water, doing her best to rein in her temper. When she was pretty certain she'd managed it, she turned back. 'I thought you weren't going to be rude anymore.'

'I did not mean to be rude. I am simply telling you the truth. If you think Marguerite has your best interests at heart, then you are sadly mistaken.'

He loathed the Funaro family. Folding her arms, she swallowed. 'What's your reading of the situation, then?'

'Marguerite's only concern is to maintain the prestige of the Funaro name, nothing more.'

She recalled that *please*, the expression in her grandmother's eyes when they rested on Lili. 'I think you're mistaken.'

'And what if I were to tell you she is already regretting the rather spontaneous request she made of me?'

Her mouth went strangely dry. 'For what reason?'

'Because it belatedly occurred to her that I might taint another of her precious granddaughters.'

Her heart pounded against the walls of her ribs. 'That's what her *quick word* was about?'

Stern lips cracked open in a humourless smile. 'It was indeed.'

Her grandmother had *warned him off*? She didn't know whether to be offended or absurdly touched.

'Succeed in resisting my masculine charms, Audrey, and the plaudits will be yours.'

He stretched out his arms as if he were a prize or a trophy. She swallowed and shifted on her seat. The thing was she couldn't deny that he had a lot of masculine charm. Not that it meant anything. She wasn't going to pursue him or anything.

'Fail and allow yourself to be seduced by me, and you'll be considered a bitter disappointment and relegated to the ranks and ignored like everyone else.'

He didn't want to seduce her, that much was clear, and yet his words and their accompanying smile sent a chill racing down her spine. Along with a traitorous and wholly unwelcome thrill.

CHAPTER THREE

UNABLE TO STARE at the incredulous expression on Audrey's far too expressive face a moment longer, Gabriel kicked the boat's engine back over with a curse and turned in the direction of his studio. He was careful, though, to keep the action of the boat as smooth as he could as an unfamiliar shame washed through him.

All of the anger and resentment he'd wanted to fling at Marguerite, all of the bitterness he felt towards Fina and the Funaro name, he'd just taken out on Audrey. Marguerite had disturbed old ghosts, but Audrey didn't deserve to bear his anger for that.

It took all his willpower not to lower his head to the steering wheel and give in to the exhaustion that crashed down on him. He and Lili had been at the Funaro estate for two weeks, and already he felt stretched to his limit. He had another ten weeks of this *imprisonment* to go. How would he bear it?

Gritting his teeth, he shoved his shoulders back. He would bear whatever was necessary for Lili's sake. He understood Marguerite's game—she hoped that if she made him uncomfortable enough, he would leave Lili with her for the duration of the summer and return to Milan.

His hands tightened on the wheel. *That* wasn't going to happen.

Blowing out a breath, he glanced at the woman beside him. Dismissing her as just another Funaro was far from fair. The stunned expression on her face just now... He shook his head. This woman was completely unaware of her position as a pawn on the Funaro chessboard.

She was still an innocent. One who believed in the sanctity of family. One who took what people told her at face value. One who clearly believed the best of people rather than the worst.

His lips twisted. Over the course of the summer, as she discovered the *delights* of the Funaro lifestyle, he had no doubts that she, too, would change and adopt their ways, become lost to the glamour, the partying... The jockeying for position and Marguerite's favour. She'd become hard and sophisticated, devious and disingenuous, shrewd and conniving. Unscrupulous.

Maybe not, a tiny voice whispered. Maybe she'd walk away when she discovered what they were.

Family should pull together and look after one another.

Or they would break her and she would flee back home.

Which he suddenly realised he had no knowledge of, beyond the fact it was Australia.

Very gently, he brought the boat in beside the studio's tiny dock, slipped a rope over the mooring post and secured it fast. After leaping out, he held a hand out towards Audrey, but she remained seated. 'Can I say something before we do this?' She nodded at the path that led to the studio.

'Of course.'

That pointed chin lifted. 'I make my own decisions about who I date and when I date.'

Dark eyes flashed, and although he stood on firm ground, he had to widen his stance to keep his balance.

'Let me make this very clear. I'm not currently in the market for either a boyfriend or a lover.'

The way her lips shaped the word *lover* had heat licking along his veins. He had to ignore it. He had no intention—*none whatsoever*—of dallying with this woman.

'And you can act as cynical and mocking as you like, but I'm fully aware that a man like you wouldn't be interested in someone like me.'

What on earth…?

'So if you *are* plotting to seduce me with a view to aggravating Marguerite, you can forget about it.'

He wasn't planning any such thing!

'I'm not going to fall for it. And you can rest assured I won't be instigating any kind of flirtation with you either, so you can stop already with the exaggerated sighs and black looks.'

With the *what*?

'I'm fully aware that I'm neither polished nor beautiful, but nor am I an idiot and—'

'Your beauty is undeniable.' Maybe he shouldn't have said it, but he couldn't allow it to go unchallenged.

She blinked.

'It's true you're not polished, but look at the land behind me.' He gestured at the unmanicured woodland that surrounded his studio and cut it off from the rest of civilisation. 'It is not polished either, but one cannot deny its beauty. One can acquire polish if they wish to.'

She stared at him as if she didn't know what to say.

'In fact, Marguerite will require it of you.'

Something in her eyes dimmed, but a moment later she shook herself, and her expression became resolute once again. 'I just wanted us on the same page about...all of that. So you've no need to be so...'

He crouched down so that they were eye to eye, and her scent rose up around him. It was wholesome and restful... familiar. It took him a moment to place it. *Lavender.* She smelled of lavender. It made him want to smile. 'No need to be so...?'

'Guarded, I suppose. Suspicious. Disapproving. You don't know me and yet I feel you've already condemned me.'

He bit back a sigh. 'If I have been sighing and glaring, it's not because of you.'

One eyebrow rose. 'I'm not sure I believe you.'

Her words were like knives and he didn't know why they should sting him so. 'I am not a dishonest man. I do not lie.'

Eyes the colour of cloves scanned his face now, but he couldn't tell if she believed him or not. 'Then what has the sighing and glaring been about?'

'Marguerite.'

Both brows shot up. 'You're still brooding about that?'

'She is manipulative and imperious. I do not like to be manipulated.' His lips twisted. 'Or given orders.'

He rose and held out his hand. 'Will you now disembark?'

She took his hand, her fingers tightening in his as the boat rocked. But she didn't panic, merely looked for him to tell her where to put her feet, and before he was ready, she was standing in front of him, swamping him in the comforting scent of lavender.

He went to release her, but her hand tightened in his. 'Please tell me you believe I've no designs on you.'

'Of course, I believe you.' And he did. 'I have been rude and boorish and you have felt threatened by me—for which I again apologise. I cannot imagine you would wish to lumber yourself with such a bad-tempered lover. No sensible woman would. And I believe that you are very sensible.'

Her lips twitched. It told him she no longer felt threatened by him, and he gave thanks for it. The thought of frightening any woman, let alone one as alone as Audrey, made him sick to his stomach.

'Also, you spoke of beauty earlier as if it were a precursor to embarking upon an affair,' he continued, 'and I cannot be accused of being a beautiful man.'

'No,' she agreed, finally releasing him. 'But there is something compelling about you.'

A pulse inside him burst to life. He ignored it. Refused to allow himself to consider her words too closely.

She cocked her head to one side. 'Beauty and attraction don't necessarily go hand in hand.'

Dio! Was she saying—?

She stiffened as if suddenly realising how her words could be interpreted. Coughing, she hastened back into speech. 'Besides, a person is so much more than what they look like. There's a woman I work with back home.'

Did she not now consider *this* her home?

'When you first meet her, you might think her plain, but when you get to know her, you realise she's one of the most beautiful people you'll ever meet.'

Affection brightened her eyes, and her lips curved in a way that had him catching his breath. When Audrey let her guard down, she—

She nothing!

He gestured for her to precede him on the path. 'Where do you work?'

'At a nursing home in Melbourne—an aged care facility.'

'You are a nurse?'

'More a nurse's aide, really. I didn't study nursing at university or anything.'

'Why not?'

She was quiet for a moment, before sending him a swift smile. 'I was busy with other things.'

He sensed she didn't wish to discuss it, and let the matter drop. After having been so ill-tempered, he needed to prove he could be a pleasant host now. Climbing the short rise in the path and then rounding the curve, his studio came into view and Audrey came to a dead halt. He only just managed to avoid walking into her.

Clasping her hands together, she stared at it with wide eyes. 'Oh, Gabriel, I think you are the luckiest man alive.'

'This is my summer sanctuary. Here I can retreat from the pressures of the Funaro family and lose myself in my art.'

At least, that had been the plan—it is what had happened in previous summers—but his art wasn't providing him with the respite, comfort or distraction it usually did. Instead, in failing him, it had become another source of tension.

He pushed that thought away. 'It is where Lili and I can come for some quiet time—to picnic and swim if we so desire.' And to sleep, too, on occasion. There were sleeping quarters here. The Funaros didn't own this land. It was his and his alone. Here Marguerite had no sovereignty, and he was determined to keep it that way.

She swung around, her face falling. 'And I'm intruding. *That's* why you've been in such a bad mood.'

He wrinkled his nose. 'I...'

'You told me you don't lie.' Her hands went to her hips. 'Don't disappoint me now.'

He stared at his studio, letting out a long breath. 'I have never invited any member of the family to my studio before. I do not wish for their dramas and demands to sully this place.'

'And you haven't invited me now, either.' With a wistful glance in the studio's direction, she turned back to him and squared her shoulders. 'Marguerite has been unreasonable, Gabriel. Come,' she said, gesturing for him to turn around. 'Return me to the villa. I'm sorry you've been put to so much trouble. I'll explain to Marguerite that she had no right to ask this of you. You can keep your sanctuary safe and—'

'I would be honoured to share it with you.'

He wasn't sure who was more surprised by his offer, him or Audrey.

'You are an artist, are you not?' he demanded, not allowing himself to dwell on why he was willing to share this special place with her.

She huffed out a laugh. 'That's debatable.'

'When you get the opportunity, do you lose yourself in your work for as long as you can? When you are working on something, do you think about it all the time? When you cannot make the vision in your head a reality and everything you do fails, and the frustration builds and builds until you think you will burst, do you keep persisting because you cannot let it go? And when you have a breakthrough, can see a way forward, does it feel like you are flying?'

Her jaw dropped. Nodding, she dragged it back into place. Satisfaction rippled through him. An artist created, and Audrey clearly created. It didn't matter if others saw value in her work or not. It didn't matter if *he* saw value in her work or not. In that moment, though, he burned with a strange curiosity to see what it was that she made.

'Would you continue with your art whether people said it was good, bad or indifferent?'

'Yes.' The word was quietly uttered, but strong for all that.

'Then, Audrey, you are an artist. It is what you do.' He gestured towards his studio. 'Would you like to see inside?'

'Very much.'

'Then come.'

Without another word, he led her to the studio door and unlocked it. 'Ready?'

'For what?' she asked, entering behind.

He flicked a switch on the wall and her eyes widened as the steel shutters on the wall of glass directly in front of them slid up to reveal the remarkable view outside. Her mouth formed a perfect O and he couldn't help but smile. She swung to him, stared at him, then turned back to the view. 'Did I mention earlier that you are the luckiest man alive?'

He laughed. Here in this space it was easy to laugh, to relax, to be himself. 'I believe you did.'

'You get to work here whenever you want.'

'Not quite. I have a warehouse studio in Milan, which is where I work on my larger pieces. It would not be practical to work on them here. But yes, this is where I work in the summer—on smaller pieces, on sketches and ideas for bigger projects.'

'Oh, Gabriel, it's absolutely amazing. Show me around.'

He gave her a tour, showing her where he kept his materials and the tools of his trade, along with the various projects he was working on. His lips twisted—*trying* to work on, he amended silently.

In her turn, she asked intelligent questions—where did he source his materials? What did he do with the scrap? How long did he spend sketching before starting a sculpture? She gazed at it all, and behind the warm, spice-brown of her eyes he sensed her mind racing.

'It's absolutely amazing—all of it. The light and the view...the tranquillity.'

The quality of the light was why he'd bought the land. Ensuring he made the most of that light had driven the specifications for the building. He'd paid a fortune for it all, but as far as he was concerned it was worth every penny. The tranquillity, though, had sealed the deal. This view looked southward. From here, one couldn't see the Funaro Villa. Nothing here rang a false note or had painful memories clamouring to the surface. All was simple and breathtaking beauty.

She pointed. 'You have a mezzanine level?'

'There are sleeping quarters up there.' He had no intention of giving her a tour of those.

She smiled. 'For when you get too caught up in your work and can't bear to leave.'

For when he needed a break from the Funaros.

'It's all very impressive. Mostly, though, I'm in awe of your work.' She gestured to the nearby bench and the finished work he'd brought with him from Milan that he'd been hoping would inspire him—an Impressionist sculpture of an oak tree in the autumn when its leaves had started to fall. 'I could look at this all day. It's a bit dishevelled and shabby but so strong, so...timeless.' She turned to him. 'You have an amazing talent.'

'Thank you.'

He had been given this compliment before, but her simple sincerity touched him in a way few previous compliments had. 'Now it is your turn to share something of your work with me.'

Her throat bobbed convulsively, and she gripped her hands so hard the knuckles turned white. 'But...' She swallowed again. 'I didn't bring any of it with me.'

He gestured to the small backpack she carried. 'You must have pictures on your phone.' He understood an artist's reluctance to share their work, their concern that it would not be understood... The fear of criticism. It was also important for an artist to overcome such fears. One could learn much from constructive criticism.

'You do not trust me with your art?' The thought pierced him.

'You're an important artist. I am a nobody.'

His brows rose. She was a *Funaro*.

'Very few people consider what I do as art.'

'This was also the fate of Vincent Van Gogh—he was considered unsuccessful and a failure. You are in good company.'

Her nose wrinkled. 'I don't have those kinds of pretensions.'

He was silent for a long moment and then gestured around. 'I have shared all of this with you willingly. Will you not share a little of your art with me?'

'You make me sound churlish.'

She nibbled on her bottom lip and he tried not to notice

the way it deepened the colour; the way that lip grew plump and inviting.

Her shoulders suddenly slumped. 'You promise you won't laugh?'

Who had laughed at her art? 'I promise.'

After pulling her phone from her bag, she opened a photo folder. Clutching it to her chest she met his gaze, grimaced. 'While you look at these, would it be okay if I were to go and explore out there?' She pointed beyond the window.

'Of course.' She didn't want to watch his face as he assessed her work. He had a good poker face, but this woman was proving surprisingly perceptive. 'The door is in the side wall there.'

Without a word, she disappeared through it.

He opened the folder on her phone.

CHAPTER FOUR

AUDREY DIDN'T PACE the path outside that extraordinary wall of glass. She ached to give vent to the nerves stabbing through her, but Gabriel would see. And she didn't want to betray herself like that.

She couldn't work him out. He'd been so rude earlier, and then shocked when she'd called him out on it. As if he'd been so deep inside his own tangled thoughts, he hadn't realised how he'd come across.

Since then, though, he'd been the perfect host.

To stop from turning and staring at him through the wall of glass, and possibly surprising him in the act of curling his lip as he flicked through her so-called *artworks*, she made her way down to the waterfront and a pretty, protected curve of bay. This must be where he and Lili sometimes swam. Kicking off her shoes, she welcomed the cool of the water against her toes.

The water was clear—unruffled and satin soft, the pebbles and sand at her feet easy to negotiate—and the forest around the lake shaded a deep healthy green, while the ridges that rose up all around were harmoniously majestic.

Across the lake the buildings of a town glowed cream, yellow and warm ochre in the late-morning sun. Tiny waves splashed against the shore, and the scent of gardenias drifted on the air.

But none of it soothed the agitation rolling through her. The elevated heart rate, the alternate hot and cold flushes. She glanced at her watch and wrung her hands. He'd been looking at the photos on her phone for fifteen minutes! *Oh, God.* She hid her face in her hands. She couldn't believe the celebrated Gabriel Dimarco was currently assessing *her* work.

I don't lie.

Well, maybe he could make an exception this one time, and tell her he thought the pieces pretty and decorative and recommend a teacher or two. Then they could change the subject and never speak of it again.

'What are you afraid you're going to hear?'

She spun to find Gabriel standing on the path above her. Her heart practically hammered its way out of her chest.

'What do you think I'm going to say?'

I don't lie.

Well then, she wouldn't, either. 'That you think the work is trivial and of no consequence.' She kept her chin high. 'Saying that, though, makes it sound as if I have delusions of grandeur when I don't.'

In two steps he was at her side though she couldn't work out how he'd moved so quickly. 'Others have belittled your work?'

'You've seen my medium.' For God's sake, what she did was glorified embroidery—*needlework*. She didn't create post-Impressionist watercolours or grand oil paintings or extraordinary sculptures. She *sewed*. 'I mean, anyone with half a brain can learn to sew, right?'

'Just as anyone with half a brain can slap paint on a canvas or make something from clay. But just because they can, doesn't mean they're good at it.'

His vehemence made her blink.

'But these—' he held up her phone '—are extraordinary, Audrey.'

Had he just said…? Folding her arms to hide the way her hands suddenly shook, she drew herself up to her full height. At five foot ten inches in her bare feet, her full height was pretty impressive, but she still had to throw her head back to meet Gabriel's gaze. 'Don't lie to me. Not about this.'

'I don't lie. This I have already told you.' He waved an impatient hand through the air. 'It is true that when Marguerite asked me to look over your work, I didn't have high hopes. At best I thought you would be a competent amateur. Until she mentioned Madame De Luca.'

'Like I said, that was just a favour for a friend.'

'She does not do such things. Her standards are too high.' Those grey eyes surveyed her with an unblinking certainty that had her pulse easing. 'She might have told you that, let you believe it for whatever reason…probably to keep you humble, but where art is concerned, Madame De Luca does not lower her standards.'

Had Aunt Beatrice deliberately let her believe it was an arrangement between friends? But why…? Oh, Lord! Had Beatrice paid the outrageous fees Madame charged and didn't want Audrey finding out, so had concocted the fiction? Oh! But—

Gabriel shook the phone in front of her face, recapturing her attention. 'I'm telling you that you have a rare talent. Your work is powerful. And while it is also true that it is sometimes raw, none of it is insipid. It is infused with life and...'

She leaned towards him, hanging on his every word. His scent once again an electrifying jolt to her senses, but this time she welcomed the oddly enlivening sting of it.

'Emotion.'

Her throat went oddly tight and she had to press a hand to her breastbone to stop her heart from falling at her feet.

'Which comes first—the subject or the emotion?'

She'd never pondered that before. 'Sometimes it's the emotion, but more often it's the subject,' she said slowly. 'But when I'm working, even if I don't want it to, the emotion takes over and directs everything.'

He nodded.

She held herself on such a tight leash in her everyday life, always had—had needed to—and art had become her outlet.

'Did not Madame De Luca tell you of your talent?'

'She told me I had an excellent technique and that my work showed promise. But I thought she was just being kind.'

He raised his eyes heavenward, exclaiming, *'Dio!'* before grey eyes skewered her to the spot once again. 'Did your family, your Australian family, belittle your work? Is that why you have feared my assessment? If I'd known how concerned you were I wouldn't have left you hanging so long.'

'No! I mean, I don't think they really understood it, none of them are artistic, but Nonna and my cousin Frankie have always been ridiculously amazed and encouraging.' So had Johanna.

'Rightly amazed,' he corrected. 'Your father?'

She shrugged, her chest clenching at the mention of her

father. 'He's more the mad scientist type. If it's not part of the imperial table of elements or has a formula an arm long, he doesn't recognise it.'

'I cannot believe you have gone undiscovered for so long.'

It was no surprise to her. 'I've never attended an art class or studied art at university. I just...dabble in my spare time. There's absolutely no reason why I should've been discovered.' She frowned. 'And you might change your mind once you see my pieces in the flesh.'

She wished she hadn't used the phrase *in the flesh*. Uttering those words at Gabriel seemed altogether too suggestive.

Something in his eyes flared, but it was quickly extinguished. 'I do not think so.'

She couldn't get her head around this conversation at all. He truly thought she had talent?

'I know of several teachers who would help you hone your craft.'

He did?

'Alas, they are all in Rome and Florence, though I think that I, too, could help.'

She moistened suddenly dry lips. 'You would consider taking me on as a student?' He was famously reclusive when it came to discussing his work. Rumour had it that many young artists had petitioned him for a mentorship, but all had been refused. Would he seriously make an exception for her?

'Our mediums are different, but many of our goals are the same.' Firm lips twisted. 'And as we're both stuck here for the summer... Think it over and—'

'I don't need to think about it. I would love to learn all I could from you, Gabriel. I'm fully aware of the compliment you pay me.'

'Good.' He nodded. 'I request, however, that you do not speak to the newspapers about this. I value my privacy.'

'You have my word.'

He stared at her for a long moment, and the air between them crackled. 'You have something else to say?' he demanded.

She chewed on the inside of her lip. 'Are you sure about this?'

His chin tilted at an unconsciously arrogant angle. 'I am not in the habit of making offers that I am not sure about. Why?'

She swallowed. 'Marguerite hasn't asked this of you, has she?' The thought of being foisted on him had everything inside her protesting.

'No. If she had I would not have made the offer.' A humourless smile touched his lips. 'In fact, she will probably be vexed by the arrangement.'

Which, as far as he was concerned, was a point in its favour, she realised.

Those grey eyes turned mocking. 'Do you dare risk her displeasure, Audrey? Which comes first—family or art?'

'Family.' She didn't even have to think about it.

He blinked.

'But I expect Marguerite will be fully cognizant of the honour you do me in offering to mentor me.' She nodded slowly, recalling the vulnerability in her grandmother's eyes. *Please.* 'I suspect she would consider me a fool if I were to refuse it.'

She *would* be a fool. This was a once-in-a-lifetime opportunity. Knowing her own weaknesses, though, knowing how much she yearned for family, if she wasn't careful the Funaro family would consume her completely. And that would defeat the purpose of being here. Accepting Gabriel's offer could help her prevent that from happening.

She wanted to be considered a legitimate member of the Funaro family, but she didn't want to lose her own identity. Or turn her back on her past. A chill chased down her spine. Accepting Gabriel's offer, having a chance to focus on her art, would give her something that was just her own, and might help her find a way to bridge past and present.

'Before we embark any further on this discussion, I need to make one thing very clear to you, Audrey.' His voice had gone chillingly serious and she met his gaze once more. 'I will not shackle myself to the Funaro family a second time.'

For a moment she didn't know what he was talking about. Then she stiffened. 'Didn't we just talk about this?'

'Is that clear?' he repeated, his brows drawing low over his eyes.

'Perfectly.' She didn't ask him why; didn't ask what made him hate the Funaro family so much. It was none of her business. 'Like I said, I'm not currently in the market for romance. For heaven's sake, look at my life!' She spread her arms wide. 'I think it's complicated enough without adding a romance to the mix, don't you?'

His lips twitched and it gave her hope that a sense of humour rested beneath that sober exterior. 'Perhaps,' he agreed.

She suddenly grinned. 'I'm a Funaro, and you're bad-tempered—it would be a most inauspicious match, don't you think? It will be much better to be colleagues, yes?'

He chuckled. '*Si*, this is true. Colleagues then. Come, let's shake on it.'

She placed her hand in his and they shook on it. Who knew? Maybe they'd even eventually become friends.

* * *

Audrey turned first one way and then the other in front of the mirror. Heavens! She eased back and twirled, only to discover her grandmother surveying her from the doorway.

She couldn't help but grin at the older woman.

'I did knock,' Marguerite said, 'but you obviously didn't hear me above that awful racket.' She pointed to Audrey's sound system.

Audrey immediately lowered the volume, but didn't turn it off. 'One day this summer, Grandmama, you and I are going to sip shandies out there on the terrace while I introduce you to the joy that is the music of Taylor Swift.'

'I will look forward to it,' Marguerite said with her customary poise, but Audrey could've sworn the older woman's eyes danced. 'In the meantime, you seem pleased with your new dress.'

She didn't just have a new dress. She had a whole new wardrobe! She'd never owned such beautiful clothes. Tonight she was to make her first appearance in public as a member of the family—at a lavish charity ball—and in its honour, Marguerite had commissioned this dress. Its folds of cream silk and pink lace made her look *beautiful*.

Or maybe that was the new hairstyle.

Or all of the makeup. She'd spent hours with a makeup artist being tutored in how to contour, shape and define each of her features. As if she were a painting or an embroidery—or a work of art.

'I feel like Cinderella,' she confided. Or Audrey Hepburn's character from *My Fair Lady*. On impulse she kissed the older woman's cheek. 'Does my appearance meet with your approval?'

'Yes.'

She'd discovered that her grandmother never gushed, but she also never lied about something as important to her as one's appearance. The hard knot at the centre of her that had been diminishing slowly over the past week eased further now. She wanted to do Marguerite proud, and tonight she meant to do exactly that. She'd be poised, polite and... Well, *polished* wasn't exactly the right word. Marguerite's level of polish came from having grown up in this world, and Audrey doubted she'd ever fully master it. But she'd be warm and kind, and she meant to enjoy every minute of the evening's festivities.

'Several other family members will be attending tonight.' She named two of Audrey's cousins and an uncle and his wife. 'And Gabriel, obviously.'

'Why *obviously*?' She hid a frown—rather well, she thought. She'd get the hang of this poise thing yet. 'He doesn't strike me as...'

Marguerite raised an eyebrow.

'The social type.'

Gabriel had decreed they'd start her lessons next week, and other than her visit to his studio, she'd only seen him one other time this week when she and Lili had spent a happy couple of hours exploring the grounds, Lili showing Audrey all of her favourite spots on the estate. That was when she'd discovered Gabriel and Lili didn't have a suite in the villa, but stayed in a cottage on the grounds instead. He'd not spoken much; had spent more time trailing behind them than taking part in the conversation.

Maybe he'd been thinking about a project he was working on.

Or just ensuring she didn't get the wrong idea and start making big moon eyes at him.

'Gabriel is a patron of this particular charity. It's one that is close to his heart.'

Shame hit her then in a hot rush. She'd been so focused on her new dress and how she looked that she'd not given a second thought to what the charity might be. What charity were they supporting tonight? She was too embarrassed to ask Marguerite.

Swallowing, she made herself smile. 'Shall we all arrive together?'

'Good heavens, no, child.'

Child? She wanted to laugh. She was twenty-six!

'You and I shall take the car together, but we're going to arrive fashionably late.'

So they could make a splash? Her stomach started to churn.

'The others have made their own arrangements. Now remember, this evening all eyes will be upon you. You will keep your shoulders back and your chin high. You are a Funaro.'

She nodded.

'And you will meet me in the foyer no later than eight o'clock.'

'I won't be late.'

With a nod, the older woman left.

Turning back to the mirror, she stared at the unfamiliar reflection gazing back at her. She pointed at it. 'You can do this.' She'd do whatever necessary to make her grandmother, and the rest of the family, proud of her.

She was in the foyer at ten to eight. She suspected Marguerite wouldn't tolerate tardiness, and she'd rather be the one kept waiting. Besides, waiting was something she was used to.

A footstep on the stair above had her turning away from surveying her face in one of the many mirrors that dotted the wall. 'Gabriel.'

He stopped dead. His eyes widened and lips thinned.

Heat rose up her neck and across her cheeks. She gestured to the mirror. 'I'm not usually so vain. I just can't believe what I look like.'

He didn't speak, but those grey eyes appraised her with a throbbing thoroughness that had her stomach clenching.

With an effort, she swallowed. 'I keep having to pinch myself to believe this is real.' She held out her inner arm to show him a red mark there. 'Which I better stop doing or I'll end up with a bruise.' And she doubted that'd meet with Marguerite's approval, either.

Gabriel stared at Audrey and couldn't utter a single damn word. At the back of his mind an ugly voice sounded: *And so it begins...* But his better self protested against the cynicism. Fina's fate didn't have to be Audrey's. It wasn't a foregone conclusion.

He was trying to protect himself. *Again.* Trying to avoid the soul-crushing disappointment of seeing another life wasted.

A hard knot squeezed his chest tight. If he'd tried harder with Fina—tried harder to break down her barriers, tried harder to make her see how self-destructive her behaviour had been—then maybe she'd be alive today and Lili would still have her mother.

He hadn't tried harder, though. He'd retreated to save himself from the pain of watching her drink herself into a stupor time and time again; retreated from her rants and rages, and from the line of lovers she'd taken such pleasure in parading in front of him. He should've realised it had been a cry for help. Instead, he'd taken righteous refuge in hurt feelings, hurt pride and his sense of betrayal.

Did he mean to bury his head in the sand again now? Did he really mean to stand by and watch another woman be ruined by the Funaro fortune and do nothing?

Rolling his shoulders, he did what he could to shake off the thought.

'Stop looking at me like that.' Audrey pressed her hands to her stomach. 'You're making me nervous. At least tell me I'm going to pass muster.'

'You look very beautiful, but then I think you already know that.'

He did what he could to keep his voice measured. She *was* beautiful. But with her hair piled up on top of her head in a sophisticated updo that showed off the elegant line of her throat, and a dress that clung to curves that had his mouth drying, the skirt floating around her legs like a dream, a deep, hard lust fired to life inside him.

It had him wanting to throw his head back and howl. He'd desired women since Fina's death, had even slept with a few, but he'd not wanted anyone with the fire that pierced him now.

It was just clothes. His hands clenched. And makeup. And a fancy hairstyle. It should make no difference. But together, all of it brought to the fore her beauty, forcing him to acknowledge it…and feel the burn of need in his very bones. It meant he could no longer hide from it.

It was her simple delight, however, her astonishment at her appearance, that eventually burned away some of the hormonal mist. Her enjoyment was oddly touching, and he did not wish to dim it.

'And here I was hoping you'd be more eloquent.' She laughed, part amusement and part shamefaced embarrassment. 'Serves me right for being so frivolous.'

He forced himself down the last few steps. 'I meant what I said. You do look very beautiful.' To his relief, his voice emerged smooth and sincere. Her gaze moved over him like a gentle touch, and his skin tightened.

'You look very debonair yourself.'

The way she suddenly glanced away to fidget with an earring betrayed the fact that she, too, was aware of him. Her frown told him she was no more pleased about it than he was.

He stared at his feet. They were adults. They could ignore this.

She sent him a tight smile. 'But we both know beauty is as beauty does. Tonight's purpose isn't about me looking beautiful.'

It wasn't?

'But supporting a good cause, like breast cancer.'

His head came up. Did she care about such things?

'Marguerite gave me to understand it's an important one to you.'

'My mother died of breast cancer.'

'Oh, Gabriel, I didn't know. I'm sorry.'

He shrugged. 'It was a long time ago now.'

Nodding, she glanced up the stairs and then back at him, a question in her eyes.

'I wanted to see Lili settled in the nursery before I left. I had planned to leave before now, but she talked me into reading her a second bedtime story.'

That made her laugh, and a whole new awareness rippled

over the surface of his skin. 'I didn't think, but of course she'd be staying here tonight.'

He didn't want to dwell on that. He knew Lili would come to no harm under Marguerite's roof. It's just he wanted, *needed*, to ensure that the Funaro influence didn't dominate Lili's life. He wanted his daughter to grow up to be whatever she wanted to be, not moulded into a cookie-cutter socialite with no anchor to keep her grounded. That lack of an anchor had destroyed Fina. He was determined Lili would find one in him, in the values he meant to instil in her, and in helping her find her purpose in life. He would do everything he could to protect her, to prevent her from feeling cast adrift, worthless and filled with despair.

'I understand we're travelling separately.'

Her frown had him chuckling. 'I suspect Marguerite will want to make a splash tonight as she introduces you to...'

She raised one marvellous eyebrow. 'Her friends?'

'High society.' He shoved his hands into the pockets of his trousers. 'And I prefer to drive myself. That way I can come and go as I please.'

An uncomfortable silence opened up then. 'You know everyone is going to want the inside story tonight. So... what's the party line?'

He'd be questioned, too, but he had the skills to deflect and the bad manners to tell people to mind their own business. Marguerite's high society only tolerated him because of his fame. He clenched his jaw so hard it started to ache. If he didn't find a way to unblock himself soon, though, he'd not have even that.

Beneath whatever perfume she wore, he still detected a note of lavender when she leaned towards him. 'The what?'

'How are you explaining the discovery that you're a Funaro heiress?'

Her lips turned down a fraction. 'Well, we're saying that my parents had an intense whirlwind affair. That resulted in...me. My father never knew my mother's true identity. She went off to see more of the world, with promises to come back, but never returned. As a result, I never knew I was a Funaro until my nonna's death when I received the letter she'd left for me.'

He wondered what the real story was. The one throbbing beneath the sanitised version. The shadows in her eyes told him there was one.

She leaned across and suddenly gripped his hand. 'I'm glad you're going to be there tonight, Gabriel. It'll help to have a friendly face in the crowd.'

Damn. Damn and blast!

He wasn't any kind of knight. Fina had proven that.

She smiled and it was as if the shadows had never been. 'I also plan to have fun this evening. In all my life, I've never been to a party like this one.'

He couldn't help feeling she was going to be sadly disappointed. And—

And nothing! She had her art. It would help when all of this tumbled down around her ears. It would be something she could fall back on. And that at least was something he could help her with.

have taken the trouble to teach their children better manners. I know you were dealing with him as efficiently as you could in the circumstance, and I suspect you didn't want to make a scene by walking off the dance floor, but it hardly seemed fair you suffer those wandering hands a moment longer.'

'I appreciate the intervention. I think he'd had a little too much to drink.'

Dio. Must this woman always make excuses for bad behaviour?

'And it's nice to dance with you, Gabriel. For once, I don't have to make small talk, sidestep impertinent questions and pretend to be...' She trailed off, but he knew what she meant.

'So Cinderella isn't enjoying the ball as much as she thought she would?'

'Oh, no, I am! I'm having the most exciting time.'

She was?

'The dinner was a revelation—I mean, *caviar*. Before tonight I'd never had French champagne, either.'

'And did you like them both?'

She nodded, those warm walnut eyes dancing. 'As my father would say, I've champagne tastes on a beer budget.'

An uncharacteristic snort shot from him, making several people glance around at him in surprise.

'What does your father think about all of this?'

When her face fell, he wished he'd not asked.

'Well, I only told him this week. Once I realised it was going to make the papers. He was a bit...shocked.'

He could imagine. Had the man really been in ignorance of Danae's true identity as a Funaro?

'But he's recently remarried and has started a new job

in the States, and it's keeping him very busy, so he won't have much time to worry.'

'Speaking of marriage... Did he and Danae marry?'

'My dear Gabriel, you're definitely going off script with that question.'

He didn't know if her chiding was serious or not.

'Apparently, the right response is *my parents had a fiery affair.*'

Marguerite's hand again, no doubt.

She bit her lip. 'I always thought they had, but maybe I was wrong.'

Or maybe...

'But if they were, it clearly wasn't legal.'

Because Danae had never divorced from her first husband.

'Nobody talks of her, you know?'

Of Danae? Of course, they didn't. And he had no intention of talking out of school, either.

Before he realised it, they'd danced another dance, and he grew aware of the speculation growing rife in the eyes of those who surreptitiously but greedily watched. *Damn.* He didn't want to be the subject of that kind of gossip or—

Though... He glanced down at the woman in his arms. Perhaps it wouldn't hurt for people to think he was interested. It'd help keep the worst of the fortune hunters and those who wanted to use her for other kinds of gains—for family and business alliances, but who wouldn't care about her as a living, breathing person—at bay.

'More champagne?'

She gave a funny little shimmy as the dance came to an end. 'Yes, please. Who knew dancing could build such a thirst?'

After seizing two champagnes from a passing waiter, he led her to one of the chairs arranged at intervals around the dance floor.

She patted the chair beside her. 'Don't loom, Gabriel. Sit.'

He was used to the women at these events who wanted to cultivate his company by raising flirtatious eyebrows and sending him long, lingering glances. Or, alternately, giving a prim thank-you as their eyes scanned the crowd for someone more biddable and civilised.

Audrey did neither of those things and as her smile informed him she was enjoying his company, he sat, then watched as an expression of bliss crossed her face when she sipped her champagne. He sipped his, too, taking the time to focus on the spark and fizz. She was right. The wine was excellent.

When had it all become old hat to him? When had he started to take it for granted? When had he started hating it?

The answer came swiftly and surely: *Since Fina died.*

'Excuse me, sir, but Ms Marguerite Funaro asked me to give you a message.'

He glanced at the uniformed waiter who appeared at his elbow. 'Yes?'

'She had a headache and has retired early. She requested you see Ms Martinelli safely home.'

'Thank you.' He did what he could not to betray his surprise.

When the man moved away, Audrey frowned. 'Are you sure Marguerite warned you off? Are you sure she's not trying her hand at some kind of surreptitious matchmaking?'

He couldn't help it. He laughed. 'I'm certain.'

She blew out a breath. 'Good.'

He rolled his shoulders, tried to dislodge an odd itch. 'Why?'

'Because you told me you hate to be manipulated. And while the motives might be benevolent, I suspect you would hate someone trying to set you up.'

Benevolent? Dear God, this woman! 'I am certain your grandmother is not trying to set us up.'

'In that case...' She took her phone from her clutch and composed a text message. No doubt telling her grandmother that she hoped she was feeling better soon. When she was done, she turned back to him. 'Is it my imagination, or does the room sit up and take notice whenever I dance more than one dance with a partner?'

'It's not your imagination.'

'So the fact we just danced two and a half dances have set tongues wagging?'

'*Si.*'

Her pleated brow told him what she thought of that.

'Were you being honest with me when you said you were not currently interested in finding yourself a husband or having a romance?'

Those walnut eyes flashed. 'Of course I was.'

He liked her all the more for the fire. 'In that case, I apologise.'

'Eventually, I'd like to fall in love, marry...have children.' She shrugged. 'But it's the farthest thing from my mind at the moment. There's just too much to learn and come to grips with.' She bit her lip. 'I don't...'

He raised his brows.

She leaned a little closer. 'I don't wish to make the same mistakes my mother clearly did.'

Her words chilled him to the bone. He didn't want that

for her, either. He *could* help. A little. 'In that case, what harm will it do if people do link us romantically?'

Her eyes grew comically wide.

The more he thought about it, the more the notion recommended itself to him. If everyone thought he and Audrey were dating, it would give her time to find her feet and work out who she could trust and who to keep her distance from.

'Are you suggesting we *lie*?'

'Absolutely not. *We* don't lie, remember? But very few people will ask the question outright. If they do, you can deny it.' They wouldn't believe her, but he kept that piece of information to himself. 'In the meantime, it will buy you time, and give you an excuse to refuse all the invitations single eligible men are going to start sending your way.'

'You think men are going to start asking me on dates?'

'I don't think, I know.'

She sipped her champagne. 'I don't want to go on dates.'

'See? My plan is pure brilliance.'

That made her laugh. 'Won't it cramp your style?'

'I am not currently interested in dating, either.'

'Why not?'

Things inside him clenched. 'I need to focus on my art and my daughter. I do not have room for other things.'

She looked as if she wanted to say something, but eventually shrugged. 'Okay.'

Her easy acceptance made him want to laugh.

'If you're going to be my lift home tonight, I want you to know I'm happy to leave the party whenever you are. Please don't change your plans to suit me. But if I don't at least sample that chocolate mousse before we leave, I'm going to regret it for the rest of my life.'

He stared at her. 'You are very easy to be with. Do you know that?'

She blinked.

'You are not—what do they say?—high-maintenance.' All the women he knew were high-maintenance.

'Low-maintenance, that's me.' She grinned. 'Apparently, I'm obliging to a fault.'

'Then I will oblige you in my turn and get you one of those chocolate mousses.'

'And then will you tell me how one goes about setting up a foundation like the one you have for your mother?'

He stared at her for a long moment, but those cinnamon-spice eyes stared back at him unfazed. What on earth was she up to? 'If you wish.'

'Thank you.'

'Which do you like better? The pink or white marshmallows?' Lili asked.

'I like the white ones best.' Audrey reached into the bowl, took a white marshmallow and popped it into her mouth.

Gabriel pretended to be immersed in his sketch—which was a joke in itself, but not one that was funny. He glared at the rose he was supposed to be sketching. It didn't speak to him at all. Maybe one of the Madonna lilies would be more suitable. He stared at the nearest one, but although it was perfection, not a ripple of enthusiasm lifted through him. Instead, his attention remained on his daughter and her aunt. They were currently stretched out on the blanket on the lawn in this sheltered corner of the garden. It was a corner few people came to, which is why he'd chosen it.

'But the pink marshmallows are *so* much prettier!'

'They are prettier, but I think the white ones taste nicer.'

He thought they tasted exactly the same. Clearly, Audrey held a contrary view on the matter.

Lili reached for a white marshmallow, then, just like Audrey had, and he bit back a smile.

'It's like clothes,' Audrey said, turning onto her back and pointing to a cloud. 'That one looks like a rabbit.'

For the briefest of moments, he imagined lying above her, staring down at her. Imagined the feel of her body; imagined the silken nakedness of her and—

Dio! He tried to banish the picture from his mind.

Lili, in perfect imitation of Audrey, lay on her back, too. 'What do you mean marshmallows are like clothes?'

'Well, Grandmama has insisted on buying me a lot of beautiful new clothes for all the balls and dinner parties and luncheons I'll be attending. And some of them are *so* beautiful. But you want to know what my favourite item of clothing is?'

Lili stared at her with wide eyes. 'What?'

'My really old jeans that I've had for a million years. I mean I know all the pretty clothes look nicer, but they're nowhere near as comfortable.' She sat up. 'Can you keep a secret?' Her eyes danced and he found himself as entranced as Lili. 'Grandmama told the maid to throw my old jeans away, but I sneaked out to the bin and retrieved them.'

Lili clapped her hands over her mouth, but girlish giggles still escaped.

'But you can't tell Grandmama! Promise?'

'I promise!'

And then Lili threw herself at Audrey, who caught her as if it was the most natural thing in the world, and who hugged her back with what looked like her entire being.

CHAPTER SIX

AUDREY'S ART LESSONS officially started the week following her society debut. Gabriel had insisted on three lessons a week—and by lessons he meant whole days spent at the studio working. It hadn't been a suggestion, more a command, but Audrey hadn't argued because, a) he was doing her a favour, and b) she wasn't used to having so much free time on her hands and she'd started to find herself searching for things to do.

Something beyond trying to work out the tangled tensions and strange undercurrents among the various Funaro family members.

They were nothing like her family back home in Melbourne. Surely, money and social standing shouldn't change family dynamics *that* much. She suddenly wished she'd taken her cousin Frankie up on her offer to come to Lake Como for moral support. Frankie was currently holidaying in Tuscany, and she had the ability to cut through nonsense and get to the heart of a matter.

Blowing out a breath, she told herself to stop being a baby. But that didn't stop the warning her grandmother had given her last night and the promise she'd extracted from weighing heavily on her shoulders.

Glancing across at Gabriel, who scowled with savage intensity at a half-finished sculpture, she had to suppress a shiver. He looked every bit as ferocious as Marguerite had claimed.

Does he, though?

Cocking her head to one side, she studied him more carefully. Maybe he was tired. Maybe he was wrestling with his muse and not happy with the way his work was going. Maybe he just had a headache.

A pulse pounded in her throat. Maybe Marguerite had misjudged him.

Chilly grey eyes lifted to hers with remarkable precision, as if aware she'd been surveying him. 'You've not managed a single stitch in the last thirty minutes.'

She shrugged and gestured at his sculpture. 'You haven't made any progress in the last thirty minutes, either.'

'I'm cogitating. What's your excuse?'

She was brooding. Not that she had any intention of telling him so. 'I'm just getting used to my new surroundings.'

'Did you have this same kind of trouble when you were working with Madame De Luca?'

No. But that was before her life had been turned upside down.

'I didn't think so.' Slamming hands to his hips, he let out an insultingly impatient breath. 'And you worked fine on Monday and Wednesday. Tell me what's bothering you.'

And just like that, without warning, anger flared. Anger she suspected she'd been tamping down for four long years. 'Stop ordering me about like some damn maidservant!'

He blinked.

She was so damn tired of being the good girl, the responsible one, the person who never rocked the boat; the one who always bent over backwards to make sure everyone else felt comfortable. Nobody here cared if she felt uncomfortable or out of her depth or *anything*. Why did she always feel as if she had to be the one to make up the shortfall?

A different expression took up residence in those grey eyes, but it wasn't one she could read. Swallowing, she waited for the customary guilt to hit her—to make her feel bad for stepping outside the lines she normally prescribed for herself. And kept right on waiting.

She let out a breath she hadn't realised she'd been holding. Maybe here in this extraordinary studio the normal rules didn't apply. It was a freeing thought.

Perfect lips pursed. 'I see we're not going to have the usual kind of teacher-student relationship.'

'I have a feeling sitting at your feet and staring adoringly up at you isn't the way to earn your respect.'

'And you want my respect?'

'Don't we all want to be respected?'

And liked?

She had a feeling, though, that Gabriel didn't care whether people liked him or not.

'It's more important to respect ourselves before we start worrying what other people think of us.' He folded his arms and widened his stance. 'I didn't mean to sound so abrupt before. I apologise if you felt I was ordering you about. I'm not used to having anyone else other than Lili in the studio.'

All of her righteous outrage dissolved at his words.

'However, I would honestly like to know what's bothering you.'

She glanced at his work in progress and then back up at

him. 'I'd like to know what's bothering you, too.' She was tired of being the only one who felt clueless, the only one who felt vulnerable.

He pulled in a long breath that had already broad shoulders broadening and a deep chest deepening, and something inside her quickened. Swallowing, she forced her gaze back to his, refusing to notice anything else.

He stared at her for a long moment. 'What's said in the studio stays in the studio?'

She pondered that then nodded. 'Okay.'

He gestured at his sculpture. 'I'm blocked. I have been for months. Eight months to be precise.'

Her jaw dropped.

'It's not something I'd like made public. I have three commissions due by the end of the year and yet... I have nothing.' That dark scowl bloomed across his face again. 'It's beyond frustrating and makes me testy.'

She couldn't think of a single word to say.

'No platitudes to offer?'

His sarcasm, she finally saw, was a shield. It wasn't directed at her personally, but at himself. She lifted a hand and let it drop. 'I'm sorry, of course, but that's hardly helpful.'

He rolled his shoulders. 'Any advice to offer?'

'Me?'

'Yes, of course you.' That scowl became ferocious again. 'Why not you? You're an artist, aren't you?'

That was debatable. She stared at the screen in front of her, at her barely started embroidery, and forced her chin up. 'You said you've been blocked for eight months. Did something happen eight months ago?' Had he suffered a trauma or an accident? 'Have you been ill or anything?'

'No.' He was silent for a moment. 'You've never suffered from a creative block?'

'I've never had the opportunity. I've only ever worked on my embroideries in my free time and in stolen moments.'

Perfect lips twisted. 'So I'm wallowing in my malcontent and wasting the good fortune I've been given. Being self-indulgent.'

'That's not what I said!' But it's how he saw himself, she realised. 'I think you need to relax a bit and stop being so tense.' *And judgemental.* 'Coffee?'

She didn't wait for an answer, but strode across to the small kitchenette and the coffee machine, glancing up briefly at the mysterious mezzanine level that hadn't been part of her tour, before busying herself making coffee. 'When was the last time you made something just for fun? Just because you wanted to?'

'I...'

She looked at him. Could he not remember? 'I've fitted my embroideries in between work and other things. It has always been a form of relaxation and play.' That had to change once it became your day job.

'What other things?'

She glanced around at the unexpected question. For a moment she was tempted to tell him, but Marguerite would hate it if she did. Marguerite had requested Audrey not tell anyone.

Ice slid in between her ribs. Her sister Johanna wasn't anything to be ashamed of. She'd reluctantly agreed not to mention her twin in the near future, though. She wanted a chance for her and Marguerite to grow close, before putting forward the memorial she had in mind for her sister.

She busied herself with the coffee again. 'Oh, you know. Family and taking care of a house and chores and all the other things normal people do.'

He ambled across to lean on a kitchen bench. 'You do not consider the Funaros normal people?'

His lips had lifted in a smile, humour lurking in his eyes, making him look younger, and she shook her head, battling a strange sense of breathlessness. 'I do not. I doubt they'd know the first thing about keeping a house clean or how to do the grocery shopping or put on a load of laundry.'

His warm chuckle lifted the fine hairs on her arms.

'Do you?' The question blurted out of her unbidden, and he sobered.

'I grew up in a working-class family. My father died when I was young and my mother was an invalid. More often than not, the household chores fell to me. As I suspect they did to you, too, if your father was a scientist. I take it that it was his house that you kept.'

She'd always thought it was hers, too. Just for a moment their gazes caught and clung. Shaking herself, she poured coffee into two mugs. 'I believe it's called character building.'

He gave another of those rare chuckles that threatened to wrap around her like a warm blanket.

Don't think about warm blankets. Or rumpled sheets.

Straightening, she forced her mind back to their conversation. 'What I'm trying to say is that embroidery has always been my escape from the real world.' She handed him a mug. 'I've never been commissioned to make something for someone else. I mean, I've made gifts for family members and friends, but I've never had to make something to measure like you. Things have to change when art becomes your work.'

'It does not feel like work. To be able to make a living from my art has been a joy.'

It was hard to associate joy and Gabriel in the same sentence.

'Is that what has been worrying you? That you now have to share your art? Is that why you haven't been able to work this morning?' His eyes narrowed, and he shook his head. 'No, that is not it.' He shrugged when she sent him an exasperated glare. 'What? You have an expressive face.'

'Then I'm going to need lessons in how to look like a closed book.'

'That is something I can help you with, too.'

She might just take him up on it. 'Yesterday afternoon Marguerite called me into her private apartment for a chat.'

His mouth flattened. 'Come, let's get some fresh air.'

He led her outside to the wooden table and benches that rested on one side of the studio. With the sun warm on her face, she sank down to a bench to gobble up the expansive views of unruffled water in various shades of silver, deep blue and navy green that spread before her. Timeless mountains rising silent and majestic all around.

'What did Marguerite say that still has you chafing a day later?'

She snapped back with a bump. 'She warned me off you.'

His face became enviously unreadable, and she swallowed. 'Remember what we agreed. What's said in the studio stays in the studio.'

'Absolutely.'

She bit her lip. 'Are you offended?'

She'd love to somehow bridge the uncomfortable gap

that existed between Marguerite and Gabriel. It'd be far more pleasant for Lili if her father and grandmother could be friends. And Lili *was* her niece. She'd do all she could to ensure the little girl was happy and content.

'Why should I be offended? As you know, she has already given me that same lecture.'

It wasn't an answer.

'Marguerite is always scheming, though. I do not trust her.'

Marguerite had likewise been far from flattering about Gabriel. She'd said that he wasn't to be trusted where women were concerned; that he'd become too angry and embittered after Serafina's death—as if he wanted revenge on the entire female population.

Revenge? Because no woman could ever live up to his memory of Serafina? The thought had made her stomach churn.

Marguerite had said she didn't want to see Audrey suffer at his hands. Audrey didn't want that, either.

'She made me promise to not fall in love with you.'

He shot to his feet. 'And you *agreed* to such an archaic directive?'

Those grey eyes glared at her, his large body bristling with outrage, but he didn't alarm her. Not anymore. She'd seen beneath the bluster. Whatever Gabriel wanted her and the rest of the world to think of him—and, again, she doubted he cared—she knew that beneath that bristling demeanour, he was a good man.

Wasn't he helping her with her art? And hadn't he rescued her on Saturday night when Alessio's hands had been straying? And the fact his daughter adored him spoke volumes. Yes, Gabriel Dimarco, despite whatever Marguerite thought, was a good man.

She lifted her chin and glared back at him. 'Of course I did. I thought you'd be pleased.'

His mouth worked but not a single sound emerged.

'Why all this outrage? Didn't you demand the same promise from me? On this one issue, at least, you and Marguerite seem to be in complete agreement.'

And so was she. He might be a good man, but to fall in love with him...

She went cold all over. She hadn't been enough for her mother and she hadn't been enough for her father. She wasn't making the mistake of falling in love with Gabriel, because she'd never be enough for him, either—not enough for him to overcome his prejudices; not enough for him to be a part of a family he loathed; not enough for him to risk getting his heart burned again. No, she was nowhere near enough for him on any level.

All she was good for was as an aunt to his daughter. One he could trust to be sensible. And that was something. She knew that. But it was a line drawn in the sand...and he wasn't even totally convinced she could be that person yet, either. She suppressed a shudder, imagining what it would be like to give your heart to such a man. He'd shred it. Oh, he wouldn't mean to, but his coldness, his inflexibility, his indifference... It would be the chilliest, loneliest of prisons.

Not going to happen.

Nonna had taught her that comfort and strength came in the shape of family. Her parents might've let her down, but her sister, grandmother, aunt and her cousin had all been there for her. She'd find strength and solace in her new family. *That* was where she needed to focus her efforts.

***

Gabriel stared at Audrey and wanted to yell; wanted to slash dark, ugly colour across a canvas. It made no sense. He had extracted the same promise. Why should it infuriate him that Marguerite would request it, too?

Because it was none of Marguerite's business who he dated or slept with.

'On Saturday night, when she saw how ably you rescued me from Mr Wandering Hands, she wanted to make sure I didn't read too much into your gallantry.'

His hand had clenched on the table beside his mug. He forced it to unclench. 'Why, then, when she could have the finest and most celebrated teachers here with a click of her fingers, would she entrust me with your artistic instruction?'

She leaned towards him as if he was hard of hearing...or slow of understanding. 'She said you are one of the most important artists of your generation. She knows what a coup it is that you've taken an interest in my education.' She folded her hands in her lap like a prim schoolgirl. 'I've been ordered to learn all I can from you.' Lovely lips twitched. 'And to not make a nuisance of myself.'

His eyes practically started from his head. 'I do not believe you.'

An eyebrow rose, but laughter still remained in the depths of those spice-coloured eyes.

'Sorry, that was a figure of speech, of disbelief, not an accusation. I know you do not lie.'

Her eyes abruptly dropped and a burning started in his chest. What wasn't she telling him? Had Marguerite told her he was a beast where women were concerned—that he used and abused his paramours before discarding them with nary a thought?

As far as the Funaros were concerned, he had never been good enough for their darling Serafina. And now he clearly wasn't good enough for their darling Audrey, either.

A sigh escaped soft lips, and things inside him tightened as his gaze fixed on those lips. Dear God, he had to stop fixating on them—their shape and texture—and wondering what it would be like to kiss them. Wondering what kind of lover Audrey would be—would she be shy or bold? He thought she would be shy, but he suspected there was fire banked beneath that unflappable exterior and he'd—

Stop!

'What's the issue between you and Marguerite anyway?' Her brow pleated. 'Is it to do with Serafina?'

He stiffened at his wife's name.

She huffed out a laugh. 'Bingo. Nobody wants me to ask questions, but this is my family. I don't understand what happened or why this has made everyone the way they are.'

'And how do you think they are?'

She stared out at the lake, rubbed a hand across her chest. 'Broken,' she finally said.

The single word made him flinch. So did the sorrow in her gaze—all this concern for these people she barely yet knew.

'Nobody speaks of either Serafina or Danae. As soon as I mention either name, the conversation is deftly changed to some other channel or people excuse themselves, because there's something that they have to *see to immediately*. If a long-lost daughter turned up to meet my family in Australia, we'd regale her with all the stories we could about the mother she'd never known...and the sister.'

He silently swore.

'Obviously, the stories are far from pretty. Obviously,

they're painful. But I don't see how keeping me in the dark is going to help.'

'I suspect Marguerite is wanting you to get used to everything else before subjecting you to the less salubrious side of the family history.'

Firm eyes met his. She might appear meek and quiet on first meeting, but there was a surprising strength to this woman, too. 'What's the deal between you and Marguerite?' she asked again.

Things inside him clenched and burned. 'Marguerite holds me responsible for Fina's death.'

Her face fell.

'While I hold *her* responsible.' She opened her mouth, but he held up a hand. 'No more for today.'

With a nod, she transferred her gaze to her coffee. 'Can I ask a side question, then? Why do you spend the summers here on Marguerite's estate?'

'Lili. It is an arrangement made between lawyers, to give her the opportunity to know her mother's family. Marguerite could insist that I drop Lili off and leave her here, but we both know Lili will be happier if I am here, too. So Marguerite tolerates me. In return, I allow her visits throughout the rest of the year.'

The smallest of smiles touched those lips.

Don't notice the lips.

'You've found a way to work together—for Lili's sake.'

'If I had my way, Lili would have no contact at all with the Funaro family.'

She frowned. 'You have to believe it's only right that she knows both sides of her family—'

'No, I don't!'

He couldn't help the savagery with which he spat out

those words. He hated himself for them when Audrey flinched, but he couldn't take them back. They were the truth. 'The Funaro family are poison.' And with everything he had, he wished he could protect Lili from them.

Her eyes throbbed into his. 'You hate them.'

He normally kept a more civilised facade on these emotions, but Audrey had somehow prised that lid off and it was taking all of his strength to hold them in check.

'I'm a Funaro. Do you hate me, too?'

Exhaustion overtook him then. 'I do not hate you, Audrey. You are not a true Funaro. You are, I suspect, very much a Martinelli.' And his hate was not so illogical.

Are you sure?

Of course he was sure. He loathed the Funaros for not believing the rules applied to them, for thinking themselves above the laws that defined and governed normal behaviour—for their excesses and entitlement and selfishness.

'There's something I don't understand.'

He frowned. 'Just the one?'

'Why *have* you agreed to take my artistic education in hand if you hate the family so much?'

The way she said *hate* made him sound like a monster. And who knows? Maybe that was exactly what he'd become. If he'd managed to corral his anger and resentment towards Fina, she might still be here. And Lili might still have her mother.

'Lili.' The single word cracked from lips that didn't want to cooperate, but he suddenly and desperately didn't want this woman to let his daughter down the way her mother had. He would do everything in his power to prevent that, regardless of what he thought of the rest of the Funaro family.

'Lili?'

She said his daughter's name with such affection. Nodding, he rubbed a hand over his face. 'She adores you.'

'I adore her, too.'

'Do you know what she said to me the other night? She said that she loved you and that she was certain her mother would be just like you.'

Audrey gave a funny little hiccup, her eyes growing suspiciously bright.

'And then she asked me if you were going to die like her mother had died.'

The soft gasp speared to the very centre of him.

'The Funaro women sometimes self-destruct, Audrey. It is what they do. It is what your mother did and it is what your sister did. Nobody talks of it because it brought shame and scandal to the Funaro name—and that is something that Marguerite finds unforgivable.'

She stared at him for a long moment. 'The reason Marguerite doesn't talk of them is because their deaths hurt her too much. She loved them and it hurts her to remember how they died.'

'You are seeing what you want to see. You only see the best in people.'

'While you only see their worst.'

She didn't say it as an accusation. Just sadly, as if she felt bad for him. An itch settled between his shoulder blades. 'I did not see what was happening to Fina. I didn't realise how close she was skating to the edge. Marguerite did not see it, either.'

'And as a result, you blame each other.'

He ignored that. 'Fina had nothing to fall back on—no

resources beyond partying ever harder and trying an ever-greater array of drugs.'

He watched her digest that.

And lovers. Fina had also taken lovers. Lots of them. He left that unsaid, though. Even now Fina's infidelity chafed at him. He'd have given her everything, but she hadn't wanted anything he'd had to offer.

All she'd wanted was to annoy her grandmother by marrying someone none of them considered suitable. He'd been nothing but Fina's act of rebellion, and the knowledge left a bitter taste in his mouth. He'd been too focused on getting a divorce, and custody of Lili, to see how far down Fina was spiralling.

He leaned towards Audrey now. If he had any say in the matter, this woman would not follow Fina's path. 'Your art will give you something to fall back on—somewhere to escape to when the pressures of life in the fast lane, the pressure of being a Funaro, become too much. I do not want you to let Lili down the way Fina let her down.'

'Oh, God, Gabriel...'

She stared at him, stricken. Reaching out, she gripped his forearm, her hand small and pale against his tanned skin. 'I am *not* a life-in-the-fast-lane person.'

'Not yet.'

'And I am *never* going to take drugs.'

'So you say now, but how can you be so certain?'

'Because I care about my health!'

She was a nurse's aide. She must've seen what drugs did to people.

'Do you take drugs? Or do you mean to in the future?'

He stiffened. 'Absolutely not!'

She glanced to where her hand rested on his arm, as if

his muscles tensing beneath her fingertips was a fascinating sensation. He flexed his arm again. The action involuntary. Her fingers firmed against him as if to test the solidity of the flesh beneath... And then she snapped away as if he burned her. The way she swallowed and glanced out at the lake had his every primal instinct firing to life.

Audrey found him attractive. And he found satisfaction in that knowledge. A deep, burning satisfaction. If he turned her face towards him, would she let him kiss her? If he kissed her with the deep, thorough hunger pouring through him now, would she kiss him back with the same abandon? Would she wrap her arms around him and press herself against him in a silent plea for more?

His breath sawed in and out of his lungs. Would she let him peel the clothes from her body and lose himself in the—

What the hell...?

This woman was off-limits. No matter how much he might wonder what it would be like to bed her, it was not a fantasy in which he could indulge. For Lili's sake. For Audrey's sake, too.

And his own.

She turned with eyes that seemed to shine with some powerful inner light. 'You've agreed to take charge of my education because you want to protect me.'

'Do not look at me like that.' He pointed a shaking finger at her. He was not a knight in shining armour.

'Like what?'

'Like I am a hero.' The idea was laughable.

'You said I like to see the best in people.'

'You will be foolish to see what isn't there.'

'Or maybe you need to start seeing yourself through eyes like mine.'

This woman had no idea, and she would be hurt, and hurt badly, if this was the way she meant to deal with the Funaros.

'I fear for you, Audrey, but I will not be drawn back into that world—the one the Funaros inhabit.'

'That sounds like a warning.'

It was. 'Why is this family so important to you?'

She folded her arms. 'Why is Lili so important to you?'

He waved that off. A child was an altogether different thing. He thought back to the things that she'd told him. 'Your nonna recently died,' he started slowly, 'and your father has abandoned you for pastures greener.'

'He hasn't abandoned me!' But her gaze slid away.

'It was his house that you kept. This I know already. You told me as much. No doubt you cooked and cleaned for him.' Cared for him.

She shrugged, but a new tension threaded through her. 'It was my home, too. It was the family home.'

His heart started to thump. She'd said her father had taken a new job in America. 'Audrey, what happened to the family home?'

She moistened her lips, not meeting his eyes. 'It was sold.'

Dio! No wonder she felt so lost, so rootless. But to pin her hopes on the Funaros... 'You are lonely, feeling at a loose end. And are now hoping this new family you've discovered will fill the holes in your life and your heart.'

She turned to him fully, a frown in her eyes. 'I want to love them and I want them to love me.' She touched a hand to her chest. 'I want to belong. What's so wrong with that?'

'The Funaros are not that kind of family.'

'So says you, and you clearly don't want to belong to

anyone. You'll have to excuse me if I take what you say on the subject with a grain of salt.'

'You want them to save you. When they cannot even save themselves. You will be disappointed and disillusioned and—'

'Let's agree to disagree on that one. Or we'll have an awful falling out and I'd prefer that we didn't.'

He'd prefer that, too.

'Do you ever sketch, Gabriel?'

The change in topic threw him. 'Yes, of course.' He made multiple sketches of his sculptures before starting them.

'Me, too. I want to sit on that rock over there and sketch out a design that's started to come to me. I want to somehow try and capture all this.' She gestured at the view.

'Very well. And once you are done you can explain your process to me.'

'Okay, but fair's fair. You need to sketch, too, and explain your process to me.'

He didn't have a process at the moment. He had nothing!

Which meant he didn't have anything to lose, either. 'Very well. I will remain here and try to capture the mountains.'

Fifteen minutes later he gave up with an exasperated sigh. Glancing across at Audrey, who sat on her rock at the other end of the small bay, he found her with head bent over her sketchpad. Picking up a charcoal, he drew a few lines to make the shape of her. Audrey was an interesting combination of frailty and strength. And as the clash between weakness and strength was what he often took as his subject…

Frowning, he drew a few more lines. And then some more. Before he knew it, his hand was flying across the page.

CHAPTER SEVEN

GABRIEL'S STICK OF charcoal raced across the page of his sketchpad as if afraid that if it didn't keep moving, the image it was trying to capture would disappear and fade to black.

Audrey wanted to go peer over his shoulder, curious to see what had finally sparked his creativity, but didn't dare disturb him. Instead, she sat on the nearby rustic retaining wall with her sketchpad in her lap and remained silent.

A breath of warm air fanned the hair at her nape and a beetle negotiated the grass and pebbles at her feet. She watched its progress, but Gabriel's earlier words continued to go around and around in her mind.

You want them to save you when they cannot even save themselves.

Her heart pounded. She'd never felt so seen—so *judged*. Was that what she wanted—for them to save her?

Losing Nonna had made her realise that there were only Aunt Deidre, Frankie and herself left of her family. Oh, she'd still have her father, but while he'd been physically present, he'd been as absent as her mother in all the ways that had counted. But if anything were to happen to Aunt Deidre or Frankie…

Her mouth dried. Did she really hope the Funaros would fill that gap?

They cannot even save themselves.

She pulled her gaze from the beetle and stared out at the water. Maybe she could do something about that. She wasn't weak and she wasn't pathetic. Her heart was big enough and strong enough to take a few knocks if the prize at the end was a family that loved each other, that pulled together.

She'd had that with Nonna and Johanna, and Frankie and Aunt Deidre. There was absolutely no reason why she couldn't have it with Marguerite and Lili and the rest of the Funaro family as well. She had no intention of replacing one family with another, but she could widen her circle. And it wasn't a one-way street. She'd be gaining them, but they'd be gaining her, too.

Something trilled a pretty melody from a nearby tree. As she turned to try and spot the culprit, she realised the scratching of the charcoal had ceased and Gabriel now stared at her, brows lowering over his eyes.

'When did you move?' The frown deepened. 'In my mind's eye you've been on that little headland for the last hour.'

She shrugged. 'Time seems to move differently here. But probably twenty minutes ago.'

He shook himself, patted the table. 'Come. Let me see your sketches.'

She moved to the seat opposite. 'May I see yours?'

He hesitated, but with the smallest of shrugs, nodded. They exchanged sketchpads.

His was still open to the final sketch he'd done. Glancing

down, her mouth dried. Turning the pages over, she followed them back to the first of his drawings before returning to the last one, her heart pounding. She knew he watched, and the weight of his stare did strange things to her insides. Moistening her lips, she tried to find something to say.

'What do you think?'

She didn't know if her opinion mattered to him or not. 'They're all of me,' she blurted out.

'Yes.'

He gave no explanation, his face giving nothing away. But... What did it mean? Why would he draw her? Why would he find her so fascinating?

Just like the sculpture in Como that had enthralled her, one couldn't tell if the figure on the rock—*her*—would remain there strong and steadfast, or whether the water would rise up to engulf it.

'It is important for you to develop an artistic sensibility. What do you think of it objectively?'

She forced herself to focus on the overall impact of the sketch—the strong lines, the ambiguity... Its strange beauty. 'Because the subject is me, and I've never been the subject for a work of art before, it's hard to be objective. This is only a sketch, but it has a real impact. It feels...alive.'

He took the sketchpad from her and surveyed it with narrowed eyes. 'Yes.' He nodded. 'This is something I can work with.'

'Why?'

He glanced up.

'Why me?'

One broad shoulder lifted. 'I was sketching the mountains, but they bored me. And then I saw you and there was something about your posture that caught my attention.

Before I knew it, I was trying to capture it in a sketch... and then sketching as if my life depended on it.'

A thrill shook her to her very core. Something about her fascinated him. To think that a man like Gabriel would find someone like her captivating... She hugged the knowledge close. Very slowly, however, the excitement drained away. The water in the drawing, so still, somehow evoked a quiet menace that threatened both woman and rock.

Some Funaros self-destruct.

That was the subject of the sketch. He feared she'd follow in the footsteps of her mother and sister. He had no faith that her strength would prevail over whatever innate weakness he thought resided in her blood. He was recording a downfall that may not happen.

A downfall that *wouldn't* happen!

Lifting her chin, she glared at him. His eyes flashed with brief amusement, before he closed his sketchpad and slapped hers on top of it. Flicking through the various sketches, his lips pursed, his gaze halting only briefly on the final drawing. Eventually, he handed it back to her. 'It will make a pretty piece.'

She blinked. 'That sounds dismissive.' What was wrong with pretty?

'Pretty has its place.'

That sounded even more dismissive. 'But?'

Leaning back, he folded his arms and it drew her attention to the rock-hard strength of his chest. She swallowed, a pulse at the centre of her starting to pound. He'd taken her as his subject, and now all she could think about was if she had the skill to commit all of that raw masculinity to an embroidery—capture it in linen, silk and wool. To wonder what it would be like to draw close enough to touch all of that raw power.

Her pulse pounded harder, making it difficult to draw breath. What would it be like to press herself against such a body? Watch as that body rippled with awareness of a feminine presence—a feminine presence that could fire it to life and exhort it to—

Dear God!

Dragging her gaze back to his face, she found those merciless eyes watching her with a narrowed chill. Had he read her thoughts? Recognised her desires? If he had, the chill in his expression told her it wasn't an attraction he reciprocated.

Heat flooded her face.

Channel Marguerite.

With an effort, she kept her chin high. Women must find Gabriel attractive all the time. It didn't have to mean anything.

She *had* to keep her guard up. For heaven's sake, he was waiting for her downfall. He didn't want it to happen, and yet he expected it. *Daily.* She might fascinate him, but he had no faith in her.

'What's wrong with pretty?' she repeated, her voice little more than a croak.

'You need to start taking risks with your art, Audrey. You need to experiment and free yourself from the usual conventions that hold you back.'

He's talking about artistic conventions.

He flicked negligent fingers at her sketchpad. 'Where is the movement? Where is the interest? What is the point?'

She stared at her sketch. She'd been so happy with it. Her

brow furrowed. Pulling the pad closer she *really* stared at it. Swallowed. He was right, darn it.

'What were you thinking when you sketched that?'

'Just...how beautiful the scenery was. The beauty here overwhelms me. It's so different from home.' She moistened her lips. 'My sketch is pretty, but it's...sterile.'

'Because the beauty does not touch you here.' He pressed a hand to his chest. 'You need to find the courage to create the things that make you feel deeply. That is what will touch other people and draw them to your work.'

Her hands gripped each other tightly in her lap. 'What were you feeling when you sketched me?'

He hesitated. 'Anger.'

She flinched.

He shrugged, but he didn't apologise. 'I didn't say I was angry *with* you.'

No, but—

'Artists channel their emotions into forms and works that have no relation at all to the source of their emotion.'

She thought of the things she'd made in the aftermath of Jo's death, and nodded slowly.

'Will you sit for me?'

The question had her stiffening, though she realised belatedly she should've expected it. Maybe she should even feel flattered. But she didn't. Instead, she prickled and itched and burned and had to fight a scowl. What would he title the piece? *Before the Fall?*

'Will you sit for me?' she shot back instead. She could call hers *Pig-headed Male*.

His head rocked back.

And she crashed back with a thump, rushed back into

speech. 'The answer is yes, of course I'll sit for you, Gabriel. It's not dependent on you sitting for me.'

He was doing so much for her, and she'd oblige him in any way she could. If something in her had helped him overcome the block that had him in its grip for the past eight months, she'd be honoured to help him.

She gritted her teeth. *Honoured*, she repeated silently.

He leaned towards her. 'You would like me to sit for you?'

'I've never thought to take a person for my subject before.' She bit her lip. 'I've no idea if I could do it.'

'You have the skill.'

His quiet certainty had her straightening. 'You have a lot of faith in my abilities.'

'I do not understand why you don't have more faith in them yourself.'

Because, until now, she'd not had anyone recognise anything particularly wonderful about them. She'd never believed Nonna and Frankie when they'd told her how amazing her creations were. Oh, she knew they believed it, but they loved her. They were biased.

'How is it you've never pursued your art further? I do not understand. You tell me it is a passion of yours. Why, then, have you not attended art classes? And before you say you had neither the time nor opportunity to study art at university, there are night courses you could've taken. Hobby groups you could have joined. There your talent would've been recognised.'

His incredulity needled her. 'A person can have more than one passion.'

'What are these other passions of yours?'

'Family.'

He stared. With a muttered curse, he rubbed a hand over

his face. 'I sometimes forget that not everyone is as caught up in their art as I am in mine. I apologise if I sounded uncompromising just then.'

She folded her arms. He was just like her father, caught up in his own world, uncaring and oblivious of anything—or anyone—else.

No, he's not.

Her heart started to thump. As soon as she'd been old enough, she'd looked after not just Johanna, but her father, too. Nonna had been getting on *and* was running a restaurant. And when Uncle Frank had died, Aunt Deidre had gone into such deep mourning, Audrey had refused to be an additional burden.

She hadn't minded looking after the house, though, and although her father had never said as much, she'd thought that he'd appreciated her efforts; she'd thought that she'd mattered to him. But she hadn't—at least, not as much as his own ambition. The way he'd just up and left for America, selling her childhood home from under her, proved that. Too late she'd realised she'd always given him more than he'd ever given her.

Was Gabriel like that? She moistened her lips. 'If you had to, would you give up your art for Lili?'

'Yes.' He watched her through hooded eyes. 'This is what you had to do for your family?' He let out a long breath. 'I'm sorry if you have been burdened with familial responsibilities and obligations that have prevented you from following your own dreams.'

She shot to her feet, her hands clenching so hard she started to shake. 'My family hasn't been *a burden*, Gabriel. Is that how you view Lili?'

His head rocked back. 'Of course not.'

'Then why would you say such a thing? I—'

Whirling away, she started to pace. She'd give up all of this—the chance to develop her art, Lake Como and all these riches—to have Johanna and Nonna back.

She swung around. 'You can't—'

Her words stuttered to a halt. He stood a hand's breadth away.

'I'm sorry.' Strong hands reached out to grip her shoulders, wrapping around them with a comforting warmth. It was the sincerity in his eyes that undid her, though. 'Audrey, I'm very sorry for upsetting you. I've blundered in with my blind judgements.' Those intriguing lips twisted. 'I'm always so sure I'm right. It is a failing of mine.'

The fight went out of her, just like that. She tried to smile and shrug at the same time but it emerged more like a hiccup. 'Forget about it.'

He led her back to the table, made her sit and then he went and made a pot of green tea and brought it out along with *chocolate biscuits*. She suddenly realised how ravenous she was.

'Please...' He gestured to the plate.

She needed no second bidding. Biting into a biscuit, she closed her eyes and let the sweetness coat her tongue. When she opened them again, she found him watching, but he quickly seized the teapot.

After pouring the tea, he pushed a cup towards her and then lifted his own and blew on it. 'I would like to hear about your family if you wish to talk of them. If Marguerite hasn't forbidden you from doing so.'

She felt a twang of sudden resentment at Marguerite. She had no right to ask her to keep Johanna a secret. Her gaze lowered to their sketchpads lying side by side. She recalled the threat that stretched through his sketch and hitched up her chin. Gabriel needed to know she had more strength than he'd given her credit for. She *wanted* him to know that.

'I had a twin.'

He froze.

'Her name was Johanna. Unfortunately, there were complications during the birth and she was starved of oxygen. She was diagnosed with cerebral palsy when she was fourteen months.'

He swore softly.

'It affected her movement and speech particularly. She could walk unassisted but it took a lot of effort so she mostly used a wheelchair. And while she could talk, it took her a long time to say what she wanted to. But she was whip smart and had a wicked sense of humour. She made you laugh at the most inopportune times.'

He smiled and she couldn't help but smile back. 'And,' she continued, 'took much delight in it, too, I might add. But she needed a lot of care.'

'And that care fell to you?'

'Nonna and Aunt Deidre helped out a lot. They basically raised us.'

'Where was your father all this time?'

'Playing the helpless male.' She rolled her eyes. 'I mean, we lived in the same house as him, which I can see now simply made more work for Nonna and my aunt. But they obviously thought it was the right thing to do—and it probably was—but single fatherhood was too much of a challenge for him, and he threw himself into his work instead.'

His lips thinned but he didn't say anything.

'We had part-time carers for Jo as well, but when I finished school I became her full-time carer. Not because anyone requested it of me, but because I wanted to. I loved her. She was my sister.'

Because of their father's preoccupation, she and Jo had become a team, had become each other's cheer squad. They'd shared everything—their hopes, dreams…secrets. She missed it more than she could say.

He nodded, no trace of judgement in his eyes. 'What happened to Johanna?'

'She died in a car accident four years ago. Just one of those freak things—a tyre blew out when they were on the freeway. The driver lost control and slammed into a truck.'

A strong tanned hand reached across and squeezed hers. 'I'm sorry.'

'Losing Johanna… That's when I realised how hard it is to love someone.'

'Because you sacrificed so much for her?'

'Because when I lost her, I felt I'd lost everything.'

That hand tightened about hers. 'Audrey, in some ways you did. You'd built your whole world around her.'

Of course he would think like that. She squeezed his hand back. 'I didn't lose everything, Gabriel. I still had Nonna and Aunt Deidre and Frankie, and Dad, even if he was rather detached. I still had the ability to work and earn a living. I had my embroideries.'

'And yet, even surrounded by all of those good things, a heart can break.'

And yet, broken hearts did mend.

She nodded at their joined hands, hers looking small and pale beside his. 'You're muscled and strong on the outside, Gabriel, while I look feeble in comparison. But don't let appearances fool you. I've had to be strong—for Johanna's sake and for my father's. And, yes, I know I'm out of my depth here in this brave new world I find myself in, but I will eventually find my feet. And I *will* be the director of my own destiny.'

Grey eyes met hers and he nodded. 'That's me put in my place, then.'

She bit her lip. 'I didn't mean it that way.'

'I know.'

To her relief he didn't look at all offended.

With one final squeeze, he reclaimed his hand and she tried to ignore the way her body protested the missing contact.

'Danae left when she discovered the issues Johanna would have to face in the future. I have no memory of her—Jo and I weren't even two years old yet.' She hitched up her chin. 'I'd never run away from the people I love. Especially when they needed me most.'

He remained silent.

'And I love Lili. I know I've only known her for a short time, but I love her. I plan to be there for her.' She shrugged, suddenly self-conscious. 'Just so you know.'

'I will sit for you, Audrey.'

She blinked at the sudden change of topic. His words and the pictures they evoked in her mind throwing her off balance. She leaned towards him. 'Really?'

'Would you like me to sit for you naked?' he said with a teasing glint in his eye.

Yes!

'No!' Heat flooded every atom of her being. Closing her eyes, she tried to shake the images from her mind. He chuckled and she knew she must be scarlet. Her eyes flew open and she pointed a finger at him. 'And I won't be posing for you naked, either.'

'What a shame.'

Her jaw dropped, but he merely threw his head back and laughed. 'Johanna would've enjoyed the joke, I'm sure.'

She snorted then, too. Seizing another chocolate biscuit, she held the plate out to him. 'Have a biscuit and stop teasing me.'

But he didn't. He'd stilled. '*That's* why you asked me about charities and how to become a patron. You want to set something up in Johanna's name.'

'Maybe.' She wished her voice didn't sound so suddenly small or defensive.

He stood and stalked to the edge of the clearing. When he turned back, he widened his stance. 'Marguerite has banned you from talking about Johanna, hasn't she?'

She didn't want to answer, but he clearly read the answer in her face. Giving a harsh laugh, he shook his head. 'I should've realised sooner. She wouldn't want the wider world knowing she'd had a granddaughter who was anything other than physically perfect. Heaven forbid anyone suspect something so shocking.'

'No,' she croaked. 'I'm sure you're wrong. I think she finds it painful she never met her.'

A sceptical look crossed his face and he folded his arms. 'How do you think you're going to get Marguerite's approval for a foundation in Johanna's name? How do you think you're going to reconcile her to you talking freely about Johanna *publicly*?'

That, of course, was the question. Because as things currently stood, Marguerite couldn't tolerate so much as the mention of Johanna's name. But it'd get better. She swallowed. It *would* get better.

If wishes were fishes...

She pushed that thought away. Marguerite *had* to reconcile herself to Audrey's talking about Johanna publicly because nobody, not even the Funaros, would have her turning her back on her sister. Even if it meant they'd disown her. 'She just needs time.'

He gave a disbelieving laugh.

Pain pounded behind her eyes. 'I'm going to talk to her about it…soon. And then you'll see.'

Those infuriating brows rose.

'You'll be eating your words before you know it.'

CHAPTER EIGHT

'Is CONVERSATION BANNED while I sit?'

Gabriel was midstretch when Audrey asked her question. If she'd asked him five minutes earlier, he'd have probably not even heard her. He hadn't been this intensely captured by a work in...

He couldn't remember.

Thankfully, his creative drought was at an end. He felt alive, invigorated, as if all of his body was breathing again.

Despite that, his instinct was to answer in the negative and demand silence as he was working. But she'd agreed to sit for him without a murmur of complaint. It'd be churlish of him to refuse.

'We can talk if you like...as long as you don't move too much.'

He had her sitting on a mound of cushions on the floor—a make-believe rock—with her face turned towards the wall of glass, side on to him. She held her sketchpad and a pencil.

She chuckled. 'You didn't complain a little while ago when I stretched out a cramp in my calf. You were clearly immersed in your drawing.'

He glanced at the clock and swore. '*Dio*, Audrey, it has been two hours! Why didn't you say something? You can get up and move if you wish.'

'I'm fine. You have me for another half an hour and then I'm done, so you might as well make the most of it.'

He picked up his pencil again. He would refine what he could in the next thirty minutes. 'In light of your patience, I'll even start a conversation.'

Those mobile lips curved upwards and he wondered how he could capture their compelling combination of softness and strength. And what would be the better material to use to capture them—steel or wood?

Doing his best to ignore the heat prickling through his veins and the persistent ache of his groin, he dragged his mind to the promised conversation. 'Why, when I asked you to wear your oldest, most comfortable jeans when you were sitting for me, did you not just wear them for the whole day? Why did you bring them to get changed into?'

She started to shrug, but stopped as if remembering she was supposed to be still. 'Because I didn't want Marguerite to see me in them.'

He scowled. 'Why would it matter if she did?'

She huffed out a laugh. 'Are you scowling, Gabriel?'

He cleared his face. 'Absolutely not.'

'Because she doesn't like them, and I don't wish to upset her.'

'You don't have to live your whole life to please her. Why even consider doing such a thing?'

'You ask the wrong question.' She turned her head a couple of inches to meet his gaze and the expression in her spice-coloured eyes had his pulse picking up speed. 'Ask yourself *why* these jeans bother her so much.'

That was simple. 'Because they do not fit the sleek, sophisticated image she would wish for a granddaughter of the Funaro family.' As far as Marguerite was concerned, the image the Funaros presented had to be perfect.

'You're wrong.' She turned to stare back out at the window, but where before the lines of her body had been passive, they were now firm—that pointed chin squared and those eyes narrowed. 'These jeans remind her that I grew up in a world far removed from hers. They remind her of all the years we didn't know each other and can't get back. The sight of my old, shabby jeans makes her grieve, because she wasn't there to help out financially or to offer any kind of emotional support when I was growing up.'

Her words made something in his chest cramp. 'You imbue her with feelings she doesn't have.'

'While you seem determined to believe she has no feelings at all.'

He rolled his shoulders. That wasn't true. Was it?

'Tell me about Serafina.'

'No!' The word shot out of him with the violence of a summer storm, and he found himself breathing hard. The request had taken him by surprise, but it shouldn't have.

Audrey flinched, but a moment later resumed the pose. 'Why not?'

'I do not talk about Fina.'

Her entire body drooped as she let out a breath. 'Nobody does. You must all miss her very much.'

His fingers tightened about his pencil. She had no idea. And he had no intention of enlightening her.

'She was so young. And so beautiful.'

Oh, yes, Fina had been very beautiful. On the outside.

'Lili is going to want to know about her, you know. Eventually, she'll start asking more demanding questions, and she won't be put off with one-word answers. She'll expect more from you.'

He knew that. But it wouldn't be for several years yet. He had time to work out what he would say. And maybe time will have softened him, and he'd be able to utter the lies without giving himself away. He scowled. 'Why are you so interested in Fina anyway?'

She turned fully around to face him. 'She was my *sister*. How would you feel if you suddenly discovered a sibling you never knew you'd had? Wouldn't you want to know all about him or her?'

'Assume the pose, please.' She did, but it didn't ease the burning in his soul. Her words had found their mark, but they didn't make him any more eager to talk about Serafina. Yes, he understood her curiosity, but if she'd ever met Fina, she'd have been disappointed in the other woman.

Bitterly.

Just as he had been.

'Fine, then tell me about Vittoria, Livia and Adriana.'

Her cousins? 'Why?'

'Because I'm having lunch with them tomorrow.'

And so it begins...

This family would engulf her, take her over and re-create her into their own image. They'd destroy her. He threw his pencil down. 'We're done here for the moment.'

She glanced around, registered the expression on his face and nodded. But as she started to rise, she winced and grabbed her calf. He immediately moved to assist her, his hand reaching down to hers. Her fingers tightened in his and she gasped and hopped. 'Gah, cramp! I'm not used to sitting so still for so long.'

As a nurse's aide, she must spend long days on her feet. He should've taken that into account and ensured she had regular stretching breaks.

Kneeling down, he brushed her hands aside, working his fingers on the calf muscle that had tightened beneath the soft denim of her jeans. She gasped, groaned and half hopped. 'Lean against my shoulder,' he ordered.

A hand immediately landed on his shoulder, and the soft weight of her and the feel of her warm flesh beneath the thin, butter-soft denim made him aware of her in a way he'd been trying to avoid all morning. Her scent swamped him, invading his lungs and moving with a slow surety to his blood, his limbs growing languid. As the tightness in her calf gave way beneath his hand, his fingers, too, became more leisurely—exploring, caressing, wanting to learn the shape of her.

He suddenly found his hands empty.

'It's all good now, thanks,' she choked out.

Rising, he found her eyes wide and dark colour staining her cheeks.

'Where did you learn to massage like that? It's very effective. I'm dying for a coffee. You?'

She was babbling and he knew why—because she felt the pull between them, too. And because of Marguerite, she was determined to ignore it.

And because of you.

Dragging a hand down his face, he nodded. He'd told her not to fall in love with him or to think of him in any kind of romantic way. Just because Marguerite was of the same mind didn't mean he had to change his.

Dio! He knew he was bitter, but what kind of man would it make him if he seduced Audrey simply to disoblige Marguerite? He was not in the habit of breaking hearts and destroying people. He left that to the likes of the Funaros.

Audrey had moved to the kitchenette and he dragged in a breath and tried to steady himself. 'I used to play football when I was younger. Not professionally. I wasn't that good. But I played for years in a local league. Cramps were common.'

When she finally turned back, her colour was normal again. Handing him a coffee, she took a turn about the studio, studying the various pieces he'd started and abandoned. 'So, Vittoria, Livia and Adriana?'

His nose curled.

'It seems to me you don't like to talk about any of the Funaros.'

'Esattamente,' he muttered. *Exactly.*

'But nor do you want me letting Lili down. You want me to be a regular fixture in her life.' She turned and pinned him with those eyes. 'So help me fit in here, Gabriel. Explain the undercurrents and all the things I'm in ignorance of.'

A dark anger pierced him. This woman deserved so much more. 'How can family mean so much to you when your own parents were the antithesis of what family stood for?' How could she still have so much faith in family?

'My parents got it wrong. For heaven's sake, why would I emulate them? Why would I make the same mistakes they did?' She pointed a finger at him. 'It was my nonna who got it right. *That's* who I want to emulate.'

With the Funaros? Was she mad?

Those dark eyes narrowed and sparks flashed in their depths as if she could read his thoughts in his face. 'Nonna gave me so much. She taught me that there's strength in a family, not to mention a sense of belonging and love. She *proved* that to me. And I'm going to do everything in my power to create that with my family here in Italy. I'll continue the legacy she gave me.'

He opened his mouth.

'And just because I wasn't enough for my father or my mother, doesn't mean I won't be enough for Marguerite or the rest of the Funaros.'

He wanted to swear.

'And just because *you* don't value family, doesn't mean the rest of us feel the same way!'

He valued family!

'And just because the Funaros aren't enough for you, doesn't mean they're not enough for me!'

He gaped at her.

'Family matters *so much*. I'd hate to think what would've happened to Jo if it weren't for Nonna and Aunt Deidre.'

Or Audrey, he added silently.

'If she'd been alone in the world...' She shuddered. 'It doesn't bear thinking about. And *I* don't want to be alone in the world, either. What if something happened to me? Who could I turn to?'

His hands clenched at the thought.

'I know you're besotted with this whole "I'm a lone wolf and untouchable" thing you've got going on.'

'My...*what*?'

'But there's a reason solitary confinement is a punishment. People weren't meant to be isolated and alone. And just because family politics are tiresome and some family members can be annoying, doesn't mean one shouldn't make the best of what they've got.'

'Have you not heard the proverb that you can't make a silk purse from a sow's ear?' he ground out.

She clenched her hands so hard she shook. 'Vittoria, Livia and Adriana?'

After dragging in a breath, he let it out slowly. He couldn't force Audrey to see what she didn't want to see. Eventually, he nodded. 'Vittoria went into business with a friend—fashion, I think... Something to do with earrings if I'm not mistaken. Anyway, she plugged a great deal of money into it, but it was a failure. Marguerite refused to bankroll her any further.'

She bit her lip. He did his best to not notice how it deepened the colour and plumped it—as if she'd just been kissed. Her colour was still high from their somewhat heated exchange and... He swallowed. Audrey would look sublime mussed up after a bout of vigorous lovemaking.

Dio! Stop imagining such things.

'Livia was at the centre of a sex scandal. An ex-boyfriend leaked a piece of naked footage he'd taken of her on his phone.'

Her eyes widened. 'That's appalling.'

'Welcome to the world of the Funaros.'

She rolled her eyes. 'And Adriana?'

'Has recently returned from drug rehab.'

Her shoulders slumped. 'Okay, so that's...a lot.'

'They each have a big black mark against their name as far as Marguerite is concerned.'

'And are all desperate to make amends.'

It was true that all of them would like to be in Marguerite's good books.

'And what about some of the older family members—my mother's contemporaries—like Caterina, Anna, Nicolo and Davide? There's going to be a dinner later in the week.'

They were the children of Marguerite's siblings. He filled her in on some of the family politics.

She listened in silence. When he was done, she pointed to one of his sculptures. 'Next time I sit for you, would I be able to look at that?'

He frowned. 'Why?'

'I don't know, but there's something about it...' She fixed him with a frown. 'Surely, it's an easy enough question—yes or no?'

'*Si*, if you wish it.'

Her shoulders and jaw relaxed. 'Thank you.'

Something inside him unhitched then, too, but for the life of him he couldn't explain what it was.

'How did your lunch with Vittoria, Livia and Adriana go?' Gabriel asked the following Monday when she was once again sitting for him.

He'd arranged the sculpture on a low table in front of her. Her attention had been fixed on it for the past hour, and it was her attitude of concentration that had caught his fancy today. He glanced down at his sketch and nodded, satisfied.

'Okay, I think. I liked them.'

That surprised him.

'And the dinner with Caterina, Anna, Nicolo and Davide?'

'Okay, too, I think.'

The brevity of her answers needled him. 'Was Marguerite at the dinner?'

Her dark hair fanned about her face when she shook her head. 'She had other plans.'

He froze. 'Marguerite left you to face the slathering horde alone?'

'I told her I was more than capable of going alone. And they're not a slathering horde.' She bit her lip. 'Though they're all a bit reserved.'

By reserved, he bet she meant rude, impenetrable and unwelcoming.

She gestured at his sketchpad. 'Are we done?' At his nod, she rose and shook out her arms and legs. 'They're not exactly a happy bunch, are they?'

'You know you could just walk away from them.' He hated the thought of her expending time and energy on people who didn't have her best interests at heart. 'You don't owe these people anything.'

She turned her back on him. 'We've had this conversation before. That's *not* what family does. And as I already know you don't want me walking away from Lili, why should I walk away from anyone else?'

She had a point even if he didn't want to admit it.

She turned. 'I'm also including you in my *not a happy bunch* comment.'

He stiffened. 'Not happy? *Me?* I'm happy!'

'Shout a little louder. I'm sure that'll convince me.'

He scowled. When he wasn't stuck at Lake Como on the Funaro estate, he was happy.

And when he didn't have a creative block.

And when he didn't have to think about Fina or the legacy she'd left their daughter.

'Gabriel, when was the last time you played football?'

He blinked to find her staring at him with her head cocked to one side. 'I... A long time.'

'Maybe you ought to take it back up again.'

'Why?'

One shoulder lifted in an elegantly eloquent shrug. 'Why

not? Exercise is good for the soul as well as the body. Maybe you've got into a rut and that's why you've been having trouble with your sculptures. Maybe you need to try new things, do different things... Have some fun.'

She might have a point, and if he could've focused on it, he might have pursued it further, but... He pointed a shaking finger at her shoulder. 'Have you been having *deportment* lessons?'

She jumped up and down on the spot, clapping her hands. 'You can tell?'

It was *awful*!

'You've no idea how wonderful it is to have your body say exactly what you want it to, to *behave* exactly as you want it to.'

She... It—

'No, scrap that.' Her soft laugh slammed into him. 'You're a master at silent communication. You know *exactly* how empowering it is.'

He had absolutely no comeback for that.

CHAPTER NINE

AUDREY CLOSED THE villa's front door as quietly as she could. Leaning against the door to catch her breath, she slipped off her high heels. What a night.

She was too keyed up for bed, even though it was the wee small hours of the morning. And she was starving. An image of the cake she'd made earlier in the day rose in her mind but before she could turn in the direction of the kitchen, footsteps sounded on the stairs.

She immediately straightened—slouching was bad, or so her deportment teacher informed her—but relaxed again when her gaze collided with the piercing grey of Gabriel's. Somewhere deep inside a tic started up.

'Do you know what time it is?' he hissed when he reached the bottom stair.

She gurgled back a laugh, pitying future teenage Lili. 'Yes, I do.' She folded her arms. 'What do you mean by staying out so late, Gabriel?'

His mouth opened but no words came out.

She took pity on him. 'Hungry?'

Not waiting for an answer, she made for the kitchen,

going to the hidden spot on the other side of the island where Anna the cook had secreted the cake. Lifting it up, she raised an eyebrow in question.

'You're having a midnight feast?'

She giggled. 'Technically, I think you'll find it's a 2 a.m. feast.'

Dark brows lowered. 'Are you drunk?'

She set the cake on the bench between them. 'A little tipsy, perhaps, but not rolling drunk. You get the milk while I cut the cake.'

His eyes practically started from their sockets. 'Milk?'

'Yes, it comes in cartons and is usually kept on the top shelf of the refrigerator, which is that huge stainless-steel monolith over there and—'

'Yes, yes, thank you.' Without another word he grabbed two glasses and the carton of milk and then hesitated. 'Do you want it heated?'

She shuddered. 'Hot milk is disgusting. Cold milk is perfection.'

With lips twitching, he set a glass in front of her and filled it to the brim. 'Do you know how many calories are in this?' He gestured at their feast.

'If that's the stance you mean to take with Lili as she's growing up, I'm afraid we're going to butt heads.'

'I...no. But Marguerite would have a fit if she could see you now.'

That made her laugh. 'Marguerite told me slim women held all the power, but I pooh-poohed that idea. I told her *healthy* women held all the power. I said, *It's the twenty-twenties, Grandmother, not the nineteen-sixties, when Twiggy was all the rage.* She found the idea...not without merit.'

He stared.

Pulling one of the plates towards her, she forked a generous mouthful of sponge into her mouth, relishing the sweet softness of cake, the hint of raspberry jam and fresh cream. 'Try it,' she ordered when he remained rooted to the spot. 'It's my signature cake.'

'*You* made this?'

'Why so surprised?'

'Everything you do surprises me,' he muttered. 'You're nothing like any of us expected.'

She was starting to think that could be a good thing.

Ignoring his fork, he lifted the cake in his fingers. A firm mouth and strong white teeth bit into it. She held her breath as he blinked, his eyes widening…and then he took another gigantic bite and swore softly in a way that sounded like a caress. 'You are a witch.'

'Why are your eyes grey? I like them, but the colour is unusual.'

'Are you sure you're not drunk?'

'Pretty sure. It's a 2 a.m. thing, I think.' She ate more cake and sipped her milk. 'People have a tendency to say things they wouldn't normally say in the wee small hours.'

'Where were you tonight?'

'Where were you?'

'Having dinner with a prospective client.'

And he'd checked on Lili before going back to his cottage. Because of course he had.

'I was out dancing with the girls.'

'The girls?'

'Tori, Livy and Ana.'

He leaned towards her. 'Who?'

'Vittoria, Livia and Adriana.'

'You've given them pet names?'

'Nicknames are a big thing in Australia—a sign of affection.' When he didn't say anything, she added, 'If you lived in Australia, you'd be called Gabe. But I prefer Gabriel. It suits you.'

'And what is your name shortened to?'

'Aud, sometimes, but that's not very pretty.'

'No, I prefer Audrey.'

They finished their cake and milk.

'Did you enjoy the dancing?'

She suppressed a yawn as she rinsed their plates and glasses before popping them in the dishwasher. 'Very much. Due to various things over the years, there hasn't been too much dancing in my life. Not that I'm complaining. But tonight was a real treat. I danced so hard I earned my cake.'

'And is that all you did?'

'Of course not. We chatted—girl talk, you know—and drank French champagne, which is *truly* delicious.' She winced. 'Though, it's wickedly expensive.' Apparently, she had the money to indulge such treats these days, but it was still hard not to count pennies when she'd been doing so all her life.

'Anything else?'

He'd gone all stiff and disapproving, and she suddenly realised what he was asking. He wanted to know if she'd indulged in any flirtations. 'That's really none of your business, Gabriel.' Normally, she was conciliatory, but he made her want to throw things with his casually negative judgements. 'Just because I go out dancing and enjoy a couple of drinks with the girls doesn't make me a bad person. It doesn't mean I'm about to self-destruct. And neither does meeting a man who might take my fancy and exploring that further. So you can take your nasty mind and its vile conclusions and shove them where the sun doesn't shine.'

His head rocked back. He opened his mouth, but she shook her head. 'You're acting like a dog in the manger. And I don't get it.' She leaned in close and his swift intake of breath speared into the centre of her, the chill in his eyes replaced with a heart-stopping heat...and that heat started to inch through her, too. She snapped back before she fell into them and did something totally *stupid*.

'It wouldn't matter if I were the most perfect woman in the world.' She said it for her own benefit as much as his. 'The fact that I'm a member of the Funaro family is a black mark I can never overcome.' He wouldn't fall in love with her on principle—because it would mean having to forgive the Funaros and he had no intention of doing that. 'In your eyes I will always be tainted by association.'

He stiffened. 'I...'

She huffed out a laugh. 'You can't even offer me friendship. I mean, if you were even so much as friends with me the world would come tumbling down, right?'

He blinked.

'So here's the thing, Gabriel. You don't get to tell me who I can and cannot date, any more than Marguerite can.'

He started to say something but she cut him off.

'Don't say a word. I repeat... It's. None. Of. Your. Business.'

With that she turned and walked away.

Audrey eased back to stare at her handiwork, the light outside that enormous window flooding the studio and haloing the piece she'd been working on. She'd created a glittering web of golds and blue, but threaded beneath it here and there were strands of black and grey—the exact same grey as Gabriel's eyes.

She glanced around, but he was working on something and had his back to her—as if deliberately ignoring her. It had been a week since that incident in the kitchen, and while he'd apologised to her the next day, the memory of it still somehow throbbed between them.

It was there when she sat for him.

It was there when he explained some detail of his methodology.

It was there when they explored the work of other fibre artists.

And it was there in his eyes whenever she spent time with Lili.

Shaking the thought off, she focused on the web and backdrop she'd created and then glanced across at the sculpture she'd studied so thoroughly while sitting for him. It was a clay model of something he'd probably hoped to eventually make on a far greater scale from recycled metal and timber. At the moment it wasn't much more than a fluid shape half a metre tall, but nevertheless, the outline suggested to her a figure wrestling with...well, itself, she supposed.

The web she'd made was supported on seven sticks she'd sourced from fallen branches outside, and she wanted to place it over the sculpture, engulfing it. She'd taken measurements, had envisaged it in place...

She now needed to see it all as one piece before she decided how she ought to continue with the backdrop, which was the piece of linen from which all the threads emanated. Glancing across at Gabriel, she bit her lip. If she was quiet, she could tiptoe over to the sculpture, set the frame in place, assess the effect and then tiptoe the frame back to her workbench. If she was quick and careful, Gabriel would be none the wiser.

She couldn't explain why she didn't want to share this with him yet. It's just...she wanted it perfect before he gave her feedback. And she didn't want to risk either his scorn or indignation that she'd improvised from a work of his. Maybe he'd think she was taking advantage of him.

She grimaced. Maybe he'd be right.

In the next moment she thrust out her chin. He'd told her to experiment. That was what she was doing.

Glancing across again and assuring herself that Gabriel was utterly immersed in whatever he was working on, she picked up her intricate web and moved silently across to the sculpture on its low table and set her frame in place.

After easing back a couple of steps, she crouched down to view it. Her pulse suddenly quickened. She'd never created anything like this before—but the moment she'd conceived it, it had consumed her.

Rubbing her nape, she nodded. She was definitely on the right track. Straightening, she went to remove the frame, when a commanding voice behind her bellowed, 'Do not touch it!'

She froze. *Damn.* She should've waited until he'd gone outside for a walk or a coffee.

Though his footsteps were silent, she could feel him moving closer. He stopped just behind her. She could feel the heat that flowed from him and the invigorating sting of his scent. Combined, they made her feel both confused and alive. Like so much about this man, her reaction made no sense.

She did what she could to channel Marguerite's unflappable calm—but inside butterflies the size of seagulls squawked and divebombed. Pressing her hands to her waist, she kept her gaze firmly fixed on the piece before them. She would *not* be the first to speak.

In fact, she shifted her weight and continued what she'd been doing in the first place—assessing the piece and deciding what else she could do to improve it. She'd take her time. Gabriel kept telling her she was an artist. Fine! She'd act like one, then.

Making a circuit around the piece, she halted at the backdrop that she was still in the process of embroidering. From the statue side the threads shot out to the rest of the frame, but on this side she was trying to create an abstract pattern.

'What are you thinking?'

He spoke from beside her, and she pointed. 'I need to remove the black.'

'And replace it with…?'

'Pink.' She frowned. Pink hadn't been part of the colour palette she'd used, but she instinctively knew it would work. It would create a contrast—not lightening the piece like gold or blue would, but softening it. 'And, actually, I'll keep a thread of black here and here.'

'Why?'

'Because it's what's true to the piece. It will make it more…human.'

They continued their circuit until they stood in front of it once again.

'What are you titling it?' When she didn't immediately answer he offered, *'Tangled Web?'*

She shook her head. There was nothing tangled about her web. It was quite deliberate. *'Ties That Bind,'* she decided.

'Audrey.'

She finally turned and met his gaze. Grey eyes raked hers and firm lips lifted. 'Excellent.'

'What?' She frowned. The piece? Her experimentation? Or...?

'You do not care what I think of this piece. It is something of which you are happy to take complete ownership. It is something of which you are proud.'

His words made her blink. 'I am proud of it,' she agreed. 'But it's not entirely true that I don't care what you think.'

'But if I told you this was rubbish?'

She shrugged. 'I'd continue to work on it.' *She'd* still like it.

'*Si*, this is what I mean.' He considered the piece again. 'But in this instance, we're in agreement. What you have done here, it is extraordinary.'

He really thought so?

'I can see how beautifully you've incorporated what you learned from our studies of both Marley and Sinestra.'

She couldn't prevent her hands from going to her hips. 'Then why haven't you called it derivative?' Which is what he'd called a piece she'd been working on earlier in the week.

'Because here you have employed the techniques in your own unique fashion.' That gaze settled on her, a crease deepening his brow. 'If my derivative comment stung, you perhaps need to grow a thicker skin.'

'And maybe you need to recognise that I work differently than you. You see something new and immediately want to experiment with it. I see something new and want to practise the technique to know that I can master it before I begin experimenting.'

He eased away a fraction farther to survey her more critically. Eventually, he nodded. 'There is a reason I am an artist and not a teacher.'

His words immediately had guilt crashing down on her. 'You're an excellent teacher, Gabriel. I shouldn't have inferred otherwise. I've learned an enormous amount from you and I'm very grateful.'

He merely shrugged. 'You are a consummate recycler, too, because I had every intention of throwing that sculpture away. Now instead, I can gift it to you.'

She gaped at him. 'You can't do that!'

He thrust out his chin at a haughty angle. 'I can do what I wish with my own work. Would you prefer that I throw it in the bin for you to retrieve later?'

'Of course not. I—'

'Then accept this gift in the spirit it was given—a gift from one artist to another. You had a vision for the sculpture where I did not. You've *earned* the sculpture.'

She stared at him, blinking.

'Simply say thank you and accept the gift.'

Drawing in a breath, she nodded. 'Thank you.' She knew precisely how extraordinary such a gift was.

Gabriel could sense how much Audrey wanted to get back to work, but he couldn't let the piece go just yet. Even unfinished, it captured the attention and held it hostage. 'This needs to be shown.'

'I beg your pardon.'

Her incredulity had him smiling. Maybe once she saw other people's reactions to her work, she would finally start to believe in herself. Before the summer was over, they might have enough of her work assembled to hold an exhibition.

'How many exhibitions have you been to since arriving in Italy?'

'Only a couple. I saw one in Rome before coming to Lake Como, and then another in Como. Though I have spent a lot of time at the art gallery.'

'Would you like to attend the new exhibition at the Galleria Pensiero with me in a fortnight?'

She started to dance on the spot. 'Are you serious? I'd give my eyeteeth to go to an opening night like that one.'

He shook his head, but he suspected his eyes might be dancing, too. 'Then you need to tell Marguerite's secretary and she will ensure you get all such future invitations.'

Her mouth dropped open. 'Just like that?'

He couldn't explain why, but she made him want to laugh; she made him feel young again. Even now she had no idea what doors her name and fortune could open for her. 'Just like that.'

'Wow.'

'But in this instance, you can come as my guest, yes? There are several people from the art world I would like you to meet.'

'Are you sure it's no bother?'

'Of course it isn't. It will be an interesting night and should be fun to compare opinions on the different pieces. Consider it part of your ongoing education.'

'Then thank you. I'd like that very much.'

'It's finally finished.'

Audrey had continued working on *Ties That Bind* for the rest of the week and Gabriel set down his tools now and moved across to where she stood.

Every time she'd left the room during the past week,

he'd found himself drawn across to it. Something in it ruffled his soul, made him feel too much. He could count on the fingers of one hand the artworks that had such an impact on him.

The finished piece was shocking. And beautiful. The longer he stared at it, the more his heart ached.

'What's wrong?'

The quiet question throbbed between them.

'Gabriel?'

His name on her lips broke the spell and had him slamming back. He swallowed and gestured. 'It is powerful.'

She sucked her bottom lip into her mouth; her forehead creased. 'I can hardly believe I created such a thing.'

He knew what she meant. He sometimes felt like that when he finished an installation. Somewhere between vision and execution, a work could take on a life of its own.

'Is that how you see yourself?' he suddenly burst out. 'Trapped behind a beautiful web and unable to break free?' Because while there was no denying the beauty of the web, it still held the figure fast inside.

Her brow pleated.

'I mean, you have made the figure strong. Or at least you have given the sculpture an appearance of strength.' But that didn't change the fact that the figure was trapped.

She stared at the piece. 'Is that how you see it?'

Did she not?

Shaking her head, she met his gaze. 'That's not me, Gabriel.'

Her face confirmed the truth of her words. He couldn't explain why, but something inside him unclenched and he was able to breathe again. He did not want her feeling trapped like that. This woman deserved to be free.

* * *

Gabriel was aware of the glances he and Audrey drew as they entered the Galleria Pensiero, but he ignored them. The gallery was built on classic lines, and the inside foyer was a soaring auditorium of Italian marble and sparkling chandeliers, the light glinting off crystal glasses balanced on elegant trays circulated about the room by stylish waitstaff.

At his side Audrey gave a dreamy sigh, and for once he agreed with her. With practised ease, he seized two champagne flutes from a passing tray and handed her one. Smiling her thanks, she touched her glass to his before taking a sip, her lids fluttering in appreciation.

In that moment he knew she would never take French champagne for granted; that she would always acknowledge the wonder of it with every sip. The knowledge lifted something inside him. Fina had knocked the stuff back like there was no tomorrow. She hadn't cared whether it was French champagne, vodka, or a nice Brunello. It had all been one and the same to her.

Maybe, just maybe, Audrey would be able to avoid the same fate as her mother and sister. For a moment he allowed himself to hope. He would do whatever he could to make sure she had all the props and supports she needed; that she had something to fall back on. Something other than drugs, alcohol and sex. And then Lili would have at least one female relative she could take as a role model.

'Thank you so much for bringing me tonight, Gabriel.'

'You have already thanked me three times. This thanks is not necessary.' He gestured for them to move towards the works on display. 'It is my responsibility as your mentor to ensure you receive ample opportunities for development, yes?'

She glanced across, a frown in her eyes. 'And what about when we are no longer mentor and mentee?'

'We will still be colleagues.' They could continue to discuss art and the projects they were working on. She would still be Lili's aunt.

'Not friends?'

When he didn't answer immediately, the light in her eyes dimmed and it left him feeling like a heel. He hated having put that expression in her eyes. But could he and this woman ever be friends?

She sipped her champagne. 'That's clearly a *no*, then.'

What if they became friends and then she followed in Danae and Fina's footsteps, after all? Where would that leave him and Lili? He swallowed, his collar drawing tight about his throat. 'I do not give my friendship quickly,' he finally said. 'I am not one of these people who needs a lot of friends. But the ones I have I take very good care of.'

'That's good to know.' But the happy sparkle in her eyes didn't return.

'I am not saying we will not be friends.'

She nodded, but didn't look at him, pointed instead at the painting they surveyed. 'That's an interesting colour combination.'

They were both silent as they assessed the painting before moving along to the next one.

'In the meantime—' she swung back, her attempt at restraint clearly failing '—you'll just keep fatalistically waiting for the worst to happen and miss out on all the good things friendships—and family—can give you?'

He choked on his wine. Was she inferring...? 'The Funaros are *not* my family.' He kept his voice low but the words shot from him like paint splatter.

'Of course they are. You married into them, didn't you? They're Lili's family.'

'But—'

'Sure, you can keep your distance and be all grumpy and broody and disapproving. But it doesn't change the facts.'

You bet your life he'd keep his distance, but he couldn't prevent a thread of curiosity from rising through him then, too. 'How, I would like to know, do you think I could—' he searched for an appropriate word '—*integrate* myself into the family?'

'By getting to know them better... Socialising and mixing with them. Like, for example, attending the surprise seventy-fifth birthday party I'm throwing for Marguerite.'

She was doing *what*? Marguerite would *hate* a surprise party.

'I don't like this piece.' She scrunched up her face at the canvas in front of them. 'Odd, as I can see the expertise, the superiority of the artist's technique.'

He found himself in accord, but he didn't say that out loud. It was strange how attuned they could be about art, and yet how out of step they were when it came to family.

'It would mean a lot to Lili.'

He knew that, but... Huffing out an exasperated breath, he glared at her. 'You are not easy company.'

'Not true! I'm very easy company when I sit for you.'

Then she thankfully seemed content with her own thoughts and kept them to herself, instead of giving voice to them and ruffling his mood.

'Ah.' He looked up. 'I just spotted Marco. I would like to introduce you to him. He is an agent and I suspect he would be very interested in what you are doing with your fibre art.'

She stared up at him with deer-in-the-headlights eyes, her throat bobbing as she swallowed.

'No.' He pointed a commanding finger at her. 'You are not going to be nervous or self-effacing. You are going to own the fact that you are an artist and that the work you are doing is unique and powerful and needs to find a greater audience.'

'Oh, but—'

'No buts! You have talent. You will project confidence and conviction in your work.'

The glass in her hand wobbled.

'Close your eyes.'

She did as he said. Staring into that beautiful face with the hair gathered up high on her head and dark ringlets falling down around her neck, a deep hunger surged through him. He ground his teeth against it. 'Picture in your mind your *Ties That Bind* piece. Recall how you feel about it—the pride you have in it and the wonder—revel in the knowledge that you created it.'

She swallowed. The glass in her hand steadied and she opened her eyes. 'Okay, you're right. I have work I'm proud of. I'll do my best not to embarrass you.'

Her words softened something at the centre of him. 'I know you won't. Even if you did, I wouldn't care. But I do not wish you to do yourself a disservice. This is all.'

Taking her arm, he manoeuvred her towards Marco. 'You once asked me about the colour of my eyes.'

She swung to him. 'I did! You never did tell me where they came from.'

'From my mother. She was half Irish.'

She stared. 'Have you been to Ireland?'

'*Si.*'

'Do you have family there?'

What was it about this woman and family? 'A couple of distant cousins.'

'How lovely. Tell me. Is Ireland as green as everyone says?'

He nodded. 'I'm sure you would find it most inspiring. Marco!' He hailed the agent. 'It is good to see you.'

He made the introductions, and with a few choice words didn't just pique the agent's interest in Audrey's work, but had him covetous to be the first agent to see it.

'Is this piece really as extraordinary as you say?' Marco demanded, handing Audrey his card.

'It's one of the most powerful artworks I have ever seen.'

Marco took Audrey's hand. 'You must contact me soon, yes? I will come view your work and then—'

'Excuse us. I just spotted someone I'd like Audrey to meet.' Gabriel smoothly detached Audrey from the other man's grip and whisked her off to introduce her to a rival agent. Marco would be the perfect agent for Audrey, but he'd appreciate her all the more if he had to fight for her.

'Oh, my God! Oh, my God!' Audrey chanted under her breath for his ears only.

'Smile. Chin up. Confident, remember?'

She gurgled back a laugh. 'Would it appal you to realise how much like Marguerite you just sounded then?'

He tried to feel affronted, but couldn't manage it. He satisfied himself with a flippant, 'Do not spoil the evening.'

Her laugh made him grin.

CHAPTER TEN

'AT BREAKFAST THIS MORNING Lili was talking about this party you're planning for Marguerite.'

Audrey halted midstretch, glancing up from the piece she was currently working on—a traditional embroidery on a piece of square linen the colour of midnight—and realised Gabriel's hammering and welding had been nonexistent for the past twenty minutes. Had he been waiting for her, not wanting to break her concentration?

Shaking herself, she completed her stretch. 'She's very excited about it. Coffee?' She started towards the kitchenette. 'Of course, when you're four, parties *are* very exciting.'

'I will make the coffee if you will cut whatever sweet wickedness you brought with you today.'

She'd cut the chocolate brownies before they'd left the villa—leaving instructions with Maria that both Lili and Marguerite had one for their morning coffee as well—but she dished them out now onto the plain white plates he kept in the cupboard.

As had become their habit, they took their midmorning coffee outside to the wooden table, sitting on the same bench so as to face the lake and drink in the view. Not so closely, though, that shoulders or thighs brushed. She could feel the heat that emanated from him, though, as warm against her left side as the sun overhead.

'Audrey, do you have much experience with children?'

'A couple of my girlfriends have children, and I enjoy their company on the odd occasion I get the chance. Why?'

A frown creased his brow and her heart plummeted. 'Have I done something wrong with Lili?' Her hands clenched. She'd never knowingly do anything to hurt her delightful little niece.

'That is not what I meant. It is just...'

He turned to face her more fully, his knee bumping hers, sending a rush of awareness streaking through her. She tried to look unmoved, but heat crept into her cheeks, no doubt turning them pink. She hoped he misread it as her horror of doing something that would harm Lili.

He shuffled away until their knees no longer touched, and it occurred to her that this awareness might not be one-sided. A pulse in her throat fluttered to life, and so did one low in her abdomen—a deep and insistent *throb-throb* that the rest of her body took up.

Dragging a breath into cramped lungs, she ordered herself to ignore it. They'd both made their positions clear. What was the point getting all hot and bothered when she couldn't do anything about it?

'Have I done anything wrong?' she asked, staring doggedly at the infuriatingly placid lake.

'Not wrong so much, as... It's just that a four-year-old doesn't fully understand yet the concept of keeping a secret.'

Blowing out a breath, she relaxed again.

'If Lili in her excitement should blurt out the secret to Marguerite, I would hate for you to be vexed with her.'

She reached out to touch his arm. 'Of course I won't be vexed.' She'd meant her touch to be a sign of reassurance. Instead, the power and heat of the man filtrated into her blood, making her want him with such an elemental fierceness she sucked in a breath. Snatching her hand back, she rubbed it against the linen of her trousers.

'Actually, Gabriel, I'm very much hoping she will let the cat out of the bag.'

That clenched hand on the table in front of him immediately loosened. He swung to her. 'You *want* Marguerite to find out?'

'Absolutely. She'd hate a surprise party, don't you think?'

'*Si.*'

'But a surprise party she knows about and can plan for...'

'You—'

He broke off, his face darkening, but she couldn't tell if it was in outrage or surprise.

'Think about it.' This time it was she who turned to him, though she was super careful not to bump him. 'This way Marguerite gets all the advantages of a surprise party, but with none of the drawbacks. Try your brownie.' It might help sweeten his mood.

With a disgruntled huff he bit into it, and as he slowly chewed, his eyelids lowered to half-mast with drowsy appreciation. Her breath caught. If she tasted him with the same lazy appreciation, would he—

Don't!

He sent her a sidelong glance from those grey eyes. 'You are a crafty harpy.'

'I'm not a *harpy*!' She feigned affront.

'A manoeuvrer then, a puller of strings.'

'But in a nice way.' She bit into her brownie, too, and groaned a little.

He gestured. 'Did you make these?'

She nodded. 'Nonna owned a restaurant and let me and my cousin Frankie help out in the school holidays. We loved it. Frankie adored being in the dining room with the customers—chatting and laughing and taking orders. But I loved to sneak into the kitchen and help out there.' It had been another haven.

He stared at her for a long moment. 'And Johanna? Did she love the restaurant, too?'

She loved that he asked, as if it'd be the most natural thing in the world that her sister would also be involved. 'Jo said nobody was tying her to a kitchen. She usually went away to camp during the school holidays—did far more exciting things like horse riding and kayaking.'

He laughed, and the sound of it made her feel happy and light, like she did when listening to her favourite pop music.

'Maria doesn't mind having you in her kitchen?'

'Not in the slightest. She understands that cooking can be a comfort. That it can help quieten the mind and soothe the soul.'

Intriguing lips pursed. She forced herself to look away.

'It has been a tempestuous time for you, yes? I had hoped the art would help, but—'

'Of course it's helped! Working here with you invigorates me. It fires me up—it's frustrating and satisfying in equal measure. But it's not *relaxing*. Do you find it relaxing?'

He opened his mouth, but closed it again with a frown. 'I find myself lost to it sometimes,' he finally said, 'and when I come back to myself, I am exhausted. But you are right.

It is not relaxing. It is good that you have an outlet that is soothing and relaxing, too. Very good.'

'It's not the only one. Spending time with Lili is a delight.'

Something in his eyes lifted. 'Yes.'

'And with other members of the family, too.'

'With *the girls* as you call them?'

She nodded. 'And Marguerite.' Though she knew he wouldn't believe her. 'And I have hopes that the older members of the family will thaw as they get to know me better.'

He dragged a hand down his face, looking suddenly tired and grey. 'Have you approached Marguerite yet about setting up a foundation in Johanna's honour?'

Her chest clenched. 'I've mentioned it. She's thinking about it.' Forcing a smile, she lifted her chin. 'She'll come around, you'll see.' It would all work out.

'Audrey, you will be disappointed—'

'It's a risk I'm prepared to take.' She nodded at his abandoned brownie. 'Eat up. You call me a puller of strings, but you're wrong. I'm not pulling strings. I'm building bridges. I'm hoping that Marguerite knows by now that there's a surprise party in store for her—and that while I'm the brains behind it, the rest of the family is helping me in every way they can.'

'And what do you hope that will achieve?'

'Goodwill.'

'Audrey...'

She rushed on before he could pour cold water on her plans. 'And in the evenings that Marguerite and I spend together, I'm asking her advice about various family members.'

She watched him wrestle with his curiosity and saw the

exact moment he surrendered to it, and it gave her a silly thrill of triumph. 'What kind of advice?'

'I asked her who I should set Livia up with. Do you know Livy hasn't dated since that awful sex scandal? No? Neither did Marguerite. I told her I thought it was dreadful what had happened, but that I didn't think it should put Livy off a relationship forever. Not all men are selfish jerks.'

'Did she suggest anyone?'

'Well, we discussed it long and hard because Livy needs someone kind-hearted and patient. We made a short list. I told her I'd get Tori and Ana's feedback, too, as they no doubt know these short-listed guys. I've told her I trust their judgement.'

His jaw dropped. 'You...'

'Bridge builder,' she provided for him. 'Also, Tori is thinking of starting up another business—she wants to help a community of women affected by domestic violence who've pooled their talents to make a range of funky T-shirts and earrings. Part of the proceeds go back into helping fund women's shelters. Tori's going to use her connections to create a more global platform for them.'

The pulse at the base of his throat throbbed. 'And Ana?'

She beamed at him. 'I'm glad you asked. Prior to her stint in rehab, she'd been working in her father's firm.'

He raked both hands back through his hair. 'You say *father's firm* like it's some kind of small holding. Audrey, it is one of the most prestigious real estate firms in all of Italy.'

'Whatever. The fact is she loved her job but her parents are so embarrassed at her downfall they'll barely speak to her, let alone give her old job back to her.'

'Yes, but—'

'She didn't steal from them, Gabriel. We all make mistakes. And we all deserve a second chance.'

'And this is the argument you presented to Marguerite?'

She bit into her brownie. 'I asked her advice for how we can best convince Ana's parents to give her her old job back.'

Autocratic lips twisted. 'I can already tell you how that went.'

'Go on, then.' She continued eating her brownie.

'If she didn't simply dismiss the idea and say it served Ana right.'

'Which she didn't.'

She licked her fingers clean of crumbs and Gabriel watched her as if mesmerised. Things inside her clenched up tight. He looked as if he'd like nothing more than to gobble her up. Shaking himself, he glared out at the water. Sagging, she seized her mug and buried her nose in it.

'Then she'd have said she would simply order Reggio and Claudia to give Adriana her job back.'

She nodded. That was exactly what Marguerite had said.

'What did you do?'

His voice was laden with doom and she couldn't help bristling a little. Why was he so sure she'd mess up and fall out of Marguerite's good graces?

'I didn't *do* anything. I simply laughed and told her I was starting to see why everyone was so terrified of her.'

His eyes widened and for a moment she could've sworn his lips twitched. 'What did she say?'

'She said that was *utter nonsense*. But I told her Nonna's motto had always been "You win more flies with honey than with vinegar."'

He choked on his coffee. 'You invoked your paternal grandmother?'

Admittedly, it had been a risk. But it had paid off. 'I suggested it might be better for domestic harmony—for Ana's relationship with her parents—if Marguerite made some throwaway comment about how well Ana seemed to be doing and suggested it might be time for her to get back to work, or something along those lines.'

'*Is* Adriana doing well?'

His face had closed up and it took a force of will not to seize what was left of her brownie and mash it against the front of his shirt. 'Of course she is! I don't lie, Gabriel. How many more times do we have to have this conversation?'

But the exhaustion that crossed his face tugged at her heart. Ana's drug addiction must remind him of Fina's. And anyone could see how badly Fina's death had marked him. How it still marked him.

'Sorry,' she murmured. 'I didn't mean to snap.'

'While I shouldn't have been so sceptical. I barely know Ana.'

She glared into her coffee. 'You hardly know any of them and yet you're happy to dismiss them wholesale as a bunch of hedonistic partygoers without a care for anyone but themselves and their own pleasure. Or in Marguerite's case that she'd sacrifice all for the family name. But you're wrong. The Funaros are like any other family—a complicated mix of good and bad. People aren't perfect, Gabriel, and it's unreasonable to expect them to not make mistakes.'

She wanted to add that what had happened to Fina wasn't anyone's fault—not his and not Marguerite's—but snapped her mouth shut. She'd already said more than she'd meant to.

'And this is what you are also trying to do between

me and Marguerite—and the rest of the family—build a bridge?' Dark eyebrows rose over flinty eyes. 'You are trying to get me to see them in a different light.'

'I *would* like you to see them in a different light,' she admitted. 'A truer light.'

'Truer for whom?'

'I'm not being dishonest.' She crumpled her paper napkin. 'I'm not lying or making things up. Everything I tell you about Marguerite is the truth.'

'As *you* see it.'

'As I see it,' she agreed. 'In a way that isn't twisted by bitterness or hate.'

'If you should continue to attempt this thing, you will be making a mistake.'

He didn't speak with anger, but his quietness was ten times worse. She pressed fingers to her forehead. She would love for him and Marguerite to loosen their grip on the prejudices they held about each other.

'And then we will not be friends. I will not allow you to be my puppet master, Audrey.'

Her chin lifted. 'And are we friends?'

For the briefest of moments, stern lips relaxed into a smile. 'I am friendlier with you than I have ever before been with a Funaro.'

Not counting Fina, of course. Though that remained unspoken.

'I'm not manipulating anyone. I'm simply providing a vision of the truth that you are uncomfortable with, and I suspect Marguerite is, too, though she does a better job of hiding it. I believe you're a lot of things, Gabriel. I suspect you can be every bit as ruthless as Marguerite claims. But

I also know you can be patient and kind. The one thing I didn't expect you to be was closed-minded.'

His jaw dropped.

'And from all you've lectured me on artistic practise, closed-mindedness is the death of art.'

If possible, his jaw dropped even farther.

She stood and planted her hands on her hips. 'Do you think I'm doing harm with this so-called string-pulling? Do you think I'm doing a bad thing? Do you think I am making a mess, making things worse?'

With a visible effort, he hauled his jaw into place. He neither glared nor yelled. Behind the grey of his eyes, she sensed his mind racing. Finally, he shook his head. 'You are trying to create harmony, and I think that in these instances—with *the girls*—you will succeed. You are looking after your friends. It is admirable. But I still think you are going to be disappointed.'

She sat again, tracked an eagle high above, circling on air currents. She kept her gaze trained on it. 'Why?'

'Because you are trying to create one big happy family here in Lake Como and that will never happen. You yearn so much for the love and security of family and are prepared to give your all for it, but you do not see how others can, and probably will, take advantage of that to promote their own agendas.'

She had to swallow. His perception—his recognition of her feelings about family—left her feeling raw and vulnerable. And yet, she wouldn't be as cynical as he was for all the world, even if the Funaros should end up breaking her heart.

'Or maybe they just need to experience someone loving them without an agenda, to understand what it's like to be loved unconditionally, to discover what it's worth. Maybe they need to be loved like that first, before they can see how they, too, can love like that.'

He swore under his breath. 'You need to develop some armour against the world, Audrey. You need—'

'I don't see your armour bringing you any joy, Gabriel, so excuse me if I don't jump on board your armour train. You are dismissing vulnerability as something to be afraid of. You don't understand what a gift it can be. Armour?' She snorted. 'Armour simply weighs one down.'

Gabriel watched Audrey return to the studio with her plate and mug, her shoulders back and her head held high, and an icy fist reached inside his chest and squeezed.

She had such faith in people. What would happen when this family took all she had to give then stomped all over her? Who and what would she turn to for solace when they refused to live up to her expectations and behaved their worst—when she felt discarded and unloved and betrayed?

She enjoyed the finest French champagne now, but would she start chugging back bottles of the stuff to take the edge off the pain? Would she lose herself to a string of love affairs and one-night stands in an effort to find a physical release from her sadness and sense of failure? Would she turn to drugs...?

Breathing hard, he ran a hand over his face. He and Lili would be there for her, and so would her art, but would it be enough? What else could he give her that would provide some comfort if this came tumbling down around her ears?

If? Don't you mean when?

Tapping fingers against the table, he realized that if things truly did go badly, he wasn't sure she'd know how to get away from the villa. Marguerite could stymie a cab driver, refuse them entrance. His lips pressed into a tight line. That at least was something he could help with.

Seizing his mug and plate, he, too, returned to the studio. 'Audrey, do you know how to drive?'

She glanced around from *Ties That Bind*. He thought she'd finished it.

'I have an Australian driver's licence, but I've not driven in Italy yet.' She shuddered. 'You guys drive on the wrong side of the road.'

He ignored the shudder. 'Would you like to learn to drive here?'

She turned around fully. 'Are you offering to teach me?'

'*Si.*'

'Why?'

'I think it is wise for every person to have as much independence as possible.' He would do for her what he'd never thought to do for Fina.

'You think there might be a situation in the future where I'll need to make a quick getaway?'

Her lips twitched as if she found him amusing. He didn't care. She could be amused all she liked as long as she was also prepared. 'It is better to be safe than sorry.'

She stared at him for several long moments, but to his relief, finally nodded. 'I'd very much like to practise my driving with someone capable. As you say, you never know when such a skill might come in handy. Thank you for the offer.'

Excellent. He gestured at *Ties That Bind*. 'I thought you had finished.'

'I did, too, but something in me refused to rest. And it just occurred to me that one can lift off my frame and the figure beneath is suddenly freed, but...that's not the truth of the piece. It's not the way things work in the real world. So now I want to send threads from here to here—' she pointed '—and here to here. So that it is all fully integrated. I know it will make the piece harder to transport. That two pieces now become one, but...' She shrugged.

He stared at the piece, and as always, things inside him clenched.

'Are you sure the figure there trapped behind that beautiful web is not you?' He wasn't sure he could stand it if that was how she felt.

'I don't feel trapped, Gabriel.'

He tried to feel relief, but it wouldn't come. 'Who *is* the figure, then?'

She frowned. 'Why does it have to be anyone?'

Because every instinct he had told him she'd created that piece with someone particular in mind. Johanna? Marguerite?

Before he could ask, her frown deepened. 'Who was the figure in *Maybe*? Who was your muse for that piece?'

'Fina.'

She flinched and it had him refocusing fully on her rather than her artwork. She stared at him with wide eyes, the colour draining from her face. How was it possible for her to grieve so hard for the dead sister she'd never known? Exhaustion swamped him and he dropped into the nearest chair. 'It was when I didn't know if she was going to overcome her addiction or give in to it completely.'

It had been during her second stint in rehab. He'd had such high hopes. They hadn't been realised, and even now the acrid taste of disappointment burned his throat.

Audrey gave a low laugh, but it held no humour. His every sense was on high alert.

'*That's* what me sitting for you has been about?'

Her mouth twisted in self-derision, as if she'd been a fool. He found himself on his feet. 'What do you mean?'

She paced the long length of the bench running the width of the room. 'You haven't wanted me to sit for you because of who I am, because there's something about *me* that speaks to you.' She thumped a hand to her chest.

What the hell...?

She swung around, eyes flashing. 'I've just been a substitute for your real muse—*Fina!*'

She had this wrong. *So* wrong.

'I thought your creative block was because you'd been trapped in your grief for so long that you'd forgotten how to have fun and enjoy yourself. I thought I'd somehow helped to pull you out of that funk—that in agreeing to be your student, I'd given you a different focus.' She flung an arm in the air. 'I thought having a female role model for Lili—a woman who would love her—had helped quieten some of your fears. I thought those things combined—'

She broke off, breathing hard. 'God, I must have an ego the size—' she gestured out the window '—of a lake!'

The magnitude of her misapprehension left him speechless. He tried to make his brain work; tried to formulate words to tell her how mistaken she was.

'Instead, all of this time I've been a substitute, a very sad second best, but a chance nonetheless for you to relive your glory days with Fina.'

The expression in her eyes pierced him to the very core.

'No wonder you didn't want to be friends. Were so intent on keeping me at a distance. You didn't want to bring the temporary fantasy that Fina still lived crashing down.'

'*You are so wrong!*'

The shouted words reverberated around the studio, reaching into the farthest, darkest corners.

'Incredibly, stupendously and momentously *wrong*!' he roared.

Her head rocked back.

He stabbed a finger at her. 'I hadn't been married to Fina a full year before I realised what a mistake our marriage was.'

The shock in her eyes was far more welcome than the previous self-loathing.

'I wanted a divorce.'

Her hand flew to her mouth.

'But then Fina became pregnant and...' He raised his arms, let them drop back to his sides. 'I hoped things would change. We had made vows. It is wrong to give up on a marriage without a fight. I wanted to be there for Fina and I wanted to be there for our child.'

Neither of them said anything for several long moments.

'My relationship with Fina was not the great romance you seem to think it.'

She took several steps towards him. 'You must've loved her once.'

'She didn't marry me because she loved me. She married me as an act of rebellion...because she knew Marguerite would not approve.'

She moved another step closer. 'But *you* must've loved *her*.'

'I must've done,' he agreed. 'But I cannot remember feeling that way now. All I remember is her destructiveness and her selfishness, and how I wished to break free of her. You are wrong, Audrey. I am not mired in grief.' He was mired in guilt. He did what he could to get his raging emotions back under control. 'However, Lili has lost her mother, and that is a great tragedy.'

'I'm sorry,' she offered quietly.

He moved across until they stood toe to toe. 'You have not been a sad substitute. You do not, thankfully, remind me of Fina in any fashion. You are ten times the woman she was.'

Her lips parted and she blinked.

He leaned down until they were eye to eye, the cleanness of her scent welling up all around him. 'I keep my distance because I am the one who demanded there be no romantic entanglement between us. And yet, when you are near, all I can think about is kissing you.'

Her throat bobbed and her gaze lowered to his lips, clove-coloured eyes darkening to walnut. 'So...' That gaze returned to his and she swallowed again. 'I haven't imagined that?'

His hands clenched to fists to stop from reaching for her. 'You haven't imagined it.' He would not undermine her confidence or sense of self the way Fina had his, no matter what the admission might cost him.

'And you know I feel the same way. That sometimes I look at you and—'

'Yes!' He cut her off before her words could inflame him further.

'So...it's safer to keep our distance.'

He tried to push another yes from his throat, but it wouldn't come.

She moistened her lips. 'What would happen if we broke those rules?' She said the words as if to herself. 'Would the sky fall in?' The pulse in her throat fluttered. It took all his strength not to lower his head and touch his lips to the spot. 'Should we amend the rules?'

This was madness, but as he stared at the line of her throat, took in the oversized man's button-down shirt she wore when she worked, the vee of the neckline hinting at shadowed cleavage, hunger roared through him. 'Amend the rules how?' The words rasped out of him.

'I still don't want a boyfriend. But I've never wanted a man the way I want you. What I feel for you is...*greedy*. I've been careful my whole life not to be greedy, but I see you and I want...'

She reached out and placed her hand on his chest. The warmth of her hand penetrated the thin cotton of his T-shirt and he sucked in a breath. 'And you want what?' he demanded.

She met his gaze and her eyes widened—at whatever she saw in his face or her own audacity, he had no idea.

'I want to claw off your clothes and feast on you, and have you feast on me. I want to be greedy.'

She spoke clearly, as if she wanted her every word to hit him with the force of a mini tornado. He couldn't move. If he did, he'd kiss her, and there'd be no going back.

'Can I kiss you, Gabriel?'

His body shook from the force of holding back. 'If we kiss, Audrey, we will not stop.' He reached out and pulled the clip from her hair. Her hair fell past her shoulders and he wrapped his hand around it, pulled her head back until her throat was exposed to him. He pressed a kiss there, grazed the sensitive skin with his teeth and she whimpered. The sound arrowed to his groin.

'Release my hair, Gabriel.'

He didn't want to, but he did as she asked. Rather than move away, though, she hooked a hand behind his head and drew his face down to hers, her eyes glittering and her breath shallow. 'We keep it here, at the studio. We don't take it back to the villa or anywhere else. Agreed?'

His heart beat so hard he thought she must hear it. 'Agreed.'

Bunching her fingers in his shirt, she dragged it over his head and then simply stared at him. 'Can I change my mind? Can I ask you to sit for me naked?'

'You can have me however you want.'

And then they were tearing at each other's clothes. It was raw and physical and primal. He wanted to slow it down, but she wouldn't let him. She seemed to know exactly how to touch him to inflame him and make him forget himself.

'Now,' she demanded, sobbing when he touched her in that most intimate of places. She was soft and wet and ready. Wrapping a hand around him, she squeezed gently and he bucked into her hand. 'Now, Gabriel, now!' she demanded. 'I want you inside me *now*.'

He went to sweep the bench clear, but it would mean disturbing her current embroidery.

He swung away to the other bench. 'We'll hurt your work,' she groaned.

Stumbling together, they hit the back wall. He took the force before swinging them around and lifting her up, her back braced against the wall as he fumbled with a condom from his wallet on the bench. Her legs wrapped around his waist and he lowered her down. They both shook as she closed around him.

They stilled, staring at each other. It felt as if not just time but the world itself stopped, and then they were moving with a greedy fervour that shook him to his core. They moved with a mutual rhythm, not once breaking stride, not once falling out of step.

Her breaths, her moans and whimpers filled his ears. Her cries as her muscles tightened and she broke around him. His name on her lips.

From somewhere far off a guttural cry sounded—him?—and then he was sucked into a swirling vortex of pleasure that shook every atom of his body with its force—breaking and then rearranging it in a different pattern.

And leaving him feeling like a new man.

CHAPTER ELEVEN

AS GABRIEL LOWERED her feet to the floor, Audrey wondered if her legs would hold her upright. *Good legs.* She praised them when they did. *Very good legs.*

Not that he let her go. They were both breathing hard. She had one arm flung around his neck; the other drifted down to rest against his ample chest. He'd wrapped one strong arm around her waist and his forehead rested beside her on the wall.

Closing her eyes, she did what she could to catch her breath. That had been...*intense.*

Eventually, Gabriel roused himself and swore softly. 'Did I hurt you?'

Her eyes flew open and she reached up to touch his face. 'You took me to heaven.'

Grey eyes met hers. He traced a finger down her cheek. 'I lost all control. You probably have bruises on your back.'

'And you probably have scratch marks on yours.' She bit her lip. 'I might've even drawn blood.'

He smiled. And it was sweet and warm and every good thing. Things inside her melted and begged and did all manner of things she couldn't begin to decipher when her mind was still so full of him, and while he remained so close.

She needed him to stay close. She didn't want him moving just yet.

'I loved your enthusiasm,' he murmured, pushing her hair from her face. 'I loved how much you wanted me.' His gaze darkened. 'You made me feel alive again.'

He'd made her feel like a wild woman. 'I didn't know it could be that good,' she whispered.

His gaze roved her face and he nodded as if in approval. 'I have dreamed of seeing you mussed like this, and it is every bit as beguiling as I knew it would be. You are an extraordinary woman, Audrey.'

She melted some more, cupped his face and kissed him. A warm kiss that he returned with the same goodwill that threaded through her.

'I meant to savour you, though.'

She bit her lip and drew back a fraction, curiosity rippling through her. What did he mean by that?

'I meant to take it slow, meant to explore every inch of your body, learning what gave you pleasure, taking my time until you were begging for release.'

Warmth flushed through her cheeks. And other places. 'What? *Now, Gabriel, now. Please!* wasn't enough begging for you?'

His chuckle warmed her all the way through. 'Next time,' he promised. 'I am afraid I will not want to do any work if we are keeping this thing here and only here.'

'It has to stay here.' They both knew it.

It had to stay here, because if they took this thing into the real world, she was afraid she'd fall in love with him. As long as they kept it within these four walls it would continue to feel like nothing more than an escapist dream, a flight of fancy—something not quite real.

Gabriel didn't want her falling in love with him. Marguerite didn't want her falling in love with him, either. An icy drip slid down her spine, and she wasn't masochistic enough to set herself up for that kind of heartache.

Gabriel would never fall in love with her. She was a Funaro, and that was something he'd never be able to overlook. He might make her body sing, but she'd be a fool to expect more. If he thought her feelings were getting involved, he'd walk away without a backwards glance—perhaps tossing her one of those blisteringly sardonic smiles over his shoulder first.

She shivered, and he rubbed his hands up and down her arms. 'Are you cold?'

Pulling in a breath, she smiled. 'No, I'm fine.'

Nobody would fall in love with anybody. They'd keep things light, they'd keep them fun...and they'd keep them separate. They'd enjoy each other, be kind to each other and remain friends when this eventually ended. Because regardless of anything else, she did feel that finally they were friends.

Over the next week Gabriel introduced Audrey to a brand-new world of sensuality. He showed her exactly what he intended when he'd said he'd meant to savour her. He made her beg as he promised he would. He made her soar. He made her feel replete. He made her feel *complete*.

In turn, she savoured him with the same slow relish; learned all she could about his body and what gave him pleasure. It made her want to pinch herself to know she had the power to affect him so greatly. To see that masculine body trembling at her touch. She made him beg, too; made him lose control...made him soar.

'How long before it burns itself out?' she asked after a particularly earth-shattering session of lovemaking. Her hand trailed a path across his naked chest as they lay on the bed in the mezzanine level he'd revealed to her the afternoon of the first day they'd become lovers. The view outside that enormous wall of glass was as spectacular as ever, but it was the man who captured her attention and held it.

'I do not know.' His fingers traced delicate patterns across her back. She wondered if she could capture those patterns and this feeling in an embroidery. 'You wish to be tired of me already?'

'Absolutely not!' But in a far-off corner of her mind, she hoped the need and intensity would soon lessen. At the villa they tried to avoid each other. Oh, she spent time with Lili, but he no longer accompanied her. They might have rules about where and when and how they could indulge their explosive chemistry, but their bodies had minds of their own.

And refused to be ruled.

The driving lessons he insisted on giving her were a special form of torture. But neither of them broke the promise they'd made. Even though she could see in the set of his jaw, the pulse in his throat and the fire in his eyes that he wanted her every bit as much as she wanted him.

'We are friends now, Gabriel, yes?'

He lifted up on one elbow, a frown in his eyes. 'Of course. I like you. I care about you.' He blinked as if the admission surprised him. 'Do you doubt it?'

She shook her head. 'I feel it in here.' She touched her chest. A hungry light came into his eyes as he glanced at her chest, making her swallow. 'I just wanted to make sure you felt it, too. Gabriel…' She hesitated. 'You know I've no desire to hurt or vex you?'

His frown deepened. 'I trust you, if that is what you ask. Why?'

'Because I want you to tell me more about Fina. What happened? How did she die?'

He sat up, a mix of emotions racing across his face as he settled back against the headboard.

She sat up, too, but rather than rest beside him, she curled against his chest, her head nestled beneath his chin, and she let out a sigh of relief when, after a moment's hesitation, his arm went around her.

'I know this sounds silly. I mean, I didn't even know I had a sister until a few weeks ago. But now that I do—not having had a chance to meet her, know her, makes me feel as if a part of me is missing.'

'Audrey.' Her name was nothing more than a murmured sigh, and when she glanced up, the tired expression in his face pricked her heart. 'Do you have this image in your mind of a lovely, warm woman with whom you could've been best friends?'

She let out a breath. 'Not anymore.'

'The things I tell you won't make you like her very much.'

'And yet they'll be the truth. And that's what I want—the truth.'

She watched him war with himself. She settled back against his chest. 'Please?' she whispered.

'Where to even start,' he murmured.

'At the beginning.' She kept her voice soft, though she wasn't sure why. 'How did you meet?'

'We were both living in Rome at the time. We met at one of my exhibitions. When I saw her—it was as if someone had punched the breath from my body. I had never met anyone more vibrant. She was very beautiful, very charismatic...and so confident.'

'She bowled you over.'

'Completely. Ours was a whirlwind romance. We were married within six months of meeting. I have never been a rash man, and yet I rushed into that marriage without thinking twice. I didn't notice—or didn't want to notice—that she was also headstrong and reckless. I thought they were simply factors of being a Funaro and that once she married, she would settle down.'

'That's not what happened?'

She glanced up to see him shake his head. 'At first, I was happy to attend the parties and society functions that she so loved, but the novelty eventually wore off. I had commissions to fill and wanted to get back to work. She kept promising we'd move to Milan, near to her family, and start living a quieter life. But that day never seemed to come. That's when I realised we barely knew one another.'

'What did you do?'

'I hired studio space in Rome so I could at least work, and then set out to woo my wife—to make her truly fall in love with me. I didn't care where we lived, but I wanted to spend time with her. And I wanted her to spend time with me.'

'That didn't turn out the way you wanted?'

Doh! Clearly, it hadn't.

He gave a mirthless laugh. 'Oh, she was more than happy to have me in her bed, but it didn't stop her partying. It didn't stop the excessive drinking or the recreational drugs.'

She winced.

'And then she became pregnant. I hoped rather than believed things would change. I seized on the opportunity to settle us into a different routine—away from the drinking and drugs. We bought a villa on the outskirts of Milan, which she spent a fortune redecorating and furnishing.'

'And were you happy?' She wanted them to have had at least a taste of happiness before it all went so terribly wrong.

He was silent for several long minutes. 'We'd moved to Milan to be closer to her family. It was where she'd grown up. I foolishly thought she would appreciate having them near, to have their support during her pregnancy, but she missed her social life in Rome. She started throwing lavish parties, which I attended to make sure she didn't drink or take drugs while pregnant. Funnily enough, she didn't seem to mind that, and the parties kept her entertained for a while. But then she became...'

'What?'

'Resentful of the changes in her body.'

She couldn't hide her dismay.

One powerful shoulder lifted. 'I did what I could to reassure her...'

The set of his jaw and the expression in his eyes told her how that had played out.

'She went into self-imposed seclusion until Lili was born. Shut herself away, refused to see anyone, including Marguerite. She'd barely talk to me—blaming me for the state she found herself in. I hired a team of doctors and nurses and they did everything they could.'

Fina had taken no joy in her pregnancy? Audrey sagged against him. It should've been one of the most joyful and exciting times of her life.

'I had heard of postpartum depression, of course. What I hadn't known is that seven percent of pregnant women also suffer from depression.'

'And Fina was one of them.'

He shrugged. 'Or maybe she was simply a selfish brat who hated anyone or anything curtailing her freedom.'

Whoa!

'Why do you say that?' she asked carefully.

'Because as soon as Lili was born, and she'd lost the pregnancy weight, she immediately started partying again. She had absolutely no interest in the baby, and when I confronted her about it, she told me that in birthing a new Funaro heiress, she'd performed her duty. And that if I didn't want the bother of a child then to hire a nanny.'

Her hand flew to her mouth.

'That was the moment I realised what a spoiled young woman Fina was. It was the moment I realised that she cared nothing for either Lili or me.'

She wrapped an arm around his waist, hugged him tight. 'I'm sorry, Gabriel.'

'She moved back to Rome, started drinking again, taking drugs…and lovers. While I started getting legal advice about a divorce and getting custody of Lili. I wanted nothing more to do with Fina. I hated her for disregarding Lili like she had, for dismissing her as if she was worth nothing. Marguerite, of course, caught wind of what I was planning and we had an awful row. She blamed me for Fina's fecklessness and I blamed her.'

Audrey winced.

'But she convinced me to come to Rome with her to confront Fina together. And then there was another row. That was when I discovered Fina had married me to spite Marguerite. I hadn't known until then that Marguerite had been against the match. I left without a backwards glance. Headed back to the lawyers in Milan. But before I could start divorce proceedings, Fina died. She'd been partying on a yacht off the coast of Portofino, had taken a cocktail of party drugs and slipped overboard. A couple of people saw her fall and raised the alarm, but they were terribly inebriated and by the time Fina was found, it was too late. She'd drowned.'

Audrey closed her eyes. Just as Gabriel had said, Fina had self-destructed.

He'd fallen headlong in love with Fina and he'd never be that unguarded again...that *wholehearted* in his emotions. The thought had her aching for him, even as a chill crept over her.

Would there be a price to pay for these stolen moments?
Don't be foolish.

This thing they shared wasn't love. It was...pleasure, respite, fun.

Actually, it felt a lot like family—the sense of belonging, the no need to be on one's guard, to be with someone with honesty and trust. It was what she'd had with Jo, Nonna, Aunt Deidre and Frankie. When this thing between them had run its course, she and Gabriel would still have that.

'The coroner said there were so many drugs in her system that she'd probably lost consciousness before she hit the water.'

And just like that, a young woman had lost her life. She shivered.

'I'm sorry, Audrey.' He rubbed her arm as if to warm her. 'It's a far from edifying story.'

'But I wanted to know. And I'm glad to know. Thank you for telling me.' She rubbed her cheek against his chest, welcoming his warmth. 'I don't think Fina and I would've become friends.'

'No.'

'I think she must've been a terribly unhappy person to act the way she did.'

'I agree.'

'But her unhappiness stemmed from a time before she met you.' She struggled into a sitting position. 'You do know that, don't you?'

He nodded.

Subsiding back against the headboard, they both stared out at the view, but things inside her continued to throb. 'Gabriel, all of that is in the past now. It happened two years ago, but as you just said, you and Fina were over long before then. Why haven't you met someone else? You're young and virile.'

And so alone.

She hated the thought of him with someone else. But she hated the thought of him being alone more.

'You listen to my ugly story and you don't judge any of us, but perhaps you should. None of us are nice people.'

'That's not true!' He'd been kind to her—gruff at times, stern, even unfriendly, but still kind. He was a generous lover. And he adored his daughter. He was a good man.

'If I had tried harder, if I might've seen beneath Fina's recklessness to the unhappy young woman she really was, I could've helped her. Instead, I let pride and hurt feelings override what I knew in my gut—that if she continued on her path, she would die an early death.'

Even though he spoke the truth, his words cut him like knives. Shoving the sheet back, he pulled on a pair of shorts and strode to the railing, not really seeing the view spread in front of him.

'It was your mother, Danae, who got her onto drugs. Did you know that? She abandoned Fina when she was two years old and didn't return until Fina was sixteen.'

'I thought Danae returned to her family here after she left Australia.'

Danae, another troubled Funaro heiress, had taken recklessness to new heights. He turned to meet Audrey's gaze. She reclined against the headboard, those walnut eyes watching him, and his body tightened and hardened at the sight. 'According to the rest of the family, she would never say where she'd been or what she'd been up to. She was missing for thirteen years, and when she came home she refused to act the mother to sixteen-year-old Fina, taking instead the role of the rebellious older sister.'

She leaned towards him. 'But to introduce your own daughter to drugs? What kind of person does that?'

'She left less than a year after she'd returned. I can see now how much that marked Fina.'

'To have your mother come back into your life simply to leave again. Poor Fina. She must've felt doubly abandoned. As if she were somehow not enough.'

It took all his strength not to flinch at her words. She hadn't uttered them as an accusation, but it was what he deserved—to be held accountable.

'I never met Danae. I found out only after Fina died what had happened to her.'

'What did happen to her?'

He didn't want to answer, but if anyone deserved the truth, it was Audrey. 'She took some mind-altering drug while she was away travelling…it addled her brain.'

'She died of a drug overdose?'

He rubbed a hand over his face. 'She's not dead, Audrey.

But her mind is lost. She's in a private clinic north of here on the Swiss border.'

She shot out of bed to stand in front of him. '*Not* dead?'

He forced himself to look at her. 'It's the Funaro family's greatest secret, and most of them don't know it.'

'But Marguerite told me she was dead.'

'She might as well be. Her body lives on, but... If you were to visit her, she'd not know you.'

'I don't want to visit her.' She dropped to the bed as if her legs would no longer hold her up. 'Did Fina know the truth?'

'No.'

She buried her face in her hands. Long moments passed, but she eventually pulled them away, her eyes murky with sorrow. 'And as a result, Marguerite bears the same burden of guilt that you do.'

He stabbed a finger at her. 'Fina should've been told the truth!'

'Because maybe then she'd have avoided taking drugs to ensure the same thing didn't happen to her?'

Yes! 'I should've known the truth!' If he'd known the truth, maybe he'd—

What? mocked an ugly voice. *Tried harder?*

He hadn't been able to get away from Fina fast enough. *That* was the truth. He hadn't *wanted* to try harder.

Wheeling around, he gripped the railing with all his strength. Feeling the weight of his own culpability. 'It is true that I blame Marguerite. But I married Fina. I was supposed to look after her. I failed her, and because of that Lili no longer has a mother and—'

'Stop it.' Warm arms slid around his waist. 'You aren't to blame for the choices Fina made. Neither is Marguerite. And if we want to be brutally honest, neither is Danae.'

Outrage made him turn, but one look at her face and he didn't have the heart to break away.

'Fina was an adult, Gabriel. A grown woman in charge of her own destiny. She had other options available to her to deal with her problems. She didn't have to turn to drugs. She made bad choices.' Her grip tightened, urging him to meet her gaze. 'Did you suggest counselling? Drug rehabilitation?'

'Of course I did. I—'

'You couldn't drag her there against her will, though. She needed to make that decision of her own free will. You couldn't impose it on her—no matter how much you wanted to save her.'

He hated her words at the same time as he hungered to believe them.

She cupped his face in both her hands, her eyes swimming with unshed tears. 'If Fina's daughter couldn't save her, Gabriel, you and Marguerite didn't stand a chance. And all of this guilt and regret, it's eating you alive. You need to let it go.'

She stood there offering him a vision of a future he didn't dare believe in. Reaching up on tiptoe, she kissed him, and he kissed her back with a need he could barely temper, wanting to lose himself in her warmth and softness and belief. She opened up to him without reservation and he took everything she gave, searching for peace and release...and absolution.

'Tomorrow is Thursday.' Thursday was one of the days Audrey didn't work at the studio.

She glanced around from pulling on the cotton sundress over her head, and Gabriel wanted to pull it back over her head, drag her back to bed and make love with her all over again. But the afternoon shadows were starting to lengthen and he would need to take her back to the villa soon.

'We've barely worked these last two weeks.'

They'd both tried to settle to their respective works in progress, and Audrey had even started a new piece, but their hunger for each other had yet to subside, and their concentration for anything work related never lasted long. 'If you wanted to come here with me tomorrow...' he offered now.

Her eyes danced. 'But would we work?'

Righting her dress, she surveyed him reclining on the bed completely naked and swallowed. A smile built inside him. He revelled in the way just the sight of him could undo her. He stretched and sent her a lazy grin.

Her breath hitched and she gave a shaky laugh. 'You stop that right now, Gabriel Matteo Dimarco!'

He loved it that she called him by his full name when she was trying to be stern with him.

'Up!' She made shooing gestures with her hands before throwing his jeans at him. 'Get dressed.'

'Why the hurry?'

'It's Wednesday night.'

Some of the brightness bled from the day. Wednesday night was the one night of the week Marguerite demanded Lili spend at the villa rather than in the cottage with him. Though if Lili was otherwise occupied...

'Would you like to come to the cottage tonight?'

She froze.

'I could cook for you.' He would like to do that. 'And—'

'I can't.'

Her voice sounded strangled and he frowned, but then she smiled and he thought he must've imagined it. But something chafed at him; something he couldn't explain. After rolling out of bed, he dragged on his jeans.

'It's date night with Lili and Marguerite.'

Standing on opposite sides of the bed, they made it, smoothing out the creases and fluffing up the pillows and the duvet until it looked smooth and fresh, as if they'd never been there. He immediately wanted to mess it up again. Mess her up and convince her to change her plans for him tonight.

Audrey stared at him across the divide of the bed. 'We agreed to keep things here, at the studio.'

'Would it matter if we stole a few extra moments elsewhere?'

'Yes.'

'Why?'

She hesitated.

'Audrey?'

'I don't want Marguerite knowing about us.'

Ice crept across his scalp. He recalled that fight between Fina and Marguerite.

'I loved how much it irked you when I married a lowbred, impoverished artist. The expression on your face when you discovered I was pregnant by him. It was worth the price I had to pay.'

His nostrils flared. His hands clenched. 'I'm fine to sleep with just as long as nobody knows. Is that it? I lack the polish the Funaros are renowned for and you don't want to be sullied by association. You'd—'

'If that's what you think, then you don't know me at all!'

Her eyes flashed, and shame, hot and hard, hit him in the gut. Audrey wasn't Fina.

'We agreed to keep this thing between us here where it's

contained and...not real. Once we take it into the everyday world, it becomes *real*. And if it becomes real it'll lead to complications.' She strode around the bed to poke him in the chest with a hard finger. 'Do you want complications, Gabriel? Because I was under the impression you didn't.'

He didn't want complications. He'd do anything to avoid those. Reaching out, he cupped her face, lowered his brow to hers. 'I am sorry. I know you are not like that. It was an appalling thing to say. Please forgive me.'

She gave a funny little hiccup. 'Why did you say it, then?'

'Frustration.' He couldn't seem to get enough of her. 'Jealousy that you're spending tonight with someone else rather than with me in my bed.' He released her with a frown. 'What happens on Wednesday nights anyway?' The words growled out of him but he couldn't help it. 'It seems as if it's some top-secret thing. It makes me suspicious. Whenever I ask Lili she says it's a girls' night.'

'Because that's what it is—a girls' night.'

Was Audrey in on this, too? Were she and Marguerite in cahoots...?

To what? He was being paranoid.

He frowned again. He had every right to be paranoid where Marguerite was concerned. She—

'If we're really friends, Gabriel, then you shouldn't mind spending time with me outside of the bedroom.'

Her words had him stiffening. 'Of course I enjoy spending time with you doing other things!' He looked forward to their driving expeditions, even though his body hungered for her the entire time. He enjoyed the conversations they had after their lovemaking, or over coffee during their breaks. He enjoyed working side by side with her. 'I value you for more than just the sex, Audrey. You must not doubt that.' He wanted her to understand that she was valuable to him on many levels.

She stuck out her hip. 'Then join us for our girls' night tonight. But if you agree, you have to understand that for the evening, you are an honorary girl. And you are not allowed to criticise proceedings or to have an opinion on what happens.'

His eyes narrowed, his suspicion radar pinging madly. 'How is it possible to not have an opinion?'

She pursed her lips. 'Okay, that's true. Then you need to agree to keep your opinions to yourself.'

Could he do that? If he didn't, it would earn her a big black mark in Marguerite's books. He might not like Marguerite, but he knew what family meant to Audrey and he wouldn't do anything to damage that.

He gave one hard nod. 'You have a deal.' He would take this chance to enter the inner sanctum and judge for himself if Marguerite was leading his daughter astray, putting pressure on her to conform to a certain image and behaviour, and grooming her for a life of a socialite when he wanted so much more for her.

As directed, Gabriel turned up at the villa at 6 p.m. on the dot. Audrey met him with a smile and led him upstairs and down several corridors he'd never ventured along before. Opening a door, she led him into...

A media room.

He couldn't have said why, but it was the last thing he'd expected. An enormous TV took up most of one wall, and four sets of three-seater sofas rested in front of it—the second row slightly raised like in a theatre. Each seat had cupholders, a table in the arm that pulled out, and each seat reclined.

'Here's our mystery guest,' Audrey announced.

Marguerite glanced up, partially hidden by a drinks cabinet, and rolled her eyes, but remained mercifully silent. Lili bounced up and down. 'Papa! You're a girl tonight.'

'I am,' he agreed gravely.

'I get to decide where everyone sits—that's my job—because I'm Princess Lili.'

His lips twitched. 'And where would Princess Lili like me to sit?'

She cocked her head to one side. 'Tonight I'm sitting here.' She pointed to the middle seat of one of the front sofas. 'Princess Nonna is sitting here.' She pointed to the seat on the right of hers and Marguerite immediately took it. 'Princess Audrey's seat is here.' Audrey sat in the seat Lili pointed to on her other side. 'And Princess Papa,' she giggled. 'You get a whole sofa to yourself.' She pointed to the sofa directly behind her. He immediately moved to it because the others had taken their seats so quickly and he didn't want to get the etiquette wrong and spoil Lili's fun.

A knock sounded on the door. Lili knelt on her seat to face him. 'That'll be the pizza.'

Pizza? Marguerite was eating pizza?

'It's Audrey's job to order the pizza and Nonna's job to serve the drinks.'

Had he entered an alternate universe? He watched Audrey race to the door to take the pizza boxes from one of the maids and realised she wore her oldest jeans.

In front of Marguerite!

Marguerite moved to the drinks cabinet again. And he

realised she wore a... Good God, the woman was wearing a tracksuit. While Lili was in her pyjamas.

'What would Princess Lili and Princess Audrey like to drink?' Marguerite enquired in her beautifully modulated voice. He felt as if he'd stepped into an alternate reality.

'Lemonade, please,' Audrey said.

'Orange juice, please,' Lili said.

'Princess Papa...' He could've sworn Marguerite uttered that with relish. 'What would you like to drink? We have sodas as well as orange, apple or pineapple juice.'

He'd kill for a beer, but that clearly wasn't on offer. 'A cola please... Princess Marguerite,' he couldn't help adding, and could've sworn the older woman's lips twitched.

Audrey handed around paper napkins and plates loaded with pizza. 'Tonight I chose a vegetarian pizza and a pepperoni pizza.'

'Lovely.' Marguerite passed around the drinks in cups with straws in them. Had he ever seen her drink out of anything but crystal or fine bone china?

With a wink in his direction, Audrey settled into her seat. 'What movie are we watching tonight, Princess Lili?'

'Ready?' Lili lifted the remote and pressed Play.

'Ooh, *Ever After*.' Marguerite rubbed her hands together as the opening credits rolled.

'I love this movie.' Audrey grinned at Lili. 'I love me a feisty Cinderella.'

'Me, too.' Lili nodded twice, even though he doubted she knew what the word meant. 'Can I be Feisty Princess Lili next week?'

'I think we should all be Feisty Princesses next Wednesday night,' Marguerite said.

Audrey nodded. 'Yes, let's.'

He watched in amazement as the three women—*princesses*—ate pizza, drank their juices and watched a fairytale movie with pure and easy enjoyment. Watched as Lili curled up first against her grandmother, and then eventually fell asleep in Audrey's lap.

He felt like Alice when she tumbled down the rabbit hole.

CHAPTER TWELVE

'I THINK THIS is where I say I told you so,' Audrey said as she passed a plate of thinly sliced ham to her grandmother the next morning at breakfast.

'I take it you're referring to our special guest last night?' Marguerite took a slice of wafer-thin ham and set it neatly on her plate.

That was one of the things she most loved about her grandmother—she didn't feign ignorance; wasn't the slightest bit coy. 'It wasn't dreadful or awkward or any of the things you were concerned about, was it?' She hadn't misread her grandmother's serenity of the night before, had she? Marguerite had still enjoyed their girls' night.

'You were right, Audrey, and I'm glad of it. Gabriel wasn't all bristling resentment as I expected.' She cut a small portion of ham and chewed it thoughtfully. 'He's a good father. It's something I never doubted. I'm glad he can put aside his own feelings to present a good face for Lili's benefit. It will be much easier for her, if her father and I can appear friendly when we're around each other.'

'It'd be best for Lili if the two of you actually stopped

being so stubborn and got to know each other properly. I'm convinced that if you did, you'd become the best of friends.'

'My dear Audrey, it's best not to wish for the moon.' Marguerite eyed her from the head of the table. 'You aren't getting too attached to Gabriel, are you?'

Something weird and hot squirmed through her, but she ignored it. 'He's become a friend—a good friend. I appreciate all he's done for me. I appreciate the fact he's promoted my relationship with Lili. And—' She broke off with a frown.

'And?' Marguerite raised an eyebrow.

She blew out a breath. 'Well, he's blisteringly honest at times, which can be confronting.'

Marguerite set her cutlery down. 'Has he hurt you?'

She sent her grandmother a swift smile. 'He hurt my feelings *dreadfully* when he called a particular piece I was working on *derivative*. I had to take a little walk along the waterfront to calm down.'

Marguerite's lips twitched.

'To make matters worse, he was right.' She pulled in a breath. 'There's an awful lot of stuff we don't agree on, but his honesty means I can trust him.'

'I can see how that could be a comfort.'

'He has a real chip on his shoulder about the Funaros—not that that'll be news to you. But he told me about Fina.'

Marguerite stilled.

Audrey soldiered on. 'And Danae.'

Marguerite didn't outwardly flinch, but she sensed her grandmother's tension. 'He had no right to speak about such matters.'

'As I said, we're friends. And friends are honest with one another.'

Marguerite's head rocked back. 'Are you saying that you and I are not friends, Audrey?'

'Absolutely not. But I know how much you want to protect me.' She reached across and covered Marguerite's hand. 'And I can't begin to tell you what that means to me.' With a squeeze, she straightened again, returned to her breakfast. 'I know you all think me naive and soft and vulnerable. And I guess I am naive in many ways, but it doesn't mean I'm weak. I'm far stronger than you all give me credit for.'

'I'm sorry, *mi cara*. It is not that I thought you couldn't deal with the truth. But it is so ugly and I wanted to spare you. I would have told you eventually.'

'I know. But I'm glad to know the truth.'

They ate in silence for a bit. 'Grandmother, I'm really sorry you've suffered so much loss—first your daughter and then your granddaughter. It makes me understand why you've ruled the rest of the family with such an iron fist.'

Marguerite stared at her, opened her mouth, but no sound came out.

'I mean, every time someone else in the family makes a mistake—when there's a divorce, a failed business venture, or some kind of tabloid scandal—it must feel as if another person is going to follow the same path Danae and Fina did.'

'I gave the two of them far too much freedom.' The older woman sighed. 'I do not wish to make the same mistake with anyone else.'

'Their choices weren't your fault, Grandmama. They both had the world at their feet. They should've valued what they had. It's on them, not on anyone else.'

She pretended not to notice when Marguerite dabbed surreptitiously at her eyes. This woman took far too much blame for what had happened when all she'd been trying to do was keep her family safe.

'I have this same argument with Gabriel. He seems to think just because Danae and Fina went off the rails, the rest of the Funaros will go off the rails, too. He takes as his proof various family members' missteps, shortcomings and scandals and says, *"See? They're going the same way."* But that's absurd. All families are complicated, and every person makes mistakes regardless of how rich or poor, famous or obscure they are, and the Funaro family is no different.'

'My word, Audrey.' Marguerite's voice was faint.

She winced in her grandmother's direction. 'Some days we're so immersed in our different projects we barely speak. But other days we seem to—' she shrugged '—cover a lot. And as I told him, he's a member of this family, too, so...'

She trailed off before reaching out to grip her grandmother's hand. 'I just wanted you to know that I know... about Fina and Danae.' She sent her a smile. 'I don't want you to worry so much about me.'

Marguerite squeezed her hand in reply.

'And to tell you that I trust Gabriel, and that I think you should, too.'

'But he doesn't trust me.'

'If the two of you would just give the other a chance, you'd see each other the way I see the both of you.'

'Well, I'll think upon what you've said. Now, speaking of letting each other into secrets...about this party you're throwing for me...'

She did her best to feign shock. 'Who spilled the beans?'

Marguerite laughed. 'I know exactly what you're up to so don't be coy with me, young lady.'

Audrey had to laugh then, too. 'Okay, so I figured you

wouldn't really want to be surprised. But the rest of the family are so enamoured of the idea.'

'Yes, I'm sure they'd love to see me at a disadvantage.'

'You're wrong, you know? This is just giving people a chance to do it the way they want to do it—and in a way they hope will make you happy.'

One imperious eyebrow lifted.

'Okay, well, maybe there's one or two people who are mean-spirited enough to enjoy seeing you at a disadvantage, but families…what are you going to do, huh? We won't give them the satisfaction.'

'May I see the guest list?'

'Absolutely, though I was keeping it small and intimate—no more than fifty people—but I'd love to know if there's anyone else I should include.'

'I'd like to make sure a couple of old school friends are on the list.'

'Also, Lili is in charge of choosing your birthday cake. Now, I can easily sway her away from the ice cream cake she has her heart set on, so if you'd rather a black forest cake or lemon gateaux, now is the time to speak up.'

'My dear granddaughter, I'm sure you'll ensure there's a variety of desserts to cater to every taste. I'm more than happy with whatever Lili chooses.'

'Excellent.' She could tick that off her to-do list. Pulling her hands into her lap, she gripped them tightly. 'Now, on a completely different topic, have you given any more thought to the foundation I'd like to set up in Johanna's name?'

'I'm sorry, Audrey.' Marguerite rose. 'I have a rather important meeting with one of my brokers. We will talk about it later.'

Marguerite swept from the room and Audrey frowned at the pastry on her plate. But later *when*?

'Are Wednesday nights the hotbed of vice you were expecting?'

Audrey trailed her fingers across Gabriel's chest. She loved the feel of him—the firm smoothness of his skin. She loved touching him after they'd made love. She couldn't explain the sense of peace that stole over her; the warm afterglow and sense of wellbeing.

She'd meant to raise the topic of Wednesday night once they'd boarded the boat. But the moment she'd slipped into the car, he'd sent her such a heated glance that speaking had become impossible, and need and desire took possession of her. The moment they'd closed the studio door behind them, they'd started tearing off each other's clothes, greedy for one another.

He pressed a kiss to the top of her head now. 'Would you like me to apologise?'

'Of course not.' Reaching across, she hugged him hard. 'You should never apologise for having Lili's best interests at heart.'

'But?'

'No buts.' She rested her chin on his chest and glanced up at him. 'Did you enjoy yourself?'

Those stern lips broke into a rare smile. 'I did. As a one-time thing. I prefer sports to romantic comedies and Disney films.'

'And beer to lemonade.'

A laugh rumbled through him. *'Si.'*

'Also, I told Marguerite at breakfast yesterday that I know about Fina and Danae.'

He stiffened.

'I just thought you should know.'

His brow darkened. 'I suppose I should now expect to be called into the headmistress's office for a dressing down.'

'I don't think so. I told Marguerite that I was glad to know the truth and that everyone needed to stop treating me like I might break—that I'm stronger than you all give me credit for. And I told her I trust you and that she should, too.'

His eyes looked like they were going to start from his head.

'She said she'd think about it.' She pressed a kiss to his chest. 'So you need to stop being an idiot and give her a chance.'

'Such lover-like words,' he growled.

She laughed and pressed another kiss to his chest. 'Tell me you'll come to her party.' She kissed her way down his stomach. 'Please?'

'Are you trying to extort an agreement from me?'

She grinned up at him. 'Will that work?'

A laugh rumbled through that powerful frame again, those grey eyes dancing. 'I think it just might.'

'Well, let's see, then, shall we...?'

The day of the party arrived. Livia's car pulled up in the villa's circular drive, and as soon as Audrey saw it, she rushed through to the ballroom where everyone was gathered. Livia and her mother, Caterina, had taken Marguerite to have her hair done—the excuse they'd used to get Marguerite out of the villa so that everyone else could secretly arrive. 'Quiet, everyone, quiet. They're here,' she said, slipping into the room and closing the door behind her.

She took her place at the head of the crowd with Lili, who

slipped her hand inside hers. Glancing back behind her, she caught Gabriel's eye. He'd secreted himself at the rear of the crowd. Then Nicolo turned off the lights and smothered them in darkness.

The outside conversation reached them clearly. 'Really, my dear Livia, your birthday is in winter. Surely, you'd prefer a party at the Milan estate.'

'Como is only forty-five minutes from Milan, and the ballroom has such beautiful views over the lake.'

Caterina's voice sounded outside. 'Why don't we just take a look?'

The door opened.

Nicolo snapped on the light.

'Surprise!' Audrey shouted, jumping up and down, grinning madly.

Taking their lead from her, everyone else also started shouting 'Surprise!' and 'Happy birthday!' in Italian and English, and then an unrehearsed but rousing chorus of *'Tanti Auguri a Te,'* the Italian version of 'Happy Birthday,' started up.

To Marguerite's credit, she looked utterly stunned. Though Audrey suspected it wasn't all feigned. Everyone did look ridiculously chuffed and excited. And the ballroom looked fabulously festive with balloons and streamers and tables laden with party food and drinks.

'A birthday party? For me?' Marguerite glanced around with wide eyes, one hand pressed to her chest.

Audrey and Lili danced up to her. 'Tell me you love it,' Audrey said, grinning at her.

'I adore it,' she said, kissing Audrey's cheek. 'Thank you, my dear.'

She said it with such tenderness, Audrey's throat thickened.

Lili hopped from one foot to the other. 'Were you surprised, Nonna? Were you?'

'Absolutely, Lili.' Her cheek was kissed, too. 'I'd have never guessed, not in a million years.'

Marguerite circulated about the room, thanking everyone and clearly enjoying herself. Which, in its turn, made everyone relax and begin to enjoy themselves as well, letting their hair down in a way Audrey hadn't yet seen them do en masse.

Before long, the French doors were opened to the terrace that had been set with an array of cast-iron tables. A game of croquet started up, and the '60s cover band Audrey had hired when she'd discovered Marguerite loved '60s music, started playing at one end of the ballroom.

People ate, chatted, danced. Marguerite exclaimed over her ice cream cake, blew out her candles and then beamed as everyone sang 'Happy Birthday.' It was the perfect party.

'You've danced with just about everyone except me.'

Gabriel's voice had all the fine hairs on Audrey's arms lifting in the most delicious manner. She turned to find him standing behind her, so close she could reach out and trace a finger down his chest.

Don't think of his chest.

'Would you do me the honour?'

Did she dare? They'd avoided each other so far—it had seemed wise. She was afraid that once she was in his arms, they'd give themselves away.

'It occurs to me that if we don't dance, it might look strange…raise questions.'

'Good point.' They didn't want to do that.

What harm can it do?

She allowed him to lead her to the dance floor. The band was currently belting out a Chubby Checker number. They wouldn't be dancing cheek to cheek, thigh to thigh.

Gabriel moved well, which shouldn't surprise her, but it had awareness creeping across the surface of her skin, and her lungs contracting. As if aware of the direction of her thoughts and wanting to break the spell, Gabriel took her hand and spun her around. She couldn't help laughing, and was breathless when the song came to an end. With a pounding heart, she waited for the next song. She'd allow herself the luxury—and exhilaration—of one more dance and then she'd continue with her hostessing duties.

The first notes of the Beatles' classic 'Hey Jude' sounded through the ballroom and she swallowed. Who didn't love this song? But it was a slower number and...

Glancing up from beneath her lashes, her pulse picked up speed as Gabriel's gaze darkened, but without a moment's hesitation, he pulled her into his arms. Everything inside her quickened. He held her closer to him and she allowed her eyelids to droop for just a moment, to relish it and breathe him in. They didn't talk. They just swayed to the music and lived in the moment.

All too soon, the song came to an end.

'Don't look around or get tense, but Marguerite's watching us,' he murmured in her ear. 'I'm going to cut in on Sergei and Paulette and we'll swap partners.'

'Excellent plan.'

They successfully avoided each other for the rest of the party. But the memory of being in his arms had burned itself into her mind. She couldn't wait for Monday to come when the two of them would be alone in his studio once more.

* * *

'Gabriel, Audrey…a word, if you don't mind?'

Everything inside Gabriel clenched at the imperious voice located somewhere behind him, but he kept his face bland and disinterested. His usual hostility where Marguerite was concerned was…well, not entirely absent, but certainly diluted.

Audrey's doing. She *had* made him see Marguerite in a different light. He just didn't know if he trusted in it yet or not.

He watched as Lili raced across to hug her great-grandmother before heading to the kitchen with the nanny. In movies and books, children were often used as a kind of barometer to indicate whether someone was good or bad beneath their crusty exterior. He reminded himself that was fiction, and how easily children could be manipulated. But even as he did, he couldn't deny the strength of the bond between his daughter and the older woman.

'Come.' Marguerite led them through several rooms on the ground floor to the library that acted as her unofficial study. She took a seat behind a large oak desk and waved them to the seats on the other side. His every sense went on high alert.

'This feels remarkably formal.'

Audrey voiced his own thoughts as they sat. It was an effort not to reach out and take her hand, to help support her through whatever ordeal was about to come. Because he was in no doubt that some confrontation was about to take place.

Marguerite laid both her hands flat on the desk and drew in a long breath. 'So…the two of you didn't heed the advice I gave to you when Audrey first arrived here.'

Audrey leaned forward. 'You're going to have to be more specific, Grandmother.'

'About the two of you not becoming romantically entangled.'

After one frozen second Audrey sat back again, lips pursed. She glanced at Gabriel. 'You don't lie.'

'No.' Though in this instance he would. If she wanted him to. And *that* realisation sent a strange kind of panic racing through him. He'd sworn to never change for another woman. It only led to heartache and—

'And I don't want to.'

The panic hurtled to a halt. He stared at her as she turned back to Marguerite. 'What gave us away?'

'You're not going to deny it?'

'Absolutely not. I've no desire to lie to you. I know you warned me off him, Grandmama, but…'

He wondered if Audrey was aware of the way her casual *Grandmama* affected Marguerite—the easy affection it indicated. The older woman hid it well, but the word sent a ripple through her every time it was uttered—like a light breeze through the fronds of a massive weeping willow.

He suddenly yearned to capture that image in wood and steel and glass.

He glanced at Audrey. This extraordinary woman waltzed into his life, and after an eight-month drought he was now brimming with inspiration. It made no sense.

'But?' Marguerite prompted.

'The thing is—' Audrey pressed her hands together '—I think you've misjudged Gabriel. And,' she continued, lifting her chin, 'I decided to follow my own instincts where he was concerned.'

Marguerite nodded, though it wasn't in agreement.

'He's not heartless or callous.'

Marguerite had told Audrey he was heartless and callous? He wanted to rail against such an assessment, but he couldn't. In their interactions since Fina had died, his ferocity had been on a tight leash, but at different times he'd allowed the older woman to see it—hoping it would keep her at a distance.

'It was our dance at the party, wasn't it?' Audrey said. 'It gave us away.'

'Does it matter?'

'No, I don't suppose so,' Audrey conceded.

Marguerite sighed. 'It was the way you so assiduously avoided each other at the party. You tell me that you and Gabriel are such good friends, and yet you do your best to not spend any time together when other people are around. It is a realisation that has been playing on my mind since our girls' night. Saturday's party confirmed it.'

'Grandmama...'

That ripple again—tree fronds moving gently in the air.

'Please don't take this the wrong way, but my relationship with Gabriel is nobody's business except his and mine.'

'I'm afraid, my dear, that's where you're wrong. What happens between the two of you has the potential to have a direct bearing on current custody arrangements pertaining to Lili.'

Audrey's jaw dropped.

'For the last two years, Gabriel and I have been walking on eggshells to avoid further unpleasantness. He would rather walk away from this family and would be delighted for Lili to not know any of us. He knows, however, that I would fight that with all the resources at my not inconsiderable disposal. We both know, as well, that such a battle would upset Lili. And we should like to spare her that.'

Audrey glanced from him to her grandmother. The distress in her eyes tore at him. 'We are all adults here,' he found himself saying.

'Fina was an adult, too,' Marguerite shot back. 'And we all know how well that turned out.'

'Fina was a fool,' Audrey said, making both him and Marguerite blink. 'From the little I know, I doubt any of us could consider her a fully functioning adult.'

Marguerite eventually shook herself, shooting a glare at Gabriel. 'I can't believe you would risk the hard-won equilibrium we have arrived at.'

Audrey gave a soft laugh. 'I'm not sure he had much choice.' Marguerite stared at her. 'Grandmama, you're a woman of the world. Have you never taken...*matters* into your own hands?'

For a moment he thought Marguerite might laugh, but the brief twinkle in her eye darkened again. 'Audrey, it would grieve me greatly to see you hurt.'

'But—'

'You tell me there is a great honesty between you and Gabriel. Does he know, then, that you have fallen in love with him?'

His every muscle stiffened in painful protest. Audrey didn't love him! Love had never been in the cards.

Audrey gaped at her grandmother.

Deny it, he ordered her silently. *Deny it!*

One of Marguerite's hands briefly fluttered to her throat, before it was once again clasped in front of her. 'You do not answer me.'

'I, um...' Audrey moistened her lips, and even through

the panic and denial, a shot of desire, hard and dark, speared through him. He still wanted her.

But he didn't want her heart.

'Audrey?' Did that voice belong to him? 'We said...' He swallowed. 'Does Marguerite speak the truth?'

'I...' Her brow furrowed. 'I don't know.'

She didn't know? How...?

He watched her mind race behind those dark eyes, saw the awful realisation filter across her face in a slow, sickening wave. His hands clenched. He wanted to throw his head back and howl.

'Yes.' She swallowed. 'I just didn't realise it until this moment.'

He believed her. With any other woman he'd suspect some hidden agenda—a hope that she could trap him into a permanent arrangement. But not Audrey.

She gave a funny little laugh. *A laugh.* How could she laugh at a time like this?

'I told myself I could control my emotions. I kept telling myself I wouldn't fall in love with you, thinking that would make it true, but—' She broke off, her eyes dark in a pale face. 'Apparently, that's not the way emotions work.'

An ache gripped his chest.

She winced and sent him an apologetic grimace. 'If it's any consolation, I didn't mean to.'

It wasn't any consolation whatsoever!

'You make me feel alive. You make me feel as if I could achieve anything. You're kind and smart and protective of those you care about. You're also demanding, and sometimes moody.'

He blinked.

'You're a generous lover, a fabulous father and...' She

shrugged. 'Of course I fell in love with you. How could I not?' She stared down at her hands. 'I guess I didn't want to face the truth because I didn't want what we had to end.'

He rubbed a hand over his face. Of course it had to end, but things inside raised a ruckus at the thought. And the knowledge that he'd hurt her twisted through him in a torturous knot of self-condemnation.

'You want to know what my real mistake was? Thinking that we were like family. That just because I felt at ease with you and because we were honest with one another and because you saw something in my art and seemed to see something in me, that meant you'd stick.'

That he'd...what?

'In the same way that me and Jo and Nonna and Frankie stuck together—there for each other through thick and thin.' She didn't raise her voice, didn't shout and rail at him. 'But that was just wishful thinking.' She shook her head, her eyes narrowed as if the glare of the truth was hard to take. 'I was never special to you.'

'That's not true. You—'

She raised an eyebrow and he bit the rest of his words back. The fact remained that he didn't love her, and to give her false hope would be unkind.

'Gabriel, if you don't want to hurt my granddaughter more than you already have...'

He lifted his head to meet Marguerite's gaze.

'You have to discontinue this affair and walk away.'

She was right. He hated it. But she was right.

Marguerite pulled in a breath. 'Unless you, too, want more?'

'My heart was never on the table.' The words fell from his lips, strangely impassive. Beside him, Audrey flinched.

'We agreed love was not part of the equation.' They'd *promised*! 'You're right, Marguerite. This needs to stop. I have no desire whatsoever to cause pain to Audrey.'

He turned to her. 'Audrey—'

'Oh, God, please don't, Gabriel. I don't want platitudes or sympathy. I already feel foolish enough.'

'You are not a fool!' Hearts had minds of their own. He was the fool for thinking they could keep emotions out of it.

Audrey rose. 'I want to assure you both that I harbour no resentment or ill feeling towards Gabriel. Nothing that has happened between us needs to affect the custody arrangements you have in place for Lili.'

She turned with eyes that were strangely flat—as if the sunshine had been bled from them. Her lips struggled into a smile. His heart burned that it should now be such an effort for her to smile at him.

'I hope you will still allow me to spend time with Lili.'

He rose, too; took her hand. 'Lili loves you. She will look to you in the future. She needs you in her life. I will do everything in my power to safeguard your relationship.'

'Thank you.' She reclaimed her hand and her graveness had a different kind of panic racing through him. Would they no longer be able to share their ideas and challenge each other creatively? Would she no longer chivvy him out of a dark mood or make him see the beauty encased in *everything*? Would they now be so distant from one another that—?

'If you'll both excuse me, I think I'd like a bit of time on my own.'

But it was Monday, and they were supposed to be working at the studio—

With a smothered oath, he crushed that thought. All of it

was now at an end, but he couldn't help grieving for what they'd lost.

Audrey stiffened and then whirled on him. 'What do *you* have to swear and be grumpy about? *Your* precious heart's still safe and sound.'

He swallowed. He understood her anger. 'I'm just sorry that—'

'No, you're not. Your world is still the safe little prison it's always been.'

His anger leapt then, too. 'We had a deal!'

'And I broke it.' Her hands slammed to her hips. 'So what? *Deal* with it.'

He gaped.

'Except you won't, will you?' She poked him in the chest. 'You won't do anything, because you're a coward. You'll run away every bit as fast as my mother and father did when things got too hard.'

He clenched his hands so hard, he shook.

'You think loving someone is a prison, but it's not. It can be wonderful and—' She broke off, breathing hard. 'You refuse to try again because it didn't work out with Fina. What kind of attitude is that? Art doesn't work like that, and neither does love or life.'

He opened his mouth, but nothing came out.

'You accuse the Funaros of being profligate, but it's better than being what you are—*a big, fat, emotional miser!* You set your heart against me before you even met me, and nothing that came after was ever going to change that. You said we were friends. You said I was special to you. You told me I was an extraordinary woman, but none of that was enough for you, was it? *Why?* Because biologically I'm a Funaro!'

She was breathing hard, but straightened and looked him

dead in the eye. 'As long as your heart remains safe, you don't care how much you hurt anyone else.'

With that, she turned and left.

Everything inside him throbbed. He wanted to yell, chop wood, kick a ball as hard as he could...swim laps until he was exhausted. Anything to rid his body of this awful tension. Instead, he thumped back down to his chair.

Marguerite sighed. 'You're a fool, Gabriel.'

'I deserve something far harsher than *fool*.' Why hadn't he taken more care? Why hadn't he—?

'A fool for letting her go.'

It took a moment for her words to sink in. 'Don't pretend you're not relieved. You warned Audrey off just as you warned Fina off. You've never considered me good enough for this family.'

The older woman rested back, her fingers steepled. 'You have it wrong, my dear.'

He gritted his teeth. He was not her *dear*.

'It was the other way around. I warned Fina off because I knew she was using you as a weapon to make a childish and selfish statement. You were young and idealistic and I knew she would hurt you...lay waste to your dreams.'

His jaw dropped.

'She was such a troubled young woman and I did not know how to help her. Or you. I failed her. Just as I failed her mother. And as I've failed you, too.'

He hauled his jaw back into place, his heart thundering. He recalled all that Audrey had said to him about Fina and straightened. 'You didn't let either one of them down, Marguerite. You gave them both every advantage life had to offer.' Rubbing a hand across his chest, he nodded. 'Audrey is right. They failed themselves, and yet, we continue to bear the brunt of the guilt and regret.' It was time to let it go.

'Audrey is not like Fina.'

No, she was unlike anyone he'd ever met.

'She would not walk all over your heart and treat you as if you were worth nothing.'

'She is kindness personified.'

'And yet, you tell me you do not love her. *That*, my dear Gabriel, is what makes you a fool.'

He gaped at her.

'Go!' She waved an imperious hand at the door. 'I have better things to do than talk with stupid men. I need to ring the girls—'

'The girls,' he parroted.

'Livy, Tori and Ana. We shall rally around Audrey, drink champagne cocktails, eat chocolate and watch some dreadful movie.'

Without him. He was being forced out and the injustice burned through him.

Marguerite glared down her nose at him. 'Broken hearts mend, and we will help Audrey's mend as quickly as possible.' She nodded once, hard. 'We will find her a new prince, and soon you shall be forgotten, and all of this will feel as if it had never happened.'

Everything inside him rebelled at the thought. He shot to his feet, but the words he wanted to shout refused to push past the lump in his throat. Without another word, he strode to the door, but before he slammed through it, he swung back.

'You call me a fool, but you'll be the bigger fool if you don't support Audrey's plan to create a foundation in her sister Johanna's name.' If he could do nothing else, he could at least make Marguerite see sense on this one issue. 'Family means everything to Audrey, but she will not betray her past family to achieve one in the present. If you make her choose, she'll walk away.'

With a heart more broken than he'd left her with. He wanted to throw his head back and howl. Who would she then turn to?

Without another word, he left.

CHAPTER THIRTEEN

AUDREY FLED TO HER ROOM, craving sanctuary and quiet, but all too soon the enforced inactivity began to grate. After dragging on her old jeans, she headed outside to the gardens. The estate was large and, if she wished it, she'd be able to avoid bumping into anyone.

She set off for the gardens farthest away from the villa, where no one would be able to spot her from the windows. She walked briefly beside the water, but that didn't help. It simply reminded her of Gabriel's studio.

If Marguerite hadn't called them into the library, she'd be at the studio now. She'd have had a chance to make one more memory to help shore her up on the lonely nights ahead. Because she didn't doubt there'd be long, sleepless nights where the longing for Gabriel would wring her dry and leave her feeling torn and empty.

Turning her back on the extraordinary view, she started down the most beautiful of avenues—tall trees and shrubs towered on either side, making her feel as if she were the only person in the world. But even that brought no comfort.

Finally, she flung herself down in a shady clearing, the

scent of wisteria and pine thick in the air. What on earth had she been thinking? Love hadn't been part of the plan.

Falling to her back, she stared up at an impossibly blue sky. She hadn't *wanted* to fall in love. It had been the furthest thing from her mind. For heaven's sake, Gabriel had been more than adamant about his feelings on the subject. It's not like she hadn't been warned.

How could she have been so stupid? So *blindly* stupid?

Pressing palms to hot eyes, she swallowed hard. She'd been so ready to believe they were friends. That what they had meant something to him. *Why?*

Because they'd been honest with each other, had shared a few secrets, had found common ground in their art? None of that had meant he cared for her. Nor did the fact that she'd helped him through his creative block, or that he saw something of value in her fibre art. She was the one who'd thought that'd meant something. Not him.

A growl left her throat. Why had she allowed herself to think it had signified something deep and lasting? Would she never learn?

She'd made that same stupid mistake with Gabriel as she had with her father—seeing something that wasn't there. Gabriel might not have meant to hurt her, but he didn't care for her any more than her father did, in a kind but careless way. As soon as something more was demanded of him, he'd turned tail and fled.

What she hadn't realised was how much loving a man like that would tear her apart.

I'm sorry, but...

A humourless laugh left her lips.

But. It was the story of her life. Gabriel had proved what she'd already known—that she'd never be enough for him.

His prejudices, his bitterness, his resentments, were all so much bigger than any feelings he might have for her. And he'd cut off all such feelings at the knees rather than dare feel anything like that for her—*a Funaro*.

But she'd finally learned her lesson. Never again would she waste that much time, energy and effort on a man who'd closed his heart. Her hands clenched. She was tired of not being enough, of being made to feel less than, being made to feel like a fool.

A hard lump stretched her throat into a painful ache. And yet, even now she ached to see him with every breath she took. Even though she knew seeing him would be like torture.

She sat up. Should she leave Lake Como?

Her heart pounded, but her mind grew suddenly clear. To leave would hurt Marguerite and she wouldn't do anything to hurt the older woman. Marguerite had become dear to her. She might not be able to have the man she wanted in her life, but she did have her family. She loved this odd assortment of people who'd come into her life. And there was strength in love, even if Gabriel couldn't see it.

And why on earth should she let him chase her away when she'd found a place to belong? If he chose to remain an outsider, that was his problem not hers.

'Fine.' She hitched her chin at a particularly spectacular pine tree. 'I need to make a new plan.'

Actually, she had the plan Gabriel had created for her for when, as he'd put it, all her hopes and wishes surrounding the family came tumbling down. Except the family *was* everything she'd wished for—that wasn't the part of her life that was tumbling down.

A lump lodged in her throat. Neither she nor Gabriel

could have envisaged then that it would be *he* who'd bring her world tumbling down. Because he lacked the courage to love.

Gritting her teeth, she ordered herself to focus on a new plan. First, she'd keep working on her art. She'd ask Marguerite for studio space somewhere on the estate. There must be a garden shed that wasn't in use that she'd be able to coopt. And she'd take classes somewhere when this summer was over and the family returned to Milan. And she'd contact that agent, too; invite him to take a look at her work. She didn't need Gabriel for any of that.

Oh, but—

She cut that thought dead, pulled out her phone and sent Gabriel an email. She needed to draw a line under all that had gone before.

Gritting her teeth, she thanked him for mentoring her—she was grateful—added a line mumbling some nonsense about remaining friends, and ended with a request for him to let her know when it would be convenient for her to collect her materials.

And just like that, it was over. She swallowed a sob, dusted off her hands, she set her phone to the ground. One: her family. Two: her art. She'd throw herself with vigour into both.

On cue, her phone pinged. Turning it over, she found a text from Marguerite.

The girls are on their way. Champagne cocktails. Chocolate. Assorted movies at the ready. Anything else?

She had to blink hard as she read the message; acknowledged the love behind it. Gabriel might not love her. Her heart might be broken. But she had a family who cared, and that was something to be grateful for.

She texted back:

Face packs and pizza.

Then she hauled herself to her feet. She refused to wear her oldest, daggiest jeans to this impromptu pity party. She could do better than that.

The moment Gabriel strode into his studio, he knew it had been a mistake to come here. He should've done something else, gone somewhere else. Audrey permeated every inch. From her coffee cup left to drain on the sink, to the container of biscuits she'd baked, to the pile of yarn on one of the workbenches. Lavender scented the air, and the current silence mocked the remembered laughter, the arguments, the earnest discussions about art.

He glanced at the mezzanine and rubbed his hands over his face, his eyes burning. Everything *ached*.

Why the hell couldn't Marguerite have left well enough alone?

Because she didn't want to see Audrey hurt.

He stilled. He didn't want that, either. The knowledge he'd hurt Audrey, even unwittingly, rubbed his soul raw.

He should never have let a Funaro into his studio. He should've realised it'd cause nothing but trouble.

Except Audrey wasn't like the other Funaros. She was warm and friendly and open-minded—

His head lifted. Marguerite hadn't been cold and unfriendly this morning. She'd been concerned. Oh, she'd torn a strip off him for hurting her granddaughter, but that was nothing more than he'd deserved.

The party on Saturday hadn't been cold and unfriendly, either. It'd been fun, a true celebration.

Walking across to *Ties That Bind* and whipping off the dustcover, he stared at it once more. Audrey was a fine artist and the world would soon discover her. But she was a sculptor, too—of people. She dug until she found the good in them and she somehow brought that to the fore so everyone else could see it, too.

Marguerite and her kin hadn't been cold and unfriendly. At least, not in recent times. Maybe the cold and unfriendly one had been him?

The thought made him swallow. Audrey was right. He'd been so determined to ensure another Funaro couldn't take advantage of him that he'd built a wall around himself with huge no-trespassing signs tacked all over it to keep the rest of the family at bay. His hands clenched and unclenched. It wasn't an edifying revelation.

It might've been better for his peace of mind now, but he didn't regret allowing Audrey entry into his sanctuary here. The only thing he regretted was hurting her. He'd move heaven and earth to make that otherwise.

You can.

His temples throbbed and his heart pounded. Wheeling away, he shook his head, but Marguerite's words sounded through his mind.

She's not Fina.

He knew she wasn't Fina! She was ten times the woman Fina was. But there was too much at stake. It wasn't just his heart he'd be risking but Lili's.

You're a fool.

Marguerite's words again, but what did she know? And—

His mouth dried. His heart thundered in his ears. Audrey *wasn't* Fina. If the worst did happen, if a romance between him and Audrey soured, Audrey wouldn't abandon Lili. He felt the truth of that in his bones. In that moment everything inside him yearned towards a future he'd never dared let himself dream about again.

Swinging back to stare at Audrey's artwork, he finally saw it in a new light—her light. The various threads crisscrossing the figure at the centre weren't shackles or restraints. Those threads were in shades of shimmering gold, peacock blue and pale pink. They *weren't* symbolic of the Funaro fortune as he'd previously thought. They were symbolic of family—of attachment, compassion...love.

These weren't ties that bound one against their will. They were the kinds of connections that anchored a person, helped them find their place in the world. These ties created a sanctuary, a safe place...a haven where a person could be themselves.

He glanced around his studio. Audrey's was the real sanctuary, not this place where he'd tried to keep the rest of the world at bay. His studio wasn't a sanctuary; it was a hideaway.

In that moment he agreed with Marguerite—he was a fool. He loved Audrey with every atom of his being; he'd just been too much of a coward to admit it.

His phone vibrated, alerting him to an incoming email. His heart leaped when Audrey's name flashed across the screen. With fingers that shook, he opened the message.

Dear Gabriel,
I'm very grateful for all you've done. Under your expert eye, my technique and artistry have improved a hundredfold. Clearly it is not going to be viable for me to continue

to study under you, given today's revelations, but I very much hope we can remain friends.

Friends? He didn't want to be friends. He wanted them to be lovers. For the rest of time.

If it's not too much trouble, I would appreciate it if you could arrange for my supplies and the pieces I've been working on to be packed up and sent to the villa. Or, if it's more convenient, please let me know a time when I can organise to do so myself.

She was already moving forward with her life—sensible, straightforward, classy. It hit him then how strong Audrey really was. She'd never needed a protector. All of this time, she'd been the warrior fighting for the family she could see beneath all the hurt and bluster and pride.

He lifted his head. It was time to stop hiding. It was time he started fighting for the life he wanted, too. And he wanted Audrey—heart, body and soul. And if he was going to convince her that he truly did love her, that he would do everything in his power to look after her and make her happy, he was going to have to prove it to her.

He stared at her artwork and knew exactly what he had to do.

CHAPTER FOURTEEN

THE BOAT POWERED across the lake with a no-nonsense speed that set Audrey's teeth on edge. She didn't sit in her usual seat. She didn't face forward as she normally would. There was nothing normal about any of this.

It made no sense, but she wanted to rail against the fact that it wasn't Gabriel driving the boat. He'd hired someone to take her across to the studio so she could oversee the packing up of her equipment.

Folding her arms, she glared at the whitewash they left in their wake. He couldn't make his stance any clearer if he'd bellowed it at the top of his lungs from a megaphone. He *didn't* want to see her. He *didn't* want to remain friends.

Jerk!

In a dim part of her mind, she knew he was only trying to save her further pain. A low growl sounded in the back of her throat. Why did everyone think she was going to fall in a heap just because she'd had her heart broken? She wasn't that pitiful.

And not seeing him—having him avoid her as if she'd *betrayed him*—

Closing her eyes, she concentrated on her breathing. The one good thing about today was not being the object of the loving but watchful gazes of Marguerite and the rest of the family. She knew they only wanted to help, but... Yesterday she'd only just managed to stop herself from yelling at everyone to stop watching her.

It will get better. It will get better.

She crossed her fingers.

The boat slowed and bumped to a rest at the tiny dock. She pulled in a breath, girded her loins before disembarking with an ease that had been alien to her two months ago. She glanced at the driver, who cleared his throat and shrugged. 'My instructions were to remain here.'

With a nod, she set off along the path that wound through the trees. The men hired to help her pack were probably already at the studio. As she rounded the curve and topped the rise, though, and the studio came into view, she stuttered to a halt.

Everything that had happened there played through her mind. The disagreements between her and Gabriel, the challenges they'd thrown at each other, the moments when they'd worked together in complete harmony. He'd called her an artist; had given her the permission to explore and experiment; had urged her to dig deeper and discover the heart of the things that moved and interested her. Here her knowledge had deepened and her skills had developed and...

He'd opened up a new world to her.

She refused to think of the other new world he'd opened up to her—a world of sensuality and pleasure and intimacy. Today she'd focus on the future. Not what had been. He'd given her the tools and the contacts to continue to develop her art. *That* was what she'd think about.

That and setting up The Johanna Foundation. This morning Marguerite had called her into the library and had agreed to support Audrey's desire to set up a foundation in Johanna's honour. She'd apologised for her tardiness and had confided her grief at never having had the chance to meet her late granddaughter. 'Whenever I began thinking about how we would set the foundation up and how to make it work, it was... I found it so painful to think about. I so wish I'd had a chance to meet Johanna the way I've had the chance to meet you. I know that I would have loved her, too. So I kept putting it off, kept trying to avoid the grief and regret. I can see now that wasn't fair to you.'

She'd also confided that it was Gabriel who'd convinced her to move forward with Audrey's plan. Apparently, that was something else she ought to feel grateful to him for.

Shaking herself, she continued along the path. Not giving herself a moment to think, she reached for the door, sighing in relief when it opened. That could've been awkward. Gabriel had never given her a key.

'Oh, like that's a surprise,' she muttered under her breath. He'd only ever given her the parts of himself he'd been comfortable sharing.

Her fleeting resentment, though, was no match for the memories that immediately assailed her—none of them to do with embroidery or art of any kind. She stared at the back wall, recalling their first time and how they'd not even fully undressed—too hungry and greedy and wild for each other.

She should have known then. Should have known that to feel so much so soon meant she was already too invested. That it would end in tears.

Shaking the thought off, she faced the room. Nothing stirred. Nobody stood to greet her or awaited instructions.

'Hello?' She moved farther inside, resolutely averting her gaze from the mezzanine level. Now wasn't the time to wallow. She could do that tonight in the privacy of her own room where no one could see.

Her voice echoed in the space, but nothing else moved. Had she misunderstood the message? Maybe she was supposed to pack her things up and leave them for someone to bring back to the villa later. Had Gabriel left a note?

She strode across to the bench where she'd worked, but there was no note there, and then across to the kettle. Nothing. Opening the side door, she glanced out, but nobody sat outside enjoying the view or the sunshine.

It wasn't until she turned back that she saw it—the easel sitting directly in front of the huge wall of glass. A cloth draped over the easel hid the picture, painting, or whatever the artwork was, from view. Was this Gabriel's current project?

Biting her lip, she glanced around. There was nobody to see if she had a peek. Gabriel had never minded sharing his work with her—unfinished or not.

Lifting one corner of the cloth, she glanced beneath... Reefing her hand away, the cloth fell back into place. Her heart pounded.

Was that...*her*?

After glancing around again, she reached out and pulled the cloth completely away to stare at the charcoal drawing encased in a simple wooden frame.

The piece had the same compelling power as his *Maybe* sculpture.

Except this time *she* was the subject. And unlike *Maybe* there was no ambiguity here—no *will she...? won't she...?* questions threaded beneath.

The sketch was of her on the rocks that jutted out into the lake. Where he'd sketched her sitting with her sketchpad all those weeks ago, she now stood, facing the water. Above her, rather than a sun hung a moon, radiating light...somehow bathing everything in the sketch in light.

She took a step closer, trying to work out how he'd done that. The man really was the most extraordinary artist.

The water in this sketch wasn't threatening. All around her it was millpond smooth, though farther out where the light of the moon couldn't quite reach, waves loomed. She took a step back again, her frown deepening. It was as if, because the water farther out wasn't under her influence, it was storm-tossed and restless. Unhappy.

What on earth did it mean?

She pressed a hand to her brow.

If—

She swallowed.

If she saw this picture in an art gallery, and if the woman wasn't her, and if the artist wasn't Gabriel, she'd think the artist had drawn the woman he loved.

But she *was* the woman. And the artist *was* Gabriel.

A footfall sounded behind her and she swung around. *Gabriel.*

Eyes as storm-tossed as the distant waters in his sketch stared at her from a ragged face in dire need of a shave; his hair a thick, tousled mess. He looked how she felt.

For a long moment neither of them moved. He opened his mouth, but she held up a hand and he closed it again. Her heart beat so hard she was sure he must hear it.

Turning to stare at the sketch once more, she forced her spine into straight lines. 'You don't lie?'

'I don't.'

'Then what does that mean?' She gestured at the sketch.

'Many things.'

Exhaustion hit her then. She didn't want to play games. If he didn't want to tell her, fine. Turning away, she made for her bench.

'It means I was wrong about you.'

She stuttered to a halt, but she didn't turn back.

'All of this time you've been telling me that you're strong enough to deal with whatever life throws at you, but I didn't believe you.'

His laugh, full of self-mockery, had her turning.

'I wanted to save you from the same fate as Fina. I couldn't save her, but by God, I'd do my utmost to save you.'

She couldn't move; stood rooted to the spot.

He took a step towards her. 'But it was the rest of us who needed saving. You were right—you are strong, stronger than the rest of us put together. I'm in awe of you, Audrey. You did the impossible—you created a family from practically nothing.'

'Not nothing.' Her voice was low. She tried to strengthen it. 'The framework was there. It just needed…fortifying here and there—the odd wall knocked down and bigger windows to let in the light.'

'You've saved this family.'

The way he said that… Her eyes narrowed. 'Are you now saying *you* feel a part of this family?'

'Yes.'

That was something at least. 'I'm glad.'

'I wanted you to know that I now see how strong you are.' He gestured at the picture. 'That was one of the reasons for the sketch.'

'Okay.' But while it was a definite compliment, it wasn't a

declaration of love. She still wasn't enough for him, and the knowledge burned like acid through her. 'Thank you.' Turning away, she seized a box and started tossing in sketchpads, pencils and yarn.

'I'm out here.'

Holding on to the threads of her temper, she glanced around again. It wasn't his fault he didn't love her. But he had to know that seeing him like this was torture.

He met her gaze—and even with at least twelve feet between them, the intensity of it hit her with the force of a cyclone. His finger pointed to the edges of the sketch where all was dark and storm-tossed. 'I'm here,' he repeated. 'But I want to be here.'

He moved his finger until it was right beside her in the sketch.

'I want to be the innermost person in your circle, Audrey.'

Her heart thundered. 'But you said...' He'd said his heart wasn't on offer. That it had never been on offer.

He moved towards her, those long legs closing the distance between them, his face unreadable.

If he wasn't offering her his heart...? She slammed her hands to her hips. 'So now you're telling me that you want to be friends?'

He halted in front of her. 'I *don't* want to be your friend.'

She rolled her eyes, knowing she was being contrary but unable to help it. 'Charming.'

'I want to be your lover.'

Her body leapt in instant excitement, but she held it in check. She couldn't do this. Not anymore. 'I want more, Gabriel.'

He shook his head. 'I do not mean in a physical sense.'

She blinked.

'I mean, I do want you in a physical sense—of course I do.' He reached out and took her unresisting hands in his. 'No woman has ever fired my blood the way you do. But I want to be your lover, your *amore*, in every sense of the word.'

She gaped at him, too afraid to hope. She pulled her hands free. 'On Monday you said your heart wasn't on offer and you don't lie and—'

He touched gentle fingers to her lips. 'Clearly, I do lie because I do love you and my heart is yours whether you want it or not.'

The world tilted.

'I lied to you and Marguerite, but only because I was lying to myself. I never wanted to find love again. You were right. It frightened me too much. I told myself one day in the future I would take the plunge again, but—'

He shrugged, his lips twisting as if in disgust. 'I told myself that my affair with you was controllable—pleasurable, but ultimately short-lived—and that it would burn itself out. The thing is, Audrey, it didn't burn itself out. It grew bigger and you became more and more dear to me.'

He was saying... Was he really uttering these beautiful words?

'Marguerite called me a fool when I let you go. Did she tell you that?'

She shook her head.

'It wasn't until you were gone that I realised that she was right.'

'I didn't go anywhere,' she whispered. She'd been mooching about the villa, pining for him.

'But you weren't here!' He gestured around the studio. 'There was no *us*. And I found myself cast adrift.'

She couldn't utter a single word.

'I do not lie, Audrey. I love you.'

Did she dare believe him?

He gestured at the picture. 'I drew that so you could see yourself the way I see you—strong and beautiful and the very heart of your family. I wanted you to know that you *are* enough, Audrey. That anyone lucky enough to have you in their lives is blessed.'

Tears blurred her eyes. The artist *had* drawn the woman he loved. Gabriel *did* love her.

Suddenly, she was in his arms and his hands were cradling her face and they were kissing each other with a desperate need that had their hips and bodies careening off the furniture.

Seizing her by her upper arms, he dragged her away, his breathing ragged. '*Dio*, I become a beast!'

'I like it when you become a beast,' she panted.

'You undo me.' He tried to frown, but there was a new lightness in his eyes that had her heart lifting. 'At the moment, though, I do not wish to lose control.'

'What a shame.'

He laughed, but sobered again a moment later. 'I love you, Audrey. I love you with all of myself. I know I let you down badly—like your father did, and your mother. I know I hurt you and made you feel less, but I will make it up to you. I swear, if you give me a chance, I will show you how splendidly and perfectly enough you are. I will do all I can to make you love me again. Please tell me I haven't ruined my chance to make amends.'

The lines in his face deepened and he turned grey as if the thought made him physically sick.

Reaching up, she cupped his face. 'I love you with all of

myself, too, Gabriel, and I will never let you go. I will always love you and I will always look after you.' She would prove to him that love could be a joy and a wonder and a sanctuary.

As she spoke, the lines in his face eased and the light in his eyes made her heart soar. Holding her gaze with his, he went down on one knee. Her heart crashed about in her chest and her lungs refused to work. 'Gabriel?'

Reaching into his pocket, he pulled out a velvet box. After snapping it open, he held up a ring—a beautifully cut pink diamond that sparkled as the light pouring in at the window caught it. A lump lodged in her throat.

'Now that I know the truth, *carissima*—that I love you—I do not want to leave you in any doubt of my intentions, or what I want for our future. I want you to marry me and be my wife. I want you to be a mother to my daughter. I hope that in time, if you desire it, we can have more children. I want to build a long and happy life with you. I want to dedicate my life to making you happy.'

His outline blurred as tears filled her eyes.

'And just so you know, I sought Marguerite's blessing, too. I did not want to cause any disharmony between you and your grandmother.'

Of course, Marguerite had known what would take place today. She gulped back a happy sob. 'This morning she told me you'd convinced her to pursue the setting up of the foundation in Johanna's honour.'

He rolled his shoulders. 'It was nothing. I simply did not want her making the same mistakes that I had. And I wanted you to have the family you deserve.'

Another sob lodged in her throat, making speech impossible.

He rose, snapping the velvet box closed. 'You do not need to give me your answer now. You can take as much time as you need. I just did not want there to be any misunderstandings or misconceptions. I have been a fool for long enough. I wish to be an open book now and—'

She reached up and pressed her fingers against his lips. 'Gabriel, are you babbling?'

'*Si*. I am very nervous. I love you. This matters a lot to me.'

She pinched herself. This strong, beautiful man really had just gone down on his knee before her. He'd offered her everything he was. Couldn't he see it made her the luckiest woman in the world? 'I would love to marry you. I can't think of anything that would make me happier than to build a life with you and Lili.'

Her words electrified him. 'You mean this?'

'With all my heart.' Reaching up on tiptoe she wrapped her arms around his neck. 'Gabriel, you have the kindest heart and the most honest soul of any person I've ever met. You make me feel seen and known…and loved. I've never felt more alive in my life than I have here in the studio with you. I know how badly your experience with Fina hurt you, but you've found the courage to love again. You're the most wonderful man I've ever met.'

He kissed her then. Warm, firm lips moved over hers, telling her how much he loved and desired her, how she, too, had brought him alive, opening up a world he'd never imagined. He kissed her until she became boneless with need and drunk on the taste of him. He kissed her with the wildness that she loved.

Lifting her head, she stared into his eyes. 'Is it okay if we lose control now?'

She gasped when he lifted her into his arms and strode towards the staircase. 'Your wish is my command,' he said, grinning down at her.

'Hmm...' She cocked her head to one side and pretended to consider his words as he carried her up the stairs. 'Aren't you being just a teensy bit derivative with that line?'

But then he did something wholly original with his tongue and his hands, and her pulse skyrocketed. 'Okay, scrap that. My mistake.'

Laughing, they fell down to the bed together into a future filled with love and laughter and family.

EPILOGUE

The following summer

DRAGGING A DEEP BREATH into her lungs, Audrey cast one last glance in the mirror before exiting the bedroom she'd been allocated. The excited voices coming from the direction of the living room told her the bridesmaids were ready. Instead of turning towards them, though, she moved down the hall to knock on the door of the master suite. 'Frankie? It's me.'

Frankie threw the door open and they stared at each other in open-mouthed amazement, before Frankie grabbed her hand and hauled her into her bedroom and closed the door.

'You look—' They both started at the same time and then laughed.

Neither she nor Frankie had ever dreamed of a big white church wedding where they wore dresses that weighed almost as much as they did. Their dream wedding had always been much simpler—a garden wedding surrounded only by the people they loved.

'Frankie, you look perfect.' And her cousin did. She'd

chosen a boho-inspired ankle-length wedding dress with peekaboo lace and intricate embroidery. The V-neckline was playful and sexy and the pink toenails peeping from their pretty sandals made her smile. 'The most beautiful bride that ever was.'

Frankie laughed. 'I love my dress, Audrey, but I think you might win the honours for most beautiful bride.'

Wrapping an arm around each other's waists, they turned to stare into Frankie's full-length mirror. 'I love my dress, too,' she confessed. The sweetheart neckline, lace bodice and A-line skirt in a soft tulle that floated about her calves were more traditional, and they made her feel like a fairy-tale princess. 'I feel like Cinderella.' She swung to Frankie. 'I'm so glad we're having a double wedding.'

Frankie's eyes sparkled. 'We embarked on this adventure together, Audrey. It's only fitting we now walk down the aisle together as brides. I can't believe it's ended so *wonderfully*. Who knew that one summer could change everything? And this—' she gestured at the two of them '—is the best happy-ever-after possible.'

Audrey's grin widened. Marguerite would probably sigh and shake her head at her granddaughter's inability to contain her happiness, but secretly she knew her grandmother loved that about her. 'I wonder if Nonna knew we'd find our destinies here.'

Frankie shook her head. 'I think she wanted to give us the opportunity to take stock of our lives and decide what was important to us...to help us choose the path that would make us happiest. But not even she could foresee how momentous this summer would prove to be.'

It had been the best gift she'd ever received. 'And are you truly happy with the path you've chosen, Frankie?'

Frankie had recently finished her medical specialty, and when she returned from her honeymoon in Venice, she'd start practising as a family doctor in the nearby village. It was a far cry from her old dream of becoming a neurosurgeon.

Frankie squeezed both of Audrey's hands. 'Totally happy, Audrey, I promise. I know it seems like an abrupt about-face, but this is the right fit for me. And I love Dante with all of my heart. Marrying him... It makes my heart sing.'

Audrey could relate to that 100 percent.

'And I don't have to ask if you're happy. I can see it shining from every pore. Gabriel is a lucky man.'

And she was the luckiest woman alive. Gabriel was everything she could hope for in a husband.

Frankie gave an excited shimmer. 'Are you ready to marry the man of your dreams?'

'I've never been readier for anything in my entire life.'

Not a single cloud marred the blue of the sky on the short drive to the vineyard where their guests—*and grooms*—waited for them. The terrace of Dante's restaurant Lorenzo's had been transformed into a fairyland with flowers and fairy lights, and Audrey and Frankie stood beneath an arbour of flowers at one end of the aisle, smiling guests seated in front of them. At the other end of the aisle against a glorious backdrop of golden hills, green grapevines and a stunning sunset, their grooms waited for them.

Lili looked enchanting as their flower girl, and Dante's sisters looked gorgeous as the bridesmaids in their identical dresses, each in a different pastel shade—Maria in rose, Sofia in peach, and Giorgia in mauve. The small crowd oohed and ahhed as the attendants moved down the aisle, and both Aunt Deidre and Dante's mother, Ginevra, began dabbing at their eyes with handkerchiefs. Even her father looked suddenly emotional and proud. Marguerite might not have a tear in her eyes, but her smile was so large it made Audrey want to sing.

Frankie held out her hand, Audrey took it and they walked each other down the aisle. They'd been each other's main support for as long as they could remember, and it only seemed fitting they should support each other now and walk boldly into their new futures together.

Despite the beauty of the setting, despite being surrounded by all the people she loved, Audrey only had eyes for one person—Gabriel. Those grey eyes never left hers as she moved towards him. Her pulse fluttered with appreciation at the way he filled out his tuxedo—but it was the expression in his eyes that held her spellbound. The desire, the possessiveness, made her skin tighten, but it was the love in his eyes that made her heart pound. For this man she was *enough*. For this man she would *always* be enough.

As they made their vows, their voices rang out sure and true.

When the celebrant pronounced them husband and wife, and told the grooms they could kiss their brides, Gabriel kissed her with such fierce conviction it stole her breath. 'I love you,' he murmured.

'I love you,' she murmured back.

He pressed a warm kiss into the palm of her hand. 'You are beautiful.'

He made her feel beautiful.

Much later, after a glorious dinner, and the cakes had been cut and the bridal waltzes had been waltzed, Gabriel whisked her off to a far corner of the terrace where a huge urn filled with roses hid them from view and pulled her into his arms to kiss her. 'I have been dying to get you to myself.'

Breathless, she reached up to touch his face. 'Happy, Gabriel?'

'*Si*. More than I ever thought possible. Loving you, Audrey, has done what I never thought possible.' He took her hand and placed it over his heart. 'You have healed my heart. I mean to cherish you every single day of our lives together. And you, *cara*? Are you happy?'

'I'm so happy there aren't words—in either English or Italian—to describe it.'

His grin made her heart soar. 'And are you still happy with our honeymoon plans?'

'Yes!'

They'd bought a beautiful old villa on the outskirts of Bellagio that had a gorgeous view of Lake Como and the surrounding mountains. The sale had only gone through last week, and on the spur of the moment they'd cancelled their honeymoon plans to spend it there. Alone. Everyone else still thought they were going to Paris.

The villa was in need of some updating, but that gave them the opportunity to make it truly their own. What's more it had a huge barn they had plans to convert into a joint studio, which might have to take precedence if they were to be ready for their joint exhibition in the autumn. Audrey still couldn't believe the acclaim her work was starting to garner.

'You will not miss the romance of Paris?'

She wound her arms around his neck. 'I can't think of anything more romantic than spending the first week of married life in our new home and truly making it our own. Besides, you have never been away from Lili for a whole week before, and while I know Marguerite has lots of exciting plans to keep her busy, we want to be near at hand in case she should need us.'

Lili's excitement that Audrey was her new mother knew no bounds, but that didn't mean there wouldn't be teething problems. Audrey wanted to make the transition as smooth for her as possible. It was the reason they'd waited a whole year to marry.

'Maybe we can spend our first anniversary in Paris,' she said.

'You are a remarkable woman, Audrey. Do you know that?' He kissed her long and deep, and when he lifted his head, she had to cling to him to remain upright. 'What do you say to leaving for our honeymoon right now?'

Reaching up, she kissed him. 'I think that's an excellent plan.'

* * * * *

Two Weeks To Tempt The Tycoon
Nina Singh

Nina Singh lives just outside Boston, Massachusetts, with her husband, children and a very rambunctious Yorkie. After several years in the corporate world, she finally followed the advice of family and friends to "give the writing a go, already." She's oh-so-happy she did. When not at her keyboard, she likes to spend time on the tennis court or golf course. Or immersed in a good read.

Books by Nina Singh

How to Make a Wedding

From Tropical Fling to Forever

Their Festive Island Escape
Her Billionaire Protector
Spanish Tycoon's Convenient Bride
Her Inconvenient Christmas Reunion
From Wedding Fling to Baby Surprise
Around the World with the Millionaire
Whisked into the Billionaire's World
Wearing His Ring till Christmas
Caribbean Contract with Her Boss

Visit the Author Profile page at millsandboon.com.au.

Dear Reader,

Oftentimes, the person we are toughest on is ourselves. Self-forgiveness does not come easy for most people. In the wake of a serious mistake, one that might have caused harm to others, we often don't afford ourselves much grace or charity.

Such is the case with Gio Santino. He's made a terrible error in judgment, one that has led to intensive damage not only to himself but also to another. He doesn't feel worthy of forgiveness, or understanding, or—least of all—love.

But both redemption and love are bestowed on him by a most unexpected source, his little sister's best friend. Gio has known Marni most of his life, didn't dare think of her as anything more than a family friend. Much to his surprise, she turns out to be the path toward atonement he didn't think he was worthy of. It takes Marni to show Gio how to forgive himself as she overcomes her own past missteps.

Along the way, they fall hopelessly in love with each other. I hope you enjoy their path.

Nina

To all those with the grace and heart to forgive.

Praise for
Nina Singh

"A captivating holiday adventure! *Their Festive Island Escape* by Nina Singh is a twist on an enemies-to-lovers trope and is sure to delight. I recommend this book to anyone.... It's fun, it's touching and it's satisfying."
—*Goodreads*

CHAPTER ONE

THERE WAS SOMEONE else here in the house with her. Maybe more than one someone.

Marni Payton's heart slammed against her chest as she shut the wooden door behind her. It had been unlocked. This was so not the welcome she'd been expecting after a long, turbulent flight and an exhausting day of travel.

But she had a more pressing matter at the moment.

Nella had warned her there might be squatters at the villa this time of year. She'd said they were usually harmless. Older kids, mostly, who were looking for a place to party. Teenagers trying to get away from under the watchful eyes of strict parents.

Which, on the surface, did sound harmless enough. Or at least it had when Nella had explained it to her a month ago, while offering Marni the use of her beachside villa in Capri for two weeks before she and her husband would need it back.

Now, however, the knowledge did little to calm Marni down. Shaking with fear, she stood in the middle of the foyer, listening to the sounds coming from upstairs. What if it wasn't a bunch of kids up there? What if the house was being robbed? Or she was about to be attacked?

Marni stepped backward, readying to flee the house, her gaze still locked to the top of the stairs. She reached for the cell phone in her back pocket to call the authorities. In her fear and panic, she yanked it out too jerkily and dropped it to the tile floor. It fell with a loud crashing sound and she watched in horror as the case popped off and the screen shattered.

So much for calling for help. The taxi that had driven her to the house was long gone. She was on her own. Marni froze in her spot, unable to move or so much as breathe.

Had the intruders heard her dropping her phone? Were they scrambling down right now to come hurt her?

Squeak. Squeak. Squeak.

Oh, God. That was definitely a sound she recognized— the unmistakable noise of the springs in a bed. Whoever was up there was using the very bed she'd be sleeping in! Marni could just guess what they were doing. A wave of indignation rose in her chest. The audacity to break into a house and then do...that! She was as sympathetic as anyone to lovesick teens, but this was miles and miles too far.

It was high time to put a stop to it.

Marni pushed aside her fear in favor of outrage. Plus, they were definitely naked. She had the element of surprise on her side. She'd just go up there, demand they get their clothes on and vacate the premises ASAP. Marni bounded up the stairs before she could change her mind. When she reached the closed bedroom door, she gave a quick knock then covered her eyes before pushing it open. Some things she didn't need to see.

"I won't tell your parents if you both get dressed and

leave right now," she said. It was an empty threat. She had no idea who their parents might be or where they lived. "Right now," she repeated.

No answer. Maybe they didn't understand English.

She repeated the bluff in broken Italian. Still nothing. And she didn't hear any scuffling about either.

Of all the nerve. Were they seriously just going to ignore her? At least the squeaking had stopped.

Marni cleared her throat, beginning to speak louder this time. "Listen, I'm going to give you exactly sixty seconds to gather your clothes and get out of this house!"

"Dio!" A sharp male voice exploded in her ears. Definitely not the voice of a teenager. A string of sharp Italian curse words followed.

Nope. That was no kid.

In fact, the voice sounded all too familiar. Marni's blood turned to ice in her veins. It couldn't be. But the next word she heard only confirmed that indeed it could.

"Gattina? Is that you?"

Oh, no. There was only one person who ever called her that. But how? Why? With great reluctance, Marni lowered her palm from her eyes and fearfully opened her lids. She immediately wanted to squeeze them shut again.

She'd been so wrong. There was no couple on the bed. Just one solitary man. To her horror, he happened to be Gio Santino. Her best friend Nella's brother. The same man she'd had a crush on for most of her life.

Well, at least she'd been right about one thing: the intruder was indeed naked.

His usual nightmare had taken quite a surprising turn. Rubbing his eyes, Gio blinked away the grogginess of interrupted sleep and tried to focus on the figure standing at the door.

Yep, it was definitely her. Marni Payton stood staring at him in shock, wide-eyed, her mouth agape. What in the world was she doing here at his sister's villa in Capri? Marni lived in Boston.

"What are you doing here?" they both asked in unison.

Gio knew what his answer to that question was. He'd been trying to get some much-needed sleep. The insomnia and nightmares were wreaking havoc on him. Not to mention the throbbing pain in his leg and torso.

Marni blinked rapidly before attempting to speak. "Nella said I could stay here. For two weeks. I just arrived."

Huh. Gio ran a hand down his face. "That's funny. Because her husband told me the same thing. That I was welcome to the villa whenever I needed."

Marni swallowed. "Well, clearly there's been some kind of misunderstanding."

"Clearly." He was tempted to throttle Antonella the next time he saw her. As much as he loved her, his sister had always been scattered and disorganized. He didn't know how her new husband dealt with it, for God's sake.

Gio sighed wearily. "Look, we're not going to solve this now." Not that he knew exactly how they *would* solve it at any other time. Other than looking for a hotel room for himself at the earliest opportunity. Which was not going to be easy. Capri was busy with tourists and vacationers this time of year. What a pain.

He was so tired of pain.

"Why don't we go downstairs and talk about this," he offered.

Marni didn't answer for several seconds. He was about to repeat the question when he noticed her gaze traveling from his face, past his shoulders, down his chest. Then lower.

She cleared her throat before speaking. "Yeah. Sure. We could do that. But do you mind getting dressed first?"

Gio flinched. He totally forgot that he'd climbed into bed completely nude. Much too tired to do more than peel off his gritty clothes before collapsing under the covers. To his horror, he saw the bedsheet and blanket had moved lower below his waist and barely sat on his hips. Reflexively, he yanked the sheet up to below his chest.

"Sure. I can do that," he answered.

"Great. I'll see you in a few," Marni replied, turning on her heel. She shut the door firmly behind her.

Gio leaned back against the pillows and threw his arm over his face. Great. Just great. Not only had his chance at some rest and recuperation just been soundly ruined, he'd almost flashed his younger sister's dearest friend.

Why did she have to be here? Now of all times? Was nothing going to go his way this year? Guessing he already knew the answer to that question, Gio begrudgingly tossed the covers aside and stood. Pulling his suitcase open, he grabbed a pair of sweats and a T-shirt then made his way down the stairs.

Marni was bent down in the doorway when he got to the first floor. In spite of himself and despite the circumstances, he found himself appreciating the view. The sight of Marni's rounded hips had his mind traveling to places it had no business going.

Whatever she was doing, she was distracted enough that she seemed unaware of him. Hopefully, she hadn't noticed just how long it had taken him to get dressed and get down here. Everything took longer to do these days. Something the doctors kept reminding he'd better get used to.

"What are you doing?" he asked Marni's back.

She straightened and turned to face him, holding something in her hand that might have resembled a cell phone at some point in time.

"I was a little startled when I heard noises upstairs. I panicked and dropped my phone." She held up the object in question and shrugged.

"Noises? What noises?"

"The bed, you were making of lot of racket up there." She pointed to the ceiling. "For someone who was sleeping…" She drifted off and a blush of color rose in her cheeks, her bright hazel eyes grew wide. As if she was embarrassed.

Gio held his hands up, offended and slightly amused at her insinuation. "Marni, it's not like that."

She shook her head, growing redder. "Oh! Of course. Whatever you say. Um… Not that there'd be anything wrong or to be embarrassed about. If that was what you were… doing." She faltered on the last word.

Gio couldn't help chuckling. "Thanks. I guess." What exactly was he thanking her for? "The truth is, I haven't been sleeping well. Lots of tossing and turning. That's if I'm lucky enough to fall asleep in the first place."

She looked unsure of what to say. Best to change the subject. "So you're here on vacation?" he asked.

Marni looked away, but not before he caught a shadow dance across her eyes. "Something like that," she answered.

Huh. He'd thought it was a casual question. But Marni clearly didn't want to talk about what exactly she was doing here, halfway across the world from her home. That suited him just fine. He didn't really want to get into his own reasons for being here either.

She finally returned his gaze. "Gio. If I'd known you were going to be here, I would have made other arrangements."

"I'd say the same. But we're both here now." The question was, what were they going to do about it?

She glanced around her. "I mean, the place is rather roomy."

Maybe. But there was still only one finished bedroom. And only the one bed. Nella and Alex had never gotten around to furnishing the entire house, having recently purchased it. Gio glanced past the foyer to the sitting area. It looked comfortable enough, but the furniture was hardly ample. He didn't think he'd be able to endure sleeping on the small love seat in the living room. The shape he was in at the moment, his body simply couldn't handle it.

And he wasn't going to ask Marni to sleep there. Old-fashioned or not, his masculine pride simply wouldn't allow it. Which lead to another complication. There was no way he was going to explain to Marni why he wouldn't be able to do the chivalrous thing and sleep on the couch.

"I would call around to see about available hotel rooms, but…" She simply held up her shattered phone to complete the sentence.

"I don't think you'd find one anyway. Places around here are booked months in advance." He rammed his hand through his hair in frustration. "Look. We're not going to solve this now," he repeated. "Why don't you go freshen up and I'll throw a snack together. I don't know about you, but I could use a bite."

As if in answer, her stomach reacted with a low grumble.

Gio had to chuckle again. For as long as she and his sister had been friends, she'd always managed to make him laugh. He couldn't even remember the last time he'd laughed since the accident. Marni had been here only a few minutes and he'd already chuckled twice.

Despite the awkward circumstances they found themselves in.

By the time Marni made it back downstairs, Gio had thrown together a rather enticing tray of snacks and munchies, if he did say so himself. He'd loaded the fridge and pantry when he'd gotten here three days ago—it was a rare instance of him planning ahead.

If only he'd lived his life being a better planner. He might be in better physical shape right now, without the throbbing pain in his side and the pronounced limp in his gait. A limp he would have to somehow try to hide now that Marni was here.

He got an appreciative sigh from her when she entered the kitchen and eyed the food tray.

"Wow. You threw together a charcuterie board," she said, then added, "I'm impressed."

A what now? "Uh, thanks, I guess. If you mean the tray of cubed cheese, tapenade, meat and grapes. Where I come from, we call it antipasto."

She smiled wide. "Whatever you want to call it, sure beats the dry granola bars I have stashed in my purse. A man of many talents. Who knew?"

Considering they'd been acquainted for most of their lives through his younger sister, he wasn't sure if he felt slighted by that.

When was the last time he'd seen Marni? Had to have been the holidays last year. He studied her now. She looked different, more mature.

And she smelled good. Some kind of spicy, citrus scent that lingered in the air. Her cheeks had filled in. He remembered her face being much more angular. In fact, she'd filled in all over. Marni was definitely curvier than he remembered, bringing to mind images of starlets from the Hollywood of old. The likes of Sofia Loren or Gina Lollobrigida. The changes looked good on her. *Marni* looked good.

And why in the world would he notice a thing like that? Gio gave himself a mental shake. Maybe his head injury wasn't as healed as he'd hoped. He had no business sniffing around his sister's best friend or waxing poetic about her curves. This was little *gattina*, for heaven's sake. "Little kitten." He couldn't even remember when he'd first given her the nickname. They'd been kids, and she'd reminded him of a kitten because she was always so playful and constantly underfoot.

She pointed to the kettle sitting by the side of the island. "Mind if I make some tea? If I know Nella, she's got some high-quality black leaf sitting around here somewhere."

He'd been about to suggest one of the bottles of high-end Chianti he'd discovered in the wine rack by the bar but tea would work. In fact, it might be better to keep sober around her given the wayward thoughts that kept popping in his head.

"Sounds good."

"I was thinking of getting ahold of Nella," she said, filling the silver kettle with water and setting it on the stove.

"To ask her if there's a friend in town who might happen to have a room."

"Good idea," he answered. Better than anything he'd been able to come up with.

"As much as I hate to bother her and Alex on their romantic trip to Paris."

"They'll have to forgive us for the intrusion."

She nodded. "I would have done it already except I have no phone." She looked at him expectedly.

Gio popped a mozzarella ball into his mouth. "Yeah, it's really too bad that it shattered like that." He really did feel bad about scaring her so badly. He should find a way to apologize. Though it was hard to say sorry about something you weren't even aware was happening at the time.

"So...uh...could you maybe do it?" Marni asked.

Gio gave his head a shake. Of course! How daft could he be? What was wrong with him? Why couldn't he suddenly think straight around a woman he'd known practically his whole life?

Had to be the lack of sleep. It was wreaking havoc on his mental faculties. He pulled his phone out of his back pocket and clicked on his sister's name. Straight to voice mail. Not surprising. "No answer," he told Marni after leaving Nella a brief message he could only hope she would check in a timely fashion. "I'll try Alex next."

His brother-in-law's phone didn't even have the option to leave a voice mail. Gio just got the "unavailable" message. He shook his head at Marni's unvoiced question.

"Sorry. Can't reach him either."

Marni's face fell, her lips forming a thin line. She was really worried. A tinge of guilt tugged in his chest. She'd be kicking back and relaxing right now with a working phone if it wasn't for him. He couldn't seem to do anything right these days.

The dejected expression on her face tore at him. Gio had a crazy urge to go to her and gather her in his arms. Lucky for him, the kettle started screeching before he could do anything so foolish. Marni silently went to brew the tea, the look on her face not easing in the least.

"We'll figure this out," he reassured her. "In the meantime, it's not so bad being here with me, is it?"

But Marni only silently smiled in answer. Whatever she was hoping to get out of this trip, it was clear Gio's presence was going to be a hindrance. His guilt grew.

Within moments, Marni had found two ceramic mugs, had brewed the tea and had a steaming mug sitting in front of them both.

"We'll try Nella and Alex again in a bit."

"Something tells me they're not going to answer their phones anytime soon." Her voice was low and forlorn.

"Then we'll make do for now and start fresh tomorrow. And first thing in the morning, we'll head into town and see about replacing that phone."

If he'd thought that was going to cheer her up at all, he was sorely disappointed. Marni barely reacted to the offer. In fact, she appeared to be deep in thought, staring at the steam rising from her mug. For as excited as she'd seemed about the food, so far she'd barely taken a bite. Yep, Gio had inadvertently ruined Marni Payton's vacation.

Nothing he could do about it now. They just had to coexist for the next few hours until he could figure out a plan of action.

And as far as sleeping arrangements for the night, heaven only knew what they would do.

***

Marni lay awake staring into the darkness. It had all been too much to hope for. Was a two-week reprieve too much to ask for from the universe? All she'd wanted from this trip was to get away for a few days and lick her proverbial wounds. Just a chance to leave the past behind and focus on herself in quiet solitude in what she'd thought would be her friend's abandoned villa on the Italian coast. No such luck. Because enter one Gio Santino.

What was he doing here in Italy, anyway? He had a major corporation to run. Santino Foods was headquartered in the North End in Boston.

As CEO of Santino Foods, Gio rarely took time off. Even after a car accident last year, he'd barely given himself time away. Last she'd heard from Nella, he was putting off the therapy and the appointments recommended for a full recovery.

Regardless of his reason for being here, now Marni would have to find alternate arrangements. And she would have to be the one to leave. First of all, Gio had gotten here first. He was already settled while she hadn't even unpacked yet. Not to mention, his blood sibling actually owned the house. Marni and Nella had been friends for years—but blood trumped friendship.

Bad enough she'd kicked him out of the bed for the night. Gio had insisted. He'd told her he was having problems sleeping as it was. Now he was lying on a pile of cushions they'd taken off the couches downstairs and turned into a makeshift mattress on the floor of one of the empty rooms. Try as she might, Marni hadn't been able to convince him to take the real bed instead of her. Not surprising. She'd known the argument was futile from the beginning because Gio wasn't wired that way.

What a mess.

But none of this was her fault. She'd been planning this trip for weeks. Since the day she'd walked away from Ander for good, Marni knew she'd have to get far away from her ex. At least for the short term. Being anywhere near him right after the breakup was a recipe for disaster.

She could only imagine what Ander's thoughts on her current predicament might be. First, he'd tell her that he'd told her so. He'd remind her how little she was capable of without his guidance. That it was no wonder she'd messed up the very first thing she'd tried to do without him by her side.

Worst of all, Ander had plenty of contacts who were all too willing to print and air his version of events. It was why she'd had to get away, to find refuge in an entirely different country.

Marni sniffled away a tear and threw her forearm over her eyes. She refused to believe that Ander might be right about her. He liked to think she was useless and incompetent without him. That was just his narcissism. Being out from under his thumb and getting far away from him was the best thing Marni could have done for herself. Something she should have done much sooner.

As soon as she figured out her living situation for the next couple of weeks, everything would fall into place.

A loud shriek cut through the darkness. Marni bolted up in bed, disoriented and alarmed. She'd been closer to falling asleep than she thought. The loud noise sent her pulse rocketing.

Gio. Something was terribly wrong with him. Had someone broken in, after all? Was he struggling with an intruder right at this very moment?

Marni scrambled out of bed and ran to his room, grabbing a heavy vase off the bureau along the way. Her heart pounding, she threw open his door. Relief surged through her when she saw no one else was in there with him. But Gio was far from okay. A small sliver of moonlight from the open window illuminated just enough of the room to allow her to see him thrashing about on the cushions, his cries of anguish echoed off the walls. Whatever nightmare he was having seemed to be torturing him in his sleep. Marni rushed over to his side and dropped to her knees.

"Gio. Wake up," she cried. "You have to wake up."

Nothing. He hadn't even heard her. The thrashing didn't let up, his cries continued jarring the night air.

"Gio! It's me!" she yelled out, louder this time. She reached for his shoulders to give him a shake.

Big mistake. Gio didn't awaken but she'd managed to startle him in his sleep. His arms thrust out and he grabbed her by the arms, yanked her down. She landed on top of his chest, their legs intertwined.

Marni's vision went dark, her voice stuck in her throat. Scramble as she might, she couldn't get out of Gio's grip.

Panic and fear surged through her until she thought she'd completely lost her breath. Images rushed through her mind—all the times Ander had grabbed her arm just a little too roughly. The times he'd been frustrated with her when they were running late and given her a nudge just hard enough to be considered a push. The many moments she'd wondered if and when he'd go too far.

Steady. Ander wasn't here. This was Gio. And he would never hurt her. He was just having a nightmare.

The more she fought, the harder Gio held her. Marni forced herself to go still and take several deep breaths. It seemed to work. Gio's grasp loosened just enough for her to roll out of his reach.

Several moments passed while she tried to regain a steady breath. Gio finally grew quiet, she was debating whether to simply stand and leave the room, when his eyes fluttered open. His gaze cast about the room, his dark brown eyes growing wide when they found her.

"Marni?"

She could only nod in response.

"What are you doing here?"

"I heard you…thought you might be hurt. Or someone might be here…" She couldn't seem to make her mind communicate with her mouth.

Gio's face tightened as he put the scenario together. Even in the dark, she could see the horror flood his features. He stood and rubbed a hand down his face. "Marni. I'm so sorry. I never meant to scare you. Again."

In two strides he'd reached the wall and flipped on the light switch. Soft yellow light flooded the room. Gio wore only pajama bottoms, hung low on his hips. Bare chested, she could see the hardened contours of his muscles.

So not the time to be noticing such a thing.

But she noticed something else. It was rather hard to miss. A large angry scar ran down the side of his torso down to his hip. It looked fresh and red.

Nella hadn't told her much about his accident. Though, truth be told, Marni had been too preoccupied with the emotional toll of her relationship with Ander to really pay attention. But judging by Gio's physical scars, the accident had been more serious than Marni had known.

No wonder Gio was having nightmares.

CHAPTER TWO

Gio wasn't in the house when she awoke the next morning. Marni had to wonder if he'd even managed to get back to sleep or if he even wanted to, given what awaited him in dreamland.

When he'd mentioned yesterday that he had trouble sleeping, she'd had no idea how violent his slumber could get. It certainly explained the squeaking she'd heard upon arrival at the house.

What exactly happened to him? The tabloids and gossip websites had moved past reporting on the story pretty quickly. The high-profile divorce of a Hollywood power couple had taken over the news feeds right around the same time. Nella didn't give away much either when Marni asked. There was a while a few months back where Nella looked particularly distracted. Worried, even. Marni hadn't wanted to pry at the time. She knew Gio and his sister were quite close. But she also knew both siblings could be withdrawn and very private.

She gave her head a brisk shake. It was too much to think

about first thing in the morning after a restless night. She made her way to the kitchen for some much-needed caffeine.

A scrap of paper sitting on the counter caught her eye. Gio had left her a note.

Gone for a walk on the beach. Let's talk when I get back.

Fine by her. They had a lot to discuss. Like exactly what the plan was if neither of them could find another place to stay.

The sound of a standard ringtone shrilling behind her cut through her thoughts. Gio had left his phone behind. The sound reminded her that her own phone sat in the bottom of the rubbish bin in several pieces. She sighed with frustration. Yet another thing to deal with and fix.

Marni glanced at the screen. Nella! As if her thoughts from a few minutes ago had conjured her. Finally.

But Gio wasn't here. Marni raced to the small window above the sink to see if he was at all nearby. They both desperately needed to talk to his sister.

No sign of him.

Marni swore under her breath then rushed to pick up the call. Gio wouldn't mind if she answered his phone. Just this once. Not in this case. Before she could change her mind, she answered.

"Hey, Nella."

Several silent pauses followed. Marni could just picture the confusion on her friend's face about a thousand miles away as she tried to figure out what was what.

Nella sounded just as confused as she'd imagined when she finally spoke. "Marni? Is that you? I thought I dialed my brother."

"It is. I mean, you did."

Far from clearing anything up, Marni's response was a jumbled mess. She took a deep breath to try again. "Yeah, it's me. But you dialed right. This is your brother's phone. He's just out right now. So I didn't think he'd mind if I answered."

That wouldn't do much to clarify things either.

Nella spoke before she could try again at another lame attempt. "Marni, what's going on? Why are you answering my brother's phone? Where are you two and what are you doing together?"

Marni scrambled for the right words. Where exactly to begin? "Well, it's a funny story actually." Except it really wasn't.

"Tell me," Nella prodded.

"See, I decided to take you up on your offer to stay at your house in Capri for the next two weeks."

"Good," Nella said immediately. "You need it."

"Right. Well, I got here last night and, to my surprise—"

Nella cut her off before she could finish. "Let me guess, Gio was already there when you arrived."

"Bingo."

Marni heard a low whistle from the other end of the line. "He's had a key since we've owned the place, with a standing offer to use it as he wished when we aren't there. Though I can't recall the last time he's actually taken us up on it."

Just her typical lousy luck, then. "I see."

"I'm really sorry, Marni. I had no idea what he planned—he's supposed to be in Chicago."

"Chicago?" As far as she knew, Santino Foods had no presence in Illinois.

Nella cleared her throat. "Never mind, the point is I would have warned you if I had any clue that he might show."

"No need to apologize. This is your house. And he's your brother."

"And you're my dearest friend."

"It wasn't your mistake," Marni reassured.

"Still, I know how much you could use a getaway. And my brother is sort of hard to ignore."

That was an understatement. Gio was larger than life. Handsome, charming, with a sharp sense of humor. He'd always had a large personality.

Nella was still talking. "But I tried to call you last night. You didn't answer."

"Yeah, that's the other thing. I sort of destroyed my phone when I got to the villa. But that's a story for another day."

Marni cringed as the words left her mouth. Anyone but her best friend would probably deem her daft or clumsy. Or both. She'd arrived at an already occupied house and then promptly smashed her phone.

"Huh. I'd definitely like to hear it."

"Right. Well, now we're figuring out where I might move out to. If you have any suggestions."

"Move out? Why would you move out? The villa is huge."

When she put it that way, Marni was hard-pressed to come up with an answer. But she just couldn't imagine herself staying here when Gio was close by. Plus, there was the whole matter of the accommodations. "For one thing, there's only one bed."

"That's easy. Signora Baraca's son owns a furniture shop in town. Every piece is handcrafted. We've been meaning to get those empty rooms furnished and never got around to it. I'll give her a call and you guys can go down and pick something."

Marni rubbed her forehead. "Nella, you should be the one decorating your house. Not me."

Nella laughed. Marni could almost see her waving her hand dismissively. "Why not? It's literally what you do for a living."

True, Marni was an interior decorator. But she usually did commercial work with plenty of input from whomever she was working for.

"I think you know me well enough to pick out pieces I'll like," Nella pressed.

Still. "I don't think Gio will agree, Nella." What if Gio needed time to himself? To deal with whatever he was trying to deal with. She had an urge to ask Nella more about the accident and Gio's scars but decided against it. Her friend would have told her before now if Marni was meant to know.

"Well, then that would be *his* problem, wouldn't it?" Nella answered. "And he'd have to be the one to find another place. He'll come around," she added after a pause. "He's not that stubborn."

"If you say so," Marni answered, not quite convinced. She'd seen Gio act plenty stubborn over the years.

"I do say so. Trust me. And, Marni?"

"Yes?"

"Please have my brother call me as soon as he gets in. I'd really like to talk to him." Was it her imagination, or did Nella sound slightly amused?

She was pondering that question several moments later when a loud sound jarred her in her seat. She took a deep breath. It was just the front door. Just Gio returning.

Honestly, she had to stop being so jumpy. She was in

Capri now. Not back home in Massachusetts where there was someone constantly hovering over her shoulder, ready to hurl an insult or some type of accusation. Someone she'd thought she'd loved once.

When she'd been naive and too trusting. Never again.

"Marni?" Gio called from the doorway.

"In the kitchen."

When Gio entered the room, he brought with him the scent of fresh pastries. He held out a white cardboard box tied with a thin string. "I thought you might want some breakfast."

"Oh. Wow. Thanks."

Without another word, he set the box in front of her. Huh. The gesture was so unexpected, Marni wasn't sure what else to say. She couldn't recall the last time someone had brought her breakfast. Or brought her anything, for no reason other than that she might enjoy it.

Ander would have never treated her to pastries. He considered such indulgences out of the question. Well, she didn't need to give his opinion another thought anymore. He would no longer be monitoring her calorie intake or anything else that concerned her. Never again.

She untied the string and lifted the cover to reveal an array of mouthwatering pastries that looked as delicious as they smelled. Croissants, bagels, a baguette, fruit-topped Danish with rich glaze. There had to be thousands of calories in this box.

But she didn't need to focus on that these days. Not unless she chose to do so. Ander didn't have the right to comment on her looks anymore or check whether she'd logged a calorie deficit or gain for the day.

"Where did you get these?" she asked, just for something to say and to pull herself out of the unwelcome thoughts.

"There's a stand on the beach. You should check it out. They have desserts in the evenings."

Marni sighed. Baked goods on the beach. Exactly the kind of thing she'd been looking forward to when coming here. Could Nella be right? Could she and Gio just stay here? Together but apart? It would solve everything. Neither one would have to worry about finding another place. The only thing they'd need to do was find a bed and some furniture.

The villa was indeed a good size.

But would Gio see it that way? He was clearly here to get away from something, much like herself. What if the last thing he wanted was his little sister's pesky best friend underfoot?

Only one way to find out.

"So, your sister called," she told him. "You just missed her."

"Oh? About time."

Marni nodded. "She wants you to call her back. As soon as possible."

Gio shook his head, reached for a glass from the cabinet and poured himself water from the sink. "She's always so bossy," he complained, but his voice held no sting. Still. He wasn't in a rush to do as Nella had asked.

"I hope you don't mind, but I answered your phone when I saw on the screen that it was her calling."

He shrugged. "I guess that's okay. As long as she's the only one you answer my phone for."

That was weird. Why would she answer it otherwise? But it was apparently important for him to set that boundary. Marni tipped three fingers to her forehead in a mock salute. "Aye, aye."

His privacy was clearly important to him, not surprisingly. Which probably didn't bode well for him agreeing to share the villa with her.

"Bet she was surprised to hear that we're both here."

"She certainly was."

"What did she have to say about it?"

Marni pursed her lips and pointed to his phone on the counter behind him. "I think you'd better call her now. Hear it all for yourself."

Well, that sounded pretty ominous. What had Nella and Marni discussed exactly? Though he'd been delaying returning Nella's call out of pure sibling pettiness—wanting him to get back to her ASAP when she'd taken her sweet time to return his call. As if.

But now his curiosity was piqued. Reaching behind him for his phone, he called up his sister's contact and dialed. When he looked up, Marni was no longer at the counter. The woman could move like a feline, as befitting his nickname for her. He hadn't even heard her leave.

His sister answered on the third ring. With a string of curse words followed by some very specific thoughts about his intelligence and stubbornness.

"Good morning to you too, sis."

"Don't give me that," she snapped back. "What the devil are you doing in Capri? Of all places."

"Sorry. I thought you said I could use this place whenever I wanted."

Nella sighed loudly into the phone. "You know that's not

what I mean. Of course any home I have is open to you at any time."

"Huh. You could have fooled me the way you answered my call."

Another Italian curse reached his ear. "Stop playing games, Gio. This isn't the time." Silence followed. A pause during which Nella's aggravation with him had been replaced by sisterly concern. "How are you, by the way?"

Gio was torn between irritation and affection. He was beginning to resent that question. It was all he'd heard for the past several weeks. From Mama, his sister, everyone who knew all the details about what had happened.

"I'm fine."

"Gio, you're not fine. You're supposed to be in Chicago seeing that orthopedic specialist and beginning rehab. Why in the world did you cancel?"

"I canceled because I'm feeling better." Not quite the truth, just a small fib. Gio pinched the bridge of his nose. Who was he kidding? It was a whopper of a lie and he deserved to be hit by a lightning bolt where he stood.

"I'm fine, Nella," he repeated. She may be his sister, but this was really none of her concern. "I just need another place to stay. Do you have any ideas? A neighbor who's away for the season? A hotel you'd recommend? I guess I could go to Naples, stay there…"

Nella sighed with clear resignation. "You don't need to go to Naples. You and Marni can both stay."

"There's only one bed."

"*Nessun problema.* I've already called the furniture store in town, told them to expect you."

Gio supposed that made sense. If Marni was okay with this arrangement, he could make it work.

Nella continued, "Having said that, dear brother, there's just one more thing."

With Nella there always was. "What's that?"

"Marni happens to be my oldest and dearest friend. She's like a sister to me."

"I know all that."

"So I trust you'll know not to toy with her."

Toy with her? She really wasn't going *there*, was she? "Nella, what in the world are you getting at?"

"Let's not pretend you don't have a reputation as a ladies' man, Gio. Marni's too important."

"You've made your point, Nella."

"Please remember it."

Gio said goodbye and ended the call, trying not to feel offended. Did Nella really think she had to warn him off Marni? Of course he'd be mindful not to cross any boundaries with her. He'd known her too long, considered her part of their family.

Given his current situation, Gio was in no position to pursue anything romantic with anyone. Let alone the dear friend who Mama and his sister loved. He'd have the two of them to answer to when things went bad, as they inevitably would. He wasn't built for long-term relationships, especially not now. And Marni deserved more than a meaningless fling.

No, the bigger issue when it came to Marni, if they were going to stay here together for the next several days, was how long he could avoid questions about what was wrong with him.

"Nella thinks we should both stay put here," Gio announced as he walked out onto the patio several minutes later.

Marni looked up from the Italy travel site she'd been perusing on her tablet. Not that she'd been able to pay attention to the colorful pictures of the many tourist attractions. She was much too preoccupied with the way Gio and Nella's phone call might have gone.

"She says the villa is spacious enough for the both of us," he continued. "And that all we need is to furnish one of the rooms."

Huh. Well, he wasn't laughing or grimacing, for that matter. It sounded like he was actually considering it.

"And what do you think?"

He pulled out the lounge chair next to her and plopped down. "It's your decision, *gattina*. I'm the one who came here unannounced."

"True. Which was very inconvenient of you by the way."

"As Nella made sure to let me know."

"But this happens to be your sister's house. And you have an open invitation to be here, unannounced or not."

Not to mention, he was clearly dealing with trauma horrible enough to have scarred his body and give him violent nightmares. A trauma he didn't seem in any kind of hurry to talk about.

"All right, *gattina*. I guess we've established that we both have a right to be here, then."

"I agree."

"Then I say we go furniture shopping," he declared, then grunted out a laugh. "Now, there's a line I never thought I'd say to a woman. And certainly not to my sister's best friend."

Marni bit down on the disappointment that washed through her at his words. His sister's friend. Little *gattina*. Gio had quite the reputation as a ladies' man. He had since he'd barely been a teenager. But he'd never see her as anything more than an extension of his sibling. A little playful kitten. Why that bothered her at this precise moment, she couldn't decide.

One theory that made sense was that her previous relationship had completely destroyed her self-esteem and confidence. So much so that she was now looking for validation from a man she should never view as anything more than a friend. And friends could be roommates. Especially if it was only a temporary arrangement.

Shutting her tablet, she rose out of her chair. "I'm ready when you are."

An hour later, Marni followed Gio out the door. But he surprised her when instead of heading toward the road, he turned toward the beach.

"Where are we going?" she asked his back, following him anyway.

"To town, remember?"

"But the road is behind us."

He turned to give her a curious glance. "But the ocean is in front of us. As is the boat."

"Boat?"

He finally turned to face her. "That's right. You know, it's a mode of transportation that's particularly useful on the water. Has these large white things called sails. And a motor."

Marni gave him a useless shove on his upper arm. He barely moved in response. "Ha ha. I know what a boat is. I just didn't realize we had one at our disposal."

"We do. And it's just as easy to sail up the coast as to try to get a taxi or catch the bus. You don't mind the water, do you, Marni?"

"I'm on an island, aren't I?"

He chuckled then turned back to the stone steps leading toward the water and continued down. Marni silently followed. They walked the beach about a quarter mile until they reached a small wooden pathway leading to the ocean. Half a dozen boats floated anchored at the end. Of course, Gio headed straight for the sleekest, newest-looking one.

"So I lied about the sails," he told her as he helped her aboard. "It's a motorboat."

The amount that Marni knew about boats could fit into a thimble. She could count on one hand all the times she'd been on one. Including the dinner cruise she'd taken with Ander last summer where he'd complained the entire time about the quality of the food and speed of service. Also, about her outfit. She remembered he'd chastised her about showing too much leg with that particular one. If she'd worn a tea-length gown, he would have found something else to complain about.

But that was nothing unusual.

Marni shook away the thoughts and allowed Gio to help her onboard. He walked over to a built-in bin and lifted the cover, removing two life jackets. He handed the smaller one to her. "Do you know how to put one of these on?"

Well, she wasn't that clueless about sailing. "Yes. But is it absolutely necess—"

He didn't even let her finish the sentence. "Yes. We don't even lift anchor unless you have it on nice and tight. Otherwise, you can just turn around and get off right now."

Marni swallowed. Everything about Gio's demeanor had just changed. As soon as she'd begun to ask the question, his eyes flashed dark and the muscles around his mouth tightened.

She hardly recognized this side of him. The Gio she knew would have made light of her resistance, made some kind of quip about not diving in to rescue her if she were to end up in the water. Gio's expression now held no mirth whatsoever.

"Harsh," she muttered, yanking the preserver out of his hands. Without another word, she put it on then clipped the holster clasps shut. Gio studied her the entire time, as if not fully trusting her to do it properly. She glared at him, lifting her arms. "Do you care to inspect it?"

The corner of his mouth lifted ever so slightly as his eyes traveled down her body.

"As tempting as that is, I've been warned against such inappropriate behavior." With that he turned to stride toward the dashboard, throwing his own life jacket on in the process.

Marni felt hot color flush her cheeks. A tingling awareness skittered over her skin.

He'd been warned? What in heaven's name did that mean?

CHAPTER THREE

GIO TURNED THE steering wheel and began to guide the boat toward the town marina. A bright orange sun hung in a crystal blue sky, and the waves shimmered like liquid gems as they moved along the surface of the water.

If someone had told him a week ago that he'd be spending the day furniture shopping with Marni Payton, he would have told said person to check their mental state. Yet, as ridiculous as it was, he was about to go pick out bedding and floor rugs with little gattina, the same girl who'd followed him around like a pest with his sister for a good chunk of his years growing up.

But she looked very different than that little girl right now. In fact, there was nothing girlish about her. The lanky teen she'd once been had grown into a strikingly attractive young woman. He'd tried hard not to notice those changes over the years. It was harder to do so now in such proximity.

Maybe this living-together thing wasn't such a great idea, after all.

He studied her from the corner of his eye while she sat stern side, her gaze studying the distant horizon. Long, chestnut brown hair secured in a tight ponytail. So tight it seemed to be pulling at the skin around her face. A collared sleeveless shirt atop pressed capri pants. Sensible leather flat-heeled shoes adorned her feet. She looked like she could be going into the office for a day full of meetings.

Did the woman even know she was on vacation?

He would have to make sure she realized it at some point. Tell her to relax, loosen up a bit.

Not that it was any of his business. He had enough to deal with on his own plate.

Still, he couldn't help but wonder what had brought her out here. Alone. And she certainly didn't seem to be in vacation mode just yet. Rather than getting away, Marni looked to be running away from something.

His thoughts led him to remember the last time he'd seen her before this trip. She'd been thin to the point of looking gaunt, dark circles had framed her eyes, her lips continually thinned in a worried line. When he'd asked his sister if Marni was okay, Nella had alluded to a bad relationship. In fact, the look on his sister's face had turned downright murderous when she'd answered his question.

What kind of demons was Marni running from? Were they as bad as his?

Suddenly, he felt like a jerk for the way he'd reacted when she'd scoffed about putting on the life jacket. He could have been gentler. But he wasn't going to risk her well-being in any way. He of all people knew how a split-second moment of carelessness could result in a monumental catastrophe with a lifetime of dire consequences.

Not on his watch. Not this time.

A chuckle rose out of him when he recalled how she'd reacted, challenging him to inspect the life jacket. How tempted he'd been to do just that. To run his fingers down her throat with the pretense of checking the clasps' tightness. To tug her tight ponytail out from beneath the vest, then run his hands through the thick, curly waves.

Whoa. Gio gave his head a shake.

"What is it?" Marni asked.

"Huh?"

She smiled at him. "You were just laughing at something," she said. "Can I get in on the joke?"

He certainly couldn't tell her where his mind had really been.

You see, Marni, I was thinking about the way your skin might feel under my fingertips, how the strands of your hair might flow over my hands, the way you smell of lemon and rose and some combination of spice I can't quite name.

No, definitely wouldn't go over well. Gio scrambled for a response. But it was hard to think with the way Marni was smiling at him as the sunlight danced along her eyes and glimmered in her hair.

What was wrong with him?

No matter. He just had to stop. Best way would be reverting to his go-to behavior when it came to Marni. Teasing her like an older cousin might.

"If you must know," he began, "I was thinking how you look like you're about to go to a board meeting as opposed to spending a carefree day on a Mediterranean island in one of the most gorgeous countries on earth."

Her mouth fell open. "What's that supposed to mean?"

He shrugged, and turned his gaze back to the water. "Start with your shoes for example."

She lifted one elegant leg and looked at her foot. "What's wrong with my shoes?"

"I think Nonno Santino owned a pair just like that, but in taupe."

She dropped her chin to her chest, glaring at him. Okay, maybe he was being a bit over-the-top. In truth, his *nonno* had worn nothing but tennis shoes.

"I'll have you know, these are quite comfortable," Marni protested.

"Is that why you shook sand out of them twice already?"

"I didn't know we'd be walking along the beach, now did I?" Her voice rose just enough to convey annoyance and irritation while remaining steady. "You could have mentioned we'd be taking a boat into town before we'd left the villa."

He nodded. "I could have. And you could have dressed less like a librarian about to begin a full shift."

Marni crossed her arms in front of her chest. "Yeah? What about the way you're dressed?" She gestured toward him with a fling of her hand.

Gio looked down at his wrinkled T-shirt, hip-hugging sports shorts and loose leather sandals. "What about it?"

"We're about to enter one of the most elegant shopping centers in Europe and you're wearing what could best be described as 'frat boy who caught the wrong flight heading to spring break.'"

Gio couldn't help it, he threw his head back and laughed at her put-down. "Touché, little gattina. Touché."

Good for her, she was giving it right back.

She'd felt safe returning Gio's barbs. Marni knew his insults weren't really meant to wound her. A world of difference existed between the way Ander's constant criticisms were delivered and Gio's good-natured joking. She was surprised she even remembered how to verbally defend herself. Leave it to Gio Santino to remind her.

Forget that she'd been totally disingenuous when teasing Gio about his appearance.

The truth was, he somehow managed to look handsome and polished despite his beyond casual attire. No one in their right mind would ever confuse Gio for an out-of-place college student. No, even dressed in a T-shirt and sandals, he looked every bit the successful tycoon and CEO of a global corporation that he was. Now, as they disembarked from the boat and made their way down the sidewalk path along the street of shops, it was clear she wasn't the only woman nearby who appreciated Gio's looks.

Tall, dark, with an angular jaw and toned, muscular body. His hair just long enough to reach his shoulders in dark waves…

Just stop.

This was not the time or place to be admiring Gio's looks or sex appeal. Heavens! Why had she even thought that last part?

Yanking her thoughts from such dangerous territory, Marni focused instead on her surroundings. Glamorous designer boutiques, mouthwatering bakery window displays, the tangy scent of citrus in the air as they passed a limoncello store. They were on a mission with a goal right now, but she made a mental note to come back into town soon and visit every one of these delightful places. Such a shame that she'd be doing so alone. The only reason Gio was here with her now was to pick out the bed one of them would be sleeping in. He'd have no incentive to play tour guide or tourist and return here with her afterward. Hadn't they agreed that the only way the cohabitation would work was to do their best to stay out of each other's way?

If that thought had her feeling downbeat and lonely, then it was no one's fault but her own. Gio wasn't her guardian. He didn't owe her anything, including his time.

Deep in thought, she nearly walked into Gio's solid back before realizing he'd stopped in front of the revolving glass door of a shop.

"This is it," he announced, then pulled the door open for her.

It was like walking into her own version of heaven. Beautiful works of art in the form of handcrafted wood furniture greeted them inside. It was hard to decide which item to study first: the beautiful bookshelf with the mahogany trim? Or the three-drawer bureau with the intricate carvings. Or maybe the standing mirror with the cherrywood base.

She was startled by a pair of snapping fingers right in her line of vision.

"Earth to Marni. You in there, Ms. Payton?"

She blinked to focus on Gio's face just inches from hers, expecting to find impatient annoyance in his impression. Instead, she found him smiling widely at her.

"Sorry, I was just admiring all the craftsmanship."

He dropped his hand, the grin still framing his lips. "I'll say. I've never seen such pleasure flood a woman's face so quickly. Not from just walking into a store, anyway." He winked at her mischievously.

Marni's mouth went dry at the innuendo. Before she could recover enough to formulate an answer, Gio had turned on his heel and walked farther into the store.

If she didn't know any better, she would think Gio Santino might be flirting with her. Which was preposterous.

In all their years of knowing one another, not once had Gio even hinted at any kind of attraction toward her, while she'd harbored a crush on and off for as long as she could remember. It didn't mean anything. Gio couldn't help himself. It was simply his nature to be charming and flirtatious. She just happened to be the only one in his vicinity at the moment. Giving her head a shake, she forced her focus back on the matter at hand: the furniture. They were here to pick something out of this gallery of masterpieces. Something told her she was going to be absolutely torn when it came to settling on just one item.

Despite her professionally trained eye, she felt like the kid in a candy store who wanted to grab everything and run home with her stash. She took her time making her way to where Gio stood, delicately trailing her fingers along the finished lines of the pieces in her path. When she reached his side, he pointed to a bed frame to his left. "What about that one?" he asked.

"What about it?"

He turned to squint at her. "Should we get that one?" he asked, as if his question should have been obvious.

Marni could only shake her head and laugh. He was approaching this outing as if they were replacing the milk carton in the fridge. Poor soul, he had no idea that they'd be in here for at least an hour, more likely much longer than that while she put a room together that would feel both cozy and pleasing to the eye of whoever inhabited it.

She shook her head at him. "Gio. You don't just come into a place like this and point."

His eyes narrowed on her face. "Why ever not? How else would we pick something?"

"We don't just pick something."

More narrowing of the eyes. "We don't?"

"No. We think about what we want the room to feel like for the inhabitant."

He crossed his arms in front of his chest. "Huh. I'd say it should feel like there's a sturdy piece of furniture in there to be able to sleep on after the day is over."

Of course, he would simplify it that way. "Okay. But beyond that, what do we want to feel when we enter that room? Warmth? Comfort? A sense of solitude?"

Gio rubbed his chin. "I'd say all of the above."

Marni threw her hands in the air. This was hopeless. She turned to walk further toward the back of the store. Gio followed close on her heels. After several moments of browsing, she could practically feel the impatience resonating off Gio's body.

"Fine," she heard him say behind her. "What about this one?"

He had to be kidding. He was pointing to a small child's bed designed to look like a pirate ship. "You can't be serious. You wouldn't even fit in that."

"When did we decide that I'd be the one to have to take the new room?"

Huh. He had a point. She hadn't actually considered that.

"Look," Gio continued. "At this point, I'd settle for a cot and a throw pillow. We've been in here for how many hours already?"

Marni made a show of lifting her wrist and staring at her watch. "We've been in here fifteen minutes."

Gio rubbed his forehead. "Huh. I was exaggerating but it feels longer than just a few minutes."

Marni sighed. As much as she wanted to linger in here,

Gio had clearly reached the end of his patience. "Fine. I think your pirate ship just might have given me an idea."

Gio smiled wide, clearly pleased with himself. "Oh, yeah? How so?"

She gave him the "follow me" sign with her finger. "Here, I'll show you." The bed frame she led him to had tall posts above the headboard, and then she pointed out a round-framed mirror that could easily be accented to look like a porthole window. Rather than bedside tables for the lamps, she picked out two wooden coffers that, with the right studding, could be made to look like treasure chests.

"What do you think?" she asked Gio, after they'd gotten a chance to look at all the pieces.

"Huh. It will be like the bottom of an old-fashioned ship."

She smiled at him. "Maybe even like a pirate ship."

Gio tilted his head, examining her. "I like it, gattina. Well done!"

Marni felt a fluttering in her chest at his approval. It made no sense. She'd simply done what she was trained to do. So how utterly silly of her to feel so giddy at having pleased him.

Unlike the sparse compliments her ex threw her way from time to time, Gio's appreciation of her talent sounded genuine.

She'd almost forgotten what that felt like.

Gio signed the paperwork for the sale of the pieces Marni had picked out and led her out of the store twenty minutes later. For all the complaining he'd done in there, he had to begrudgingly admit that he'd actually enjoyed himself. Observing the way Marni's mind worked out a theme and put together a design had been more entertaining than he would have guessed. Watching her work had exposed him to a side of her he hadn't witnessed or even thought about before. She was smart, talented and had a clear enthusiasm for her chosen field.

Envy blossomed in his chest. He was a man of wealth and vast resources, but despite all his professional success, he couldn't recall the last time he'd felt accomplished and fulfilled.

Most times, he simply felt empty. Directionless.

Maybe that was why he took so many risks with his life, both physically and financially. Simply to *feel* something on any scale. It was that recklessness that had led him to fast cars and racing. Look how that had turned up. He'd damaged his body and hurt an innocent bystander to boot.

"Where to now?" Marni asked, pulling him out of the black hole of his thoughts.

In perfect timing, his stomach answered with a short growl. Marni's chuckle in response had him laughing as well. "How about we grab a bite?"

She pointed to his midsection. "I don't dare argue after that."

Within minutes they were seated at an outside table of Pescare Delfino seafood restaurant. Later afternoon had turned the sky a bluish gray. Two servers in black bow ties and buttoned vests appeared at their table before they'd so much as pulled in their chairs. One lit a large round candle in the centerpiece while the other poured limoncello in two small shot glasses.

Gio ordered a bottle of his favorite Pinot Grigio then held up his glass of limoncello once both waiters had left. "A toast."

Marni lifted her drink and clinked it to his. "What are we toasting to?" she asked.

"We are now officially roommates. For one."

They both took a sip of the refreshing liqueur, though Marni's could be described as more of a drop. Probably smart. The limoncello in Italy could be potent.

"What else?" Marni asked.

"To your stellar skills as an interior decorator. I'm sure you'll reach the highest pinnacles of success with your talent."

Something flashed behind her eyes, a darkness that shadowed the light that had been behind them since they'd first entered the furniture store.

"Um...thanks," she murmured, setting her glass down without another drink. She looked off into the distance.

Was it something he said? Gio had only meant to pay her a compliment.

Gio went the feigned ignorance route. "Do you not like the limoncello?" he asked, knowing full well that disappointment in her drink wasn't what had dimmed the brightness in her eyes from just moments before.

She immediately shook her head. "No. It's delicious. I guess I'm just hungry."

Sure. That wasn't the issue either. Talking about her professional success had completely soured her mood. Did her career have anything to do with why she was here in Capri for the next several days? Maybe a job she'd done had gone wrong and her ego had taken a hit.

Well, he wasn't one to push. Marni clearly didn't want to talk about her job. That was fine since he definitely didn't want to talk about his accident.

And if he ignored the pain and fought hard enough to continue hiding the limp, he wouldn't have to.

Marni searched for a change of topic. She wasn't in the mood to discuss the train wreck that was her current professional situation. If Ander Stolis had his way, she'd be persona non grata in all the circles that mattered as far as the interior design profession was concerned. And he'd make sure that would be the case for the foreseeable future.

Served her right for falling for the lead architect of the firm she'd worked for. At first, Marni had thought their budding relationship was so romantic. An office romance. Exciting and slightly taboo. Just like in all those rom-coms. Little had she known, she'd be living more of a drama-tragedy.

"Do you know what you're having?" Gio asked across the table, breaking into her thoughts.

"A good heap of regret with a side of crow," she answered, then immediately clasped a hand to her mouth. What in the world was wrong with her? She hadn't meant to say the words out loud. The limoncello couldn't be that strong, for heaven's sake. She'd barely had one sip!

Gio reached out his arm across the table and covered her free hand with his.

"Hey, is everything all right with you?"

He asked so gently, with such care and interest, that Marni felt a lump of emotion form in her throat. She forced a smile on her lips. "I'm fine. Really."

He looked less than convinced and gave her wrist a small squeeze. His palm and fingers felt strong and warm over her hand. The eyes looking into hers held a wealth of concern. "You know you can tell me, gattina. If you want to."

Marni closed her eyes and blew out a deep breath. Gio didn't need to hear how stupid and blind she'd been. How she'd ignored all the warning signs as well as the good advice of her friends and family. The way she'd been certain she knew better than all the people who were only trying to protect her.

But it was so tempting to get some of it off her chest for once. "I made some bad decisions over this past year," she finally managed to answer. "Countless errors of judgment that caught up to me. The gist of it is that I trusted the wrong man."

Gio merely nodded, no judgment clouded his eyes, no subtle admonishment. That made it a bit easier for her to continue.

"I took longer than I should have to break things off with him. When I did, he used his considerable influence and high-profile contacts to smear my name and professional reputation."

She didn't miss the clench of Gio's fists on the table. "I see."

Swallowing, she continued. "He's a highly respected architect with several clients who are members of the media. I know it wouldn't be above him to sully my name in the professional magazines and websites. That's the last thing I need at this point in my career."

"That's why you're here."

She nodded. "That's right. Not only to get away from it all until people lose interest. But also to try and regroup. Figure out how to climb out from under the mountain of mistakes and all their consequences."

Gio swore. "I'm sorry, Marni. If it makes you feel any better, you don't have the corner on bad decisions." He gestured to his chest with his thumb. "Your new roomie here has made a few doozies himself."

Profound hurt resonated in his voice. Gio clearly had his own mountain to climb. Perhaps he would understand her predicament better than most.

Marni turned her hand over under his, reflexively intertwining her fingers with his so that they were holding hands atop the table. She didn't let go until the server arrived to take their order.

CHAPTER FOUR

A SURGE OF protectiveness so strong rushed through Gio that he had to will himself to clamp it down. Marni was gripping his hand as if starved for strength and comfort.

What a lousy stroke of luck for her. He hardly had either of those for himself. He should let go of her, pull his arm back by his side. Find a way to lighten this conversation that had suddenly grown so heavy and deep.

He wanted badly to ask more about the man who'd caused her such deep hurt. But it was her prerogative to share as much or as little as she was ready to. Still, the curiosity didn't settle well in his gut. It was no use trying to tell himself it was none of his business. This was Marni. She'd practically grown up with the Santinos as part of the family. She was the only child of a single mother, and Gio knew how much she'd endured to simply survive her younger years. They'd met her when her mom worked briefly for Santino Foods decades ago.

Despite Marni's disadvantages, she'd grown up to be a successful, confident woman with a list of accomplishments. He didn't know the details but someone had come along and ruined all that for her.

If he ever found out who it was and what exactly he'd done to her...

The waiter arrived with his scratch pad to take their order. They both pulled their hands away at the same moment; a rather awkward moment tempered only by the presence of their server.

When their salads arrived a few minutes later, that awkwardness still hung in the air. Finally, Marni was the one who broke the silence.

"You mentioned your own mistakes," she began, poking at the vegetables on her plate rather than eating any of them. "Do those mistakes have anything to do with your sleepless nights?"

Gio swallowed the plum tomato he'd been chewing, though not tasting. His mind juggled a confusion of thoughts. He didn't know how to talk about the accident and, so far, he hadn't wanted to with anyone. It was bad enough having to go through the details with every doctor and nurse who'd had to evaluate him in the days since. And he couldn't even quite remember all the details.

Where would he even begin to try and tell Marni? The reckless decision to race the car in the first place? How lucky he was that his passenger hadn't been killed? That the man may never walk again thanks to Gio?

Or maybe he could begin with how he might never have full use of his leg, no matter how many long hours of rehab he was made to endure. The dull ache in his thigh muscle mocked his train of thought. Marni picked up on his hesitation.

"You don't have to tell me," she said. "But know that you

can," she added. "Same goes for you, because I'm little gattina, remember? Your sister's old friend."

Gio forced a smile he didn't feel. The trouble was, he was starting to view Marni as less and less of his little sister's old friend with each passing moment.

Such a dangerous development. Because the way he *was* beginning to view her spelled nothing but trouble for them both.

On the boat ride back to the villa, the early evening sky had turned navy, full of twinkling bright stars. The day had gone by in the blink of an eye. As tired as she was, Marni didn't quite want it to end. The hours she'd spent in town with Gio had been the most relaxed she'd been since her "walk of shame" through the office hallway. A shudder racked her body at the memory.

"You cold?" Gio asked, mistaking her shiver for physical discomfort.

He took her silence as a positive answer. Lifting open a center console, he removed a thick, zippered hoodie bearing the logo of the Los Angeles Angels across its back. He draped it over her shoulders, giving them a squeeze for good measure. Though it should have felt bulky and uncomfortable over the life jacket, Marni found herself snuggling into the soft fabric. It smelled of him: spicy, woodsy and oh so masculine. She buried her face in the collar, inhaling as she did so.

Suddenly horrified that Gio might have witnessed the small action, she yanked the fabric off her face. A glance in his direction told her he hadn't seen. He was focused on guiding the boat back to their destination. Marni breathed a sigh of relief. That was much too close. She'd be beyond embarrassed if Gio had any hint of her reemerging girlish crush.

It couldn't happen. Her emotions were already strung tight. She had no business crushing on a man so far beyond her reach. Sure, he was easy to talk to and they had a history of being friends. She felt lighter after having confided in him as much as she had about her fiasco of a relationship.

But their differences were plenty. Gio was several years older, and had been linked to women like starlets and models and heiresses. She knew better than to pine for someone like him. She'd just turned twenty-six last month for Pete's sake. She was too old for a schoolgirl crush. How had she not grown out of it already? Then there were the close familial ties. She wouldn't be able to bear it if there was tension between her and the Santino clan for any reason whatsoever.

No, better to just ignore her feelings and hope they went away.

It was just her mind trying to distract her. It had to be. Her brain was trying to stall figuring out all the things she had to deal with as soon as she got back to reality. Like how she might begin to restore her professional reputation. Whether she wanted to remain in Boston or relocate so she could put the past year behind her and move forward with her life.

Then there was the dream of starting her own design business. If she had the wherewithal or the resources or even the motivation to attempt such an undertaking. Another failure might completely undo her.

She was so deep in her thoughts, she hadn't even realized Gio had docked the boat and dropped anchor.

"You're not falling asleep on me, are you?" he asked.

"Guess that dinner was more filling than I thought, not to mention the strong cocktail. I do feel pretty lethargic."

"Then you're in luck," he told her while he finished securing the boat. "Because I happen to make a mean cappuccino. Not too strong, with plenty of frothy milk. It'll perk you right up without keeping you up all night."

Maybe it was wishful thinking, but it sounded as if Gio didn't quite want the night to end either.

"Sounds great." She decided to broach the subject they still hadn't gotten around to solving until the new furniture arrived. "I think you should sleep in the room tonight," she began as they made their way up the stone steps. "I'll be perfectly fine on the couch cushions."

Gio immediately shook his head. "Absolutely not. The bed is all yours."

She wasn't the least bit surprised that he'd immediately refused the offer. "It's only fair," she tried to argue. "I had it last night."

Gio didn't answer until they reached the top of the cliffside. He took her by the shoulders and turned her to him. "Marni. I'm not even sleeping for any stretch of time. Wasting the bed on me doesn't make sense."

Marni knew any further argument would be useless. With a sigh of resignation, she followed him down the path that led to Nella's villa. When they got to the house, Gio fired up the espresso machine while she indulged in a hot shower. He had a steaming mug waiting for her when she emerged a little while later.

"Want to enjoy these outside by the pool?"

That sounded like a delightful idea. Nella's outdoor lounge chairs were so plush and comfortable. And the night was warm with a soft, gentle breeze. Marni couldn't think of a single reason to turn down his offer.

"Lead the way," she answered, taking her cappuccino in hand.

Marni winced when they reached the patio and she eyed her tablet still sitting on the cushion. She'd forgotten her device out here when they'd left earlier. "Darn it."

"What's the matter?"

"I meant to charge that. Hopefully there's enough battery left."

"For what?" Gio asked, dropping onto one of the other chaise lounges.

She ducked shyly. "Don't laugh. But there's a Bollywood show I'm addicted to. I downloaded the latest episode and was looking forward to watching it later tonight."

"A bolly what now?"

She had to laugh at his confusion. "Bollywood. Filmed in India. The script is full of drama and intrigue with lots of song and dance thrown in for good measure."

"How do you understand it?"

She shrugged. "Captions, of course. It's like reading and enjoying an engrossing movie at the same time. You should try it."

Gio gave her a skeptical look. "I don't know. It doesn't really sound like my genre of entertainment."

Marni flipped the lid of her tablet and turned on the device. To her surprise and delight, she had a good amount of battery life left.

Pulling a chaise lounge next to him, she called up the show. "Here. Just try a few minutes. You might be surprised."

He tilted his head. "Sure. Why not. What else have I got to do?" he asked then scooched his chair closer while she touched the play icon. "Just don't tell my sister, or anyone else for that matter, that you talked me into watching a foreign film with captions."

Marni pressed her fingers to her mouth. "My lips are sealed. Our secret."

Gio shifted in the lounge chair and kicked out his legs to give them a good stretch. On instinct, he braced himself for the sharp pain that was sure to shoot down his thigh at any second. But the ache stayed dull and low. That was different. Usually, no matter how gentle the stretch, it always resulted in knifelike pain for several seconds.

In surprise, he blinked one eye open. Huh. The sun was out. But how could that be? The last thing he remembered, he and Marni were watching something on her tablet. A show it would normally never occur to him to watch. It had been close to midnight when the last thing he remembered—a funny dance number—had come on.

Which meant he must have fallen asleep right here. Outside on the lounge chair. More surprisingly, he'd apparently stayed asleep until sunrise…for several hours. A rarity that hadn't happened since the accident.

So that was a bit of stunning news that would take some processing.

It was when he tried to rise that he noticed an unfamiliar weight snuggled against his side. That could only mean one thing. Forcing both eyes open, Gio bit down on a groan at the sight that greeted him. He hadn't been the only one to fall asleep out here. Marni was snuggled against his length, her eyes closed shut in slumber.

Don't you dare react. Don't so much as move.

Not yet. He had no idea what he might say to Marni if she were to wake up right now. He was having trouble putting it all together himself. Besides, what would be the harm in letting her get some more rest? Something told him Marni had had her own share of restless nights recently.

He thought back to the dinner they'd shared the night before, the strain in her voice when she'd talked about her hurtful relationship, the way her lips had grown tight, her eyes clouded over with sadness. She'd trusted the wrong man. Hardly the first woman to do so. At least she hadn't made the kind of mistake that had almost cost someone else their life.

Sweet gattina, how hard are you punishing yourself anyway?

A seagull soared overhead, suddenly dropping to land on the patio by their feet. The noise was enough to have Marni stirring in his arms. Maybe he was being cowardly, but Gio immediately shut his eyes and feigned sleep. Why not spare them both some awkward embarrassment if it could be helped?

He sensed the moment she must have opened her eyes and discovered their positions. He felt her whole body go tense, a small gasp sounded beneath his ear. It took all his will not to open his eyes out of sheer curiosity. It might be worth it to see the expression on her face.

Gio felt her move softly out of his arms and scramble off the chair. The seagull squawked above and he almost reflexively opened his eyes in response. But somehow managed to continue the pretense until he heard the screen door leading to the house open before it softly shut closed again.

He gave her a good twenty minutes before finally following her inside. Marni stood at the counter of the kitchen, brewing tea. She'd changed into a pair of loose gray sweats and a tunic-length shirt that fell low off one shoulder to reveal a small triangle of smooth skin. His nerve endings tingled as he recalled how that skin had felt in his arms moments ago.

How the woman managed to look so sexy in sweats and a loose T-shirt, with her hair a tangled mess, Gio couldn't explain. Her eyes grew wide when she saw him.

"Morning," Gio said before she could speak. "Can you believe I fell asleep outside?" He shook his head as if amused with himself. "I must have been so tired."

Marni nodded. "Actually, I—"

He pretended not to hear her as he made a show of stretching his arms overhead while executing a perfectly believable loud yawn. Maybe one day they would laugh about the way they'd fallen asleep in each other's arms. He just didn't have it in him to do it today. Not after the way he'd reacted to having her body so close to his. Something told him Marni wouldn't be up for such a conversation either. "Hard to believe, but it's the best night's sleep I've had in forever."

"Huh."

He dropped his arms. "Guess I'll go take a shower."

She blinked several times in rapid succession but didn't say anything: Bingo. He'd been right. Marni was just as content to ignore the fact that they'd fallen asleep in each other's arms as he was. What was the point in dwelling on it? It wasn't as if anything physical had happened between them, after all. No boundaries had been breached whatsoever. And thank God for that. He had enough to deal with right now without crossing any lines with his kid sister's best friend. Nella's warning echoed in his head. *If you do anything to hurt her or make her uncomfortable...*

He pointed to the kettle, which started steaming. "Can you spare some of that for me when I get back?"

Marni nodded. "Of course, I'll have a mug waiting for you."

"Thanks."

See, all casual. Nothing amiss. Just two old friends who happened to be sharing the same living space for a few days. Then they would both go their separate ways and this would just be one more memory of Marni Payton that he'd add to all the other ones.

No one had to know that the shower he'd be taking would be a cold one.

Gio stood under the steaming hot spray, relishing the soothing flow of water over his skin. After a punishing blast of it at ice cold to get his libido under control, he'd turned the nozzle completely the opposite way to the hottest setting.

Not that the cooler water had helped at all. His mind kept going back to that one exposed shoulder. The way the tunic shirt had draped her curves in all the right places.

The way she'd felt in his arms when he'd awakened to find her nuzzled against his side.

Gio swore and pushed the wayward thoughts away, then squeezed more of the soap onto his hand. He usually massaged his sore leg every morning in the shower, the one piece of medical advice he'd taken so far. But the bruised and tattered muscles still felt remarkably less sore.

Had he taken a pain pill and forgotten? No. He hadn't been that out of it. Besides, he did his best to avoid the pills unless he was in absolute agony. The more likely scenario was that he'd done less thrashing about with his legs because he'd subconsciously known that he'd disturb Marni. Or maybe one good night of sleep at last had done both his spirit and body a world of good. Somehow, falling asleep next to Marni while watching a fun, mindless show had given him that rare gift.

Gio sighed and braced his hands against the tile wall. Too bad it couldn't happen again.

Spending time with her was good for him, there was no denying. But there was no way he was going to take advantage of her for his own selfish needs.

The truth was, on his best day, he wouldn't have been worthy of Marni Payton. And these days he was far from his best. Not since the race that had changed him forever.

Before he could suppress them, an onslaught of visions flooded his brain. Losing control of the wheel, veering off at too high a speed toward the other car. The flash of light as the flames burst forth.

He knew he was lucky to be alive. But he felt a mere partial version of the man he used to be. Why would he subject any woman to what his future had waiting for him? Countless days in therapy. A permanent limp. The certain frustration and resulting poor temperament all that was sure to bring out in him.

No. Marni deserved better than that. She deserved better than *him*.

Why was he even traveling down this road of thought?

He and Marni as any kind of item were out of the question. He had enough to figure out about his own life without the complication of a romantic relationship. Let alone with someone who meant as much to his family as Marni did.

Nella had warned him about not pursuing this very thing.

That was it. The shower was doing nothing to relax him at this point. Rather than soothing him in any way, now the steam felt oppressively hot and the stall felt suffocating. He pushed aside the glass door and grabbed the thick Turkish towel he'd hung up before his shower.

His phone sounded an alert in the other room. One he'd assigned to his assistant.

Might want to check your email, boss.

Gio did as her message said then cursed out loud. A reporter for New England magazine was asking questions about the accident again after all this time. The last thing Juno needed as he tried to recover was any kind of media attention. The man deserved his privacy as he healed. Gio had to find a way to shut this down as soon as possible.

He was about to text a reply when another message appeared on his screen. This one from his sister.

How are you today?

Honestly, she had to stop asking him that. He wasn't even going to bother to respond to the question. He asked one of his own instead.

Do you know when the new furniture might arrive?

The floating bubbles appeared on the screen once more.

No update yet.

Gio pinched the bridge of his nose and sighed. Nella was still typing.

But I just got word that there's a villa available to buy. If you're still interested in getting your own place in Capri.

CHAPTER FIVE

WELL, IF SHE'D harbored any illusions that Gio was in any way affected by her, she'd been proven sorely mistaken.

He hadn't even noticed her presence next to him last night. She might as well have been a teddy bear he'd been cuddling.

Whereas she couldn't stop thinking about the feeling of being in his arms, the warmth of his body surrounding hers. The scent of him filling her senses when she'd awakened with her head on his chest.

Now she couldn't seem to stop thinking about him upstairs in the shower. Surrounded by steam, water and soapy suds flowing down his hardened muscles.

Marni groaned out loud. This couldn't be happening. She couldn't be reviving her childhood crush, it was completely one-sided. It had to be. Gio may have seemed to be flirting with her sometimes, but that was just his nature, it was how he reacted with any woman in his vicinity.

How could she be lusting after a man who hadn't even realized he'd fallen asleep with her against his side?

Her breath hitched in her throat when she heard him shut

the door upstairs and make his way down the stairs. If she was going to squelch this crush, she would have to start with not becoming breathless when she so much as heard the man. He entered the kitchen a moment later, looking fresh and clean, his hair damp. He smelled of pine and mint and his own distinctive masculine scent.

She greeted him with what she hoped was a convincingly friendly smile. "Just in time. Your tea was about to get cold."

"Would have come down sooner, but I was delayed."

"Oh?"

"Nella messaged. Says hello. She tried to call you but I guess you haven't set up your phone yet."

She'd meant to. But she'd been much too distracted last night and this morning. By him.

"I'll make sure to get ahold of her later."

"Sounds good." He took a sip of his tea. "So, how'd you sleep?"

Was it her imagination, or was there a slight smirk to his lips when he asked the question? As if he was teasing her about something.

Maybe Marni was wrong to assume that he wasn't aware of their sleeping positions last night. She felt a slight heat creep up to her cheeks. Well, she certainly wasn't going to bring it up. She'd be horrified if she was wrong.

Besides, Gio was always teasing her in one way or another.

Better to just change the subject. "Too bad we're all out of those yummy pastries from yesterday." It wasn't as if she was lying, she wouldn't exactly turn down a croissant right now.

He shrugged. "We can always go get some more."

"Too wicked, isn't it? To have rich, sugary pastries two days in a row?"

Gio threw his head back and laughed. He winked at her when his gaze met hers again. "Darling, you and I have very different ideas about what we would define as *wicked*."

See, there it was. She was right. He only enjoyed teasing her. It was just his personality.

"Weren't you and Nella having junk food–laden movie nights not that long ago? I seem to recall walking into the viewing room at the house to find the two of you surrounded by snacks and candy. You didn't seem to think rich and sugary were wicked back then. What's changed?"

She ducked her head. He was too observant by far. "It's a rather recent habit. One I'm trying my best to unlearn."

Gio set his mug down. His eyes roamed over her face, full of concern. She shouldn't have given him such a loaded answer. Maybe one day she'd tell him about how Ander had even tried to control her eating habits. But she didn't have it in her right now.

Before he could ask anything more, she jumped off her stool and flashed him another wide smile. "You're right. I am on vacation and can have all the pastries I desire. Finish your tea and let's go get some."

Gio opened his mouth, clearly about to press her, but must have decided against it. He took a long swallow of his drink then offered her his arm. "Let's go."

He led her past the pool and patio area to the stone steps leading to the beach.

"What a gorgeous morning," Marni remarked. It was the truth. Crystal blue water crashed gently against golden sparkling sand in soft waves. A bright, round sun sat majestically above a cloudless horizon. As far as small talk went, it was a handy topic.

What she really wanted to do was ask him about the obvious limp he was trying so desperately to hide. And if it had anything to do with his nightmares and tortured sleep. He must have forgotten how well she knew him after all these years. The Gio she remembered from before this trip was characterized by a flurry of activity. He'd always been a man who moved quickly, never one to sit still or stroll leisurely, no matter the circumstances. That version of Gio would have challenged her to a race down the beach.

How could he think she wouldn't notice the difference?

So maybe he'd overdone it with the amount of pastries he'd ordered. Two of everything the stand offered might have been a bit much.

Silently, he handed Marni another biscotti after she'd finished the sugared almond croissant. She sat on a big boulder, her legs dangling inches off the ground while he leaned his back against it. Gio tried hard to focus on his breakfast but it was hard not to stare at Marni. Her hair had come loose, that all too enticing shoulder remained exposed and there was a smidge of powdered sugar above her lip. It took all the will he had not to reach over and rub it off with his thumb. Or maybe with his mouth.

Instead, he silently handed her a napkin from inside the box. She dabbed at her lips and the smidge disappeared. Thank God for lessened temptation.

A seagull flew overhead, past sandy beach and over the water. Marni shielded her eyes, watching its flight. She sighed deeply. "I know I keep talking about what a beautiful morning it is, but it really is picture-perfect. Like something out of a painting."

"I can't recall a single day it's rained in the week since I got here."

"You were right, Capri is paradise."

"It really is. I'm actually thinking of getting my own place here." He hadn't even realized he'd meant to share that with her.

She snapped her head in his direction. "How exciting, Gio! I think you should do it."

He bit down on the last of his biscotti, licked the crumbs off his thumb. "Nella mentioned a villa that's up for sale right now. Maybe we can look at it together."

Her mouth formed a small O in surprise. "I'd really like that. Just say when."

He couldn't quite place why, but somehow the moment had grown heavy. Something pivotal had just happened. Though he wouldn't be able to articulate why. Other than the understanding there was something rather intimate about viewing houses together. Something personal.

Gio gave his head a shake. He was being ridiculous. Two friends checking out a villa one of them might buy was purely platonic. Why in the world was he overanalyzing everything all of a sudden when it came to Marni?

"That was delicious," she finally declared after several more moments of chewing, steering the conversation back to lighter fare. "But I think I need to work off some of this sugar high."

Bouncing off the boulder, he watched as she removed her sandals and rolled up her capri pants to above her knees. Then she skipped, actually skipped, toward the water. A chuckle rose out of his chest at the image.

"You coming?" she asked with barely a backward glance.

He couldn't think of a single reason not to.

Kicking off his own sandals, he followed her into the crashing waves. She playfully kicked a splash of water in his direction when he reached her side, just enough to wet the bottom trim of his sports shorts.

"Why, Miss Payton," Gio began in a mock-serious tone. "How utterly childish of you."

Her response was a hearty laugh while she did it once more, getting him wetter this time.

He didn't mind. It was a dry, warm and sunny day. The water felt refreshing on his skin. He tried to think of the last time he'd been on the beach, simply frolicking in the water. Not a single instance came to mind. Not even from his childhood. In his before life, he'd have dived into the waves and began a series of laps, pushing himself harder and harder with each one.

What exactly had he been pushing for all those times?

"I wish I'd brought a swimsuit," Marni said, though she seemed to be getting rather wet enough despite being fully clothed.

"We can always come back."

She nodded with enthusiasm. "Yes! Let's do that. But I don't want to leave just yet."

Neither did he. In fact, he could stand out here and watch her frolicking in the water for hours. The thought both annoyed and amused him. What would he be doing right now if Marni had never arrived at the villa? No doubt, he'd be sitting at Nella's patio table poring over a spreadsheet or making phone calls. He certainly wouldn't be kicking around on the beach after having gorged on pastries.

When he looked up again, Marni had rolled her pants up higher, clear up to the tops of her thighs. She was several feet deeper in the water, much farther away than where he stood near the sand. A particular large wave appeared out of nowhere at that very moment.

Marni seemed to lose her footing as it crashed into her legs. Gio's vision blurred. There was no way he could reach her if she toppled over and got dragged under the water. Was Marni a proficient swimmer? How did he not know?

His heart hammered in his chest as he leaped to try and reach her before she could fall. With his bruised leg and weakened arm, he might not be able to pull her out if she went under and got in trouble. He'd barely made it to her side when he realized that not only had she remained upright, she was bent over laughing, her shoulders shaking with mirth.

Relief surged through him but it was quickly replaced by fury. What if she *had* fallen, what if the wave had taken her under and she'd been caught in the current.

"Did you see that?" she asked him, with amusement dancing in her eyes.

"Yeah. I saw how reckless and foolish you just were." Gio spit out the words, both unable and unwilling to temper his tone. She could have gotten seriously hurt. Or worse. And he would have been nearly helpless to do anything about it.

Her brows furrowed together, confusion clouding her eyes. "What?"

"You could have fallen in the water, Marni. I don't know how strong the current is." He thrust a hand through his hair. "I can't even remember if you're a good swimmer."

A slight breeze blew over Marni's skin as she exited the water. Goose bumps rose along her arms and legs but she couldn't tell if it was from the cold or the sheer terror she'd just witnessed on Gio's face. He was a step behind her when she turned to face him.

"Gio. What just happened? What got into you?" She

tucked a wet curl of hair behind her ear. "All those vacations to Cape Cod I took with your family. Those three times I tagged along to the Bahamas with you all. How can you not remember if I can swim?"

Gio huffed out a breath of air and closed his eyes. "I just got nervous in the moment, all right? I thought you might get hurt and I wasn't sure if I'd be able to—" He looked away, never finishing the sentence.

She reached for him then, placing her hand on his forearm. He honestly had been frightened for her. Not that she could surmise why for the life of her. "You had to know I wasn't in any real danger."

Only he clearly hadn't known. "I just—" He broke off again, at an obvious loss for words. Marni found herself torn between genuine curiosity about what was going on with him and the need to be sensitive to his boundaries. If he didn't want to share with her what was causing all these changes in him, who was she to push?

"Look, never mind," he said, turning away. "Let's just forget it happened, okay?"

Right. Like she had any hope of being able to do that.

"I think we should head back now," he announced, then didn't so much as spare another glance in her direction when he walked away.

Marni clenched her hands tight at her sides. She had no reason to feel guilty about how the morning had suddenly gone so sour. She hadn't done anything wrong. She refused to accept the burden of responsibility when it wasn't hers to bear. She'd made a vow to rid herself of the habit when she'd left Ander for good. He'd blamed her for anything and everything that had gone wrong in his life or career. No more.

Whatever Gio had plaguing him at this juncture in

his life—and she felt for him, she really did because he was obviously dealing with something major and life-changing—she just didn't have it in her to play the fall guy. Not anymore.

They walked the rest of the way in silence, only broken when Gio handed their remaining pastries to a young mother visiting the beach with her two toddlers. The children hopped up and down with glee when they dug into the box.

A pang of longing shot through her chest as she watched the scene. The mom looked harried and tired, but happy to be with her children. She didn't know if she'd ever have that. Not with the mess her last relationship had turned out to be. She mentally scoffed. What was it with her and her faulty judgment when it came to men? Look at her inconvenient crush on current company. It was wrong enough on the surface, given their past history. But especially now considering whatever was going on with Gio that had him acting so uncharacteristically.

When they reached the house, she didn't bother to let him know that she'd be heading to the shower to clean up and dry off. It would probably be better if they spent the day apart. Obviously, it had been a mistake to deviate from the original plan on day one: stay out of each other's way. Well, she knew better now. Another vow she'd made was to stop making the same mistakes over and over.

Marni took her time in the shower. The stall smelled of him, his aftershave, his soap. The woodsy scent of the shampoo he used. How many times had she imagined running her fingers through the mass of dark curls that fell over his forehead. How often had she resisted the temptation to lean closer to him and inhale deeply of the minty scent of that aftershave?

She was heading down a dubious path here. Maybe it was just as well that they'd had that little falling-out at the beach. It served as a stark reminder that she needed to keep herself in check when it came to Gio Santino.

Still, she couldn't help the temptation to reach for her new phone when she returned to the bedroom and noticed it was finally fully charged. She knew Nella's number by heart.

If her friend had wanted her to know what was really going on with her brother, wouldn't she have told her by now? Although Marni had to admit Nella might have been hesitant to burden her with her family problems given all that Marni had been dealing with the past few months. Maybe that's why Nella hadn't said anything about Gio.

Marni reached for the phone and dialed the first three numbers before she hesitated. Rubbing a hand down her face, she tossed it onto the mattress and plopped down on the edge. No, she couldn't do it. She refused to call her best friend to ask her to dish about her older brother. How middle school cringe of her to even consider it.

Besides, didn't it also say quite a bit that he didn't trust her enough to tell her himself?

An hour later, try as she might, she couldn't stand to stay in the room any longer. This was silly. They could stay out of each other's way but they would still need to be civil over the next few days. Besides, she was thirsty. Marni would simply acknowledge him if she did run into him downstairs, explain that she hadn't meant any upset, get her drink and go about her day. But when she reached the first floor, Gio was sitting on the armchair facing the stairs, as if he was waiting for her.

He spoke before she could tell him any of the things she'd decided on upstairs. "Nella tells me you're a good listener."

Gio motioned with one hand to the love seat opposite where he sat. Marni forgot all about her thirst as she made her way into the sitting room and took a seat. They must have jinxed the weather the way they'd spoken about it earlier, because now the sky had grown dark and cloudy, throwing shadows on the walls. It fit the current mood perfectly.

Gio blew out a breath before speaking. "I scared you that first day you arrived. And I know I just scared you again earlier this morning," he began.

"You were concerned," Marni offered. "I under—"

Gio held up a hand to stop her before she could continue. "Please, just let me get through this. Before I have a chance to change my mind."

Marni nodded in agreement, remaining silent. Looked like she might finally be getting some answers, far be it from her to hamper that.

"You know I'm active in the various charities that Santino Foods sponsors."

"Yes, I know." As soon as he'd graduated college and joined the family company, Gio had taken on the responsibility of running the many charitable functions the family global company supported. But what did that have to do with anything that was happening with him now?

"There's an annual event called the Mangola Rally. It's a race across eastern Europe ending in a small town in Turkey. Santino Foods was asked to sponsor a racer. We would donate money and draw attention to benefit a good cause, in this case, a refugee crisis organization." He stopped to rub a hand across his eyes.

Marni waited for him to continue, not daring to interrupt.

Gio went on, "Rather than sponsor someone, I decided I would participate myself. I'd gotten into racing cars a couple years back. Had even come in first in a few amateur motorsport events. Felt pretty confident behind the wheel. It was for a good cause. Plus, it sounded like fun. So I convinced the organizers I was qualified."

"You always were one to take risks," she offered, not surprised in the least that he'd opted to participate himself.

Gio flinched at her words. Marni wanted to suck them back in somehow.

"Well, it was one risk too many it turns out."

Oh, no.

"About the halfway mark, somewhere in the roughly terrained vicinity of the Austrian border, I lost control of the car."

Gio squeezed his eyes shut as he continued. "I don't even know what happened. I must have hit a boulder, or some other obstruction. The car was going much too fast because I had to be the one who came in first, as usual. I couldn't regain control of the car no matter what I tried."

Gio's hands were clenched tight against his thighs. A muscle worked along his jaw. She hated that he was reliving this, especially considering it was for her sake.

He sucked in a breath and continued. "I must have hit my head at some point, I blacked out. When I came to, the car was upside down."

She could guess the rest. "Oh, Gio. I'm so very sorry." Try as she might, there was nothing else she could think of to say.

"One of the other drivers came upon us eventually and called for help."

Us? Had she heard him correctly?

"You weren't alone in the car?"

Gio went pale and a shadow crossed his eyes. "That's the worst part. I had a codriver in the car with me to navigate the route. A family man with small children."

Marni's blood grew cold. "Is he...?" She couldn't bring herself to finish the sentence. Lucky for her, she didn't have to.

Gio shook his head. "He survived. Thank God." He sucked in a gulp of air. "But there's a question as to whether he'll ever walk again. And that's on me."

The enormity of what he'd just told her registered in her mind. It explained so much, no wonder Gio was in such a state. The nightmares, the restlessness, the tortured look behind his eyes when he thought she wasn't looking. No wonder he'd come here and secluded himself from everything and everyone he loved.

Not only had he suffered a catastrophic accident that could very well have killed him, he blamed himself for destroying someone's life.

A shudder racked through her core. He could have been killed. She felt shaken and unsettled at the realization. He'd been a constant in her life for so long, the thought of not having him in it made her want to weep. She'd been so clueless as to what he'd been dealing with. "I had no idea."

He nodded. "For Juno's privacy while he tries to recover, I did my best to keep it out of the papers and gossip sites. Only close family knew all the details. Luckily, the media lost interest except for a few initial reports. Until very recently, that is."

"Until recently?"

He nodded. "Unfortunately. And I need to figure out

a way to make sure the details continue to stay out of the news cycle."

She tried hard to fight it—none of this was about her, after all—but a small, selfish part of her homed in on one undeniable truth: he hadn't thought to include her in that small circle of people he'd entrusted with the full story.

Gio couldn't bring himself to look at Marni's face as she took in all that he was telling her for fear of what he might find on her expression. At best, she'd look pitying and he couldn't handle that. At worst, she'd be horrified at what his carelessness had led to.

He cleared his throat to explain some more. "So you see, that's why I panicked when I thought you might fall in the water and hurt yourself. I might not have been able to help you if you got in trouble. My left leg is shattered, I broke several bones, some of which are still healing, I wouldn't have been able to move too well."

Her chin lifted. "I wouldn't need saving. But I understand."

Good to know. He didn't need to tell her then that the agony of watching her get hurt while he was helpless to help would have broken what was left of his soul once and for all.

He finally lifted his gaze to meet hers. There was nothing behind her eyes but concern.

"Is there nothing they can do?" she asked. "About your friend?"

"I have him set up in a specialty hospital in his native Switzerland. They're doing all they can, cutting-edge treatments. I pray every day that they find a way to heal him."

She nodded solemnly. "And what about your leg?"

He didn't want to get into this now, wasn't in the mood

for any lectures. But in for a penny and all that. "I've undergone three different surgeries. The next step is rehab, which was recommended I do in Chicago with a world-renowned team of professionals who specialize in injuries like mine. I'll need more surgery after that."

"When do you start?"

He shrugged, bracing himself for the inevitable fallout when he told her. "I haven't made the appointment yet."

To his surprise, Marni merely nodded. No words of consternation followed, no warning that he was being dumb or stubborn. Could it be that she actually understood why he might be putting off the inevitable? Might she be the only person in his life who understood that he was capable of deciding for himself when and how quickly he'd be able to heal?

For the first time in several months, Gio felt a lightness come over him. The anguish coiled in his gut since the accident loosened. As difficult as it had been to get the words out, he felt as if a heavy anvil was lifted off his chest. He hated when his sister was right. Talking to Marni had in fact lessened some of the burden. He'd seen no judgment on her face, no accusation whatsoever.

Gio felt lighter but also thoroughly worn and spent. The conversation had brought all the dark memories up front and center when he'd been trying so hard to keep them at bay.

As if to match his mood, the afternoon had grown considerably darker since Marni first came down the stairs. The bright sunny morning they'd spent on the beach seemed so long ago. Hard to believe it had only been a few hours since they'd returned. The sun wasn't shining now, no seagulls could be heard outside. A bolt of lightning suddenly flashed outside the window followed by a loud blast of thunder.

"What were you saying earlier about the lack of rainy days?" Marni asked, walking to the screen to slide it shut. She closed it just in time. Fat, heavy raindrops began falling from the sky before she'd had a chance to latch the knob.

"Guess we were due."

She lifted a shoulder. "Darkness and rain have to appear some time."

Despite the seriousness of the moment, Gio had to bite his tongue to keep from laughing. Had she really just made such a blatantly obvious metaphor?

Marni must have come to the same realization, the corner of her mouth lifted ever so slightly.

"Too much?" she asked, the smile lingering on her lips.

"I'll say."

She bowed her head in mock shame. "As reparation, I offer to throw together some lunch for us," she stated, then glanced out the window. "Since it doesn't look like we'll be going out to eat this afternoon."

"Accepted."

"I'll cut up that baguette we picked up yesterday, throw it on a board with some cold cuts and that delicious mozzarella you have in the fridge. Do you mind grabbing a bottle of wine from Nella's rack downstairs? I'll replace it the next time we go out."

"Sure. Maybe for entertainment we can watch another episode of that Bollywood series." Huh, he had no idea he would suggest such a thing. Or that he'd actually thought about watching that show ever again.

Her eyebrows lifted toward her hairline. Yeah, well, he was pretty surprised at the suggestion himself.

"Sure, my tablet's in my room. I'll go get it before I pull the food together."

He wasn't sure how she'd managed it, but somehow he'd gone from suffering the crushing weight of memories of the accident, to looking forward to a relaxing afternoon watching a show while listening to the rain. And it was all Marni's doing.

He couldn't resist teasing her yet again. "But please try not to fall asleep again. You have a tendency to snore."

She turned on her heel to glare at him. "What? How would you possibly know that?" He watched her eyes widen as the realization dawned on her.

"Why you sneak," she threw out, her hands on her hips, though there was no bite in her tone.

"Why whatever do you mean?"

She pointed a finger in his direction. "That night, on the lounge chairs. You knew the whole time. Pretending you were clueless."

He crossed his arms over his chest. "Miss Payton, I have no idea what you are talking about."

"Right. Sure, you don't."

He laughed in response. "Go get your tablet. I'm dying to know what happens after the last dance battle."

CHAPTER SIX

THE NEXT MORNING Marni awoke to a noise she barely registered. Sunlight poured through the half-open blind on her window. She hadn't gotten much rest. It felt as if she'd just fallen asleep moments ago. How was it possible that it was morning already? She'd been plagued by disturbing dreams involving fiery crashes and being trapped in a car after it flipped. If simply hearing about Gio's accident had invaded her dreams, she couldn't imagine how nightmarish his nights must be.

Vaguely, she recalled a late-night disagreement about who would get the bed. The new furniture had yet to arrive, delayed by the freak storm yesterday. Both had insisted the other get the bed and room. She'd won by losing. Or maybe she'd lost by winning. Hard to tell. Gio wouldn't budge, insisted on sleeping on the couch.

Her heart ached for him and all he was dealing with. Maybe she'd been too quick to try and lighten the mood yesterday after he'd told her everything, but she would have given anything to help ease the pain so evident in his face.

There was the noise again. She finally recognized it as

knocking. With a groan, she sat up. Why in the world was Gio knocking on her door first thing in the morning?

"Come in."

The door creaked open about a foot and Gio poked his head in. "You decent?"

"I said come in, didn't I?"

He shrugged, stepping into the room. "Didn't want to assume, sweetheart."

The endearment shot through to her center. It was way too early to be hearing sweet nothings from Gio Santino. She hadn't even had any caffeine yet.

"Sorry to wake you," he said. "But I waited and you didn't come down. And we only have a small window."

She blinked at him. "Gio. What in the world are you talking about?"

"The management agency called early this morning. About the villa that's available to buy. They said a rep can be there to let us in until about noon. If you'd rather go back to sleep, I understand."

Noon? Marni glanced at the bedside clock for the first time. It was approaching ten thirty! She couldn't recall the last time she'd slept so late.

"Of course, I'll be down in a fast minute."

Gio's shoulders seemed to drop three inches and he grinned. "Great. I'll see you in a bit."

He appeared relieved that she didn't turn him down. And he'd waited for her instead of just heading to the villa by himself. Did he value her opinion that much? Or maybe he just wanted her company. Either way, she couldn't help the sense of pleasure that pulsed through her.

In her line of work, she visited houses all the time. So

why was she practically feeling giddy about visiting this one with Gio Santino?

He was waiting on the patio for her. "It's just up the coast, past town," he informed her.

So another boat ride, then. The sky was clear and blue once again. As if yesterday's storm had never happened.

When they boarded, Gio once again handed her the life jacket. She took it without question this time. Another piece that made more sense now. Gio's adamant insistence that she wear it the first time they'd sailed up the coast the other day.

Now she studied his profile as he steered the boat. Without warning, he turned his head in her direction. Great. She'd been caught staring. *Gawking* might actually be a better word for it.

"What?" he asked, his smile warm and friendly.

No way she could tell him the truth about what she'd been really thinking. "I was just curious about manning a boat. Do I refer to you as captain while we're on it?"

He gave her a mock salute. "I like the thought of you referring to me as your captain."

So he was back to the teasing, flirtatious version of himself Marni was so familiar with. After what she'd leaned yesterday, she would take it. Not that their situations even compared, but it seemed the past year had been life changing for them both.

"Come here," Gio said, motioning her over to his side. "Give it a try if you're so curious."

She stood without hesitation. "You mean I can be the captain for a bit?"

"Let's not get ahead of ourselves."

Marni stood in front of him and gingerly took the wheel. The unexpected vibration threw her off for the first second.

He left one hand on it as he helped her to steer. "Steady, we're just gonna keep going straight for a bit."

Marni could feel the strength of the water through her fingertips as she guided the boat over it. The cliffside rose majestically out of the ocean to their left, giving her the feeling of being yards below civilization. Which she supposed would be an accurate description. Sailing the ocean in Capri felt nothing like driving on land.

She hadn't even noticed until that moment that Gio had removed his hand off the wheel.

"You're a natural," he said into her ear.

That enticing scent of mint and sandalwood drifted to her nose. Even through the life jackets, she could feel the warmth of his body against hers. Her breath caught in her throat. Between the headiness of sailing the boat and the effect of Gio's proximity, her senses were in overdrive.

Finally, Gio reached for the wheel. "I should probably take it from here. We're almost at the shoreline."

Marni reluctantly let go and stepped away. As soon as she got her life sorted and figured out her next career move, she might have to see about sailing lessons back in the States.

Not that anything would compare to what she'd just experienced. For one thing, no lesson was going to feel the same as having Gio guide her.

It wouldn't even come close.

Gio had been looking forward to touring the villa more than he could explain. That had everything to do with Marni. In fact, if she wasn't here in Capri with him, he probably would have sent a representative and asked for pics. After they docked, he guided Marni up the stone steps to the property where a realty agent who introduced herself as Angela let them in.

She led them to the main sitting area first. "I think this would be an ideal vacation home for a couple such as yourselves," she said, her smile wide.

Marni's hand flew to her chest as she began to correct the other woman. "Oh! We're not—"

Gio interrupted her protest in Italian, quickly changing the subject. A germ of an idea forming in his mind. He and Marni certainly made a convincing picture of a couple touring a home they might share. Cupping Marni's elbow, he motioned for the agent to lead them through the area.

After a quick tour around the rest of the house, Angela allowed them some time to observe the villa alone.

"Well, what do you think?" he asked.

They were standing in what would be his sitting room if he made the purchase. It was spacious with high ceilings and a shiny polished hardwood floor.

"I think you're lucky to be able to afford this. This place is gorgeous."

He would have to agree. Gio never forgot that he'd been born under a lucky star. He was the first son of a prosperous family, who'd managed to grow his own personal wealth. He'd often wondered if he deserved his good fortune. Especially over the past few months.

Marni continued, walking the length of the wall. "I mean, it's roomy and allows in a lot of light. I can think of all sorts of ways to decorate." She turned on her heel to face him, biting her lip. "That wasn't meant as any kind of plea that you hire me. I hope you know that. I'm just making observations. I hope you understand." She seemed genuinely concerned that her innocent statement might have landed wrong. Gio wanted to strangle the person who had done this to her. At times such as this one, she seemed horrified that she'd made some kind of mistake.

"I understand completely." She might not have meant it as a plea, but he would certainly consider it an offer. Of course he would. Who else would he get to help him furnish this place if he bought it?

A look of relief flushed over her features and she continued walking, trailing her fingers along the wall. When she got to the corner of the room, she tilted her head, studied the wall. "There appears to be a gap here, in the wallpaper. Though why anyone would wallpaper these days is beyond me."

She glanced toward the door, as if on the lookout.

"Something wrong?" Gio asked.

"I just want to see what's under this paper, there's some kind of pattern. Let me know if you see the agent approach. I don't want her to think I'm trying to tear the paper off."

Gio had to laugh. Somehow their visit to see an available property had turned into some kind of covert operation. Everything he did with Marni seemed to take on a special or unusual turn. Life was going to seem so flat and boring after they parted ways.

"I've got you covered," he assured her, his eyes trained to the door.

He heard the scrape of her fingernail. "Oh, my God," she said breathlessly a few seconds later.

"What is it?" Gio gave up on guard duty and strode to her side. She was picking at a spot on the wallpaper that had partially come off.

"If I'm not mistaken, there's a genuine mosaic under all this paper. Probably handcrafted."

Gio had no idea what that might mean. Was it a good thing?

"When did you say this place was built?" Marni asked.

He hadn't, it hadn't come up before now. "I think the details online said late nineteenth century."

She tapped the paper back in place and stepped away, her eyes alight with enthusiasm. "You could have a real work of art under all this. I can't imagine for the life of me why anyone would cover it up with plain beige wallpaper."

He wished there was a way to bottle up her excitement. He couldn't remember the last time he'd been so affected by a discovery. Let alone a wall. Maybe that was why he kept looking for ways to take risks. Just to be able to feel things the way someone like Marni did.

He recalled the way she'd reacted when he'd let her steer the boat. Such a mundane task as far as he was concerned. But Marni had been practically buzzing.

"I would kill to see what the entire thing might look like under that paper," Marni added.

He could only think of one way that would be possible.

"I wonder what other delightful discoveries a place like this might hold," she said, palming the wall with a faraway look on her face.

Gio figured she just might find out.

Angela's words echoed through his head...*a couple such as yourselves.*

Gio pushed the thought away. For now.

Twenty minutes later he and Marni were sitting outside on the vast patio by a sparkling blue infinity pool. The realty agent had locked up the house and left, asking them to shut the locked gate once they left.

The pool area felt like a mini paradise, complete with

marble statues of cherubs and a plot of colorful flowers in each corner. Marni took her shoes off and sat at the edge of the pool, soaking her feet up to her ankles. The image looked right to his eyes, as if she belonged here.

As far as property went, it wouldn't be a bad purchase. He'd wanted a place in Capri for a while now, ever since his sister and husband had inherited their estate. He could picture himself lounging out here by the pool. Could picture having his morning espresso while seated at the bay window overlooking the cliffside. Funny thing was, in none of those pictures was he alone. The woman splashing her feet in the pool was central in every single one.

What that might mean for his psyche, he didn't even want to analyze. So much in his life was in turmoil right now. Marni was at a daunting crossroads herself. He had no business envisioning her in any part of a future he was so uncertain about.

Marni reached in the pool and cupped a handful of water then splashed his legs with a playful giggle.

One thing he was certain of, regardless of what the future held, Gio planned to be the next owner of this villa.

Marni sighed and took another look back at the villa they'd just toured. The place really was rather remarkable. What she would give to use her skills to decorate a place like that. Who was she kidding? Even if Gio did buy the place and hire her to decorate it—and those were pretty big ifs—she'd have to do it virtually from thousands of miles away in the States. She couldn't stay here in Capri long term. She had to get back and see about putting her life back in order.

Still, a girl could dream.

"Are you in any rush to get back to Nella's?" Gio asked from the bow without looking away from the horizon.

"Not particularly," she answered. "Why?"

"There's something I want to show you. If you're up for it."

His wide smile of enthusiasm was enough for her.

"Sure."

Gio turned the boat in the other direction and ramped up the speed. Within half an hour they approached a cavernous opening on the cliffside. A slew of motorboats, small yachts and rowboats surrounded it in the water.

"Let's hope the wait won't be too long," Gio said, then picked up his cell to make a phone call. She couldn't make out any of the Italian.

"What exactly are we waiting for?" she asked.

"You'll see," he answered with a mischievous gleam in his eyes. "Have some patience."

Moments later, Gio got a phone call and maneuvered their boat around the other craft. One of the men in the rowboats close to the cavern opening was waving them over. Gio navigated to his side then turned off the motor.

"Let's go," he told Marni, offering her a hand then helping her onto the rowboat before jumping on himself.

"This is Mario," he introduced, "he'll be our tour guide and rowboat driver."

Tour guide?

Marni cleared her throat. "Wait. Are you telling me we're about to sail into that massive cave in the cliff wall?"

"That's right. This is the Grotta D'Abruzzo. Wait till you see what it's like inside."

Excitement mixed with fear churned in her chest. She'd never been great at closed-in places. Exploring a water cave wasn't exactly what she'd had in mind when she agreed earlier to this outing. But Marlo was grinning and gesturing for them to be seated.

Marni swallowed her trepidation and sat down on one of the rungs. Then jolted in surprise when Gio took the one behind hers. Not so much because he'd sat behind her, but because of the closeness of their bodies in the small space. Her bottom was nestled against his inner thighs, his chest close against her back.

Suddenly, her trepidation about entering the cave was completely overtaken by the fire that shot through her system at the close contact.

Heat crawled over her skin, her nerve endings afire with the intimacy of their positions. Surely, Gio had to feel it too. She was practically sitting on his lap, for God's sake. His legs spread out, tight against her hips.

She froze when he leaned in to murmur in her ear, "Comfortable?" Marni didn't imagine the mischief in his tone. His breath felt hot against her cheek, tickled her earlobe. How in the world was she supposed to answer that?

Marni closed her eyes, willed herself to focus on her breathing.

Gio leaned into her shoulder once more. "Breathtaking, isn't it?"

Oh, she was breathless all right. But no doubt he was referring to whatever was in the cavern. Marni opened her eyes and blinked when she focused on the view before her.

Was she seeing things? The cave was alight with a bright neon blue. The water below them glowed, the rock walls glittered indigo. It was as if they'd entered a monochrome painting that somehow lit up from the inside.

"Oh, my," was all she could muster in response.

"Quite a sight, huh?" Gio asked, his chin bopping against her bare shoulder.

"I've never seen anything like it. What is this place?"

"They say it used to be the private swimming hole of Emperor Tiberius of the Roman Empire." From the corner of her eye, she saw him point upward. "His castle was built above us."

"How is it lit up in blue fluorescence?"

She felt him shrug behind her. "I'm not sure about the exact physics." He asked Marlo a question in Italian. The other man replied with several accompanying hand gestures.

Gio translated when he was done. Something about holes in the cave wall and capturing the sunlight through the openings. But God, it was so hard to concentrate between his closeness, the feel of his breath against her skin and the spellbinding sight before her.

"Imagine having this as your private swimming pool," Gio said after several minutes spent simply admiring the view.

Marni could imagine it all too easily. Had the king come down here for a late-night skinny-dip with his queen? Had they stolen private moments in the water, surrounded by this heavenly light, simply enjoying the pleasure of each other's company? As well as other much more intimate pleasures?

The vignette morphed into more personal images in her mind's eye. Only now it wasn't the Roman king and queen she was picturing. Oh, God, it was her and Gio. What would it feel like to frolic in this water, in the dark, while held in his arms? To have his lips on hers in such a secluded and private setting? Heat rushed to her cheeks. She silently said a small prayer of thanks that Gio couldn't see her face.

No! For all that's holy. No, no, no!

Gio spoke again softly over her shoulder. "I see the sight has left you breathless," he said. "You're practically gasping for air."

If he only knew the truth.

His leg was angrily throbbing. Bolts of pain shot through his thigh down to his knee. It was almost bad enough that he could ignore the more constant ache in his side and rib cage. Almost.

He'd overdone it today.

A voice in his head wholeheartedly agreed. It listed the litany of things he'd done when he should have known better. Climbing stone steps, both at this villa and the one he would be buying. All that walking as he and Marni toured the property. Jumping into a rowboat.

That last one was probably the nail in the proverbial coffin. A perfect comparison since he felt like the pain might actually kill him if it didn't subside significantly.

"You're hurting, aren't you?"

He hadn't even seen Marni come out to the patio.

"What makes you say that?" he said in as light a voice as he could manage. It wasn't easy.

She lifted an eyebrow. "Oh, just the way your face is scrunched up as if you're pushing a heavy boulder up a steep cliff. Or maybe how you keep rubbing the spot above your knee. All sorts of clues I'm sharp enough to pick up on."

That was the problem. She was too sharp by half.

"It's nothing, Marni," he said with a forced chuckle. "Nothing a night's rest won't help. I'll be much better in the morning."

"But you haven't been getting any kind of good rest, have you?"

Well, she had a point there. He should have come up with a better way to assuage her.

"I'll be fine," he repeated, for lack of anything else to say.

"We did too much today. I wondered what you were thinking, jumping onto that boat."

Yeah, the thing was, he hadn't been thinking at all. Just anticipating the joy he might bring to Marni by taking her to the grotto. He was certainly paying for it now.

She walked over and sat down on the lounge chair next to him. "I just wish the new furniture would get here already."

"Hopefully soon. Though things tend to move slower in Europe. Especially this time of year, during vacation season."

Marni's spine straightened and she lifted her chin, as if she was prepping for a fight. "Listen, Santino. If you think for one minute I'm going to take the bed tonight while you try to sleep on the couch or this lounge chair or on a bunch of cushions, you better think again."

Gio rubbed a hand down his face. How often were they going to go through this? Although, this time, he was actually tempted given the thousands of small knives stabbing his leg muscles at the moment.

"I will not argue about this. It's settled."

"Marni—"

"No!" Her tone was sharp enough that he was somewhat surprised. "I said it's settled. In fact, if you don't take the bed, then I won't either. We'll both be uncomfortable while there's a perfectly good bed upstairs sitting empty."

He tried to argue, but found he just didn't have it in him. The pain medication he'd been given left him groggy and disoriented, a sensation he'd hated. And Marni was right, the thought of trying to endure this pain while lying horizontal on anything other than a mattress would no doubt result in a night of absolute agony.

"All right," he said, blowing out a resigned sigh.

"Don't you—" She stopped. "Wait. Did you just agree?"

He nodded. *"Sì. Hai vinto."*

Her eyes roamed over his face. "Huh. I win, huh? That tells me how much you must be hurting."

"Because I actually agreed with you?"

Marni shook her head. "No. That you reverted to speaking Italian."

"Okay. I admit. My leg doesn't feel real great right now. But I don't see why you have to sleep down here."

Marni practically rolled her eyes. "I knew that was too easy. I thought you just said you agreed that you should take the bed."

"I did. But I think you should too."

Her eyes grew wide and her brows lifted clear to her hairline. Her shocked expression made him chuckle out loud. "Marni, it's a very large bed. And I'm hardly in any position to—"

She held her hand up to stop him. "I see what you're getting at. And you're right. We've both had an enjoyable yet tiring and long day. There's nothing wrong with two old friends getting a good night's sleep on the same mattress. Not much different than all those slumber parties Nella and I had at your house."

Gio's ego took a bit of a hit with that one. But she was right. For the most part. "Can we do each other's hair and paint our nails? Write in our journals?"

She nodded. "Sure, we could do all that. Or we could watch another episode of *Lotus Dreams*."

"That works too."

"Sounds like a decent plan to me. I'll go cue it up on the tablet."

"Can't wait." He was aiming for a sarcastic tone but realized he actually was looking forward to the night they'd just planned. Something about watching a mindless television show with Marni by his side was more appealing to him these days than a night out on the town. Or a night scuba diving or parasailing or dirt biking...or any of the countless, rather extreme ways he'd been entertaining himself throughout most of his adulthood.

"Before I do that, I'll go get you some ice for that leg."

There wasn't enough ice in the kitchen, maybe in all of Capri, that would do any good given the condition he was in right now. He was about to tell her not to bother, but she'd already left to go get it for him.

CHAPTER SEVEN

MAYBE THIS WASN'T such a great idea. Gio sighed as quietly as possible so as not to disturb Marni. He desperately wanted to toss and turn but didn't want to risk waking her. One of them should be able to get some shut-eye. They'd just retired half an hour ago. It was sure to be a long night.

"It's okay..."

He heard Marni's soft voice in the dark.

"I know you're not asleep."

"Are you?" The ridiculous question garnered a low laugh out of her.

"Guess," she answered.

Gio chuckled and turned to her. He'd been so concerned about moving toward her in his sleep that he was practically on the edge of the mattress. There was a good three feet of distance between them. "I'm sorry, for keeping you up."

She released a breath, turned over onto her back. "You're not the reason I haven't drifted off. I have a lot to think about and I can't seem to shut my mind off."

Boy, could he relate. It was better for both of them to just do their best to fall asleep. So he surprised himself when he opened his mouth to ask the next question. "What was it about him?"

Gio sensed her discomfort at the question. Finally, she turned her head to face him. "I don't exactly know why. I can only say that he was very charming at first. Until he wasn't."

"Tell me."

She was silent for so long, he figured she had no intention of sharing. Finally, she sighed and began to speak. "I told you about leaving my job, you remember?"

He remembered every bit of their conversations. Something that tended to happen when he truly enjoyed someone's company. "I do.

"All because you broke things off with your former..." He hesitated. He couldn't seem to use the word *lover* when it came to Marni's past relationship. Referring to her as someone else's lover felt wrong on his tongue.

"With your ex?" he finished.

"You do remember. Only I didn't just work with him. I worked *for* him."

"He had the nerve to fire you for breaking up with him?"

"More or less an accurate assumption."

A bolt of rage shot through his chest for a man he'd never laid eyes on. The damage he'd done to Marni was unforgivable.

"What would make it more accurate?"

"He was one of the head architects at the firm I worked for. Interoffice relationships weren't explicitly forbidden but everyone knew they were frowned upon by the higher-ups."

"I see."

"I got lots of disapproving glances and a few outright glares by the other partners."

Gio shook his head. It took two to be in a relationship. "That's pretty unfair."

"Then there was all the snickering and gossip from the other decorators. I could just guess what they were saying behind my back every time I was assigned a job."

He could also guess.

"That I slept my way to getting the assignment," she confirmed.

Again, wholly unfair. But it was the way of the world, wasn't it? Unfortunately, women were the ones who were often the target of bitterness in scenarios such as the one Marni was in. Kudos to her for having the good sense to remove herself from such a toxic situation.

Only, she hadn't walked away unscathed, without any battle wounds.

"What happened?" Gio prompted. He had the feeling it would do her good to get some of this off her chest. And maybe it was selfish of him, but he had to acknowledge it did him a bit of good as well to focus on someone else's woes for a while. If that was indeed self-serving, at least it was a win-win.

"I knew I had to end the relationship. Between the way it was affecting my work environment and the way Ander… treated me. It was all too destructive to my well-being."

"How so?"

"He tried to control what I wore, how I dressed. What I ate, how much I ate. And nothing I did was ever enough to please him."

"Do I have to take a trip back to Mass?" he asked, completely serious and more than willing to do just that. "To pay this guy a visit?"

Marni puffed out a breath of air. "He's not worth it. Believe me. I would much rather just forget he existed."

That was fine with him.

Marni continued, "Only, that's proving hard to do since I was fired on his behalf."

"On his behalf?"

He felt her head bop up and down in a nod. "Ander wasn't happy about the breakup. He didn't try to hide it. In fact, he made sure the tension was thick and heavy every time we had to be in the same room together."

"Not exactly conducive to a work setting."

"Nope. He didn't care, he knew he could get away with it."

"And you were the one who ended up paying for it." Job or no job, Gio believed wholeheartedly that she was better off far away from that sorry excuse for a man.

"That's right," Marni said. "Out of nowhere, I was told they needed to do some cost cutting and could do with one less decorator. Never mind that I had seniority over two of the other decorators who got to stay."

Gio swore in Italian.

Marni repeated the epithet with a thick American accent, earning a guffaw out of him.

"I reached out to colleagues for other opportunities right away. But got a lot of cold-shouldered responses. I guess the gossip was too much for me to overcome. I am persona non grata right now in the Boston interior design scene."

"I'm really sorry, Marni," he said, his heart breaking for her.

"So now, thanks to Nella, I have two weeks to try and put it all behind me."

"If I know my sister, she insisted."

"You would be right," Marni said with a laugh. "But she only has my best interest at heart. And she's smart—what better way to regroup than to do it in paradise?"

He had to agree on that score. It was why he was here in Capri too, after all.

Marni had been through so much. Was still dealing with the vengeful manipulations of a jilted lover. The same nagging thought in his head since they'd toured the villa for sale resurfaced once again. It was hairbrained and ridiculous and nonsensical.

But maybe, just maybe, it might be a way to address both their dilemmas.

Who would have thought she'd be grateful for a bout of insomnia? Marni glanced at the digital clock behind Gio on the bedside table. They'd been simply lying there in bed, just talking, for over an hour. She'd had no idea just how badly she'd needed to purge herself of all that had happened in the past few months. Gio was a good listener. He offered no judgment, didn't pretend to know any of the answers. He simply listened quietly. Turned out, that was exactly what she needed right now.

Nella had been there for her, of course. As always, she was only a call away and checked on her often. But she had her own life to live, now as a newlywed no less, and Marni hadn't wanted to burden her. As for her mom, well, her mom was just too tired these days to care.

"What do you think you'll do?" he asked her now. "When you get back after the two weeks?"

That was the question, wasn't it? She had no plans other than to keep reaching out to people she knew in the field, sending out her CV and hoping for the best.

Except for those times when that one other option floated through her brain. But that was mere fantasy. How she would attempt to pull it off, she had no idea. Didn't even know where to start.

So she surprised herself when she answered Gio's question the way she did. "Well, during more wishful moments, I fantasize about branching out on my own. If I can figure out how."

"Like opening up your own place?"

"Yeah. But it's a big *if*."

"Marni, I think that's a great idea."

She rubbed her forehead. "I don't know. It would be a lot. I'd have to figure out how to finance it. I'm barely scraping by as it is."

"There are ways to find investors for this kind of thing. Plus, you can start small."

Valid points. Her credit history was pretty good. A small business loan from the bank wasn't out of the question. But what if she failed? Again.

Then she'd be jobless and further in debt. Her school loans were enough to keep her finances in the red for years still.

"Let's pretend you have all the logistics figured out," Gio suggested. "What would you call the business?"

Marni's gut tightened at the question. She was nervous even pretending about having her own place, something she'd wanted so badly for so long. "Nothing fancy," she answered. "Probably Marni's Interior Design. Something along those lines."

"Where do you think you'd set up shop?"

Now that she'd voiced her pretend business name out loud, her stomach muscles loosened just a little. What was the harm in just pretending? "If I had to pick right now, I might say Somerville. Or Medford. Those towns are really growing fast right now. But not enough that I'd be priced out of leasing a place."

Huh. She hadn't even realized the thought had occurred to her.

"What kind of sign would you have above your door?"

"See, that's where I might get fancy. It would have to be big and colorful. With my name displayed cleaRLY in huge, artistic lettering."

The image flashed clearly in her mind as she spoke the words as if a physical sign hung before her at this very moment in the dark. So real, she thought she might be able to reach out her hand and touch it.

"What might your slogan be?" Gio asked.

She surprised herself by coming up with something right then and there. "Comfort, quality and personal attention guaranteed."

"I think that's perfect."

She kind of liked it too. "One of the things about working in such a large firm was not really knowing the clients enough to gage for certain exactly what they would find homey," she explained. "I never knew if I was creating a home interior that went with their innermost personality."

"With your own place, you can personally ensure that happens."

She slapped her palm on the mattress. "Exactly!"

Marni closed her eyes, now fully immersed in the make-believe world she'd just created—sitting at a big mahogany desk, speaking to a client, taking notes about how best to furnish their home. She couldn't guess how much time had gone by when she snapped her eyes open at a grunt from

Gio. The moon cast just enough light in the room that she could see him gripping his thigh as well as clenching his lips. In fact, his whole body had gone rigid and tight. He was in pain still.

Marni cupped a hand to her mouth as a realization hit her. "I'm so sorry, Gio."

"What in the world are you apologizing for?"

"Here I am practically wailing about my misfortune then waxing poetic about my dreams. All the while you're lying there literally in pain. I'm being so selfish."

He chuckled. "You're hardly wailing. And you most definitely aren't selfish. Far from it. If anything, you've managed to take my mind off the pain for a bit."

If he really meant that, Marni was beyond grateful that she might have been able to provide even a small iota of comfort, albeit small, especially considering all he'd just done for her. For the first time since leaving the firm, she felt a glimmer of hope for her future. Maybe she'd never be able to start her own place, but the dream was enough to keep her afloat during the tough times.

"Thank you for that. And thanks for indulging in my fantasy design firm creation."

Though she'd be darned if it didn't seem just a bit more real now.

Gio reached over and tapped a playful finger to her nose. "You're welcome, gattina. Anytime."

She couldn't have heard him correctly.

Marni sat up on her blanket-size beach towel and shielded the sun from her eyes. Gio's shadow loomed large on the golden sand beside her. She'd spent the morning lounging by the water. Now he was here handing her a sweaty glass of lemonade.

And also apparently to make a suggestion that seemed too far-fetched to be real. "I'm sorry, I could have sworn you said that we should pretend to be a couple for the next several days."

He crouched down to one knee next to her, so close his scent mingled with the salty sea air. His forearm brushed her shoulder, raising goose bumps despite the heat of the day.

Focus.

"I must have heard wrong," she said now with a soft chuckle.

"Hear me out," he began. "I think a little pretense might be beneficial for both of us."

Marni studied his face, no signs of joking or humor in any of his features. He really was serious. "What kind of pretense?"

"We pretend we're here together intentionally. That we're dating."

Marni shifted in her position. "That settles it, no more of that Bollywood show for you. What you're suggesting sounds like a plot right out of its storylines."

"But it makes sense, gattina. We're seen doing the tourist thing together. Everyone assumes we're a couple. There's no speculation about either of us."

"Speculation?"

Gio sighed and sat down all the way next to her. "It must be a slow news week. Because there's a journalist for a regional publication who's been calling to find out more about the accident. My guess is that others will follow. For Juno's sake, I need to make sure to shut it down before it starts."

"So you want to pretend you're simply vacationing, but

why the farce about us being together?" Marni had to swallow after uttering the last few words.

"This way, we avert any interest in digging up the past and give them something new and shiny to focus on. They'll drool at the human interest angle. A local CEO who narrowly avoided death and has now found love. One who's seen how tenuous and fragile life can be and wants to settle down and give up his playboy lifestyle."

"Huh."

"And you show the world that your previous relationship is well in your past."

His suggestion was still preposterous, but Marni was beginning to see the logic behind the plan. He didn't need to explain how it would be beneficial for her to have the world believing they were an item. It would certainly quiet down the rumors Ander was spreading about her. She would look like a woman who'd truly moved on. "You want it to look like you're simply on some kind of romantic vacation."

He tapped her nose playfully. "Right. What do you say? Do you want to think about it before you make your decision?"

Marni shook her head. "I guess it's worth a try. I mean, we have nothing to lose by giving it a shot."

Gio's grin in response had her insides quivering. "That's my gattina," he said. "All we need to do is just make sure to be seen around town, like we're on holiday together. Visiting attractions, playing tourist. It would settle down all the gossip about the both of us. No one really knows the true circumstances of why we're here except for Nella and Alex."

"How do we explain all this to them?"

He shrugged again. "If they even get wind of it, we'll just tell them the truth. That it's not real."

It's not real. Gio was merely suggesting they playact, put on a show for the rest of the world. So why was her mind flooded with images of the two of them together enjoying the sights and attractions of one of the most romantic places on earth?

Her mind knew it wouldn't be real. But her heart was already wishing it could have been.

Maybe Marni had been right. Maybe this idea was completely insane, a story straight out of the plot of a soap opera. Either way, Gio figured they had nothing to lose by giving it a try. A few leaks to some gossip sites, a few photos floating in the social media sphere, a well-placed comment here or there. That should be more than enough to still the wagging tongues on both his and Marni's behalf.

This dinner cruise along the Capri coast aboard a yacht was a good first stop. Judging by Marni's expression, she was enjoying herself to boot, which was icing on the cake. Wait until they arrived at their destination. She was sure to be stunned.

Speaking of being stunned, Marni's black wraparound dress draped over her curves and brought out her tanned skin. She'd done her hair up in a simple style that somehow made her look both elegant and casual. The woman sure did clean up well.

He'd instructed the captain to specifically have them go by the *faraglioni* rocks on their way to Il Faro, the famous lighthouse on the southern coast. This way, Marni could experience their majestic beauty as well as the lighthouse itself and its views. Just because they were on this outing for practical reasons didn't mean they couldn't make the most out of it. He could show her the beauty that was the Amalfi coast while they were at it.

Her jaw dropped when they approached the sight. "Oh, my," she whispered breathlessly.

He could hardly blame her wonder. The *faraglioni* rocks in Capri were one of the most captivating landscapes in the world. Towering out of the deep sea, waves crashing at their base with a beautiful view of verdant land in the distance.

"It's breathtaking," Marni added, not taking her eyes off the scene before them.

When the waiter appeared at their table to take their order, Gio fished his phone out of his pocket and handed it to the man. "Would you mind?"

Draping his arm around Marni, he pulled her closer to his side, the majesty of the rocks setting the scene behind them. "Smile for the photo, *cara*," he told her.

Taking his phone back, he glanced at the image on the screen. "Picture-perfect," he said to Marni. "This should work just fine."

Picture-perfect. Marni took a deep breath and tried to still the racing of her pulse. That's all this was, just a picture she and Gio were trying to project onto the world. One based on a complete falsehood. So why had her heart quickened when Gio put his arm around her and pulled her close? For his part, Gio seemed single-mindedly focused on their true objective—playing up their false relationship.

Well, she could do the same. She'd force herself to not be distracted by the scent of his aftershave or the way his silver-gray suit brought out the dark specks in his eyes and highlighted the darker streaks in his wavy hair.

No. She'd ignore all that and focus on the now. In the

meantime, she'd enjoy this once-in-a-lifetime early evening dinner cruise aboard a luxury yacht.

The food arrived in short order, helping in her efforts at distraction. Fresh lemon dill sea bass and homemade pasta with a side of grilled vegetables. A few months ago she would have pushed the pasta aside, making sure to only eat the lean fish and veggies. All to maintain her calorie goal in case Ander asked.

What a relief not to have to worry about such things now. Marni's mouth watered. She wasn't sure what her expression must have held but when she looked up Gio was staring at her with concern.

"Is that not to your liking? We can ask for something else?"

"No, it's absolutely perfect," she answered, sticking her fork in the pasta first. "I can't wait for dessert."

Several minutes later, the boat gradually slowed as they approached a redbrick building. Atop it sat a tall lighthouse. They came to a stop just as a waiter appeared with a tray that held two silver goblets half-full of golden liquid. "For the viewing," he said in a charming Italian accent.

Marni took one of the offered drinks and sniffed. They nutty aroma of almonds and spice tickled her nose. "What exactly are we viewing?" she asked Gio after the server walked away.

But he simply winked at her then said, "You'll see."

"Why can't you just tell me?"

"Because there's no way to describe it, *gattina*."

Marni realized just how true that statement was once they'd disembarked and walked up a stone pathway toward the lighthouse.

"La Punta Carena," Gio announced. "The best place in the world to watch the sun setting over the Mediterranean."

Marni slowly sipped her drink and watched the horizon as the sun began to lower in the sky. Gio's words had not been an exaggeration. The horizon was a striking hue of red and orange, the water beneath it sparkling like jewelry. It was like watching a live-action view of a masterpiece painting.

Pretense or not, this was one of the most breathtaking scenes she'd ever witnessed. One she'd never forget.

Sighing deeply, Marni leaned back against Gio's chest and simply enjoyed the view, surrounded by his scent and heat.

CHAPTER EIGHT

"I THINK WE'VE floated enough photos out there for this plan to work," Gio announced the next morning. She'd come out to the patio to admire the now familiar view of the ocean in the horizon past the infinity pool. She was going to miss this ritual when she had to return to Boston in a few days. "Combined with the leak that we were seen touring an available villa together, I think we've got a solid foundation for our fake relationship."

Why did she cringe inside every time she heard those last two words?

Gio continued, "But just in case, I've got one more outing planned for us this afternoon."

Marni lowered her sunglasses to study him. "Another outing, huh?"

Gio nodded, his smile growing. If she didn't know any better, she might think he was actually enjoying all this activity. Still, she'd been growing more and more concerned about whether he was overtaxing himself. He'd insisted on walking along the pathway at the base of the lighthouse yesterday so that Marni got the full experience. But she was loath to say anything to him. Gio seemed to take any hint at his vulnerability as some kind of affront.

She could only hope whatever he had planned for today wouldn't involve too much physical effort. For his sake.

"What kind of activity?"

"The Gardens of Augustus. No trip to Capri would be complete without a visit there." He plopped himself down on the lounge chair next to her. "And it will give us another chance to be seen out and about together. The gardens are usually full of visitors this time of year. It's a beautiful day so today will be no different."

Gio was proven right about the crowd size when they arrived by private car two hours later to the winding pathway that led up to the world-renowned botanical garden.

Marni made sure to walk as slowly as she could so that Gio wouldn't overwork his sore leg, taking several breaks along the way. The breaks weren't all that contrived, like the ones yesterday, these views were equally stunning, taking her breath away.

The park's layout consisted of different sections, each made to look like a terrace full of botanicals overlooking the coastline and ocean beyond. Grand statues dotted the landscape, as if a museum of sculptures had its pieces scattered throughout a magnificent garden. Marni had never seen anything like it. She was having trouble deciding exactly which visual feast she should focus her eyes on.

"What do you think?" Gio asked as they stood in a terrace full of colorful dahlias and luscious green leaves. Marble statues flanked them on either side, a cherub to the right and a maiden carrying a load of fruit on the left.

"I think I might have died and am right at this moment

walking through Eden," she answered, the awe in her voice clear to her own ears.

A commotion sounded from the pathway a few feet behind them. Excited voices, male and female alike, speaking in what sounded like German.

Marni turned to watch as a bridal procession made their way past the terrace. Half a dozen tuxedoed young men walking alongside elegantly styled women in sapphire blue gowns. Trailing behind them was a bride clad in layers of white silk and delicate lace walking alongside her groom. The couple seemed totally engrossed in one another, oblivious to anything around them, including their own bridal party.

The scene could have been a picture straight out of a bridal magazine. What an absolutely idyllic venue for a wedding. How lucky these two people were, to have found love and were now able to celebrate it with a union bonded in paradise. A bubble of envy formed in her chest, mixed with longing. How could she ever hope to do the same given her disastrous romantic history?

She released a long sigh, which came out sounding much louder than she would have anticipated. Sure enough, when she turned her head, Gio leveled a curious look her way. Maybe it was irrational, but she found herself getting defensive.

"What?" she asked, her tone on the side of aggressive. "Is it so odd to appreciate young love?"

"Is that what you were doing, gattina? Appreciating?" He tilted his head, a slight smile to his lips. He was teasing her!

"Do you mean to tell me that you've never entertained the idea of your own wedding? Where it might be? Not even once?" She found herself asking, against her better judgment.

His smile grew smirk-like. "Oh, sure, we talk about it every time me and the boys get together. Then us guys draw hearts all over our notebooks and sign the names of our crushes on our palms."

"That's ridiculous."

Gio turned with a chuckle to face the view of the Marina Piccola in front of them, crossing his arms in front of his chest. "Fine. To answer your question, no I never gave much thought to my wedding. Or marriage in particular. There was never an occasion to."

So there'd never been a woman who'd inspired thoughts of marriage. Heaven help her, Marni felt a twinge of relief at that notion. Which made absolutely no sense whatsoever.

But she was deflated by the next words out of Gio's mouth. "Now I can't even entertain the thought. Not for a long while," he said solemnly, his gaze narrowing on the horizon.

"Why is that?" she asked. Again, probably another dumb question she didn't really want to hear the answer to.

He shrugged, his jawline tensing. "How could I even think of that? The state I'm in, on top of all my regular responsibilities, how could I even consider tying myself to another person?"

A lump formed in Marni's throat. She had no business feeling so dejected by his words. She was only his pretend girlfriend.

How silly of her to take any of it personally.

For the third time during the span of a week, Gio opened his eyes to the brightness of sunshine rather than watching the onset of dawn. He'd been able to fall and stay asleep. Despite the pain.

Marni. He had her to thank. Again.

As his focus continued to clear, he realized exactly why he'd slept so comfortably. She was nestled against him and he was holding her in his arms. Sometime during the night, Marni had shifted to his side of the bed. He must have instinctively wrapped his arms around her.

This is wrong. This shouldn't be happening.

His subconscious was simply blurring the lines, had lost sight of what was real and what was pretend. A whisper-soft voice in his head tried to tell him all this but he gave it no need. He made no effort to move or push her away. It didn't help that Marni had been asking him about matrimony and romantic marriage proposals just yesterday.

But...it felt right, lying next to her this way. The scent of her brought to mind roses and fresh berries. The warmth of her body spread over his skin, right through to his soul. The sunrays shining through the window behind her cast her in a halo of light. Several tendrils of her hair fell around her face. She was utterly enchanting. His fingers itched to reach for her, to gently caress those untamed curls. His gaze fell to her lips: full and rose red, puckered slightly in her slumber.

Not for the first time, he wondered what she would taste like if he kissed her. Sweet as honey, no doubt. With a touch of those berries he always smelled whenever she was near.

He sensed more than saw it when she opened her eyes. They widened in surprise before heat darkened their depths. She made no effort to move out of his grasp. And he wasn't even remotely inclined to push her away.

They were a hair's breadth apart. Her eyes roamed over

his face and he nearly groaned out loud when they landed on his lips. Did she want him to kiss her, maybe even as much as he craved doing so?

The voice grew louder, more adamant. Repeating the warnings he was trying so hard to ignore.

"Gio?" She spoke softly, her voice low and thick. The sound of his name on her lips had something shifting in his middle. He gave himself permission to gently trail his fingers around the frame of her face, to tuck back a couple of those wayward locks behind her ear.

"Good morning, sweetheart."

Her response was to shift even closer, then tilt her face up toward his. Heaven help him, he wouldn't even have to move his head to take her mouth with his, to finally succumb to the longings he'd been pushing away for so long. A low hungry groan sounded in his ears and he realized it was coming from him. Just one kiss.

Stop. This. Now.

This time, the voice was too loud and too harsh to ignore. Because he could no longer deny how wrong going down this path would be for them both.

With all the will he could summon, Gio moved back away from her, then sat up. Her look of confusion had him cursing inside, made him yearn to return to her. To take those lips with his own the way he so badly wanted to.

But then what?

The possible answers to that question were much too dangerous to explore. What if they didn't stop with one kiss. A very real possibility given his body's reaction and the way Marni had been looking at him just now.

Summoning the last vestiges of his control, Gio turned to sit on the edge of the bed with his back to her. "I should get up. There are some emails I need to check on."

Not exactly a lie. For one thing, he wanted to check for any updates on Juno's recovery progress. For another, he was going to follow up on when that blasted bed might finally arrive.

The sound of her rustling behind him told him Marni was getting up as well. He waited without breath in case she said something, tried to stop him.

She remained silent.

He should have been relieved. Instead he felt a heavy brick of disappointment settle in his chest.

He took his time to get showered and dressed but then there was no longer any reason to delay the inevitable. He would have to face Marni sooner or later. Damn him for not having the sense to turn her down about sharing the bed last night. He would have preferred an uncomfortable and pain-inducing night on the sofa. Too late now.

When he made it downstairs, Marni was curled up on the love seat, still wearing her nightclothes, her hair up in that too tight ponytail again. What he wouldn't have given to set it loose and run his fingers through the strands the way he had moments ago.

"Good morning," he said by way of greeting, then cringed. He'd already said that to her upstairs.

She didn't quite meet his gaze when she responded in kind. Gio swallowed a curse. This was exactly what he'd wanted to avoid. This awkwardness between them. She wasn't even meeting his eyes. So different from before. They'd been so comfortable with each other last night, their conversation so easy.

Now the air was thick with the tension of all that was and had to remain unspoken.

Or he could just go sit next to her, take her in his arms

and tell her honestly how badly he wanted to kiss her. Then he would oblige if she said she wanted the same.

No. That was the last thing he should do, as tempting as it was.

"I'm about to brew some coffee. Can I get you some?" he offered.

She shook her head.

"How about some breakfast?"

"No, thank you."

Gio went about the business of getting himself caffeinated and fed. Looked like things were going to remain awkward between them, for now, anyway.

Because he couldn't think of a darn thing to say to make it any better.

Were they just going to ignore what had almost happened between them?

It seemed so, Marni figured as she watched Gio go about his morning as if nothing had changed. He brewed his espresso, offered to make her one or brew some water for her tea, then moved to the patio with his phone to check on those all-so-important emails that he'd used as an excuse to rush out of the bedroom this morning.

While she was still shaking with desire inside. While she was still imagining what it might feel like to have his stubble rub against her cheek. While she longed to be in his arms once more.

When she'd woken up briefly to find herself wrapped tight in Gio's embrace, she'd stayed where she was wrapped in the cocoon of his warmth. He'd seemed in no rush to let her go.

Now Gio was behaving as if none of it had even happened.

Well, he had the right of it, didn't he? He was actually thinking straight as opposed to the way she was letting her emotions run rampant. It had to be their surroundings.

This was Gio. Nella's brother. She'd practically grown up with him. They'd always had an easy camaraderie, even during all those times she and Nella were being pesky little tagalongs. Surely, they could get back to that dynamic.

Marni scrunched her face and blew out a breath.

Who was she kidding? As if. Even now, she itched to run her hands over his chest, touch her tongue to his lips, ask him to wrap his arms around her the way he had last night.

All this pretending they'd been doing was blurring her reality, bringing to the surface all the attraction she'd tried so hard to curb.

So going back to the way they'd been before this trip was wishful thinking. Still, things between them couldn't remain as tense as they were. She still had eight days here before her return flight. She would need every one of those days to figure out what she intended to return to.

Marni had to forget about the almost kiss like Gio apparently had.

So when Gio finally left the patio to announce he wanted to take a walk along the beach, she didn't hesitate. "I'd like to come with you if you don't mind the company."

He quirked an eyebrow at her in surprise. "You sure? My leg's stiffening up just sitting out there. I might be kind of slow."

"A slow and leisurely stroll. Sounds perfect. Let me just throw some shorts and a T-shirt on."

He tilted his head. "Take your time."

He was waiting for her by the pool when she came back down dressed less than five minutes later.

He hadn't been kidding about being slow. It took him much longer to get down the stone steps this morning. Maybe they should have just stayed put or floated around in the pool rather than tax his already strained leg any more.

She was about to ask him when he spoke before she could. "Feels better already, just being out here by the water in the sunshine."

Why did she get the feeling he wasn't telling the entire truth?

Marni decided not to press, the whole point of walking with him was to overcome the awkwardness between them after the almost-kiss.

"It's beautiful," she agreed. "I wore my swimsuit underneath...the water looks pretty inviting."

So there was that bit of small talk out of the way, then. Now what?

"Have you thought any more about your pretend design business?" Gio asked as they made their way along the water.

Marni waved her hand in dismissal. "Oh, that was just a bit of fun on my part, answering your questions like that. None of it is real." *Like a lot of other things that may have happened last night*, she added silently.

"But it could be," Gio countered. "I thought we established that."

Marni stared out at the horizon. She knew Gio meant well, but dwelling on a pipe dream wasn't going to do her any good right now. She had to get practical and figure out a manageable path forward.

"Maybe," she finally answered. "But I think for now I'll

stick with plan A or B. My own shop is probably more like plan Z in the overall scheme of things."

"Huh."

Was it her imagination, or did that one tiny sound hold just a hint of judgment? She felt a prickle of irritation.

Truce, she reminded herself.

"If I understood correctly last night, your plan A seems to be to keep looking for another job like the one you had."

And lost. "That's right."

"So what does plan B involve, then?"

She shrugged. "I thought maybe I'd travel to New York City to try my hand there. It's a much bigger market. With more opportunities."

"Is that what you want? To live in New York?"

Why was he asking her all these questions? This was supposed to be a stress-free stroll together to reestablish their friendship. She hadn't realized her very motivations would be poked and analyzed.

"New York is a thrilling place to live," she said noncommittally. "The Big Apple and all that."

"Yeah, but it's not your home."

She had to veer this conversation in another direction, away from herself. It was only fair to discuss Gio for a while. Besides, hadn't she shared enough about herself last night?

"What about you?" she asked.

"How do you mean? I'm still CEO at Santino Foods."

"I know that. But you have to admit the life you're going back to won't be the same one you left."

That was one thing they had in common.

Gio wasn't sure why but his pulse had quickened at Marni's words. The truth was, he hadn't really planned for much past this trip. For the first time in his life, he found himself focusing only on the short term. He just wanted to monitor Juno's recovery and continue pursuing his goals for Santino Foods. The company had a highly efficient and competent staff of employees. But with the loss of his father a decade ago and Nella having no interest in the business, the brunt of the responsibility fell on his shoulders. His mother did what she could to help, but with her advanced age she could only do so much. So many people depended on him for their livelihoods. He had a board of directors he had to answer to. Which just made his careless risk-taking that much worse.

Well, he'd learned his lesson.

"The only change I can be certain of is not participating in any more road races for the foreseeable future," he answered, squinting in the bright sunlight.

"I'm glad to hear it," Marni answered. "Nella will be too."

Gio didn't miss that she'd just put herself in the same context as his sister. That had to be intentional. If she thought that was going to make him forget his desire for her, they were way past that stage. He would just have to make the best of the new dynamic and try to ignore the inconvenient feelings he'd developed.

Easier said than done. He had to try. For both their sakes.

"What made you do it?" Marni asked the question completely out of the blue. "I mean, I know you've always been a bit of a daredevil. But why a charity race across rough terrain through several countries?"

He shrugged. "The organization it was meant to support was struggling to find participants that might draw the kind of attention and publicity they needed for the race to be successful."

Having the Santino name attached to the race had done

a lot toward that end, but it wasn't enough. Not until he'd actually been announced as one of the drivers did they see big dollar amount donations.

"Ah, I get it," Marni said. "You knew that if the CEO of an international conglomerate was an actual participant, the publicity alone would bring in more money."

She'd always been clever.

He nodded. "That's right. And there were all those friends and colleagues who wanted to pay for the privilege of taunting me if I didn't win."

Marni laughed. "I'm sure in a very good-natured way."

Despite the seriousness of the conversation, the sound of her laughter lightened some of the heaviness in his chest. See, there was no reason to let any sort of awkwardness continue between them. They could continue as villa mates until she had to leave. He had to admit, he was going to really miss her company when she left in a few days. He probably wouldn't stay much longer after that himself.

The bright yellow tank top she wore cinched at the waist and brought out the golden specks of her irises. Her denim shorts showed off her shapely thighs. Thank God she wasn't wearing those plain leather flats today. The sandals she had on were much more enticing, showing off the bright pink polish on her toes.

When had he ever noticed a woman's toenail polish before? Not a single time he could recall. Maybe he wasn't completely over his concussion, after all.

He focused on the waves splashing near his feet to get his mind to behave. "For the most part," he said.

"So you had the most noble of intentions."

"I guess you could say that." He certainly had in the beginning. The race seemed like a fun way to support a good cause. But it all went so terribly wrong. Now there was a young man laid up in a hospital while he was in pain every night.

She paused and touched his forearm. Gio braced himself, certain he wasn't going to like what was about to follow. "Gio, if you don't mind my asking, what do the doctors have to say?" She swallowed, clearly nervous about asking the question.

He was right, he really didn't want to go down this path of questioning. He shrugged. "The normal doctorly stuff."

"What does that mean? And you don't have to tell me if you don't want to."

Her bright hazel eyes clouded with concern. How could he not give her something?

He shrugged. "Like I told you. There's at least two more surgeries they say I need. But the muscles need to heal first. In the meantime, they prescribe constant and regular physical therapy appointments. Which I'm sure will continue for the foreseeable future."

Marni's hand lingered on his arm. For a crazy second, he wanted to take it in his, lift it up to his lips and plant a gentle kiss on her palm. And wasn't this a fine time to be thinking of doing something so silly and inappropriate for the moment?

"I meant, what are they saying about when you should start the therapy. So that you can move forward with the surgeries."

He was supposed to start them a week ago but had canceled every single scheduled appointment. "When I get around to it. I'm not in any rush."

No need to tell her that decision ran completely against all the medical advice he'd been given. Or that the last surgeon had bluntly and unwaveringly told him that Gio was certain to make his condition worse by delaying the treatment.

But it was as if Marni could read his mind. Her lips thinned into a tight line, and her eyebrows drew together over those piercing hazel eyes. There was no mistaking the disappointment that washed over her features. Along with a solid dose of worry. It was the worry that annoyed him most. "You've been putting it off, haven't you? The therapy and the surgeries."

Like he'd thought earlier, the lady had always been very clever.

"There's no need to look at me like that," Gio said and resumed walking but at a much faster pace—which had to hurt his leg. And for what? Marni wondered. It wasn't as if he was going to get away from her on this beach.

She began to follow fast on his heels and caught up to him in a second. "Like what? How do you think I'm looking at you?"

"Forget it, Marni. Let's just turn around and go back."

A bit late for that. She slammed her hands on her hips. "No. I'd like an answer," she demanded, not even sure why she was pushing him this way. The conversation was getting way too heated. So much for that truce she'd been after. "So tell me."

"I don't know," he bit out. "Why are you badgering me? As if I've tried to drown your pet squirrel in that ocean or something." He thrust his thumb in the direction of the water.

In spite of her frustration with him at what she'd just learned, Marni's mouth quivered with the onset of a laugh.

She squashed it. "Why in the world would I keep a pet squirrel?"

He turned to her then, rammed a hand through the hair at his crown. "Didn't you at some point or other have a small furry rodent? I remember Nella having to pet sit."

"That was a guinea pig, Gio. Completely different animal than a squirrel."

How in the world had they gotten so off topic anyway?

He crossed his arms in front of his chest. "Never mind. I suppose you're going to tell me, like everyone else that I'm being stubborn and stupid for not trying to get better as fast as I can."

"No, I wasn't going to say any of that. And I'm not going to ask you why either, for that matter."

Both eyebrows lifted and his jaw tightened. "You're not?"

She shook her head. "I think I can guess. Plus, I'm sure you wouldn't answer me anyway."

He narrowed his eyes on her. "You're right, I wouldn't answer. As for the first part, don't be so sure. You don't know me as well as you think you do."

Ouch. Marni sucked in a breath at the taunt. If he'd meant to be cutting and harsh, he'd hit the mark perfectly. Any trace of amusement flowed out of her. In her head, she knew he was just lashing out because he'd been forced to admit something he didn't want to share with her. But her heart did a little flip at the cruelty.

"Right," she said. "I suppose you're also going to tell me it's none of my business."

He reached for her shoulders, took them in a gentle but firm grip. "Don't put words in my mouth, Marni."

Her mouth went dry at the contact. This was so not the time to notice the fullness of his lips, the way his dark hair curled messily over his forehead, blowing about his face in the breeze. His dark brown eyes blazed with emotion. And something else. Something that had her blood zinging in her veins. Her heart began to pound in her chest.

She somehow got her mouth to work. "So you're saying you are my business, then?"

"I've known you a long time." His answer wasn't really an answer at all.

Suddenly, her own tenuous grasp on her emotions snapped like a dry twig. Marni knew she should step away, out of his grasp. Instead, she did the opposite. She moved forward until they were toe to toe, her face a mere inch from his. Marni knew she was playing with fire, but couldn't seem to help herself.

Once again, her mouth was within a hair's breadth from Gio's. But unlike this morning, there was nothing gentle about the way he was looking at her.

He looked like he could devour her on the spot.

That dangerous, wayward thought had her breath catching in her lungs. Gio noticed, because his lips formed a knowing smile. "What's the matter? Something wrong, gattina?"

Oh, God. Never before had the nickname sounded quite so sexy to her ears. She would never hear it the same way again after this moment.

Yes! she wanted to cry out. All sorts of things were wrong. Like how badly she wanted his lips on hers even though she was beyond angry at him for the way he was risking his health by delaying getting medical treatment. Or how much she wanted to thrust her fingers in his hair and bring his mouth down to hers. How disappointed she'd been that he'd left the bed this morning instead of just kissing her then.

She couldn't even be sure which one of them moved first. Maybe they both did. But suddenly, what she'd been fantasizing and dreaming about was somehow happening. Gio's lips found hers in a crushing, shattering kiss. His hands moved from her shoulders to wrap around her waist and pull her closer. Her hair was suddenly free from its binding with Gio's fingers threading her loose strands before pressing his mouth into hers harder.

She couldn't get close enough, wanted to feel the length of him even tighter up against her body. Good thing they were out in the open on a beach where anyone could walk by. Or Marni would have been unable to keep herself from tearing his shirt off to run her hands down his chest, over his washboard stomach. Then lower.

This was why he'd been smart not to kiss her in the bedroom earlier. She had no doubt she wouldn't have been able to stop herself from going further, as far as he would let her.

Marni leaned into him now, savoring the taste of him. His warmth seared her skin. Heat and longing curled in her belly and moved lower, and every nerve ending tingled with electricity. The world around her ceased to exist. Nothing mattered but Gio Santino and the way he was kissing her.

She never wanted it to stop.

CHAPTER NINE

How could he have lost control like that? Gio bit down on the curse that formed on his lips when he finally let Marni go. Which took way too long.

And he'd gone way too far.

He'd been naive to think they could simply gloss over what had happened between them this morning. Walking away from the bed this morning, rather than facing reality then and there, had only led to a slow simmering of tension between them that had just blown up in spectacular fashion. He had to figure out a way to put out the fire.

He dared to meet Marni's gaze now. His breath caught in his throat at the sight of her. Her hair fell in a mess around her face and shoulders, her lips were swollen. Her cheeks flushed berry red. God help him, she looked ready and waiting for him to do it again.

She looked like some sort of modern goddess, standing on the golden sand. The bright sun highlighted the streaks of golden bronze in her hair. The sparkling blue water of the ocean served as a background as if she were the center of some classic painting. Everything about her called to him, made him want her more.

How totally inconvenient.

It took several moments to get his mouth to work. "Marni, look, I'm so—"

She held a hand up to stop him before he could finish, her eyes ablaze. "Don't you dare finish that sentence, Gio Santino. Don't you dare apologize to me right now."

Gio rubbed his palm down his face. "What do you want me to say?"

She didn't answer, simply glared at him some more. Several beats passed by in silence, the air between them heavy. Gio clenched his fists at his sides to keep from reaching for her again, wiping that angry glare from her face with another deep satisfying kiss.

No! Enough already.

Kissing her again was the last thing he should be thinking about. Instead, he should be trying to figure out how they were going to get past this. Not just for this week but for the rest of their lives. Marni was practically family. They couldn't spend the rest of their days uncomfortable around each other just because he hadn't been able to control himself the brief period of time they'd been alone together.

Marni turned on her heel. "I think I'm done walking now."

Gio watched her retreating back as she made her way toward the house. He debated following her but the tension in her shoulders and the rigid set of her spine told him she wouldn't welcome his presence right now. Just as well, it was probably best for them both to be alone for a while.

Maybe for a long while at that.

***

Within minutes of docking the boat and arriving in town, Gio's phone vibrated in his pocket and he recognized his sister's ringtone. He pinched the bridge of his nose, not really up for a conversation with anyone right now let alone his chatty sibling. But guilt had him pulling out the device and answering just before it went to voice mail.

Her face appeared on the screen. "Hey, big bro."

Gio did his best to summon a smile and leaned back against the brick wall of a seafood store. Why did she have to place a video call now of all times? "Hey yourself."

Nella's eyes traveled behind him. "You're not at the house?"

"I'm in town for a couple of errands."

"Is Marni with you? She didn't answer when I called her just now. I wanted to speak to you both actually."

Again, she'd called her friend first. Not that he was offended in any way. It just confirmed what he already knew about their relationship. Nella and Marni didn't share any blood, but in every other sense they were true sisters.

Which only proved just how wrong it was to kiss her this morning. His sibling's soul sister should be completely off-limits, no matter how much he was attracted to her.

"Nope. I'm by myself."

Nella rested her chin on her hand. "Why didn't you bring her with you? Marni loves to shop."

He wasn't about to get into any of that. But Nella could be relentless about getting answers when she was curious about something. And she was like a bloodhound if she thought she detected a lie.

Gio really regretted answering the phone. He'd have to give her something. "I just had to come into town for a couple things. Just decided to do it by myself," he answered, hoping it was enough to placate her while still being vague.

No such luck. She straightened in her chair, obviously not buying it. "Well, it was rude of you not to invite her."

Rude. Ha! As if that was the worst of it.

"She wouldn't have wanted to come." Mistake. It was the wrong thing to say.

Nella's head lifted with concern, the casual smile fading from her lips. "Is she feeling okay? She's going through a lot, right now."

Those words only upped his guilt level several notches. Marni was going through a lot. And instead of being a supportive friend Marni could lean on, he was toying with her emotions.

"She's fine, Nella," he quickly assured.

Nella leaned closer to her laptop. Even through the screen it was as if she could see clear to his soul.

"What is it? What aren't you telling me?" she demanded to know.

"Nothing. I mean, you're right. I should have asked her to come."

Nella's eyes narrowed on him, all too knowing. "Giovanni Santino. I swear if you've done anything to upset her."

"Listen, Nella. I have to go. My order's up." So what if he was fibbing. He hadn't actually ordered anything from anywhere. He just had to find a way off this call.

"Fine. But I'm not happy with you right now, big bro. I'll call you later this evening. Both of you," she added in an ominous tone.

Gio ended the call and slipped the phone back into his pocket. Then he made a beeline for the furniture store. Whatever he had to do, that bed needed to be at the villa before tonight. He would hire the delivery van and find a driver if he had to.

Heck, if necessary, he would haul the bed back to the villa himself.

What do you want me to say?

How could he have asked her that? How could he not know?

Marni pounded the dough harder on the counter, trying to vent some of her frustration. Usually, the vigorous kneading and pounding calmed her nerves. Today it wasn't working so great toward that end.

The gall of that man. First to act like she had no business asking about his recovery. Then to kiss her so passionately that she'd actually felt her knees buckle.

And then the audacity of him to try and actually apologize for it.

Where was he, anyway? It had been hours since their little fiasco on the beach.

She'd already made the new bed—it had arrived a couple of hours after she'd gotten back to the villa following their eventful walk. Then she'd spent some time tidying and dusting. She'd even had a chance to watch another episode of her Bollywood show, which hadn't been nearly as enjoyable now that she was used to having company. Another mark against Gio Santino. He'd ruined her favorite pastime.

Now she was almost done with her kneading and he still wasn't back. She pounded the dough once more for good measure.

"Please tell me you're not picturing my face on that as you smack it that hard."

Startled, Marni whirled around to find Gio standing behind her in the doorway. She hadn't even heard him come in.

"Didn't mean to startle you," he added, walking farther into the kitchen.

Her irritation warred with the urge to run into his arms, and she silently berated herself. She could be such an idiot when it came to this man.

"What are you doing, anyway?"

"Making bread."

"I could have picked some up for you in town. You should have called and asked."

So that's where he'd been all this time. Marni pushed aside the dough and turned to face him, leaning her back against the counter. "And you could have called and told me where you were."

The corner of his mouth lifted. "Why? Were you worried about me?"

Of course she'd been worried. The man had a bad leg and other internal injuries he was just barely recovering from. But she wasn't about to take the bait.

"Of course not," she lied. "Just pointing out the polite thing to do when you're sharing a house with someone."

Gio visibly cringed. "You're the second person today to accuse me of being impolite. Which reminds me, Nella called earlier. Wants to talk to both of us later this evening."

Marni's eyebrows rose. "Is everything okay?"

He lifted his hand in reassurance. "She sounded fine. Just wanted to tell us both something. I was going to ask her more but our conversation got a little waylaid."

Huh. Curious.

What did he mean about a waylaid conversation with his sister? And what would Nella want to tell them both at the same time? So many questions and so few answers. Somehow, her life seemed so much more complicated during this trip when it was supposed to be a way for her to try and find some clarity about her future.

"The bed arrived," she told him, changing the topic. "I've already made it up with some fresh sheets I found in the linen closet."

Gio's response to that bit of news was surprisingly low-key. He merely nodded, then plucked a grape out of the fruit bowl and tossed it in his mouth. "Thanks. What else did you do today?"

So more small talk, then. So be it. She'd play along. For now. "I tidied, started this bread. And watched another episode of *Lotus Dream*."

Gio stopped chewing and swallowed, then tilted his head. "You...you watched an episode without me?" Marni almost felt a twinge of guilt at the dejection in his tone. Almost.

She shrugged. "Guess you'll have to catch up at some point."

"Guess so."

What do you want me to say?

His question from earlier echoed in her mind. So many words he might have come up with rather than asking it. Like, maybe he could have told her that he was just as confused as she was but not sorry about whatever it was happening between them. Or maybe tell her that he cared for her and always would, that they would figure things out together. He could have even told her that he'd enjoyed their kiss as much as she had, but needed time to process.

But Gio hadn't said any of those things. And he probably never would.

What did it matter at this point? In a few short days,

she would be on her way back to the States. She'd maybe see Gio four or five times a year when Nella invited her to various family functions. It would be as if this time spent together in Capri never happened.

Her eyes began to sting so she made a dramatic show of working the dough again, not that it needed it. In fact, if she pounded it any more at this point, the bread was sure to be a rubbery, chewy mess.

"Can I have some of that bread when it's done?" Gio asked, a charming, wide smile over his lips. "I'll trade you for some fresh fish I bought in town that I'm grilling for dinner."

She lifted her chin, not quite ready to accept any kind of olive branch. "I'll think about it."

Marni swam the length of the pool then lingered in the deep end just allowing herself to float. She let the warm water wash over her skin and soothe her tense muscles.

Why hadn't she done this before? A serene early evening swim to settle some of her frazzled nerves was exactly the ticket. The salty scent of the sea and the steady sound of the crashing waves in the distance added to the tranquility she'd so desperately needed.

With a relaxed sigh, she immersed herself fully in the water then held her breath for as long as she could. As if she could shut off the rest of the world, if only for the briefest of moments.

Finally popping up for air, she opened her eyes and gasped: Gio crouched by the edge of the pool. Honestly, he had to stop startling her like that. So much for relaxing, her pulse was rocketing again.

"You were under there quite awhile," he remarked. "I was about to jump in to get you."

Unbidden images flashed in her mind of the two of them frolicking in the pool together. Skin to skin. With complete privacy, unlike at the beach earlier.

She blinked the vision away. Her pulse now a rapid staccato.

"I was about to get dinner started," Gio informed her.

"That's fine. The bread should be done baking. I'll go get it." She swam over to the edge where Gio stood waiting for her. He'd grabbed her towel and was holding it out to her.

When she climbed out, Gio had the towel spread wide in his hands, waiting for her to step in it. Marni swallowed. Nothing to read in the gesture. The man was simply helping her dry off. She walked up to him and turned around, allowing him to drape the thick terry cloth over her shoulders. His hands lingered just long enough. She could feel the warmth of his palms through the fabric, the strength of his grasp. It took all her will not to move back closer against his chest and nestle herself against his length.

Instead, she savored the feel of his fingers on her shoulders. But it was over all too soon. He moved away and the chill of his loss immediately settled over her skin.

"I'll go get the coal grill fired up," he said behind her. "Take your time drying off."

She would need time. Not to dry off, but to quell the yearning in her core that must be written on her face. She could only do so much to hide her feelings for this man. It was exhausting her to try.

"Back in a few," she threw over her shoulder, before walking to the screen door and into the house.

When she returned a few minutes later dressed with her

hair in a topknot, Gio was spooning the fish onto two plates. He'd poured them each a glass of wine. A sharp knife of sadness pierced through her heart at what might have been as she took in the sight. In a different life, they might have been a real couple about to enjoy a quiet evening enjoying each other's company, followed by a not so quiet night.

There she went again. Thinking in ways she had no business doing.

Taking a second to compose herself, Marni walked to the table and set the basket of bread in the center, next to the salad and antipasti.

"Fresh and hot," she announced with a casualness she didn't feel. She could only hope it wasn't the texture of gum given the way she'd punished the dough.

Gio pulled her chair out for her, then took the seat across the table. The fish was good, really good. Gio had kept it simple with just a couple of spices and a generous splash of lemon on each filet.

Why did the man have to be so good at everything he did? It was hard to stay angry at someone who'd made this great of a meal for you.

She was about to grudgingly compliment his cooking when he reached for the loaf and broke off the end piece then handed it to her wordlessly. The Santinos always gave Marni the end piece, it was the part she liked most.

When he went to bite his own slice, his eyes widened and his eyebrows furrowed. He chewed once. Then again. Then he stilled.

Marni took a bite and it confirmed her fears. The bread was chewy and dense. "Okay, so it's not my best work."

"I'll say. Not even a whole stick of butter would salvage this."

And he wasn't going to pull any punches.

"I'm sorry, Gio," she said, surprising herself as well as him given the way he set his fork down and focused on her face.

"Marni, you don't have to apologize for messing up bread. We have plenty else for dinner."

Marni put her fork down as well. "I guess that's not what I'm really apologizing for." Now that the words were out, she realized they needed to be said.

"Then what?" he asked gently.

"I think you know. I shouldn't have pushed you earlier today. You clearly don't want to talk about what you're doing to recover." *Or not doing*, she added silently. "It wasn't my place to pressure you about it."

Gio pushed his plate away. Great, now she could feel guilty that she'd ruined their appetites.

"Marni. You have to realize how important you are to us. To me, my sister, my mother. And my father before we lost him."

She swallowed. "I'd like to think I am. As important as the Santinos have always been to me."

"You remember how strict our parents were growing up. They were hard on both Nella and me."

She nodded. "I remember."

"You were the only one who stuck around, put up with how rigid my parents' rules were. Nella would have no friends if it weren't for you."

The same could be said about her. Her mom was always at work and her dad had long ago left them. The Santinos were more family to her than anyone else.

Gio continued, his eyes imploring her to understand. "So

you have to see why I can't break my sister's heart by having a meaningless fling with her best friend."

Ouch. He might as well have thrown the porcelain plate at her. Well, she'd be damned if she was going to let him see just how much he'd cut her with those words.

She plastered a forced smile on her face. "Of course. You're right, Gio. I completely agree."

Gio wanted to suck his words back in as soon as they left his mouth. He hadn't meant to sound quite so heartless. Just direct and unwavering. Damn. Why did he keep tripping up over himself when it came to Marni? He couldn't seem to stop messing things up with her.

She rose from the table before he could find a way to smooth over the edges of the words he'd used. "I'll take your plate if you're done," she offered, without so much as a glance at him.

Of course he was done. As if he could continue eating now. His delivery may have been shoddy, but surely she had to see the logic of what he'd been trying to say. Gio had nothing really to offer a woman right now, especially not one like Marni. For one thing, he was a wreck physically with nothing to look forward to but months, maybe years, of treatment and surgeries ahead of him. Some days he could hardly manage to walk without cringing in pain. He had no idea how he would juggle all that while manning the helm at Santino Foods.

Marni didn't wait for his answer about his plate. She took her own, grabbed the bread basket and walked into the house.

With a curse, Gio collected the remaining dishware off the table and joined her at the sink. They silently went about washing each piece as he scrambled his brain to think of something to say.

The sound of her phone ringing came from the other room. "That must be Nella," Marni said, shutting off the water and toweling her hands dry. She motioned for him to follow. "You said she wanted to talk to both of us."

For the first time in his life, Gio found himself grateful for a call from his chatty sister. Anything to distract from the tension between him and Marni right now.

He peered over her shoulder as she accepted the video call. Nella's smiling face greeted them on the screen. Her husband, Alex, joined in the frame an instant later.

"Hello, you two," Nella said with a finger wave.

"Hi, Nella," Marni answered and a genuine smile lit up her face, her first one of the day that he could recall.

"Are you both sitting down?" she asked. "I think you need to sit down for this."

Marni cast a curious glance in Gio's direction. He shrugged in response. Damned if he had any clue or insight.

His sister's wide smile suggested that there was no need for alarm. But what exactly was she about to say that was so earth-shattering?

"Go sit," Nella insisted when they still hadn't moved.

Once they obliged, his sister actually squealed before speaking. "So, Alex and I have some big news to share with the two of you," she began.

To his surprise, Marni squealed just then too. "Oh, my God! Nella, really?" she asked.

Really what? What was all this about? Marni sounded as if she'd figured it out already. For the life of him he couldn't figure out how. Nella hadn't even said anything yet.

"Really, Marn," Nella said with a delighted laugh.

"That's wonderful!" Marni clasped a hand to her cheek. "You and my brother are about to become godparents."

Godparents? But that would mean...

His sister confirmed before he could finish the thought. "I'm pregnant!"

Gio felt his jaw drop. His little sister. His *baby* sister was going to have a baby herself.

"Congratulations you two!" Marni exclaimed. "I'm so happy for you both."

Gio could only manage a nod and a feeble "Me too."

No one else seemed to notice just how dumbfounded he was. "We're only telling immediate family right now," Nella said, glancing up at her husband for confirmation. He gave it to her with a quick peck on her forehead.

His sister's eyes found his on the screen. "Well, what do you think, big bro?"

What he thought was that he was going to need some time to let the news sink in. Somehow, he found a better response for Nella's sake.

"I think you should be prepared for me to spoil this kid rotten. Right before I hand him back to you and take off."

Nella wagged a finger at him. "Or her. We don't know yet, Uncle Gio."

Uncle Gio. His new title. The phrase added another jolt to his already shocked system.

After several more minutes of happy chatter, Nella finally said her goodbyes and Marni exited the call, tossing her phone on the couch. Then she threw her arms around his neck and embraced him in a tight hug. Gio's arms reflexively went around her waist.

"I'm going to be an uncle," he said against her cheek,

testing the words out himself, hardly able to believe they were coming out of his mouth.

Marni pulled back to beam him a dazzling smile. "And a godparent. Like me."

That's right. That was the other large piece in all this. He and Marni had yet one more major tie to each other. Nella's pregnancy was not about him of course, but he couldn't help but think it was yet another sign from the universe.

He couldn't play fast and loose with the woman he'd be sharing godparent duty with for the rest of his life.

CHAPTER TEN

MARNI STARED UP at the ceiling in her borrowed bedroom, still abuzz with the news. She was genuinely over the moon for her friend. Nella Santino deserved every bit of happiness. She was the purest, most genuine person Marni had ever met.

She and Alex were perfect for each other. Nella adored her new husband and the feeling was definitely mutual.

Nella's announcement certainly put things in perspective. Her friend had a fulfilling life with a doting, loving husband and she was about to be a mother. Whereas Marni's current relationship was completely made up for the sake of some media clicks. Speaking of which, she reached for her phone and scanned all the relevant websites. No photos of her and Gio, not yet, anyway. Clearly, their selfies weren't having much of an impact.

Marni sighed and turned over to her side, her thoughts returning to her friend's big news. What must it be like to have found the love of your life? To be starting a family with him? Nella was lucky enough to have found her soul mate, and that couple in the Gardens of Augustus had looked so in love as well.

These days, Marni doubted such good fortune would ever be in the cards for her. Just look at her past romantic history. Albeit short, it included a man who'd mistreated her then ruined her career prospects. On the heels of that disaster, she'd somehow managed to fall in love with a man completely out of her reach.

Whoa.

Where had that come from?

Marni bolted upright. She had inadvertently wandered into dangerous territory. Gio Santino had been her crush for years, she rationalized. Her attraction to him was simply at the forefront of her mind now because of their proximity and the romantic setting. She couldn't go believing she'd somehow really fallen in love with the man.

Or maybe you've always been in love with him.

Marni rubbed her eyes, squeezing them shut under her fingers. She needed some air. Despite the late hour, she threw on a thin sweater and made her way downstairs.

The light on the patio was already on when she reached the first floor. Gio was out there, sitting by the pool. She debated turning right around, heading back to the room, but too late, his head snapped up and he gave her a small wave.

With a resigned sigh, Marni went over to the screen door and stepped outside. Silver moonlight bathed the patio and beach in the distance. Bright stars dotted the dark sky like diamonds on dark velvet. If she had to paint a picture of the perfect setting for a romantic interlude, this was exactly what she might put to canvas. Complete with the man of her fantasies sitting front and center.

"My insomnia must be catching," Gio told her once she reached his side.

"I'm too excited for Nella to sleep." That was close enough to the truth. "What about you," she asked, "Don't tell me the new bed isn't comfortable."

He shook his head. "It's perfect. Definitely beats the lounge chair."

"So why are you out here on said chair instead of upstairs in the comfortable bed?"

"Thought I could use the air."

"Hmm."

"You didn't seem all that surprised, about Nella expecting."

Marni shrugged. "I saw how in love she and Alex are with each other. I know family has always been a big part of your sister's life. I guess I just saw it coming sooner or later."

"Well, it was much sooner than I would have expected. Not that I'd given it much thought."

Marni wasn't surprised. Men could be so unaware sometimes. Even about those closest to them. "You'll get used to the idea."

Gio scoffed. "It's still sinking in. Though there might be an advantage for me here with this new development."

"Yeah? How so?"

"Maybe Mama will go easier on the pestering for me to settle down and start a family."

The thought of Gio with a wife, sharing children with some to-be-determined woman, had Marni's stomach clenching in knots. She could just picture him with a doe-eyed, dark-haired beauty as they held hands with their little ones. Maybe she'd be one of the models or actresses he'd been linked to in the past, not that it was any of her business. Marni pushed the image aside.

She was not in love with him! All the pretending was warping her perception of reality.

"She must be over the moon," she said. Signora Santino might have been strict and demanding, but she'd always been one to show deep affection. Marni couldn't think of anyone more fitting for the Italian grandmother role. Straight out of central casting.

Gio shifted his chair to turn and face her. "Listen, Marni. I think this is a good time to get some things straight. I don't want things to be strained between us."

Uh-oh. Marni was afraid to guess where this was leading.

"Especially now," Gio continued. "We're going to be godparents together. Nella's going to need us both to be there for her. And her child is going to need us for the rest of his or her life."

Nothing to argue with there.

"Let's do what we need to, to put whatever started this rift between us in the trash bin. Forget it ever happened."

He meant their kiss. He wanted to pretend he'd never kissed her. Would it be so easy for him to do as he was suggesting? To just wipe from his mind that he'd been shaking with need while he'd held her in his arms with his lips on hers?

What a fool she was. That one kiss had changed everything for her. She went to bed thinking about it at night and woke up with it on her mind the next morning.

"I think that would be for the best," she answered, even as her heart ached in her chest.

He stood suddenly. "Stay put, I'll be right back."

"Where are you going?"

"Since neither of us can sleep, I say we do some celebrating. I thought I saw some nice champagne in the cellar when I first got here. If you're up for it. I know it's rather late."

She was indeed up for it, Marni decided. After all, it wasn't like she was going to get to sleep anytime soon. "Sure," she answered. "Why not? Let's toast to Nella's news."

He flashed her a dazzling smile. "And we can toast to our newfound understanding too."

Two days later Gio entered the house with a fresh box of pastries, rather pleased with himself. He'd gotten to the bakery stand early enough to get all of Marni's favorites. More importantly, since their little chat on the patio the other night, things between them felt pretty much back to normal. It helped that they had a common interest and desire to talk all the ways they planned on spoiling his niece or nephew.

Well, things were mostly normal, if he didn't count all those times he caught himself noticing the fullness of Marni's lips after she applied her favorite lip balm. Or how her hair became curlier from seaside humidity after she spent time on the beach. Or how her skin was growing more golden with each passing day, leading him to wonder about what tan lines she might have underneath her clothes.

Six days. She'd be leaving in six days. He only needed to hold it together for that long. The thought should have been a comforting one. But the idea of being here at this villa without her didn't exactly hold the appeal it should have. There'd be no one to share pastries with, to grill fish for. To spend sleepless nights with on the patio sipping on champagne or iced tea.

Gio was about to set the box down and transfer the goodies onto a serving plate when a loud thud sounded from upstairs. The sound was followed by a harsh feminine cry. Marni. Something was wrong. Gio tossed the box onto the counter then ran for the stairs and jogged up them to her room, ignoring the bolt of pain that shot through his muscles at the effort.

He found her door open and Marni sitting on the bed. Her hands were clenched at her sides, her cheeks red with a look of horror on her face.

"What's wrong?"

She swallowed, tears welling up in her eyes, and pointed to the floor. Gio followed her finger to where her tablet lay screen down on the carpet.

"That rat!" Marni cried, her voice full of anguish. For a split second, Gio thought maybe she was speaking literally. Had a rodent gotten in the house? But Marni didn't look scared, she looked angry. And panicked.

So a figurative rat then.

Gio bent down and reached for the device. The page Marni must have been reading was still up on the screen. He scanned it just enough to see what Marni was so worked up about. She had every right. In fact, his own blood pressure had skyrocketed as he read the words.

"Why the son of a—"

Marni stood and began pacing the room. "He's making up all sorts of lies about me."

Gio scanned more of the article. It was a piece in a trade mag. Ander Stolis was the featured subject. "Your ex is quite a piece of work."

Marni slammed a fist on the bureau, enough to make her toiletries jump. "He says he was particularly stressed working on his latest designs because of a young colleague who was obsessed with him. That she practically stalked him after he broke things off with her." She laughed bitterly. "What complete bull." She pointed to her chest. "Everyone knows who he means. Me!"

"Marni, you can send out a statement." He held the tablet up. "Email this editor. Tell him this is all a load of crock. You can set the record straight."

"How?" she demanded, her eyes blazing with fury and shiny wet with unshed tears. "It's his word against mine. And he has much more clout in that world than I do."

Gio clenched his fists tight. If the lowlife were standing in front of him right now, Gio had all sorts of ideas about what he might do. All of it too good for the likes of such a liar.

He knew for a fact none of the claims quoted in the piece were even remotely true. How in the world would Marni be pleading with Ander to get back together? For one, she'd been with *him* almost constantly since she'd arrived on the island.

"He says I sent him countless emails and messages and called repeatedly, begging him to take me back. All conveniently erased I might add. Because he wanted to erase all reminders of me as it was too upsetting and interfering with his work."

"People will have to see how suspect that is."

"Some might. Plenty of others won't. Ander has all the advantage here. I'll have no hope of finding another design position. Most definitely not in Boston. And probably not even in New York now. Not after all these accusations. He makes me sound downright unstable. Who would take a risk on hiring someone like that?"

"This is complete character assassination. He can't get away with it."

Her response to that was to throw her head back and release a guttural groan full of frustration and misery. "So much for our playacting. It's being completely ignored. No one seems to care."

Gio reached for her, pulled her against him, began rubbing her upper arms. "I guess we'll just have to be more convincing. Our initial attempts at getting our pictures out there clearly haven't been impactful enough. We need to do more."

She leaned back to meet his eyes. The tightness around her mouth loosened ever so slightly. "What does that mean?"

He shrugged. "Clearly, we need to be more high profile about our romance."

Marni wasn't sure she liked the sound of this. What exactly did Gio mean by higher profile? "I'm not really following, Gio."

"Think about it. This Arfin, or whatever his name is—"

"Ander," she corrected, though she could think of plenty other choice words to call the man.

Gio waved his hand dismissively. "Whatever. He's claiming you're still hung up on him. That you've made his life miserable because you can't stand that he's dumped you. We need to be more convincing. And more visible."

"I'm listening," she prompted.

"No more staged photos and appearances in the hope that we might get noticed."

"And we do what instead exactly?" she asked, her eyes still shiny with anger.

"We go to places and events that are sure to be covered. A place where there's sure to be VIPs."

She nodded. "Celebrities and famous people."

"Exactly. Capri is practically a celebrity magnet. And where there's celebrities…" He motioned for her to complete the sentence.

"There's paparazzi."

"Bingo. Then it's just a matter of my social media people sending anonymous notes to various magazines and sites. With the photos to round out the story."

Marni could only nod, trying to fully process all that he was saying.

Gio continued, "Far from a jilted ex who can't let go, you'll be shown as a happy, fulfilled woman who's moved on and found real love. And I'll be able to further redirect any media attention about me to my newfound relationship, as opposed to my near fatal accident. Love conquers all, as they say."

Good thing Marni wasn't drinking or eating anything at the moment. The way Gio kept saying "love" while referring to the two of them would have no doubt made her choke.

"Plus, there's an event we can attend. One with guaranteed cameras present."

"What kind of event?" she asked, focusing on the bare logistics of this plan of his.

"It so happens Santino Foods has an event in Naples in a couple of days."

"I'm listening."

"Every year, we host a charity gala to raise money and awareness for displaced children of wars and global conflict."

"I remember hearing and reading about it. Santino does a lot for worthy causes." Like the one that had led him to personally race in a rally.

He nodded. "Like most years, it's being held at the exclusive Grande Napolitano Hotel and Resort. Black tie, formal, live entertainment. There's always plenty of press there."

"You never mentioned a gala."

He shrugged. "I wasn't planning on going but I'll tell them I've changed my mind."

"You weren't going to go to your own annual event? You're the CEO."

He sighed wearily, rubbed a hand down his affected leg. "People understood why when I sent my regrets. I have plenty of high-level managers and PR people who don't need me there."

Marni let that knowledge sink in. Something fluttered in her chest. Gio had no intention of going to a major company event. He was too bruised and battered to be there. But he was going now. For her.

"I don't know what to say," she told him. The day so far had been a roller coaster of emotion. Waking up to that awful article and all those terrible lies about her had felt like a wrecking ball to her midsection. Now she felt touched and grateful at all that Gio was willing to do to help her make it all go away. "Except to tell you thank you…for being willing to do all this."

He nodded once. "I'm doing it for my sake too. And for Juno's."

Maybe, Marni thought. But she wasn't naive. Gio could have probably found a much easier way to garner some publicity than a sham relationship. No, the pretending was mostly for her benefit.

She looked up to find his hand waving in front of her face. "Marni? Where did you just drift off to?"

"I was just thinking whether we can pull this off."

He cast a smile her way that had her insides quivering.

"Of course we can. I know just where to start tomorrow night."

"Where?"

"There's a nightclub in town. Owned and run by a trained musician. Every weekend night he plays live music with a full band. At least one or two international celebrities are bound to show up."

"Which means cameras and picture taking."

He winked at her. "You got it. We can go tomorrow night. Make it a night on the town."

"Gio, I don't know. For one thing, are you up for it? You were in so much pain after the grotto."

His eyes narrowed on her, and a dark shadow passed over his face. "Don't worry about me, gattina. I can handle it."

Great. She'd offended him. She was about to tell him that acknowledging his injury was nothing to be insulted by. Did Gio honestly think himself lesser because of his injuries? Before she could get a word in, he thrust the tablet toward her until she took it.

"The only question is what will you decide to do," he told her, his voice challenging. "Are you going to push back and defend yourself? Or are you going to let him continue to get away with taunting you?"

With that, he turned away and left the room, shutting the door firmly behind him. Marni heard a slew of Italian words and curses as he descended the stairs.

Marni flopped backward onto the bed and swiped the slanderous article off the screen. Then she deleted the entire app for good measure.

No. She certainly wasn't going to let Ander Stolis get away with repeatedly smearing her name.

She *would* push back. She *would* defend herself.

* * *

Her friend was positively glowing. Even through her computer monitor Marni could see plainly how radiant and happy Nella appeared.

"You look great, Nella. Pregnancy definitely agrees with you."

Nella flashed her a wide smile. "Thanks, Marn. It may appear so, this time of day anyhow."

Concern flushed through Marni's core. "What do you mean? Are you not feeling well?"

Nella placed her palm above her rib cage. "The morning sickness is kind of kicking my behind. Takes me a good two hours to get past the queasiness and get out of bed."

Oh, no. Nella had always been a morning person. Being hampered the first part of her day had to be difficult for someone like her.

"I could use some of your vanilla pancakes. Been craving those," Nella told her.

"As soon as I'm back, I'm going to make them for you every morning."

"Thanks." Nella wagged a finger at her. "But don't even think about coming back early on account of me. You promised me you'd take it easy for the full two weeks."

If Nella only knew. This vacation had been less "take it easy" and more "what curve ball is next?"

"Don't you dare renege," Nella added.

"I won't. Promise."

"Good. Besides, Alex is trying his hand at those pancakes and he's getting better every day."

The twist of Nella's lips indicated that Alex might still have a way to go. How sweet of him to try for his wife. A wave of sadness rose in her chest. She couldn't recall any time a man she'd been involved with had tried to make her breakfast.

Though Gio made sure to keep the breakfast pastries in full supply. Hardly the same thing. Still...

"So, what's new?" Nella wanted to know, pulling her out of her thoughts. "You just calling to check on me and the bambino?"

Primarily. "Of course."

"And?"

"I just wanted to tell you that if you see anything online, about Gio and me, that it's not real. We're just trying to put on a show. I'll explain more later. You have enough going on right now."

Nella tilted her head. "Okay..."

She had to laugh at her expression.

"What else?" Nella asked.

Her friend could always read her so well. Marni wasn't surprised she'd picked up on the fact that there were more than a couple reasons for this call.

"Actually, there is one more thing," Marni began. "I also had a question."

"Shoot."

"I was wondering where you went in town to get your hair done. And where you'd shop if you needed a new dress."

CHAPTER ELEVEN

SOON AFTER HANGING up with Nella, Marni walked the mile and a half down the beach to the water taxi station her friend had informed her about. Gio was deep in emails on his laptop, so she'd simply left him a note.

She did some mentally calculations taking into account her bank balance, upcoming expenses and the exchange rate. Depending on how much the beauty salon was going to charge, she would no doubt have to skimp on the dress. One thing was certain, there was no way Marni could afford the upscale boutique Nella had suggested. She'd have to make do and find something relatively inexpensive.

A text popped up on her phone screen while she waited for the taxi boat. It was as if Nella was reading her mind.

Tell Gio to charge the salon and dress to a company expense account. You're attending a corporate function so it checks.

Marni smiled with appreciation but there was no way she was going to take the Santinos up on that. She wouldn't type that to Nella, however. Or she'd end up having to ditch the other woman's calls all day. She sent the heart emoji instead.

The floating dots appeared immediately on the screen.

You're not going to do it, are you?

Of course she wasn't. This time Marni sent a smiley face.

When she reached town twenty minutes later, the salon was only a brief walk away.

Using the translation app on her phone, along with the rudimentary Italian she'd learned spending so much time with the Santinos, Marni explained what she was after.

The stylist, a stunning brunette with bright red lips and dark wavy hair, gave her a dubious look.

"Sei sicuro?" the other woman asked.

Marni nodded. *"Sì."* Yes, she was sure.

She'd given this a lot of thought. No matter what happened with this little facade of theirs, Marni planned to go into it as a different person. She would start with her looks. She couldn't remember the last time she'd altered her appearance. Marni was due.

The woman who'd allowed Ander to control and belittle her, with hardly a word in her defense, was gone for good. Never to return. She was different now.

Marni was going to make sure to look the part.

Something on her face must have convinced the stylist, because she grinned and got to work. Marni spent the better part of the afternoon in the chair. When she was finally done three and a half hours later—transforming yourself was a long process—she nearly squealed in delight at the results.

The stylist was a genius. She'd taken what Marni had said and expanded on it. The result was a stunning and modern hairstyle that brought out the shape of her face. If she did say so herself. Despite her measly bank account, she gave the woman a generous tip. The stylist had earned every penny.

Let's see Gio make fun of her ponytail now… She stopped herself mid thought. No. These changes were for her and her alone. Gio's reaction was sure to be just a bonus.

So why did her heart pound with nervous anticipation at the thought of what he might say about her new hair?

Marni would find out soon enough. Right now, she had to move on to the next phase of her trip into town. The dress.

Even looking at the window display of the boutique Nella had recommended was enough to confirm what she already knew. Her credit card might not have been declined, but it would take Marni a good long time to pay it off.

It didn't help that everyone around here was impeccably dressed in the latest styles. Her simple beige wraparound dress fell far short. Particularly compared to the young lady Marni eyed sitting alone sipping a coffee at the café next door to the shop.

Marni shoved away her shyness and walked over to the woman. What did she have to lose?

"Scusa," she began, approaching the woman's table. "Er… *Dove posso trovare*." She indicated the woman's outfit with her hand.

With a warm, friendly smile, the woman gestured for Marni's phone. When she handed it back, a name and address had been typed on the screen.

"Un piccolo negozio. Poco costoso," the woman said, pointing across the piazza to a side street.

Marni wanted to hug the other woman with appreciation. *A small store. Not too expensive.* Exactly what she was looking for.

The next time she saw herself in the mirror of a small

dressing room, Marni had to pinch herself to confirm it was really her in the glass.

The new her.

Gio heard the door shut from the first-floor study and finished off his email then hit Send. Finally. Marni had been gone most of the day. With nothing but a note informing him she'd gone into town.

Why hadn't she asked him to take her?

They could have had lunch together. Done some sightseeing. Plus, they needed to talk about their exact plans for this evening. Shouldn't they discuss how they wanted to act? The image they wanted to project to the world?

Gio knew tonight would be all for show. But he wanted it to go smoothly. For Marni's sake.

Right. As if that was the only reason. It had been so long since he'd been out with a woman, and he'd never had to do so while in pain before. What if Marni had been right to ask about his readiness. What was he going to do if the pain became too much? It wasn't as if he could find a bag of ice or elevate his foot as he fought the waves of agony. Could he keep the pain at bay for a few hours given the stakes?

Well, before the night was over, he'd find out one way or another.

By the time he rose and went out to the sitting room, she had already dashed upstairs. A moment later, he heard her voice echoing from above. She must have called Nella.

Great. Marni had been gone all day and now she was holed up in her room talking to his sister, a conversation that could very well take over an hour. Those two always spent forever talking to each other once they got started.

And now that Nella was pregnant, there was a litany of baby topics they could chat about.

Gio swore and went back to his laptop. His mood had been sour all day, now it was downright acidic. He couldn't even explain why.

He didn't need to spend every day with Marni. They'd be together all evening, after all.

It wasn't as if he'd missed her while she was gone.

Gio adjusted his tie and glanced at his watch, a ritual he must have completed at least a half dozen times in the last hour. He and Marni would have to leave in a few minutes if they wanted to make any kind of noticeable entrance.

He debated icing his leg yet again but decided against it. It was on the brink of frostbite as it was.

Instead, he loosened the knot of his tie for the umpteenth time. He was out of practice as far as wearing one. The last time he'd gone out in a suit was before the accident. He'd been a completely different person then. His highest priority had been the next growth opportunity for Santino Foods and his main concern the latest sales figures and profit margins.

He still paid attention to those things, of course. Gio still made sure to monitor the industry, kept up with the distributors and read up on all the newest, trendiest Italian restaurants in major cities across the world. But numbers on a spreadsheet seemed much less life-and-death now. He supposed his turnabout was hardly surprising, given that he'd survived an actual literal life-and-death scenario.

What was taking Marni so long? He'd heard the shower shut off a good forty-five minutes ago. Was she stalling? Losing her nerve to go through with this?

After about ten more minutes of waiting, Gio made the decision to go check on her ETA. The turn of her doorknob sounded just as he reached the first step and he sighed in relief. He hadn't realized until that moment how nervous he'd been that she'd changed her mind about tonight. Which made no sense whatsoever. It wasn't as if he was looking forward to being gawked at on his first night out since the accident.

And then Marni descended the stairs and he lost all ability to think at all.

"I'm ready to go," she announced but he could hardly hear over the pounding in his ears.

Marni was…different. Her hair was cut and set in a completely different style with subtle bronze highlights throughout. It fell around her face in soft willowy strands, the ends reaching just above her shoulders. The waves were no more, replaced by a straightened thick mane that glittered where the light hit it.

He cleared his throat, finally managed to summon some words. "You, uh, got your hair cut."

Her hand reached up and she ran a finger through the fringe of her bangs, also new. "A good four inches. What do you think?"

What he thought was how much he wanted to be the one running his hands through those tresses. Of course, he wasn't about to actually say that. Trouble was, he couldn't come up with anything *to* say.

Marni's eyes widened with what looked like alarm. "You don't like it? Is it too drastic a change?"

Oh, no. He couldn't have her go thinking he didn't like it. He did. He liked it very, very much.

Then there was the dress. Gio ran his gaze down the

length of her. Whisper-thin straps sat over golden tanned shoulders. The navy silky number draped over her curves in all the right ways, the skirt coming to a stop right above her knees. Her legs were bare but, heaven help him, did they have some kind of glittery powder on them? He didn't even know that was a thing. Strappy dark blue high heels adorned her feet. The pink polish was gone, replaced by a scarlet red that reminded him of the finest Toscana Rossa.

"Gio," she asked, "what do you think?" She gestured toward her midsection. "Will this do for tonight?"

Somehow, he kept himself from yelling outright that Yes! it would more than do. The only problem with it was how much he wanted to slip the dress off her and then proceed to muss up her stylish hair in all manner of ways.

Marni pointed to her head. "Is it the hair? Or the dress?"

That had him dumbstruck. It was the whole package. Where had all this come from? Where had this Marni come from? Gone was the familiar, conservatively dressed prim and proper gattina he'd grown up with. In her place stood a strikingly stunning woman who could easily fit walking down a runway or featured in a magazine fashion spread.

Marni had always been pretty. But now she was absolutely beautiful.

He had to stop gawking somehow and find something to say.

When he met Marni's gaze again she was staring at him, her lips tight with apprehension.

"Should I change?" she asked. "Or wash out my hair to bring the curls back?" She searched his face. "Both? Should I change all of it?"

The question had him snapping out of his stupor. "Don't

even think about it, Marni," he finally managed. His voice sounded thick and strained to his own ears. "Don't you dare change a thing."

She felt like a princess on her way to the royal ball. Her companion certainly fit the image of the handsome prince. Of course, she'd seen Gio dressed up in the past. Prom night came to mind, and various formal functions she'd attended as a guest of the Santino family. But never before had she been the one on his arm.

The thought made her light-headed. She stole a glance at him now as they made their way into the club. In a dark navy suit Marni was certain was custom-tailored, Gio looked polished and devilishly handsome. A light gray shirt topped with a silk tie rounded out the image. He looked every bit the successful, coveted bachelor that he was. How unexpected that she was the woman he'd be spending the evening with.

Steady there, girl. This is all just for show, don't forget.

Still, she couldn't help but think of the way Gio had stared at her as she made her way down the stairs, and the memory sent feminine pleasure surging through her chest. He'd truly appreciated her new look. No doubt, her ex would have found a way to put down her makeover. Or even mock her for trying something different with her appearance.

Marni gave her head a shake. No more thoughts about Ander tonight. He wasn't worth it.

The band wasn't onstage yet but already the place was packed. Not one empty table. She wondered how Gio had snagged the last one.

The place was decorated to look like an ancient roman

castle. A large mural painting of the Parthenon covered one wall.

Marni scanned the others in attendance: definitely an A-list crowd. Subconsciously, she fingered the costume jewelry earring on her earlobe. The other women in here were decked out in high-karat diamonds and other precious stones.

Who did she think she was fooling?

The better question was whether she was only fooling herself thinking she could fit into a place like this, with her bargain dress and faux leather shoes.

Gio must have sensed her self-doubt, maybe her expression had given him a clue. "You look beautiful, Marni. Absolutely beautiful," he said. A darkness settled over his eyes that left her insides quivering. His compliment served as a boost to her wavering confidence, and Marni suspected that was exactly what Gio had intended.

"Thanks, Santino. You clean up pretty nice yourself."

"Good thing. Because I haven't worn a suit in ages and I feel like I'm wrapped like an Egyptian mummy." Gio stuck his finger in his collar and made a choking sound.

He was trying to get a laugh out of her, must have sensed how nervous she was. Marni reached for his other hand on the table. "Thank you, Gio. For doing all this." She meant it. He was uncomfortable and achy, out on the town when he should be home resting his bruised and battered body. For her.

Gio's hand clenched under hers. "You can thank me by trying to relax and have a good time. Just because we're here on a mission doesn't mean we can't enjoy it."

"I'll try." She knew she should pull her hand away right

then but let it linger, skin against skin. Finally, she pulled her arm back to her side when their server arrived.

Marni understood enough of the language to know that Gio ordered the night's special cocktail for them both and a bottle of champagne to share, along with an antipasto tray. Within moments of getting their food and drinks, the band appeared onstage and took their seats.

Soon the sound of traditional Neapolitan music filled the air. Before the end of the first song, several couples had already moved onto the dance floor.

Gio leaned over to speak in her ear. "Do you recognize the young lady in the leopard print dress?" he asked her.

Marni zoned in on the subject of his question. A petite blonde in impossibly high stilettos. She definitely looked familiar. It dawned on her why in a few seconds. "She's the latest addition to the cast of those superhero movies."

Gio nodded. "That's right. I'm certain at least a dozen people are snapping pictures of her right now. Pictures that will find themselves onto various gossip sites by morning."

Marni scanned the crowd. He certainly wasn't wrong. Several cell phones were held in the young actress's general direction.

"So if we want to be in any of those pictures, and hence on the websites, we should go up there now."

Marni swiveled her head and blinked at him. Was he suggesting that they actually join her on the dance floor? What about his hurt leg?

Before she could figure out how to ask without offending him again, Gio had stood up and was holding his hand out to her.

"Dance with me, gattina."

Marni's heart jumped in her chest. Silly as it might have

been, it had never occurred to her that they'd be dancing together at some point tonight. Gio remained standing with his hand extended. He tilted his head questioningly when she still didn't rise out of her seat.

She swallowed, shoved her doubts away and stood, taking his hand. Gio's shoulders dropped with relief. He led her onto the dance floor. And then she was in his arms, her cheek against his shoulder, his arms around her waist.

The song was a soulful melody. She may not have understood all the lyrics but she knew the tempo of a love song when she heard it. Reflexively, she nestled closer against Gio's frame, allowed herself a deep inhalation of his aftershave.

Gio rubbed his cheek against the top of her head. Being in his arms again felt like being home. She hadn't even realized how badly she'd wanted to be there.

The song ended but Gio didn't let her go. Instead, he lifted her chin with his finger, then placed the gentlest of kisses on her lips. Marni's heart stopped, a jolt of electricity shot through her core. She wanted to ask him to do it again. But for longer this time, so that she could once again savor the taste of him. The way she had on the beach that day.

A small flash of light shone in the corner of her eye.

"There it is," Gio said with a satisfied tone and it hit her then: someone had snapped a photo. That was the whole reason he'd been kissing her in the first place. Shame and embarrassment had heat rushing to her face. When would she learn? It served her right. A reminder of why they were here. How could she have forgotten for even a moment that all of this was meant for the photos?

None of it was real.

* * *

He was in no mood.

Nella had picked the wrong time to tease him. He wasn't even going to bother replying to her text. She may be pregnant, but she was still the pesky little sister who knew exactly how to get under his skin.

Saw the pictures from last night online. You and Marni make quite a striking couple.

That part wasn't so bad. It was the kissy face emojis, at least a dozen of them, that she'd stuck on at the end that rankled his nerves. Nella knew why he and Marni had been out last night. She'd even called yesterday to tell him he was a sweetie and a *tesoro* for helping Marni to thwart her ex's toxic campaign against her.

What Nella didn't know, nor Marni for that matter, was just how real it had all felt in the moment. On the dance floor, he'd simply meant to pose for a picture when he'd planted that kiss on Marni's lips. Just another way to continue the facade. But something had shifted in his center when he'd had his lips on hers. Their momentary loss of control on the beach had been full of emotion, with tensions running high for them both.

In contrast, the kiss last night had felt tender, delicate. Yet all the more powerful somehow. It had shaken him to the core the way he'd wanted to take her mouth again. Right there on the dance floor. He hadn't even cared that they were in a crowded nightclub, surrounded by strangers. And he no longer cared about getting some silly photo to send to a magazine.

She appeared in the doorway a moment later. Gio did a

double take when he saw her, still not quite used to her new look. Short hair suited her. He hoped she kept it that length.

What was wrong with him?

The way Marni wore her hair was none of his business. And he had no business wallowing about a chaste little kiss they'd shared in the middle of a dance floor.

"Anything yet?" She pointed to his phone.

Gio shook his head. "Yes and no. It's just hitting the mainstream sites now. It'll take a couple more days before people figure out who you are and it gets to the trade mags."

She pushed her bangs off her forehead and blew out a frustrated breath. "It stinks that we have to do this. I wish there was some other way."

Did she mean having to go out with him? He thought she'd had fun last night. Enjoyed his company.

Last night was the most fun he'd had since the accident. Maybe even before it. Despite the way his leg and torso had screamed all night at the punishment of dancing.

He ignored the lump of disappointment that seemed to have formed in his gut. "We'll just have to get through the launch party tonight. Hopefully it will generate more publicity and attention."

She blew out a breath. "I really hope so. Then we can be done with this farce once and for all."

Gio flinched where he stood, hoping Marni didn't notice.

CHAPTER TWELVE

MARNI RAN THE brush through her hair one last time and adjusted the scarf around her neck. Last night had been magical. Until she'd realized that like most magic, it was all smoke and mirrors. All the joy and thrill she'd experienced burst like a needle-pricked balloon in that moment. Then she'd just wanted it to be over.

At least she was more mentally prepared this time. She wouldn't allow herself to get carried away like a schoolgirl if Gio kissed her again. Or fake-kissed her, that was.

When she made it downstairs, Gio was dressed and waiting. He offered her a rather weak smile that didn't quite seem genuine.

"Ready to go?" he asked. Unlike last night, he didn't offer her his arm this time.

"As I'll ever be. The sooner we get there, the sooner we get this over with."

He gave her a curt nod and led her out the door.

Hard to believe but he looked even more dashingly handsome than he had at the club. Tonight he wore a tux that matched the black of his hair. He'd used some kind of gel to keep it in place, whereas yesterday it fell in waves over his forehead. If the man ever got tired of this business tycoon thing, he definitely had a future as a men's cologne model.

She, for one, would be ready to buy anything Gio Santino was selling.

A speedboat with a uniformed skipper awaited them when they reached the beach. Gio helped her onboard and led her to a comfortable seating area below deck with a circular table larger than the one she had in her apartment. A tray of fresh fruit and a variety of cheeses sat in the center, along with an airing bottle of wine and two stem glasses.

Gio poured them each a glass but she only took a sip, guzzling from the frosty water bottle instead. Best to try and keep her wits about her for as long as she could manage.

"I've never been to Naples before," she said by way of conversation. Gio was being oddly quiet. She wished he would tell her more about what to expect. The last Santino function she'd been to was a corporate Christmas party when she was seventeen in the North End, Boston's equivalent of Little Italy. This one tonight would actually be in Italy.

The motor roared to life and soon they were making their way across the ocean, the craft accelerating gradually until they reached a speed that had the scenery outside the windows zipping by.

For the second time in two nights, Marni wondered if she was going to be underdressed. Maybe she should have saved last night's dress for this evening instead, it was just a tad fancier. But last night, she'd been concerned about impressing Gio. Such a wasted effort on her part.

She checked her reflection in a side panel mirror. And thought she heard Gio snort.

Her eyes snapped on his face to find him looking at her with pursed lips and darkened eyes. "Something wrong?"

"You seem overly concerned again about your appearance. I told you yesterday you looked beautiful. How many compliments are you fishing for?"

Marni felt her jaw drop and her chest stung with a sudden flash of anger. "What?"

Gio rubbed his jaw. "Never mind. Forget I said anything. You look great, okay? Stop worrying about it."

Well, he'd seen to that. Now all she'd be worried about was why he was being so surly and offensive. Clearly, he didn't want to be here on this boat on his way to a function he'd had no intention of attending if it hadn't been for her. None of that was her fault, damn it.

"May I remind you that all this was your idea?"

His eyes bore into hers and he shook his head. "No, you don't need to remind me. And I'm sorry it's so taxing for you to go through with it."

Marni sucked in a breath. Where was all this coming from? "I never said that."

"You didn't exactly have to spell it out."

The chime of an incoming text interrupted her reply. From Nella.

Too bad it can't be real.

She'd attached a well-known meme of a disappointed cartoon character. Marni squinted at her screen. What exactly was that supposed to mean? Damned if she could guess. Honestly, the Santino siblings were insistent on testing her nerves tonight.

She was about to text her back to ask for some clarity

when Gio spoke. "We're here." He then stood, adjusting his gold cuff links.

Marni was surprised to look out the window and see the spectacular sight of Naples. Bright lights reflected off the water and lit up the clear night sky. She might have been looking at colorful fireworks somehow suspended in the air. The scene took her breath away. She imagined this was what Mount Olympus might look like.

Marni couldn't help but gawk at the sight as Gio led her off the boat and into a waiting limousine.

Less than ten minutes later, they arrived at the circular driveway of a sprawling resort. Marni could have sworn she'd seen this exact hotel in a spy movie not too long ago. Definitely worth an internet search to confirm as soon as she got a chance.

They walked down the brightly lit hallway toward the open double doors of a ballroom. The party appeared to be in full swing already.

Gio guided her through the entry with his hand at the small of her back. Marni forced herself not to react to his touch.

Even now, when she was furious with his behavior and at a complete loss to guess what might have caused it, she felt a current of electricity travel from the palm of his hand, clear through her skin and up the length of her spine.

The room seemed to still as they entered, the noise level decreased several decibels. Many heads turned in their direction at once. Marni supposed it made sense, the CEO had just arrived, after all. But there was something else she sensed in the air, a wave of curiosity.

She heard Gio utter a curse in Italian under his breath.

On instinct, she reached for his hand and gripped it tight behind her back. He squeezed back.

"Let's get a drink."

"All right." Sounded good to her; she was beginning to regret turning down the wine on the boat. Being the subject of such widespread scrutiny was not a comfortable feeling, nor one she was used to.

"I'm afraid we're going to have to mingle," Gio told her after he'd ordered them a couple of cocktails.

Sure. She could do that. All she had to do was smile and nod, right? Gio was the main attraction here, not her.

He looked less than pleased about it.

But he didn't falter. No less than half a dozen people approached him as they waited for their drinks. A couple simply wanted to say hello. The rest had urgent grievances and important matters and weren't going to waste this opportunity to bend the boss's ear.

Gio listened patiently, offered solutions or provided follow-up guidance. He really knew his stuff and was good at what he did.

Not that she'd ever doubted it.

Still, it was something else to see him in action. No wonder the company had grown several-fold under his guidance. Santino Foods was lucky to have him.

It was after they'd gotten their drinks and were headed toward their reserved table that the world shifted. Marni felt a splash of ice-cold liquid over her arm and middle. A heavy weight pushed against her side, followed by a hard thud by her feet. Marni's heart stopped as she processed what was happening: Gio had lost his balance. In horror, she looked down to find him braced on one knee gripping the base of a nearby table to keep from, going all the way down. His face a tight mask of agony.

"Oh, my God! Gio! Are you okay?" She dropped down next to him, reached for his arms. "Here, let me help you up."

The look he gave her had her breath catching in her throat. Red-hot anger burned behind his eyes. His voice was low and thick when he spoke. There was no mistaking the fury behind his words as he bit them out through tightly gritted teeth. "Marni. Don't."

Never in his worst nightmares had Gio imagined the scenario he found himself in. A room full of his colleagues and his employees, all present to see his horror. Then there was Marni. She'd had a front-row seat to it all.

His leg had actually given out, refused to support him. It had happened in a split second, without any kind of warning.

Check that. He had been warned, hadn't he? Warned by all the doctors, nurses and specialists.

He couldn't even bring himself to look around and see who might have observed his literal downfall. Clenching his teeth against the pain and embarrassment, he put as much weight as he could on his good leg, then used the thick base of the table to rise to a standing position.

Marni rose immediately as well and the look of worry on her face had competing forces warring in his chest. He was both touched by her concern and shamed that she'd witnessed such a stunning moment of weakness.

"Gio?"

He clenched his fists at his sides, here came that question again. *Are you all right?*

Marni didn't voice the words out loud, just continued scanning his face, her eyes imploring. He had to give her something. He thought about lying, telling her he'd tripped over some nonexistent object that was now miraculously gone or over a leg of a table. But what was the use? For one, she'd see right through the lie.

"I think I just put too much pressure on my bad leg. It'll be fine in a few moments."

Marni opened her mouth before closing it again, clearly at a loss for words.

He gestured to her middle. "Sorry about the drink. Your dress is all wet." Luckily, he'd ordered a vodka tonic for himself, at least she wouldn't have to walk around with a large stain on her dress. Just a large wet spot.

She blinked. "It will dry."

Gio finally dared to look about the room. No one seemed to be paying them any attention. If anyone had witnessed what had just happened, they had the good sense not to stare.

Still, he had to get out of this room. He didn't think he could handle even one person approaching him. "Excuse me for a few moments," he told Marni. "I'd like to get some air."

He turned away before she could respond.

Marni watched Gio's retreating back and debated what to do. Should she follow him? What if he fell again? She gave her head a small shake. No, he needed time alone and appeared steady enough on his feet as he navigated the crowded ballroom.

She would give him a minute. If she knew Gio, he was stinging with an imagined hit to his pride, which was ridiculous. He couldn't help what had just happened. He'd overdone it, pushed himself too far and ignored the fact that he wasn't one hundred percent. It had all taken a toll at the worst time.

But Gio Santino had never been one to show any weakness. And to think, Nella had said a couple days ago that he wasn't so stubborn. Ha! If she only knew just how stubborn her brother was acting these days.

A twinge of guilt fluttered in her chest. A lot of what he'd done had been on her behalf. Marni wanted to kick herself. She should have never agreed to this silly plan, should have just taken her lumps from Ander's conniving and not involved anyone else in her problems.

Along with an apology, she was going to tell Gio all that as soon as he returned.

Marni pulled her phone out of her clutch purse and mindlessly scrolled through various sites to kill the time until he returned, not paying any kind of real attention to what she read. Several moments passed and she continued scrolling.

Gio still hadn't come back. She dialed his number but he didn't pick up. No shocker there. Marni couldn't decide whether to be annoyed or more worried.

Finally, when she couldn't take any more anxious wondering, she went to look for him. Gio wasn't in the lobby nor was he outside by the main entrance. She ran back through the lobby area and down the opposite corridor to the back of the hotel facing the beach.

Lit fire torches dotted the sand beyond a wide stone patio furnished with cushioned wicker furniture. All of the chairs and sofas sat empty.

Marni strained her eyes down the length of the beach. Countless people were walking along the water or enjoying an evening swim. It could take her hours to find Gio if he was down there. He'd had quite a head start.

A deep, masculine voice sounded behind her. "Looking for me?"

Marni clasped her hand to her chest, her heart racing. It was anybody's guess whether that was caused by Gio unexpectedly materializing from behind her or because of the figure he posed. Framed in shadows, he looked almost ethereal.

She sucked in a breath and forced her mouth to work. "Gio. There you are. You startled me."

He stepped out of the darkness into the pool of light cast from a nearby lantern. "My apologies."

She knew better than to ask him if he was all right. That had never worked out quite so well in the past.

"I'm guessing you don't want to go back into the party just yet."

He thrust his hands in his pockets, tilting backward on his heels. "You would be correct."

Good. Because neither did she. Marni stepped to the wicker seat closest to her and dropped into it, then tucked her feet under her. The fresh air felt good on her skin, the ballroom had grown much too stuffy.

Gio didn't make any kind of move to sit himself, he merely lifted an eyebrow. She couldn't help but notice that most of his weight was solidly on his good leg. Saints give her patience with this man. He thought he'd appear weak by sitting down.

Oh, Gio. You don't have to prove anything to me.

"So when are you making the call?" she asked, feeling a little disconcerted with the height difference now that she'd taken a seat and he'd remained standing.

"Call?"

"The hospital in Chicago. To schedule those appointments finally. First thing tomorrow morning, I hope."

His head tilted. "I told you a few days ago. I'm in no rush."

He couldn't be serious. But there was no sign of joking on his face. "But that was before—"

He cut her off. "I'll call when I'm ready."

Marni covered her face with her palms, hardly able to believe what she was hearing. "Gio, you need to get started on those therapy sessions. And then you need to go through the surgeries. You can't put it off any longer."

"Is that your expert opinion?"

Marni's temper flared. How could he take this so lightly? It made absolutely no sense.

"Please explain to me why you plan to put this off any longer than you already have. Especially after what just happened."

A muscle jumped along his jaw. "Nothing happened, Marni. I lost my footing. It happens to everyone."

Maybe so, but it didn't often happen while simply walking on a flat surface. "Are you trying to convince yourself of that or trying to convince me?"

He shrugged. "I don't have to convince you of anything."

Marni pushed past the hurtful barb, one meant to imply that this was none of her business. She'd deal with the wound it caused to her soul later. Right now, she really wanted to learn why Gio was doing something so harmful and dangerous to himself.

She took a deep calming breath. "I'm just trying to understand. Don't tell me you don't believe the doctors can be of help? Gio, you have to trust in the professionals who have spent their lives helping heal others."

He scoffed at that. "Of course I have faith in doctors and professionals. I'm in regular contact with Juno's medical team. I'm making sure that he gets the best care and that he's being seen by the best specialists this side of the world."

It dawned on her then. Suddenly, all the puzzle pieces fell into place and everything made sense. She'd been so wrong in all her assumptions. Gio wasn't only putting off his recovery because he was too proud to admit he was wounded. He was delaying to punish himself. For the accident he'd caused which had tragically altered the life of a young father with a family who needed him. It was a vicious circle—he refused to get the treatment he needed because of his guilt, which only grew his frustration at his injuries. He was going around and around and couldn't even see it.

"Gio, it was an accident." She emphasized the last word. "You didn't intend harm. You have to see that."

His eyes hardened on her face. "Marni, let this go."

She couldn't. For his sake. "What if I don't want to?"

His jaw visibly tightened. "It's not up to you."

She knew he was simply lashing out, but his coldness still broke her heart.

"Good night, Marni," he said in a flat voice. "The limo and speedboat are waiting to take you back to the villa whenever you're ready."

Marni's mouth went dry. He was really doing this. He was really pushing her away because he'd rather keep punishing himself than move on with his life and his future. A future that might have included *her*.

"I've decided to stay here in Naples for the time being," he added with finality.

Gio didn't even wait for a response before walking away without so much as a glance back.

Sitting in the *piazetta* sipping coffee wasn't doing much to settle her emotions. But Marni had had to get away from the villa. She'd been going stir-crazy wandering around the grounds all morning, waiting for word from Gio. The throngs of people bustling about the square and those enjoying the cafés and shops should have made for a worthy distraction of people watching. But Marni hardly noticed her surroundings.

The biscotti she'd ordered with her cappuccino was one of the freshest and most flavorful she'd ever tasted. But she might as well have been nibbling on cardboard.

Not a peep from him since their disastrous argument last night. Not so much as a text or a phone call, despite several attempts to reach him. His silence had Marni torn between anger and worry. What if his leg had gotten worse? What if he was holed up in a hotel room right now, lying on the mattress in agony and pain?

A shudder of anxiety racked through her at the image in her head. Still, even that drastic scenario, heaven forbid it be real, wouldn't have prevented him from sending her a quick text.

No, he was ignoring her because he wanted to. Because he clearly thought Marni had overstepped when she'd insisted he get the medical care he needed.

Gio thought she had no right to weigh in on his decisions. Her opinion or thought held no import for him. And here she'd gone and foolishly fallen further in love with the man. There was no denying that now. If she couldn't admit it before, she damn well had to face reality now. She'd always loved him, since they were preteens. Now she was head over heels.

A hiccup of anguish tore from her chest and her eyes stung behind her sunglasses. She reached for her phone once more, but she wasn't holding her breath. It pinged just as she glanced at the screen. Heart pounding, Marni unlocked the message only to have her hope plummet. It wasn't Gio but his sister.

Your plan was a success! You and Gio are all over the sites.

Marni tossed the phone back on the table as if it had burned her palm. The plan. What an insignificance. Little did Nella know she could care less now about the blasted plan. Even less about what the world thought about her. She'd take her chances to get her career back on track. If that meant leaving home and moving to New York then so be it.

Right now, regaining her professional career was pretty much all she had in her life. But she'd do it on her own terms. Without a pretend boyfriend.

One challenge at a time. For right now, she had to focus on herself and the best way to move forward toward her future.

She'd done it again—carelessly trusted her heart to the wrong man. Unlike Ander, this particular man would be impossible to get over.

Gio was the one who'd made her feel like a princess. The one who'd encouraged her to dream of more for her future and told her he had faith that she could accomplish it. He was the only man who'd sent shivers down her spine when he so much as touched her.

No matter what the future held for her, Gio Santino would

forever claim her heart. All the more tragic given the family connection.

They were to be co-godparents for heaven's sake! How in the world would she even navigate that? How would she hide her true feelings and keep from shattering inside every time they were in the same room together?

With trembling fingers, she reached for her cup and took a tentative sip. Well, she was done waiting. There was no sense staying in Capri any longer either. Her goal to come here and take two weeks to recharge and regroup had completely backfired. She had nothing to show for herself but a broken heart. Looked like her days in paradise were over. Gio had clearly moved on.

Somehow, some way, so would she.

He sensed it as soon as he let himself in the front door. Gio didn't need to walk through the villa to know that she was gone. He should have answered her calls. But he couldn't bring himself to do it, couldn't for the life of him figure out what he might say. Now that he was ready to find her, it was much too late.

He knew that made him all kinds of a coward.

He'd spent hours wandering the city last night until his leg had screamed at him to stop. When he finally returned to the hotel, Gio hadn't been able to fall asleep, hadn't even bothered to crawl into bed. Just simply sat on the sofa in his hotel room, staring into the dark until the sun rose. And it had nothing to do with the regular insomnia that had plagued him since the accident.

When his eyes had finally drifted shut sometime late in the afternoon, his mind played reels of images in his head: Marni pouncing into his bedroom that first day she'd arrived; the marvel on her face as they'd sailed over blue water in the grotto; how her eyes had widened in the Gardens of Augustus... The way her lips had tasted on his.

With a curse, he strode to the patio and dropped down on the lounge chair only to have more memories of her flood his mind. He even replayed the moment in the garden when the wedding procession had walked by. Only, the bride in his mind was Marni. And he was her groom. He had to push the vision away. Because it was complete fantasy.

Maybe it was just as well she was gone. She was better off without him. He wasn't anywhere near the man he used to be.

Marni deserved better than the man he was now. Broken both inside and outside. Unable to tell the woman he loved how he really felt. Too broken for the likes of someone like her. Hopefully, one day she would see the truth of that and forgive him for his cowardness.

Heaven knew, he didn't deserve such grace from her. Just like he didn't deserve *her*.

CHAPTER THIRTEEN

Four months later

MARNI READ THE email once more, then rubbed her eyes to make sure she wasn't imagining the message. Was it really possible that they were about to be hired by their first client?

"Huh," she said out loud, scanning her laptop screen once more.

"What is it?" Nikita Murtag asked from her desk across the small office. Nikita was Marni's new business partner of approximately three weeks now. A former colleague at Marni's old firm, the other woman had contacted her the day Marni left Capri. Niki told her how low morale had turned at her old place of business. How most of the female employees knew Ander to be a predatory liar and didn't want to be next in his crosshairs. So Niki had quit. Somehow, within days after Niki's call, the two women were co-signing a business loan and painting the walls of their new shop in Boston's South End.

The signage even worked out, just as Marni had envisioned in her fantasy that night. Her mind reflexively pushed the memory aside before it could fully form. Any thoughts of the time she'd spent with Gio Santino were too painful and raw to entertain. Her heart couldn't take it.

What mattered now was that Mar-Ni Designs was officially open for business. And if this email wasn't some king of spam or junk, they might even have their first client.

"Come look at this," she told Niki, then turned the laptop toward her when the other woman reached her desk. Niki read the message over her shoulder then let out a whoop.

"We have a job!"

It certainly seemed so. "It's odd, isn't it, though?" Marni questioned. "We've barely been open more than a few days."

"Word of mouth is a powerful force, Marni. Don't discount it."

"They sent the email through the new website."

"Looks like they're asking for you specifically." Niki gave her shoulder a squeeze. "You must have impressed somebody through the years. Go ahead and confirm."

Within minutes of her replying, another message popped up.

"You're not going to believe this," she told Niki. "Whoever this potential client is, it says they're in a hurry and want a meeting this afternoon if possible."

"Are you going to say yes?" Niki asked.

Marni shrugged one shoulder. She couldn't think of one reason to turn down a potential opportunity. "Why not?" she answered. "It's not like I have anything else to work on just yet."

Three hours later, Marni made her way to the most exclusive restaurant in Boston's Seaport District, the requested meeting place, with her portfolio tucked under her arm. The dining room was relatively empty given the early afternoon so she was surprised when the maître d' led her to a private room on the top floor.

Whomever this potential client was, looked like he carried a lot of clout in the city. Marni took a seat at the large mahogany dining table, nervous anticipation humming through her veins.

A shadow fell over the table from behind her seat. A familiar scent carried in the air.

It couldn't be. Marni squeezed her eyes shut, afraid to turn around.

"*Ciao, gattina.*"

That voice. *His* voice.

Her mind had to be playing tricks on her, trying to conjure a false reality she wanted so badly to be true. Gio Santino wasn't really here, standing behind her.

Only one way to find out.

Sucking in a shaky breath, she made herself get up and turn around.

Even as her eyes fell on him, she couldn't quite believe what she was seeing. Gio stood in the doorway, his shoulder leaning against the doorframe. He flashed her a devilishly handsome smile that made her heart skip a beat.

"Gio?"

"*Sì, bellisima.* It's me."

Marni felt as if her mouth had filled with sawdust and her tongue felt too heavy to move. Somehow she managed to form a single word. "Why?"

Gio squeezed his eyes shut, tilted his head up toward the ceiling. "You have every reason to be upset, *cara*."

That got her mouth working. "Of course I do! You—you just left me. Without a goodbye. Not a word!"

He paused before returning his gaze to her face. "I know.

For the life of me, I couldn't come up with a thing to say to you. Please know that I will spend the rest of my life trying to make up for that."

A sudden war was being waged in her soul. Every cell in her body wanted to tell him he was forgiven, that she was overjoyed to see him. But a calmer, saner part reminded her how hard she'd worked these past few months to focus solely on her own growth and fulfillment.

Whatever his intentions were for being here, she had to set him straight on at least that one thing. "You can't just walk back into my life, Gio. It's not that simple. I've done a lot since we last saw each other."

He took a step closer, his eyes dark and compelling beneath those black lashes.

Focus.

"I know. From all outward appearances, it seems your new business is exactly what you'd envisioned. You should be so proud of yourself."

Her chin lifted. "I am. And I don't have room or time to waste if my feelings are one-sided."

Gio moved closer to her once more. Something nagged at the back of her mind when he took several more steps. It took a beat, but she finally figured out what her brain was trying to tell her. "Your limp," she began. "It seems to be better."

He gave her a thin smile. "It should. After the countless hours of therapy and all the grueling muscle building exercises."

Marni sucked in a breath. "You went to Chicago."

He nodded.

"You were right to push me that night. And I was so

wrong to push you away. I'm so sorry, *mi gattina*. Please forgive me for being such a *stolto*."

She couldn't help herself, didn't even realize what she'd intended until she was across the room and in his arms. He wrapped himself around her, nuzzled his chin against the top of her head.

"You're really here," she said against his chest, savoring the feel of him, inhaling deeply of that scent she'd missed so much.

"I had to come. To find the woman I love."

The woman he loved? If this was indeed a dream, Marni didn't want to ever come back to reality. Gio Santino had traveled across the country to be with her, to tell her he loved her.

But there were so many things as yet unsettled. She couldn't celebrate until she had the answers she'd been asking for that night in Naples. Marni made herself pull away. "What about your treatments?" If she was remembering correctly, he still had surgeries to complete after the therapy was over. "Don't you have to go back to Chicago for the surgeries?"

He tilted her chin. "Chicago is so far, *mi amore*."

She was about to argue when he pressed a finger to her lips. "I'm already seeing a specialist. Right here in Boston. I refuse to be so far from you again. I intend to stay right here and do all I can to work on becoming the man you deserve."

Marni thought her heart might burst in her chest. Then she couldn't think at all as his lips found hers.

When he pulled away all too soon, he took her by the hand to the table. "Now, let's get down to business, shall we?"

Marni blinked at him in confusion. "What business?"

He chuckled. "You're here about an assignment, aren't you?"

Marni didn't miss the mischief behind his eyes. What was he getting at?

"I thought that was just a ruse to get me here." As if she'd turn him down if he'd just asked her. He couldn't have really thought so.

He shook his head. "No ruse. There's a property that needs a professional decorator. As a fan of your previous work, I believe you'd be perfect for the job."

Marni tilted her head, whatever game he was playing, she'd play along. "What property?"

"Here, let me show you." He reached for a leather binder sitting in the center of the table, pulled it toward her and lifted the cover.

Marni knew immediately what she was looking at. "This is the villa in Capri. The one that was for sale." He must have bought it.

She looked more carefully at the photos and paperwork. "There's a mistake here," she said, pointing at one of the documents. "This has my name listed as the owner."

Gio flashed her a wide smile. "No mistake. The villa is yours."

Before Marni could so much as absorb that bit of information, he continued, "Consider it a wedding present for my new wife. That's if she'll have it." He took her hand in his over the table. "And if she'll have me. What do you say?"

Marni thought her heart might burst in her chest with joy. It had nothing to do with any villa. And everything to do with the man she'd loved for as long as she could remember.

"Sì, mi amore," she answered, wrapping her arms around his neck. "I say yes!"

EPILOGUE

UNLIKE THE LAST time they were here at the Gardens of Augustus, the sky was dark and overcast. In fact, it appeared as if it might rain any second. But none of that hampered the joy flooding through her heart and soul.

Let it rain, Marni thought. An all-out thunderstorm would not be enough to dampen the celebration of her wedding day by so much as even a fraction.

As she approached the man who would soon be her husband, Marni fought the urge to pinch herself to prove all of this was real. Gio stood beneath a circular archway of flowers, the view of the ocean behind him. He looked so devastatingly handsome, his eyes shining with so much love that Marni thought her heart might burst in her chest. His sister stood next to him, beaming. Cradled in her arms was Marni's infant goddaughter, surely the cutest flower girl to have ever been in a wedding. The grand view of the Faraglioni rocks framed them.

Marni's eyes stung with happy tears. She was surrounded by love and affection and everyone who'd ever mattered in her life. The Santinos had always been her family. Now it was simply official.

Her tears refused to be contained as she reached Gio's side and they began their vows. Marni felt like she was living a true fairy tale, right down to marrying her own prince.

Afterward, through a blur of happy emotion as they began posing for their wedding photos, Gio gently took her elbow. He leaned in to whisper in her ear after the photographer snapped several pictures. "I've been thinking, *cara*. Something has occurred to me and I can't seem to get it out of my head."

Marni couldn't help but giggle at the clearly exaggerated mock seriousness in his voice. "What thought might that be, dear husband?" She had to suppress a cry of glee at the last word as it left her lips.

"I was thinking how much little Alexandra would appreciate a cousin to play with. Wouldn't you agree?"

Marni gave him a useless shove on his upper arm. "Gio!"

The photographer was trying to direct them in another pose but it was so hard to process the man's direction. She was utterly, wholeheartedly focused on her new husband.

Gio continued, "As responsible godparents, it behooves us to give our little niece all that she may desire."

"Anything you say, my love."

His expression turned suddenly serious. The photographer had apparently given up at this point and stepped to the side to wait patiently before continuing.

"Of course, the timing is entirely up to you," Gio told her. "I know you're quite busy with your growing clientele back in Boston."

"I am quite busy," she said, just to tease him.

He tapped her playfully on the nose, then dropped a soft

kiss on her lips. "That's fine. Just gives me something to look forward to."

Marni cupped his face in her hands and rose on her toes to give him a deeper, longer kiss. She felt breathless and heady when they finally pulled away.

"Me too, my love," she whispered against his lips. "I'm looking forward to all of it. All that we have in front of us."

* * * * *

ew release – out next month!

The Rough Rider
by
NEW YORK TIMES BESTSELLING AUTHOR
MAISEY YATES

Return to Four Corners Ranch for a marriage of convenience between two unlikely souls — a hopeless romantic and a man who has long given up hope.

NEW RELEASE

In stores and online August 2023.

MILLS & BOON
millsandboon.com.au

MILLS & BOON

Want to know more about your favourite series or discover a new one

Experience the variety of romance that Mills & Boon has to offer at our website:

millsandboon.com.au

Shop all of our categories and discover the one that's right for you.

MODERN

DESIRE

MEDICAL

INTRIGUE

ROMANTIC SUSPENSE

WESTERN

HISTORICAL

FOREVER
EBOOK ONLY

HEART
EBOOK ONLY

f @millsandboonaustralia @millsandboonaus

ıbscribe and
ll in love with
Mills & Boon
ries today!

ı'll be among the first
read stories delivered
your door monthly
d enjoy great savings.

WE
SIMPLY
LOVE
ROMANCE

MILLS & BOON SUBSCRIPTIONS

HOW TO JOIN

1

Visit our website
millsandboon.com.au/pages/print-subscriptions

2

Select your favourite series
Choose how many books. We offer monthly as well as pre-paid payment options.

3

Sit back and relax
Your books will be delivered directly to your door.

MILLS & BOON

JOIN US

Sign up to our newsletter to stay up to date with...

- Exclusive member discount codes
- Competitions
- New release book information
- All the latest news on your favourite authors

> Plus...
> get $10 off your first order.
> *What's not to love?*

Sign up at **millsandboon.com.au/newsletter**

@millsandboonaustralia @millsandboonaus